Praise for #1 *New York Times* bestselling author

NORA ROBERTS

"When Roberts puts her expert fingers on the pulse
of romance, legions of fans feel the heartbeat."
—*Publishers Weekly*

"Roberts's style has a fresh, contemporary snap."
—*Kirkus Reviews*

"With clear-eyed, concise vision and a sure pen,
Roberts nails her characters and settings with
awesome precision, drawing readers into a vividly
rendered world of family-centered warmth and
unquestionable magic."
—*Library Journal*

"Her stories have fueled the dreams
of twenty-five million readers."
—*Chicago Tribune*

"A superb author…Ms. Roberts is an enormously
gifted writer whose incredible range and intensity
guarantee the very best of reading."
—*Rave Reviews*

"Nora Roberts is among the best."
—*Washington Post's* Book World

Dear Reader,

The heart chooses whom the heart wants—and that's not always who our head says is right for us. These classics from bestselling author Nora Roberts show us once again that no matter how different two people may be, or how far apart their worlds are, love has a way of conquering all.

In *Secret Star*, Lieutenant Seth Buchanan is facing his toughest investigation yet—the mystery of Grace Fontaine. The beautiful heiress obviously has plenty of secrets, and though Seth's head tells him she's trouble, his heart won't let him walk away. Not until he knows the whole truth. And not until she's in his arms for good.

In *The Law is a Lady*, Hollywood director Phillip Kincaid finds not only the perfect location for his next film, but also the woman of his dreams. Unfortunately for him, Sheriff Victoria Ashton is not looking for romance—especially with a city slicker like him. But Phillip sees the passion beneath Tori's cool demeanor and he's determined to make her his leading lady before he leaves town.

We hope you enjoy these tales of two unlikely couples finding everlasting love, and that they inspire you to keep your heart open to every possibility.

The Editors

Silhouette Books

NORA ROBERTS

NOT WITHOUT YOU

Silhouette® Books

Published by Silhouette Books
America's Publisher of Contemporary Romance

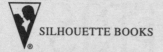 **SILHOUETTE BOOKS**

Recycling programs
for this product may
not exist in your area.

NOT WITHOUT YOU

ISBN-13: 978-0-373-28173-2

Copyright © 2013 by Harlequin Books S.A.

The publisher acknowledges the copyright holder of the individual works as follows:

SECRET STAR
Copyright © 1998 by Nora Roberts

THE LAW IS A LADY
Copyright © 1984 by Nora Roberts

Visit Silhouette Books at www.Harlequin.com

Printed in U.S.A.

CONTENTS

SECRET STAR

To generous hearts

Chapter 1

The woman in the portrait had a face created to steal a man's breath and haunt his dreams. It was, perhaps, as close to perfection as nature would allow. Eyes of laser blue whispered of sex and smiled knowingly from beneath thick black lashes. The brows were perfectly arched, with a flirty little mole dotting the downward point of the left one. The skin was porcelain-pure, with a hint of warm rose beneath—just warm enough that a man could fantasize that heat was kindling only for him. The nose was straight and finely sculpted.

The mouth—and, oh, the mouth was hard to ignore—was curved invitingly, appeared pillow-soft, yet strong in shape. A bold red temptation that beckoned as clearly as a siren's call.

Framing that staggering face was a rich, wild tumble of ebony hair that streamed over creamy bare shoulders.

Glossy, gorgeous, generous. The kind of hair even a strong man would lose himself in—fisting his hands in all that black silk, while his mouth sank deep, and deeper, into those soft, smiling lips.

Grace Fontaine, Seth thought, a study in the perfection of feminine beauty.

It was too damn bad she was dead.

He turned away from the portrait, annoyed that his gaze and his mind kept drifting back to it. He'd wanted some time alone at the crime scene, after the forensic team finished, after the M.E. took possession of the body. The outline remained, an ugly human-shaped silhouette marring the glossy chestnut floor.

It was simple enough to determine how she'd died. A nasty tumble from the floor above, right through the circling railing, now splintered and sharp-edged, and down, beautiful face first, into the lake-size glass table.

She'd lost her beauty in death, he thought, and that was a damn shame, too.

It was also simple to determine that she'd been given some help with that last dive.

It was, he mused, looking around, a terrific house. The high ceilings offered space and half a dozen generous skylights gave light, rosy, hopeful beams from the dying sun. Everything curved—the stairs, the doorways, the windows. Female again, he supposed. The wood was glossy, the glass sparkling, the furniture all obviously carefully selected antiques.

Someone was going to have a tough time getting the bloodstains out of the dove-gray upholstery of the sofa.

He tried to imagine how it had all looked before whoever helped Grace Fontaine off the balcony stormed through the rooms.

There wouldn't have been broken statuary or ripped cushions. Flowers would have been meticulously arranged in vases, rather than crushed into the intricate pattern of the Oriental rugs.

There certainly wouldn't have been blood, broken glass, or layers of fingerprint dust.

She'd lived well, he thought. But then, she had been able to afford to live well. She'd become an heiress when she turned twenty-one, the privileged, pampered orphan and the wild child of the Fontaine empire. An excellent education, a country-club darling, and the headache, he imagined, of the conservative and staunch Fontaines, of Fontaine Department Stores fame.

Rarely had a week gone by that Grace Fontaine didn't warrant a mention in the society pages of the *Washington Post,* or a paparazzi shot in one of the glossies. And it usually hadn't been due to a good deed.

The press would be screaming with this latest, and last, adventure in the life and times of Grace Fontaine, Seth knew, the moment the news leaked. And they would be certain to mention all of her escapades. Posing nude at nineteen for a centerfold spread, the steamy and very public affair with a very married English lord, the dalliance with a hot heartthrob from Hollywood.

There'd been other notches in her designer belt, Seth remembered. A United States senator, a bestselling author, the artist who had painted her portrait, the rock star who, rumor had it, had attempted to take his own life when she dumped him.

She'd packed a lot of men into a short life.

Grace Fontaine was dead at twenty-six.

It was his job to find out not only the how, but the who. And the why.

He had a line on the why already. The Three Stars of Mithra—a fortune in blue diamonds, the impulsive and desperate act of a friend, and greed.

Seth frowned as he walked through the empty house, cataloging the events that had brought him to this place, to this point. Since he had a personal interest in mythology, had since childhood, he knew something about the Three Stars. They were the stuff of legends, and had once been grouped in a gold triangle that had been held in the hands of a statue of the god Mithra.

One stone for love, he remembered, skimming through details as he climbed the curved stairs to the second level. One for knowledge, and the last for generosity. Mythologically speaking, whoever possessed the Stars gained the god's power. And immortality.

Which was, logically, a crock, of course. Wasn't it odd, though, he mused, that he'd been dreaming lately of flashing blue stones, a dark castle shrouded in mist, a room of glinting gold? And there was a man with eyes as pale as death, he thought, trying to clear the hazy details. And a woman with the face of a goddess.

And his own violent death.

Seth shook off the uneasy sensation that accompanied his recalling the snippets of dreams. What he required now were facts, basic, logical facts. And the fact was that three blue diamonds weighing something over a hundred carats apiece were worth six kings' ransoms. And someone wanted them, and didn't mind killing to gain possession.

He had bodies piling up like cordwood, he thought, dragging a hand through his dark hair. In order of death, the first had been Thomas Salvini, part owner of Salvini, gem experts who had been contracted by the

Smithsonian Institution to verify and assess the three stones. Evidence pointed to the fact that verifying and assessing hadn't been quite enough for Thomas Salvini, or his twin, Timothy.

Over a million in cash indicated that they'd had other plans—and a client who wanted the Stars for himself.

Added to that was the statement from one Bailey James, the Salvinis' stepsister, and eyewitness to fratricide. A gemologist with an impeccable reputation, she claimed to have discovered her stepbrothers' plans to copy the stones, sell the originals and leave the country with the profits.

She'd gone in to see her brothers alone, he thought with a shake of his head. Without contacting the police. And she'd decided to face them down after she shipped two of the stones to her two closest friends, separating them to protect them. He gave a short sigh at the mysterious minds of civilians.

Well, she'd paid for her impulse, he thought. Walking in on a vicious murder, barely escaping with her life—and with her memory of the incident and everything before it blocked for days.

He stepped into Grace's bedroom, his heavy-lidded gold-toned eyes cooly scanning the brutally searched room.

And had Bailey James gone to the police even then? No, she'd chosen a P.I., right out of the phone book. Seth's mouth thinned in annoyance. He had very little respect and no admiration for private investigators. Through blind luck, she'd stumbled across a fairly decent one, he acknowledged. Cade Parris wasn't as bad as most, and he'd managed—through more blind luck, Seth was certain—to sniff out a trail.

And nearly gotten himself killed in the process. Which brought Seth to death number two. Timothy Salvini was now as dead as his brother. He couldn't blame Parris overmuch for defending himself from a man with a knife, but taking the second Salvini out left a dead end.

And through the eventful Fourth of July weekend, Bailey James's other friend had been on the run with a bounty hunter. In a rare show of outward emotion, Seth rubbed his eyes and leaned against the door jamb.

M. J. O'Leary. He'd be interviewing her soon, personally. And he'd be the one telling her, and Bailey James, that their friend Grace was dead. Both tasks fell under his concept of duty.

O'Leary had the second Star and had been underground with the skip tracer, Jack Dakota, since Saturday afternoon. Though it was only Monday evening now, M.J. and her companion had managed to rack up a number of points—including three more bodies.

Seth reflected on the foolish and unsavory bail bondsman who'd not only set Dakota up with the false job of bringing in M.J., but also moonlighted with blackmail. The hired muscle who'd been after M.J. had likely been part of some scam of his and had killed him. Then they'd had some very bad luck on a rain-slicked road.

And that left him with yet another dead end.

Grace Fontaine was likely to be third. He wasn't certain what her empty house, her mangled possessions, would tell him. He would, however, go through it all, inch by inch and step by step. That was his style.

He would be thorough, he would be careful, and he would find the answers. He believed in order, he believed in laws. He believed, unstintingly, in justice.

Seth Buchanan was a third-generation cop, and had worked his way up the rank to lieutenant due to an inherent skill for police work, an almost terrifying patience, and a hard-edged objectivity. The men under him respected him—some secretly feared him. He was well aware he was often referred to as the Machine, and took no offense. Emotion, temperament, the grief and the guilt civilians could indulge in, had no place in the job.

If he was considered aloof, even cold and controlled, he saw it as a compliment.

He stood a moment longer in the doorway, the mahogany-framed mirror across the wide room reflecting him. He was a tall, well-built man, muscles toned to iron under a dark suit jacket. He'd loosened his tie because he was alone, and his nightwing hair was slightly disordered by the rake of his fingers. It was full and thick, with a slight wave. He pushed it back from an unsmiling face that boasted a square jaw and tawny skin.

His nose had been broken years before, when he was in uniform, and it edged his face toward the rugged. His mouth was hard, firm, and rare to smile. His eyes, the dark gold of an old painting, remained cool under straight black brows.

On one wide-palmed hand he wore the ring that had been his father's. On either side of the heavy gold were the words *Serve* and *Protect*.

He took both duties seriously.

Bending, he picked up a pool of red silk that had been tossed on the mountain of scattered clothing heaped on the Aubusson carpet. The callused tips of his fingers skimmed over it. The red silk gown matched the short robe the victim had been wearing, he thought.

He wanted to think of her only as the victim, not as

the woman in the portrait, certainly not as the woman
in those new and disturbing dreams that disrupted his
sleep. And he was irritated that his mind kept swimming back to that stunning face—the woman behind
it. That quality was—had been, he corrected—part of
her power. That skill in drilling into a man's mind until
he was obsessed with her.

She would have been irresistible, he mused, still
holding the wisp of silk. Unforgettable. Dangerous.

Had she slipped into that little swirl of silk for a man?
he wondered. Had she been expecting company—a private evening of passion?

And where was the third Star? Had her unexpected
visitor found it, taken it? The safe in the library downstairs had been broken open, cleaned out. It seemed logical that she would have locked something that valuable
away. Yet she'd taken the fall from up here.

Had she run? Had he chased her? Why had she let
him in the house? The sturdy locks on the doors hadn't
been tampered with. Had she been careless, reckless
enough to open the door to a stranger while she wore
nothing but a thin silk robe?

Or had she known him?

Perhaps she'd bragged about the diamond, even
shown it off to him. Had greed taken the place of passion? An argument, then a fight. A struggle, a fall. Then
the destruction of the house as cover.

It was an avenue, he decided. He had her thick address book downstairs, and would go through it name
by name. Just as he, and the team he assigned, would
go through the empty house in Potomac, Maryland,
inch by inch.

But he had people to see now. Tragedy to spread and

details to tie up. He would have to ask one of Grace Fontaine's friends, or a member of her family, to come in and officially identify the body.

He regretted, more than he wanted to, that anyone who had cared for her would have to look at that ruined face.

He let the silk gown drop, took one last look at the room, with its huge bed and trampled flowers, the scatter of lovely old antique bottles that gleamed like precious gems. He already knew that the scent here would haunt him, just as that perfect face painted beautifully in oils in the room downstairs would.

It was full dark when he returned. It wasn't unusual for him to put long, late hours into a case. Seth had no life to speak of outside of the job, had never sought to make one. The women he saw socially, or romantically, were carefully, even calculatingly, selected. Most tolerated the demands of his work poorly, and they rarely cemented a relationship. Because he knew how difficult and frustrating those demands of time, energy and heart were on those who waited, he expected complaints, sulking, even accusations, from the women who felt neglected.

So he never made promises. And he lived alone.

He knew there was little he could do here at the scene. He should have been at his desk—or at least, he thought, have gone home just to let his mind clear. But he'd been pulled back to this house. No, to this woman, he admitted. It wasn't the two stories of wood and glass, however lovely, that dragged at him.

It was the face in the portrait.

He'd left his car at the top of the sweep of the drive,

and walked to the house sheltered by grand old trees and well-trimmed shrubs green with summer. He'd let himself in, turned the switch that had the foyer chandelier blazing light.

His men had already started the tedious door-to-door of the neighborhood, hoping that someone, in another of the big, exquisite homes, would have heard something, seen anything.

The medical examiner was slow—understandably, Seth reminded himself. It was a holiday, and the staff was down to bare minimum. Official reports would take a bit longer.

But it wasn't the reports or lack of them that nagged at his mind as he wandered back, inevitably, to the portrait over the glazed-tile hearth.

Grace Fontaine had been loved. He'd underestimated the depth friendship could reach. But he'd seen that depth, and that shocked and racking grief in the faces of the two women he'd just left.

There had been a bond between Bailey James, M. J. O'Leary and Grace that was as strong as he'd ever seen. He regretted—and he rarely had regrets—that he'd had to tell them so bluntly.

I'm sorry for your loss.

Words cops said to euphemize the death they lived with—often violent, always unexpected. He had said the words, as he had too often in the past, and watched the fragile blonde and the cat-eyed redhead simply crumble. Clutching each other, they had simply crumbled.

He hadn't needed the two men who had ranged themselves as the women's champions to tell him to leave them alone with their grief. There would be no questions, no statements, no answers, that night. Nothing he could say or do would penetrate that thick curtain of grief.

Grace Fontaine had been loved, he thought again, looking into those spectacular blue eyes. Not simply desired by men, but loved by two women. What was behind those eyes, what was behind that face, that had deserved that kind of unquestioning emotion?

"Who the hell were you?" he murmured, and was answered by that bold, inviting smile. "Too beautiful to be real. Too aware of your own beauty to be soft." His deep voice, rough with fatigue, echoed in the empty house. He slipped his hands in his pockets, rocked back on his heels. "Too dead to care."

And though he turned from the portrait, he had the uneasy feeling that it was watching him. Measuring him.

He had yet to reach her next of kin, the aunt and uncle in Virginia who had raised her after the death of her parents. The aunt was summering in a villa in Italy and was, for tonight, out of touch.

Villas in Italy, he mused, blue diamonds, oil portraits over fireplaces of sapphire-blue tile. It was a world far removed from his firmly middle-class upbringing, and from the life he'd embraced through his career.

But he knew violence didn't play favorites.

He would eventually go home to his tiny little house on its postage-stamp lot, crowded together with dozens of other tiny little houses. It would be empty, as he'd never found a woman who moved him to want to share even that small private space. But his home would be there for him.

And this house, for all its gleaming wood and acres

of gleaming glass, its sloping lawn, sparkling pool and trimmed bushes, hadn't protected its mistress.

He walked around the stark outline on the floor and started up the stairs again. His mood was edgy—he could admit that. And the best thing to smooth it out again was work.

He thought perhaps a woman with as eventful a life as Grace Fontaine would have noted those events—and her personal feelings about them—in a diary.

He worked in silence, going through her bedroom carefully, knowing very well that he was trapped in that sultry scent she'd left behind.

He'd taken his tie off, tucked it in his pocket. The weight from his weapon, snug in his shoulder harness, was so much a part of him it went unnoticed.

He went through her drawers without a qualm, though they were largely empty now, as their contents were strewn around the room. He searched beneath them, behind them and under the mattress.

He thought, irrelevantly, that she'd owned enough clothing to outfit a good-size modeling troupe, and that she'd leaned toward soft materials. Silks, cashmeres, satins, thin brushed wools. Bold colors. Jewel colors, with a bent toward blues.

With those eyes, he thought as they crept back into his mind, why not?

He caught himself wondering how her voice had sounded. Would it have fit that sultry face, been husky and low, another purr of temptation for a man? He imagined it that way, a voice as dark and sensual as the scent that hung on the air.

Her body had fit the face, fit the scent, he mused, stepping into her enormous walk-in closet. Of course, she'd helped nature along there. And he wondered why a woman would feel impelled to add silicone to her body to lure a man. And what kind of pea-brained man would prefer it to an honest shape.

He preferred honesty in women. Insisted on it. Which, he supposed, was one of the reasons he lived alone.

He scanned the clothes still hanging with a shake of his head. Even the killer had run out of patience here, it seemed. The hangers were swept back so that garments were crowded together, but he hadn't bothered to pull them all out.

Seth judged that the number of shoes totaled well over two hundred, and one wall of shelves had obviously been fashioned to hold handbags. These, in every imaginable shape and size and color, had been pulled out of their slots, ripped open and searched.

A cupboard had held more—sweaters, scarves. Costume jewelry. He imagined she'd had plenty of the real sparkles, as well. Some would have been in the now empty safe downstairs, he was sure. And she might have a lockbox at a bank.

That he would check on first thing in the morning.

She'd enjoyed music, he mused, scanning the wireless speakers. He'd seen speakers in every room of the house, and there had been CDs, tapes, even old albums, tossed around the living area downstairs. She'd had eclectic taste there. Everything from Bach to the B-52s.

Had she spent many evenings alone? he wondered. With music playing through the house? Had she ever curled up in front of that classy fireplace with one of the hundreds of books that lined the walls of her library?

Snuggled up on the couch, he thought, wearing that

little red robe, with her million-dollar legs tucked up. A glass of brandy, the music on low, the starlight streaming through the roof windows.

He could see it too well. He could see her look up, skim that fall of hair back from that staggering face, curve those tempting lips as she caught him watching her. Set the book aside, reach out a hand in invitation, give that low, husky purr of a laugh as she drew him down beside her.

He could almost taste it.

Because he could, he swore under his breath, gave himself a moment to control the sudden upbeat of his heart rate.

Dead or alive, he decided, the woman was a witch. And the damn stones, preposterous or not, only seemed to add to her power.

And he was wasting his time. Completely wasting it, he told himself as he rose. He was covering ground best covered through rules and routine. He needed to go back, light a fire under the M.E., push for an estimated time of death. He needed to start calling the numbers in the victim's address book.

He needed to get out of this house that smelled of this woman. All but breathed of her. And stay out of it, he determined, until he was certain he could rein in his uncharacteristic imaginings.

Annoyed with himself, irked by his own deviation from strict routine, he walked back through the bedroom. He'd just started down the curve of the stairs when a movement caught his eye. His hand reached for his weapon. But it was already too late for that.

Very slowly, he dropped his hand, stood where he was and stared down. It wasn't the automatic pointed at his heart that stunned him motionless. It was the fact that it was held, steady as a rock, in the hand of a dead woman.

"Well," the dead woman said, stepping forward into the halo of light from the foyer chandelier. "You're certainly a messy thief, and a stupid one." Those shockingly blue eyes stared up at him. "Why don't you give me one good reason why I shouldn't put a hole in your head before I call the police?"

For a ghost, she met his earlier fantasy perfectly. The voice was a purr, hot and husky and stunningly alive. And for the recently departed, she had a very warm flush of temper in her cheeks. It wasn't often that Seth's mind clicked off. But it had. He saw a woman, runway-fresh in white silk, the glint of jewels at her ears and a shiny silver gun in her hand.

He pulled himself back roughly, though none of the shock or the effort showed as he met her demand with an unsmiling response. "I *am* the police."

Her lips curved, a generous bow of sarcasm. "Of course you are, handsome. Who else would be creeping around a locked house when no one's at home but an overworked cop on his beat?"

"I haven't been a beat cop for quite some time. I'm Buchanan. Lieutenant Seth Buchanan. If you'd aim your weapon just a little to the left of my heart, I'll show you my badge."

"I'd just love to see it." Watching him, she slowly shifted the barrel of the gun. Her heart was thudding like a jackhammer with a combination of fear and anger, but she took another casual step forward as he reached two fingers into his pocket. The badge looked real enough, she mused. What she could see of the identification with the gold shield on the flap that he held up.

And she began to get a very bad feeling. A worse sinking in the stomach sensation than she'd experienced when she pulled up to the drive, saw the strange car and the lights blazing inside her empty house.

She flicked her eyes from the badge up to his again. Damned if he didn't look more like a cop than a crook, she decided. Very attractive, in a straight-edged, buttoned-down sort of fashion. The solid body, broad of shoulder and narrow of hip, appeared ruthlessly disciplined.

Eyes like that, cool and clear and golden brown, that seemed to see everything at once, belonged to either a cop or a criminal. Either way, she imagined, they belonged to a dangerous sort of man.

Dangerous men usually appealed to her. But at the moment, as she took in the oddity of the situation, her mood wasn't receptive.

"All right, Buchanan, Lieutenant Seth, why don't you tell me what you're doing in my house." She thought of what she carried in her purse—what Bailey had sent her only days before—and felt that unsettling sensation in her stomach deepen.

What kind of trouble are we in? she wondered. And just how do I slide out of it with a cop staring me down?

"Have you got a search warrant to go along with that badge?" she demanded.

"No, I don't." He'd have felt better, considerably better, if she'd put the gun down altogether. But she seemed content to hold it, aiming it lower now, no less steadily, but lower. Still, his composure had snapped back. Keeping his eyes on hers, he came down the rest of the stairs and stood in the lofty foyer, facing her. "You're Grace Fontaine."

She watched him tuck his badge back into his pocket, while those unreadable cop's eyes skimmed over her face. Memorizing features, she thought, irritated. Making mental note of any distinguishing marks. Just what the hell was going on?

"Yes, I'm Grace Fontaine. This is my property, my home. And as you're in it, without a proper warrant, you're trespassing. As calling a cop seems superfluous, maybe I'll just call my lawyer."

He angled his head, and unwillingly caught a whiff of that siren's scent of hers. Perhaps it was that, and feeling its instant and unwelcome effect on his system, that had him speaking without thought.

"Well, Ms. Fontaine, you look damn good for a dead woman."

Chapter 2

Her response was to narrow her eyes, arch a brow. "If that's some sort of cop humor, I'm afraid you'll have to translate."

It annoyed him that she'd jarred the remark out of him. It wasn't professional. Cautious, he brought a hand up slowly, tipped the barrel of the gun farther to the left. "Do you mind?" he said, then, quickly, before she could agree, he twisted it neatly out of her hand, pulled out the clip. It wasn't the time to ask if she had a license to carry, so he merely handed her back the empty gun and pocketed the clip.

"It's best to keep both hands on your weapon," he said easily, and with such sobriety that she suspected amusement lurked beneath. "And, if you want to keep it, not to get within reach."

"Thanks so much for the lesson in self-defense." Obviously irritated, she opened her bag and dumped the gun inside. "But you still haven't answered my initial question, Lieutenant. Why are you in my house?"

"You've had an incident, Ms. Fontaine."

"An incident? More copspeak?" She blew out a breath. "Was there a break-in?" she asked, and for the first time took her attention off the man and glanced past him into the foyer. "A robbery?" she added, then caught sight of an overturned chair and some smashed crockery through the archway in the living area.

Swearing, she started to push past him. He curled a hand over her arm to stop her. "Ms. Fontaine—"

"Get your hand off me," she snapped, interrupting him. "This is my home."

He kept his grip firm. "I'm aware of that. Exactly when was the last time you were in it?"

"I'll give you a damn statement after I've seen what's missing." She managed another two steps and saw from the disorder in the living area that it hadn't been a neat or organized robbery. "Well, they did quite a job, didn't they? My cleaning service is going to be very unhappy."

She glanced down to where Seth's fingers were still curled around her arm. "Are you testing my biceps, Lieutenant? I do like to think they're firm."

"Your muscle tone's fine." From what he could see of her in the filmy ivory slacks, it appeared more than fine. "I'd like you to answer my question, Ms. Fontaine. When were you home last?"

"Here?" She sighed, shrugged one elegant shoulder. Her mind was flitting around the annoying details that were the backwash of a robbery. Calling her insurance agent, filing a claim, giving statements. "Wednesday afternoon. I went out of town for a few days." She was more shaken than she cared to admit that her house had been robbed and ransacked in her absence. Her things touched and taken by strangers. But she slid him a smiling glance from under her lashes. "Aren't you going to take notes?"

"As a matter of fact, I am. Shortly. Who was staying in the house in your absence?"

"No one. I don't care to have people in my home when I'm away. Now if you'll excuse me…" She gave her arm a quick, hard jerk and strode through the foyer and under the arch. "Good God." The anger came first, quick and intense. She wanted to kick something, no matter that it was broken and ruined already. "Did they have to break what they didn't cart out?" she muttered. She glanced up, saw the splintered railing and swore again. "And what the devil did they do up there? A lot of good an alarm system does if anyone can just…"

She stopped her forward motion, her voice trailing off, as she saw the outline on the gleaming chestnut wood of the floor. As she stared at it, unable to tear her eyes away, the blood drained out of her face, leaving it painfully cold and stiff.

Placing one hand on the back of the stained sofa for balance, she stared down at the outline, the diamond glitter of broken glass that had been her coffee table, and the blood that had dried to a dark pool.

"Why don't we go into the dining room?" he said quietly.

She jerked her shoulders back, though he hadn't touched her. The pit of her stomach was cased in ice, and the flashes of heat that lanced through her did nothing to melt it. "Who was killed?" she demanded. "Who died here?"

"Up until a few minutes ago, it was assumed you did."

She closed her eyes, vaguely concerned that her vision was dimming at the edges. "Excuse me," she said, quite clearly, and walked across the room on numb legs. She picked up a bottle of brandy that lay on its side on the floor, fumbled open a display cabinet for a glass. And poured generously.

She took the first drink as medicine. He could see that in the way she tossed it back, shuddered twice, hard. It didn't bring the color back to her face, but he imagined it had shocked her system into functioning again.

"Ms. Fontaine, I think it would be better if we talked about this in another room."

"I'm all right." But her voice was raw. She drank again before turning to him. "Why did you think it was me?"

"The victim was in your house, dressed in a robe. She met your general description. Her face had been… damaged by the fall. She was your approximate height and weight, your age, your coloring."

Her coloring, Grace thought on a wave of staggering relief. Not Bailey or M.J., then. "I had no houseguest while I was gone." She took a deep breath, knowing the calm was there, if only she could reach it. "I have no idea who the woman was, unless it was one of the burglars. How did she—" Grace looked up again at the broken railing, the viciously sharp edges of wood. "She must have been pushed."

"That has yet to be determined."

"I'm sure it has. I can't help you as to who she was, Lieutenant. As I don't have a twin, I can only—" She broke off, her color draining a second time. Now her free hand fisted and pressed hard to her stomach. "Oh, no. Oh, God."

He understood, didn't hesitate. "Who was she?"

"I— It could have been… She's stayed here before while I was away. That's why I stopped leaving a spare key outside. She might have had it copied, though. She'd think nothing of that."

Turning her gaze away from the outline, she walked back through the debris, sat on the arm of the sofa. "A cousin." Grace sipped brandy again, slowly, letting it ease warmth back into her system. "Melissa Bennington— No, I think she took the Fontaine back a few months ago, after the divorce. I'm not sure." She pushed a hand through her hair. "I wasn't interested enough to be sure of a detail like that."

"She resembles you?"

She offered a weak, humorless smile. "It's Melissa's mission to *be* me. I went from finding it mildly flattering to mildly annoying. In the last few years I found it pathetic. There's a surface resemblance, I suppose. She's augmented it. She let her hair grow, dyed it my color. There was some difference in build, but she… augmented that, as well. She shops the same stores, uses the same salons. Chooses the same men. We grew up together, more or less. She always felt I got the better deal on all manner of levels."

She made herself look back, look down, and felt a wash of grief and pity. "Apparently I did, this time around."

"If someone didn't know you well, could they mistake you?"

"A passing glance, I suppose. Maybe a casual acquaintance. No one who—" She broke off again, got to her feet. "You think someone killed her believing her to be me? Mistaking her for me, as you did? That's absurd. It was a break-in, a burglary. A terrible accident."

"It's possible." He had indeed taken out his book to note down her cousin's name. Now he glanced up, met her eyes. "It's also more than possible that someone came here, mistook her for you, and assumed she had the third Star."

She was good, he decided. There was barely a flicker in her eyes before she lied. "I have no idea what you're talking about."

"Yes, you do. And if you haven't been home since Wednesday, you still have it." He glanced down at the bag she continued to hold.

"I don't generally carry stars in my purse." She sent him a smile that was shaky around the edges. "But it's a lovely, almost poetic, thought. Now, I'm very tired—"

"Ms. Fontaine." His voice was clipped and cool. "This victim is the sixth body I've dealt with today that traces back to those three blue diamonds."

Her hand shot out, gripped his arm. "M.J. and Bailey?"

"Your friends are fine." He felt her grip go limp. "They've had an eventful holiday weekend, all of which could have been avoided if they'd contacted and cooperated with the police. And it's cooperation I'll have from you now, one way or the other."

She tossed her hair back. "Where are they? What did you do, toss them in a cell? My lawyer will have them out and your butt in a sling before you can finish reciting the Miranda." She started toward the phone, saw it wasn't on the Queen Anne table.

"No, they're not in a cell." It goaded him, the way she

snapped into gear, ready to buck the rules. "I imagine they're planning your funeral right about now."

"Planning my—" Her fabulous eyes went huge with distress. "Oh, my God, you told them I was dead? They think I'm dead? Where are they? Where's the damn phone? I have to call them."

She crouched to push through the rubble, shoving at him when he took her arm again. "They're not home, either of them."

"You said they weren't in jail."

"And they're not." He could see he'd get nothing out of her until she'd satisfied herself. "I'll take you to them. Then we're going to sort this out, Ms. Fontaine— I promise you."

Grace didn't speak as he drove her toward the tidy suburbs edging D.C. He'd assured her that Bailey and M.J. were fine, and her instincts told her that Lieutenant Seth Buchanan was saying nothing but the truth. Facts were his business, after all, she thought. But she still gripped her hands together until her knuckles ached.

She had to see them, touch them.

Guilt was already weighing on her, guilt that they should be grieving for her, when she'd spent the past few days indulging her need to be alone, to be away. To be somewhere else.

What had happened to them over the long weekend? Had they tried to contact her while she was out of reach? It was painfully obvious that the three blue diamonds Bailey had been assessing for the museum were at the bottom of it all.

As the afterimage of that stark outline on the chestnut floor flashed into her head, Grace shuddered once again.

Melissa. Poor, pathetic Melissa. But she couldn't think of that now. She couldn't think of anything but her friends.

"They're not hurt?" she managed to ask.

"No." Seth left it at that, drove through the wash of streetlights and headlights. Her scent was sliding silkily through his car, teasing his senses. Deliberately he opened his window and let the light, damp breeze chase it away. "Where have you been the last few days, Ms. Fontaine?"

"Away." Weary, she laid her head back, shut her eyes. "It's one of my favorite spots."

She jerked upright again when he turned down a tree-lined street, then swung into the drive of a brick house. She saw a shiny Jaguar, then an impossibly decrepit boat of a car. But no spiffy MG, no practical little compact.

"Their cars aren't here," she began, tossing him a look of distrust and accusation.

"But they are."

She climbed out and, ignoring him, hurried toward the front door. Her knock was brisk, businesslike, but her fist trembled. The door opened, and a man she'd never seen before stared down at her. His cool green eyes flickered with shock, then slowly warmed. His flash of a smile was blinding. Then he reached out, laid a hand gently on her cheek.

"You're Grace."

"Yes, I—"

"It's absolutely wonderful to see you." He gathered her into his arms, one of which was freshly bandaged, with such easy affection that she didn't have time to register surprise. "I'm Cade," he murmured, his gaze meeting Seth's over Grace's head. "Cade Parris. Come on in."

"Bailey. M.J."

"Just in here. They'll be fine as soon as they see you." He took her arm, felt the quick, hard tremors in it. But in the doorway of the living room, she stopped, laid a hand over his arm.

Inside, Bailey and M.J. stood, facing away, hands linked. Their voices were low, with tears wrenching through them. A man stood a short distance away, his hands thrust in his pockets and a look of helplessness on his bruised and battered face. When he saw her, his eyes, the gray of storm clouds, narrowed, flashed. Then smiled.

Grace took one shuddering breath, exhaled it slowly. "Well," she said in a clear, steady voice, "it's gratifying to know someone would weep copiously over me."

Both women whirled. For a moment, all three stared, three pair of eyes brimming over. To Seth's mind, they all moved as one, as a unit, so that their leaping rush across the room to each other held an uncanny and undeniably feminine grace. Then they were fused together, voices and tears mixing.

A triangle, he thought, frowning. With three points that made a whole. Like the golden triangle that held three priceless and powerful stones.

"I think they could use a little time," Cade said quietly, and gestured to the other man. "Lieutenant?" He motioned down the hall, lifting his brows when Seth hesitated. "I don't think they're going anywhere just now."

With a barely perceptible shrug, Seth stepped back.

He could give them twenty minutes. "I need your phone."

"There's one in the kitchen. Want a beer, Jack?"

The third man grinned. "You're playing my song."

"Amnesia," Grace said a little time later. She and Bailey were huddled together on the sofa, with M.J. sitting on the floor at their feet. "Everything just blanked?"

"Everything." Bailey kept her hold on Grace's hand tight, afraid to break the link. "I woke up in this horrible little hotel room with no memory, over a million in cash, and the diamond. I picked Cade's name out of the phone book. Parris." She smiled a little. "Funny, isn't it?"

"I'm going to get you to France yet," Grace promised.

"He helped me through everything." The warmth in her tone had Grace sharing a quick look with M.J. This was something to be discussed in detail later. "I started to remember, piece by piece. You and M.J., just flashes. I could see your faces, even hear your voices, but nothing fit. He's the one who narrowed it down to Salvini, and when he took me there... He broke in."

"Shortly before we did," M.J. added. "Jack could tell the rear locks had been picked."

"We got inside," Bailey continued, and her tear-ravaged eyes went glassy. "And I remembered, I remembered it all then, how Thomas and Timothy were planning to steal the stones, copy them. How I'd shipped one off to each of you to keep it from happening. Stupid, so stupid."

"No, it wasn't." Grace slid an arm around Bailey's shoulders. "It makes perfect sense to me. You didn't have time for anything else."

"I should have called the police, but I was so sure I could turn things around. I was going into Thomas's office to have a showdown, tell them it was over. And I saw..." She trembled again. "The fight. Horrible. The lightning flashing through the windows, their faces. Then Timothy grabbed the letter opener, the knife. The power went out, but the lightning kept flashing, and I could see what he was doing...to Thomas. All the blood."

"Don't," M.J. murmured, rubbing a comforting hand on Bailey's knee. "Don't go back there."

"No." Bailey shook her head. "I have to. He saw me, Grace. He would have killed me. He came after me. I had grabbed the bag with their deposit money, and I ran through the dark. And I hid down under the stairs. In this little cave under the stairs. But I could see him hunting for me, blood all over his hands. I still don't remember how I got out, got to that room."

Grace couldn't bear to imagine it—her quiet, serious-minded friend, pursued by a murderer. "The important thing is that you did get away, and you're safe." Grace looked down at M.J. "We all are." She tried a bolstering grin. "And how did you spend your holiday?"

"On the run with a bounty hunter, handcuffed to a bed in a cheap motel, being shot at by a couple of creeps—with a little detour up to your place in the mountains."

Bounty hunter, Grace thought, trying to keep pace. The man named Jack, she supposed, with the bronze-tipped ponytail and the stormy gray eyes. And the killer grin. Handcuffs, cheap motels, and shootings. Pressing fingertips to her eyes, she latched on to the least disturbing detail.

"You were at my place? When?"

"It's a long story." M.J. gave a quick version of a handful of days from her first encounter with Jack, when he'd tried to take her in, believing her to be a bail jumper, to the two of them escaping that setup and working their way back to the core of the puzzle.

"We know someone's pulling the strings," M.J. concluded. "But we haven't gotten very far on figuring that out yet. The bail bondsman-cum-blackmailer who gave Jack the fake paperwork on me is dead, the two guys who came after us are dead, the Salvinis are dead."

"And Melissa," Grace murmured.

"It was Melissa?" Bailey turned to Grace. "In your house?"

"It must have been. When I got home, the cop was there. The place was torn up, and they'd assumed it was me." It took a moment, a carefully indrawn breath, a steady exhale, before she could finish. "She'd fallen off the balcony—or been pushed. I was miles away when it happened."

"Where did you go?" M.J. asked her. "When Jack and I got to your country place, it was locked up tight. I thought…I was sure you'd just been there. I could smell you."

"I left late yesterday morning. Got an itch to be near the water, so I drove down the Eastern Shore, found a little B-and-B. I did some antiquing, rubbed elbows with tourists, watched a fireworks display. I didn't leave until late today. I nearly stayed over another night. But I called both of you from the B-and-B and got your machines. I started feeling uncomfortable about being out of contact, so I headed home."

She shut her eyes a moment. "Bailey, I hadn't been

really thinking. Just before I left for the country, we lost one of the children."

"Oh, Grace, I'm sorry."

"It happens all the time. They're born with AIDS or a crack addiction or a hole in the heart. Some of them die. But I can't get used to it, and it was on my mind. So I wasn't really thinking. When I started back, I started to think. And I started to worry. Then the cop was there in my house. He asked about the stone. I didn't know what you wanted me to tell him."

"We've told the police everything now." Bailey sighed. "Neither Cade nor Jack seem to like this Buchanan very much, but they respect his abilities. The two stones are safe now, as we are."

"I'm sorry for what you went through, both of you. I'm sorry I wasn't here."

"It wouldn't have made any difference," M.J. declared. "We were scattered all over—one stone apiece. Maybe we were meant to be."

"Now we're together." Grace took each of their hands in hers. "What happens next?"

"Ladies." Seth stepped into the room, skimmed his cool gaze over them, then focused on Grace. "Ms. Fontaine. The diamond?"

She rose, picked up the purse she'd tossed carelessly on the end of the couch. Opening it, she took out a velvet pouch, slid the stone out into her palm. "Magnificent, isn't it?" she murmured, studying the flash of bold blue light. "Diamonds are supposed to be cold to the touch, aren't they, Bailey? Yet this has…heat." She lifted her eyes to Seth's as she crossed to him. "Still, how many lives is it worth?"

She held her open palm out. When his fingers closed

around the stone, she felt the jolt—his fingers on her skin, the shimmering blue diamond between their hands.

Something clicked, almost audibly.

She wondered if he'd felt it, heard it. Why else did those enigmatic eyes narrow, or his hand linger? The breath caught in her throat.

"Impressive, isn't it?" she managed, then felt the odd wave of emotion and recognition ebb when he took the stone from her hand.

He didn't care for the shock that had run up his arm, and he spoke bitingly. "I imagine this one's out of even your price range, Ms. Fontaine."

She merely smiled. No, she told herself, he couldn't have felt anything—and neither had she. Just imagination and stress. "I prefer to decorate my body in something less…obvious."

Bailey rose. "The Stars are my responsibility, unless and until the Smithsonian indicates otherwise." She looked over at Cade, who remained in the doorway. "We'll put them in the safe. All of them. And I'll speak with Dr. Linstrum in the morning."

Seth turned the stone over in his hand. He imagined he could confiscate it, and its mates. They were, after all, evidence in several homicides. But he didn't relish driving back to the station with a large fortune in his car.

Parris was an irritant, he reflected. But he was an honest one. And, technically, the stones were in Bailey James's keeping until the Smithsonian relieved her of them. He wondered just what the powers at the museum would have to say about the recent travels of the Three Stars.

But that wasn't his problem.

"Lock it up," he said, passing the stone off to Cade. "And I'll be talking with Dr. Linstrum in the morning, as well, Ms. James."

Cade took one quick, threatening step forward. "Look, Buchanan—"

"No." Quietly, Bailey stepped between them, a cool breeze between two building storms. "Lieutenant Buchanan's right, Cade. It's his business now."

"That doesn't stop it from being mine." He gave Seth one last, warning look. "Watch your step," he said, then walked away with the stone.

"Thank you for bringing Grace by so quickly, Lieutenant."

Seth looked down at the extended, and obviously dismissing, hand Bailey offered him. Here's your hat, he thought, what's your hurry. "I'm sorry you were disturbed, Ms. James." His gaze flicked over to M.J. "Ms. O'Leary. You'll keep available."

"We're not going anywhere." M.J.'s chin angled, a cocky gesture as Jack crossed to her. "Drive carefully, Lieutenant."

He acknowledged the second dismissal with a slight nod. "Ms. Fontaine? I'll drive you back."

"She's not leaving." M.J. jumped in front of Grace like a tiger defending her cub. "She's not going back to that house tonight. She's staying here, with us."

"You may not care to go back home, Ms. Fontaine," Seth said coolly. "You may find it more comfortable to answer questions in my office."

"You can't be serious—"

He cut Bailey's protest off with a look. "I have a body in the morgue. I take it very seriously."

"You're a class act, Buchanan," Jack drawled, but the sound was low and threatening. "Why don't you and I go in the other room and…talk about our options?"

"It's all right." Grace stepped forward, working up a believable smile. "It's Jack, isn't it?"

"That's right." He took his attention from Buchanan long enough to smile at her. "Jack Dakota. Pleased to meet you…Miss April."

"Oh, my misspent youth survives." With a little laugh, she kissed his bruised cheek. "I appreciate the offer to beat up the lieutenant for me, Jack, but you look like you've already gone several rounds."

Grinning now, he stroked a thumb over his bruised jaw. "I've got a few more rounds in me."

"I don't doubt it. But, sad to say, the cop's right." She pushed her hair to her back and turned that smile, several degrees cooler now, on Seth. "Tactless, but right. He needs some answers. I need to go back."

"You're not going back to your house alone," Bailey insisted. "Not tonight, Grace."

"I'll be fine. But if it's all right with your Cade, I'll deal with this, pick up a few things and come back." She glanced over at Cade as he came back into the room. "Got a spare bed, darling?"

"You bet. Why don't I go with you, help you pick up your things and bring you back?"

"You stay here with Bailey." She kissed him, as well—a casual and already affectionate brush of lips. "I'm sure Lieutenant Buchanan and I will manage." She picked up her purse, turned and embraced both M.J. and Bailey again. "Don't worry about me. After all, I'm in the arms of the law."

She eased back, shot Seth one of those full candle-power smiles. "Isn't that right, Lieutenant?"

"In a manner of speaking." He stepped back and waited for her to walk to the door ahead of him.

She waited until they were in his car and pulling out of the drive. "I need to see the body." She didn't look at him, but lifted a hand to the four people crowded at the front door, watching them drive away. "You need—She'll have to be identified, won't she?"

It surprised him that she'd take the duty on. "Yes."

"Then let's get it over with. After—afterwards, I'll answer your questions. I'd prefer we handle that in your office," she added, using that smile again. "My house isn't ready for company."

"Fine."

She'd known it would be hard. She'd known it would be horrible. Grace had prepared herself for it—or she'd thought she had. Nothing, she realized as she stared down at what remained of the woman in the morgue, could have prepared her.

It was hardly surprising that they'd mistaken Melissa for her. The face Melissa had been so proud of was utterly ruined. Death had been cruel here, and, through her involvement with the hospital, Grace had reason to know it often was.

"It's Melissa." Her voice echoed flatly in the chilly white room. "My cousin, Melissa Fontaine."

"You're sure?"

"Yes. We shared the same health club, among other things. I know her body as well as I know mine. She has a sickle-shaped birthmark at the small of her back, just left of center. And there's a scar on the bottom of her left foot, small, crescent-shaped, in the ball of her foot, where she stepped on a broken shell in the Hamptons when we were twelve."

Seth shifted, found the scar, then nodded to the M.E.'s assistant. "I'm sorry for your loss."

"Yes, I'm sure you are." With muscles that felt like glass, she turned, her dimming vision passing over him. "Excuse me."

She made it nearly to the door before she swayed. Swearing under his breath, Seth caught her, pulled her out into the corridor and put her in a chair. With one hand, he shoved her head between her knees.

"I'm not going to faint." She squeezed her eyes tightly shut, battling fiercely against the twin foes of dizziness and nausea.

"Could have fooled me."

"I'm much too sophisticated for something as maudlin as a swoon." But her voice broke, her shoulders sagged, and for a moment she kept her head down. "Oh, God, she's dead. And all because she hated me."

"What?"

"Doesn't matter. She's dead." Bracing herself, she sat up again, let her head rest against the cold white wall. Her cheeks were just as colorless. "I have to call my aunt. Her mother. I have to tell her what happened."

He gauged this woman, studying the face that was no less staggeringly lovely for being bone-white. "Give me the name. I'll take care of it."

"It's Helen Wilson Fontaine. I'll do it."

He didn't realize until her hand moved that he'd placed his own over it. He pulled back on every level, and rose. "I haven't been able to reach Helen Fontaine or her husband. She's in Europe."

"I know where she is." Grace shook back her hair, but didn't try to stand. Not yet. "I can find her." The thought of making that call, saying what had to be said, squeezed her throat. "Could I have some water, Lieutenant?"

His heels echoed on tile as he strode off. Then there was silence—a full, damning silence that whispered of what kind of business was done in such places. There were scents here that slid slyly under the potent odors of antiseptics and industrial cleaning solutions.

She was pitifully grateful when she heard his footsteps on the return journey.

She took the paper cup from him with both hands, drinking slowly, concentrating on the simple act of swallowing liquid.

"Why did she hate you?"

"What?"

"Your cousin. You said she hated you. Why?"

"Family trait," she said briefly. She handed him back the empty cup as she rose. "I'd like to go now."

He took her measure a second time. Her color had yet to return, her pupils were dilated, the electric-blue irises were glassy. He doubted she'd last another hour.

"I'll take you back to Parris's," he decided. "You can get your things in the morning, come in to my office to make your statement."

"I said I'd do it tonight."

"And I say you'll do it in the morning. You're no good to me now."

She tried a weak laugh. "Why, Lieutenant, I believe you're the first man who's ever said that to me. I'm crushed."

"Don't waste the routine on me." He took her arm,

led her to the outside doors. "You haven't got the energy for it."

He was exactly right. She pulled her arm free as they stepped back into the thick night air. "I don't like you."

"You don't have to." He opened the car door, waited. "Any more than I have to like you."

She stepped to the door, and with it between them met his eyes. "But the difference is, if I had the energy—or the inclination—I could make you sit up and beg."

She got in, sliding those long, silky legs in.

Not likely, Seth told himself as he shut the door with a snap. But he wasn't entirely sure he believed it.

Chapter 3

She felt like a weakling, but she didn't go home. She'd needed friends, not that empty house, with the shadow of a body drawn on the floor.

Jack had gone over, fetched her bags out of her car and brought them to her. For a day, at least, she was content to make do with that.

Since she was driving in to meet with Seth, Grace had made do carefully. She'd dressed in a summer suit she'd just picked up on the Shore. The little short skirt and waist-length jacket in buttercup yellow weren't precisely professional—but she wasn't aiming for professional. She'd taken the time to catch her waterfall of hair back in a complicated French braid and made up her face with the concentration and determination of a general plotting a decisive battle.

Meeting with Seth again felt like a battle.

Her stomach was still raw from the call she'd made to her aunt, and the sickness that had overwhelmed her after it. She'd slept poorly, but she had slept, tucked into one of Cade's guest rooms, secure that those who meant most to her were close by.

She would deal with the relatives later, she thought, easing her convertible into the lot at the station house. It would be hard, but she would deal with them. For now, she had to deal with herself. And Seth Buchanan.

If anyone had been watching as she stepped from her car and started across the lot, he would have seen a transformation. Subtly, gradually, her eyes went from weary to sultry. Her gait loosened, eased into a lazy, hip-swinging walk designed to cross a man's eyes. Her mouth turned up slightly at the corners, into a secret, knowing female smile.

It wasn't really a mask, but another part of her. Innate and habitual, it was an image she could draw on at will. She willed it now, flashing a slow under-the-lashes smile at the uniform who stepped to the door as she did. He flushed, moved back and nearly bobbled the door in his hurry to open it for her.

"Why, thank you, Officer."

Heat rose up his neck, into his face, and made her smile widen. She was right on target. Seth Buchanan wouldn't see a pale, trembling woman this morning. He'd see Grace Fontaine, just hitting her stride.

She sauntered up to the sergeant on duty at the desk, skimmed a fingertip along the edge. "Excuse me?"

"Yes, ma'am." His Adam's apple bobbed three times as he swallowed.

"I wonder if you could help me? I'm looking for a Lieutenant Buchanan. Are you in charge?" She skimmed her gaze over him. "You must be in charge, Commander."

"Ah, yes. No. It's sergeant." He fumbled for the sign-in book, the passes. "I— He's— You'll find the lieutenant upstairs, detective division. To the left of the stairs."

"Oh." She took the pen he offered and signed her name boldly. "Thank you, Commander. I mean, Sergeant."

She heard his little expulsion of breath as she turned, and felt his gaze on her legs as she climbed the stairs.

She found the detective division easily enough. One sweeping glance took in the front-to-front desks, some manned, some not. The cops were in shirtsleeves in an oppressive heat that was barely touched by what had to be a faulty air-conditioning unit. A lot of guns, she thought, a lot of half-eaten meals and empty cups of coffee. Phones shrilling.

She picked her mark—a man with a loosened tie, feet on the desk, a report of some kind in one hand and a Danish in the other. As she started through the crowded room, several conversations stopped. Someone whistled softly—it was like a sigh. The man at the desk swept his feet to the floor, swallowed the Danish.

"Ma'am."

About thirty, she judged, though his hairline was receding rapidly. He wiped his crumb-dusted fingers on his shirt, rolled his eyes slightly to the left, where one of his associates was grinning and pounding a fist to his heart.

"I hope you can help me." She kept her eyes on his, and only his, until a muscle began to twitch in his jaw. "Detective?"

"Yeah, ah, Carter, Detective Carter. What can I do for you?"

"I hope I'm in the right place." For effect, she turned her head, swept her gaze over the room and its occupants. Several stomachs were ruthlessly sucked in. "I'm looking for Lieutenant Buchanan. I think he's expecting me." Gracefully she brushed a loose flutter of hair away from her face. "I'm afraid I just don't know the proper procedure."

"He's in his office. Back in his office." Without taking his eyes from her he jerked a thumb. "Belinski, tell the lieutenant he has a visitor. A Miss…"

"It's Grace." She slid a hip onto the corner of the desk, letting her skirt hike up a dangerous inch. "Grace Fontaine. Is it all right if I wait here, Detective Carter? Am I interrupting your work?"

"Yes— No. Sure."

"It's so exciting." She brought the temperature of the overheated room up ten more degrees with a dazzling smile. "Detective work. You must have so many interesting stories."

By the time Seth had finished the phone call he was on when he was notified of Grace's arrival, shrugged back into the jacket he'd removed as a concession to the heat and made his way into the bull pen, Carter's desk was completely surrounded. He heard a low, throaty female laugh rise out of the center of the crowd.

And saw a half a dozen of his best men panting like puppies over a meaty bone.

The woman, he decided, was going to be an enormous headache.

"I see all cases have been closed this morning, and miraculously crime has come to a halt."

His voice had the desired effect. Several men jerked straight. Those less easily intimidated grinned as they skulked back to their desks. Deserted, Carter flushed from his neck to his receding sandy hairline. "Ah, Grace—that is, Miss Fontaine to see you, Lieutenant. Sir."

"So I see. You finish that report, Detective?"

"Working on it." Carter grabbed the papers he'd tossed aside and buried his nose in them.

"Ms. Fontaine." Seth arched a brow, gestured toward his office.

"It was nice meeting you, Michael." Grace trailed a finger over Carter's shoulder as she passed.

He'd feel the heat of that skimming touch for hours.

"You can cut the power back now," Seth said dryly as he opened the door to his office. "You won't need it."

"You never know, do you?" She sauntered in, moving past him, close enough for them to brush bodies. She thought she felt him stiffen, just a little, but his eyes remained level, cool, and apparently unimpressed. Miffed, she studied his office.

The institutional beige of the walls blended depressingly into the dingy beige of the aging linoleum floor. An overburdened department-issue desk, gray file cabinets, computer, phone and one small window didn't add any spark to the no-nonsense room.

"So this is where the mighty rule," she murmured. It disappointed her that she found no personal touches. No photos, no sports trophies. Nothing she could hold on to, no sign of the man behind the badge.

As she had in the bull pen, she eased a hip onto the corner of his desk. To say she resembled a sunbeam would have been a cliché. And it would have been incorrect, Seth decided. Sunbeams were tame—warm, welcoming. She was an explosive bolt of heat lightning— Hot. Fatal.

A blind man would have noticed those satiny legs in the snug yellow skirt. Seth merely walked around, sat, looked at her face.

"You'd be more comfortable in a chair."

"I'm fine here." Idly she picked up a pen, twirled it. "I don't suppose this is where you interrogate suspects."

"No, we have a dungeon downstairs for that."

Under other circumstances, she would have appreciated his dust-dry tone. "Am I a suspect?"

"I'll let you know." He angled his head. "You recover quickly, Ms. Fontaine."

"Yes, I do. You had questions, Lieutenant?"

"Yes, I do. Sit down. In a chair."

Her lips moved in what was nearly a pout. A luscious come-on-and-kiss-me pout. He felt the quick, helpless pull of lust, and damned her for it. She moved, sliding off the desk, settling into a chair, taking her time crossing those killer legs.

"Better?"

"Where were you Saturday, between the hours of midnight and 3:00 a.m.?"

So that was when it had happened, she thought, and ignored the ache in her stomach. "Aren't you going to read me my rights?"

"You're not charged, you don't need a lawyer. It's a simple question."

"I was in the country. I have a house in western

Maryland. I was alone. I don't have an alibi. Do I need a lawyer now?"

"Do you want to complicate this, Ms. Fontaine?"

"There's no way to simplify it, is there?" But she flicked a hand in dismissal. The thin diamond bracelet that circled her wrist shot fire. "All right, Lieutenant, as uncomplicated as possible. I don't want my lawyer—for the moment. Why don't I just give you a basic rundown? I left for the country on Wednesday. I wasn't expecting my cousin, or anyone, for that matter. I did have contact with a few people over the weekend. I bought a few supplies in the town nearby, shopped at the gardening stand. That would have been Friday afternoon. I picked up some mail on Saturday. It's a small town, the postmistress would remember. That was before noon, however, which would give me plenty of time to drive back. And, of course, there was the courier who delivered Bailey's package on Friday."

"And you didn't find that odd? Your friend sends you a blue diamond, and you just shrug it off and go shopping?"

"I called her. She wasn't in." She arched a brow. "But you probably know that. I did find it odd, but I had things on my mind."

"Such as?"

Her lips curved, but the smile wasn't reflected in her eyes. "I'm not required to tell you my thoughts. I did wonder about it and worried a little. I thought perhaps it was a copy, but I didn't really believe that. A copy couldn't have what that stone has. Bailey's instructions in the package were to keep it with me until she contacted me. So that's what I did."

"No questions?"

"I rarely question people I trust."

He tapped a pencil on the edge of the desk. "You stayed alone in the country until Monday, when you drove back to the city."

"No. I drove down to the Eastern Shore on Sunday. I had a whim." She smiled again. "I often do. I stayed at a bed-and-breakfast."

"You didn't like your cousin?"

"No, I didn't." She imagined that quick shift of topic was an interrogation technique. "She was difficult to like, and I rarely make the effort with difficult people. We were raised together after my parents were killed, but we weren't close. I intruded into her life, into her space. She compensated for it by being disagreeable. I was often disagreeable in return. As we got older, she had a less…successful talent with men than I. Apparently she thought by enhancing the similarities in our appearance, she'd have better success."

"And did she?"

"I suppose it depends on your point of view. Melissa enjoyed men." To combat the guilt coating her heart, Grace leaned back negligently in the chair. "She certainly enjoyed men—which is one of the reasons she was recently divorced. She preferred the species in quantity."

"And how did her husband feel about that?"

"Bobbie's a…" She trailed off, then relieved a great deal of her own tension with a quick, delighted and very appealing laugh. "If you're suggesting that Bobbie—her ex—tracked her down to my house, murdered her, trashed the place and walked off whistling, you couldn't be more wrong. He's a cream puff. And he is, I believe, in England, even as we speak. He enjoys tennis and never misses Wimbledon. You can check easily enough."

Which he would, Seth thought, noting it down. "Some people find murder distasteful on a personal level, but not at a distance. They just pay for a service."

This time she sighed. "We both know Melissa wasn't the target, Lieutenant. I was. She was in my house." Restless, she rose, a graceful and feline movement. Walking to the tiny window, she looked out on his dismal view. "She's made herself at home in my Potomac house twice before when I was away. The first time, I tolerated it. The second, she enjoyed the facilities a bit too enthusiastically for my taste. We had a spat about it. She left in a huff, and I removed the spare key. I should have thought to change the locks, but it never occurred to me she'd go to the trouble of having copies made."

"When was the last time you saw her or spoke with her?"

Grace sighed. Dates ran through her head, people, events, meaningless social forays. "About six weeks ago, maybe eight. At the health club. We ran into each other in the steam room, didn't have much conversation. We never had much to say to each other."

She was regretting that now, Seth realized. Going over in her head opportunities lost or wasted. And it would do no good. "Would she have opened the door to someone she didn't know?"

"If the someone was male and was marginally attractive, yes." Weary of the interview, she turned back. "Look, I don't know what else I can tell you, what help I can possibly be. She was a careless, often arrogant woman. She picked up strange men in bars when she felt the urge. She let someone in that night, and she died for it. Whatever she was, she didn't deserve to die for that."

She brushed at her hair absently, tried to clear her mind as Seth simply sat, waiting. "Maybe he demanded she give him the stone. She wouldn't have understood. She paid for her trespassing, for her carelessness and her ignorance. And the stone is back with Bailey, where it belongs. If you haven't spoken to Dr. Linstrum yet this morning, I can tell you that Bailey should be meeting with him right now. I don't know anything else to tell you."

He kicked back for a moment, his eyes cool and steady on her face. If he discounted the connection with the diamonds, it could play another way. Two women, at odds all their lives. One of them returns home unexpectedly to find the other in her home. An argument. Escalating into a fight. And one of them ends up taking a dive off a second-floor balcony into a pool of glass.

The first woman doesn't panic. She trashes her own home to cover herself, then drives away. Puts distance between herself and the scene.

Was she a skilled enough actress to fake that stark shock, the raw emotion he'd seen on her face the night before?

He thought she was.

But despite that, the scene just didn't click. There was the undeniable connection of the diamonds. And he was dead sure that if Grace Fontaine had caused her cousin's fall, she would have been just as capable of picking up the phone and coolly reporting an accident.

"All right, that's all for now."

"Well." Her breath was a huff of relief. "That wasn't so bad, all in all."

He stood up. "I'll have to ask you to stay available."

She switched on the charm again, a hot, rose-colored light. "I'm always available, handsome. Ask anyone." She picked up her purse, moved with him to the door. "How long before I can have my house dealt with? I'd like to put things back to order as quickly as possible."

"I'll let you know." He glanced at his watch. "When you're up to going through things and doing an inventory to see what's missing, I'd like you to contact me."

"I'm on my way over now to do just that."

His brow furrowed a moment as he juggled responsibilities. He could assign a man to go with her, but he preferred dealing with it himself. "I'll follow you over."

"Police protection?"

"If necessary."

"I'm touched. Why don't I give you a lift, handsome?"

"I'll follow you over," he repeated.

"Suit yourself," she began, and grazed a hand over his cheek. Her eyes widened slightly as his fingers clamped on her wrist. "Don't like to be petted?" She purred the words, surprised at how her heart had jumped and started to race. "Most animals do."

His face was very close to hers, their bodies were just touching, with the heat from the room and something even more sweltering between them. Something old, and almost familiar.

He drew her hand down slowly, kept his fingers on her wrist.

"Be careful what buttons you push."

Excitement, she realized with surprise. It was pure, primal excitement that zipped through her. "Wasted advice," she said silkily, daring him. "I enjoy pushing new ones. And apparently you have a few interesting buttons just begging for attention." She skimmed her gaze deliberately down to his mouth. "Just begging."

He could imagine himself shoving her back against the door, moving fast into that heat, feeling her go molten. Because he was certain she was aware of just how perfectly a man would imagine it, he stepped back, released her and opened the door to the din of the bull pen.

"Be sure to turn in your visitor's badge at the desk," he said.

He was a cool one, Grace thought as she drove. An attractive, successful, unmarried—she'd slipped that bit of data out of an unsuspecting Detective Carter—and self-contained man.

A challenge.

And, she decided as she passed through the quiet, well-designed neighborhood, toward her home, a challenge was exactly what she needed to get through the emotional upheaval.

She'd have to face her aunt in a few hours, and the rest of the relatives soon after. There would be questions, demands, and, she knew, blame. She would be the recipient of all of it. That was the way her family worked, and that was what she'd come to expect from them.

Ask Grace, take from Grace, point the finger at Grace. She wondered how much of that she deserved, and how much had simply been inherited along with the money her parents left her.

It hardly mattered, she thought, since both were hers, like it or not.

She swung into her drive, her gaze sweeping over

and up. The house was something she'd wanted. The clever and unique design of wood and glass, the gables, the cornices, the decks and the ruthlessly groomed grounds. She'd wanted the space, the elegance that lent itself to entertaining, the convenience to the city. The proximity to Bailey and M.J.

But the little house in the mountains was something she'd needed. And that was hers, and hers alone. The relatives didn't know it existed. No one could find her there unless she wanted to be found.

But here, she thought as she set the brakes, was the neat, expensive home of one Grace Fontaine. Heiress, socialite and party girl. The former centerfold, the Radcliffe graduate, the Washington hostess.

Could she continue to live here, she wondered, with death haunting the rooms? Time would tell.

For now, she was going to concentrate on solving the puzzle of Seth Buchanan, and finding a way under that seemingly impenetrable armor of his.

Just for the fun of it.

She heard him pull in and, in a deliberately provocative move, turned, tipped down her shaded glasses and studied him over the tops.

Oh, yes, she thought. He was very, very attractive. The way he controlled that lean and muscled body. Very economical. No wasted movements. He wouldn't waste them in bed, either. And she wondered just how long it would be before she could lure him there. She had a hunch—and she rarely doubted her hunches where men were concerned—that there was a volcano bubbling under that calm and somewhat austere surface.

She was going to enjoy poking at it until it erupted.

As he crossed to her, she handed him her keys. "Oh,

but you have your own now, don't you?" She tipped her glasses back into place. "Well, use mine…this time."

"Who else has a set?"

She skimmed the tip of her tongue over her top lip, darkly pleased when she saw his gaze jerk down. Just for an instant, but it was progress. "Bailey and M.J. I don't give my keys to men. I'd rather open the door for them myself. Or close it."

"Fine." He dumped the keys back in her hand, looking amused when her brows drew together. "Open the door."

One step forward, two steps back, she mused, then stepped up on the flagstone portico and unlocked her home.

She'd braced for it, but it was still difficult. The foyer was as it had been, largely undisturbed. But her gaze was drawn up now, helplessly, to the shattered railing.

"It's a long way to fall," she murmured. "I wonder if you have time to think, to understand, on the way down."

"She wouldn't have."

"No." And that was better, somehow. "I suppose not." She stepped into the living area, forced herself to look at the chalk outline. "Well, where to begin?"

"He got to your safe down here. Emptied it. You'll want to list what was taken out."

"The library safe." She moved through, under an arch and into a wide room filled with light and books. A great many of those books littered the floor now, and an art deco lamp in the shape of an elongated woman's body—a small thing she'd loved—was cracked in two. "He wasn't subtle, was he?"

"I say he was rushed. And pissed off."

"You'd know best." She walked to the safe, noting the open door and the empty interior. "I had some jewelry—quite a bit, actually. A few thousand in cash."

"Bonds, stock certificates?"

"No, they're in my safe-deposit box at the bank. One doesn't need to take out stock certificates and enjoy the way they sparkle. I bought a terrific pair of diamond earrings just last month." She sighed, shrugged. "Gone now. I have a complete list of my jewelry, and photographs of each piece, along with the insurance papers, in my safety box. Replacing them's just a matter of—"

She broke off, made a small, distressed sound and rushed from the room.

The woman could move when she wanted, Seth thought as he headed upstairs after her. And she didn't lose any of that feline grace with speed. He turned into her bedroom, then into her walk-in closet behind her.

"He wouldn't have found it. He couldn't have found it." She repeated the words like a prayer as she twisted a knob on the built-in cabinet. It swung out, revealing a safe in the wall behind.

Quickly, her fingers not quite steady, she spun the combination, wrenched open the door. Her breath expelled in a whoosh as she knelt and took out velvet boxes and bags.

More jewelry, he thought with a shake of his head. How many earrings could one woman wear? But she was opening each box carefully, examining the contents.

"These were my mother's," she murmured, with a catch of undiluted emotion in the words. "They matter. The sapphire pin my father gave her for their fifth anniversary, the necklace he gave her when I was born.

The pearls. She wore these the day they married." She stroked the creamy white strand over her cheek as if it were a loved one's hand. "I had this built for them, didn't keep them with the others. Just in case."

She sat back on her heels, her lap filled with jewelry that meant so much more than gold and pretty stones. "Well," she managed as her throat closed. "Well, they're here. They're still here."

"Ms. Fontaine."

"Oh, call me Grace," she snapped. "You're as stuffy as my Uncle Niles." Then she pressed a hand to her forehead, trying to work away the beginnings of a tension headache. "I don't suppose you can make coffee."

"Yes, I can make coffee."

"Then why don't you go down and do that little thing, handsome, and give me a minute here?"

He surprised her, and himself, by crouching down first, laying a hand on her shoulder. "You could have lost the pearls, lost all of it. You still wouldn't have lost your memories."

Uneasy that he'd felt compelled to say it, he straightened and left her alone. He went directly to the kitchen, pushing through the mess to fill the coffeepot. He set it up to brew and switched the machine on. Stuck his hands in his pockets, then pulled them out.

What the hell was going on? he asked himself. He should be focused on the case, and the case alone. Instead, he felt himself being pulled, tugged at, by the woman upstairs—by the various faces of that woman. Bold, fragile, sexy, sensitive.

Just which was she? And why had he spent most of the night with her face lodged in his dreams?

He shouldn't even be here, he admitted. He had no

official reason to be spending this time with her. It was true he felt the case warranted his personal attention. It was serious enough. But she was only one small part of the whole.

And he'd be lying to himself if he said he was here strictly on an investigation.

He found two undamaged cups. There were several broken ones lying around. Good Meissen china, he noted. His mother had a set she prized dearly. He was just pouring the coffee when he sensed her behind him.

"Black?"

"That's fine." She stepped in, and winced as she took a visual inventory of the kitchen. "He didn't miss much, did he? I suppose he thought I might stick a big blue diamond in my coffee canister or cookie jar."

"People put their valuables in a lot of odd places. I was involved in a burglary case once where the victim saved her in-house cash because she'd kept it in a sealed plastic bag in the bottom of the diaper pail. What self-respecting B-and-E man is going to paw through diapers?"

She chuckled, sipped her coffee. Whether or not it had been his purpose, his telling of the story had made her feel better. "It makes keeping things in a safe seem foolish. This one didn't take the silver, or any of the electronics. I suppose, as you said, he was in too much of a hurry, and just took what he could stuff in his pockets."

She walked to the kitchen window and looked out. "Melissa's clothes are upstairs. I didn't see her purse. He might have taken that, too, or it could just be buried under the mess."

"We'd have found it if it had been here."

She nodded. "I'd forgotten. You've already searched through my things." She turned back, leaned on the counter and eyed him over the rim of her cup. "Did you go through them personally, Lieutenant?"

He thought of the red silk gown. "Some of it. You have your own department store here."

"I'd come by that naturally, wouldn't I? I have a weakness for things. All manner of things. You make excellent coffee, Lieutenant. Isn't there anyone who brews it for you in the morning?"

"No. Not at the moment." He set his coffee aside. "That wasn't very subtle."

"It wasn't intended to be. It's not that I mind competition. I just like to know if I have any. I still don't think I like you, but that could change." She lifted a hand to finger the tail of her braid. "Why not be prepared?"

"I'm interested in closing a case, not in playing games with you…Grace."

It was such a cool delivery, so utterly dispassionate it kindled her spirit of competition. "I suppose you don't like aggressive women."

"Not particularly."

"Well, then." She smiled as she stepped closer to him. "You're just going to hate this."

In a slick and practiced move, she slid a hand up into his hair and brought his mouth to hers.

Chapter 4

The jolt, lightning wrapped in black velvet, stabbed through him in one powerful strike. His head spun with it, his blood churned, his belly ached. No part of his system was spared the rapid onslaught of that lush and knowing mouth.

Her taste, unexpected yet familiar, plunged into him like hot spiced wine that rushed immediately to his head, leaving him dazed and drunk and desperate.

His muscles bunched, as if poised to leap. And in leaping, he would possess what was somehow already his. It took a vicious twist of will to keep his arms locked at his sides, when they strained to reach out, take, relish. Her scent was as dark, as drugging, as her flavor. Even the low, persuasive hum that sounded in her throat as she moved that glorious fantasy of a body against his was a tantalizing hint of what could be.

For a slow count of five, he fisted his hands, then relaxed them and let the internal war rage while his lips remained passive, his body rigid in denial.

He wouldn't give her the satisfaction of response....

She knew it was a mistake. Even as she moved toward him, reached for him, she'd known it. She'd made mistakes before, and she tried never to regret what was done and couldn't be undone.

But she regretted this.

She deeply regretted that his taste was utterly unique and perfect for her palate. That the texture of his hair, the shape of his shoulders, the strong wall of his chest, all taunted her, when she'd only meant to taunt him, to show him what she could offer. If she chose.

Instead, swept into need, rushed into it by that mating of lips, she offered more than she'd intended. And he gave nothing back.

She caught his bottom lip between her teeth, one quick, sharp nip, then masked an outrageous rush of disappointment by stepping casually back and aiming an amused smile at him.

"My, my, you're a cool one, aren't you, Lieutenant?"

His blood burned with every heartbeat, but he merely inclined his head. "You're not used to being resistible, are you, Grace?"

"No." She rubbed a fingertip lightly over her lip in a movement that was both absent and provocative. The essence of him clung stubbornly there, insisting it belonged. "But then, most of the men I've kissed haven't had ice water in their veins. It's a shame." She took her finger from her own lip, tapped it on his. "Such a nice mouth. Such potential. Still, maybe you just don't care for...women."

The grin he flashed stunned her. His eyes glowed with it, in fascinating tones of gold. His mouth softened with a charm that had a wicked and unpredictable appeal. Suddenly he was approachable, nearly boyish, and it made her heart yearn.

"Maybe," he said, "you're just not my type."

She gave one short, humorless laugh. "Darling, I'm every man's type. Well, we'll just chalk it up to a failed experiment and move on." Telling herself it was foolish to be hurt, she stepped to him again, reached up to straighten the tie she'd loosened.

He didn't want her to touch him, not then, not when he was so precariously perched on the edge. "You've got a hell of an ego there."

"I suppose I do." With her hands still on his tie, she looked up, into his eyes. The hell with it, she thought, if they couldn't be lovers, maybe they could be cautious friends. The man who had looked at her and grinned would be a good, solid friend.

So she smiled at him with a sweetness that was without art or guile, lancing his heart with one clean blow. "But then, men are generally predictable. You're just the exception to the rule, Seth, the one that proves it."

She brushed her hands down, smoothing his jacket and said something more, but he didn't hear it over the roaring in his ears. His control broke; he felt the snap, like the twang of a sword violently broken over an armored knee. In a movement he was hardly aware of, he spun her around, pressed her back against the wall, and was ravaging her mouth.

Her heart kicked in her chest, drove the breath out of her body. She gripped his shoulders as much for balance as in response to the sudden, violent need that shot from him to her and fused them together.

She yielded, utterly, then locked her arms around his neck and poured herself back.

Here, was all her dazzled mind could think. Oh, here, at last.

His hands raced over her, molded and somehow recognized each curve. And the recognition seared through him, as hot and real as the surge of desire. He wanted that taste, had to have it inside him, to swallow it whole. He assaulted her mouth like a man feeding after a life-long fast, filled himself with the flavors of her, all of them dark, ripe, succulent.

She was there for him, had always been there—impossibly there. And he knew that if he didn't pull back, he'd never be able to survive without her.

He slapped his hands on the wall on either side of her head to stop himself from touching, to stop himself from taking. Fighting to regain both his breath and his sanity, he eased out of the kiss, stepped away.

She continued to lean back against the wall, her eyes closed, her skin luminous with passion. By the time her lashes fluttered up and those slumberous blue eyes focused, he had his control snapped back ruthlessly in place.

"Unpredictable," she managed, barely resisting the urge to press both hands to her galloping heart. "Very."

"I warned you about pushing the wrong buttons." His voice was cool, edging toward cold, and had the effect of a backhand slap.

She flinched from it, might have reeled, if she hadn't been braced by the wall. His eyes narrowed fractionally at the reaction. Hurt? he wondered. No, that was ridiculous. She was a veteran game player and knew all the angles.

"Yes, you did." She straightened, pride stiffening her spine and forcing her lips to curve in a casual smile. "I'm just so resistant to warnings."

He thought she should be required by law to carry one—Danger! Woman!

"I've got work to do. I can give you another five minutes, if you want me to wait while you pack some things."

Oh, you bastard, she thought. How can you be so cool, so unaffected? "You toddle right along, handsome. I'll be fine."

"I'd prefer you weren't in the house alone for the moment. Go pack some things."

"It's my home."

"Right now, it's a crime scene. You're down to four and a half minutes."

Fury vibrated through her in hot, pulsing beats. "I don't need anything here." She turned, started out, whirling back when he took her arm. "What?"

"You need clothes," he said, patient now. "For a day or two."

"Do you really think I'd wear anything that bastard might have touched?"

"That's a foolish and a predictable reaction." His tone didn't soften in the least. "You're not a foolish or a predictable woman. Don't be a victim, Grace. Go pack your things."

He was right. She could have despised him for that alone. But the frustrated need still fisted inside her was a much better reason. She said nothing at all, simply turned again and walked away.

When he didn't hear the front door slam, he was satisfied that she'd gone upstairs to pack, as he'd told her to. Seth turned off the coffeemaker, rinsed the cups and set them in the sink, then went out to wait for her.

She was a fascinating woman, he thought. Full of temperament, energy and ego. And she was undoing him, knot by carefully tied knot. How she knew exactly what strings to pull to do so was just one more mystery.

He'd taken this case on, he reminded himself. Riding a desk and delegating were only part of the job. He needed to be involved, and he'd involved himself with this—and therefore with her. Grace's part of the whole was small, but he needed to treat her with the same objectivity that he treated every other piece of the case with.

He looked up, his gaze drawn to the portrait that smiled down so invitingly.

He'd have to be more machine than man to stay objective when it came to Grace Fontaine.

It was midafternoon before he could clear his desk enough to handle a follow-up interview. The diamonds were the key, and he wanted another look at them. He hadn't been surprised when his phone conversation with Dr. Linstrum at the Smithsonian resulted in a testimonial to Bailey James's integrity and skill. The diamonds she'd gone to such lengths to protect remained at Salvini, and in her care.

When Seth pulled into the parking lot of the elegant corner building just outside D.C. that housed Salvini, he nodded to the uniformed cop guarding the main door. And felt a faint tug of sympathy. The heat was brutal.

"Lieutenant." Despite a soggy uniform, the officer snapped to attention.

"Ms. James inside?"

"Yes, sir. The store's closed to the public for the next week." He indicated the darkened showroom through the thick glass doors with a jerk of the head. "We have a guard posted at every entrance, and Ms. James is on the lower level. It's easier access through the rear, Lieutenant."

"Fine. When's your relief, Officer?"

"I've got another hour." The cop didn't wipe his brow, but he wanted to. Seth Buchanan had a reputation for being a stickler. "Four-hour rotations, as per your orders, sir."

"Bring a bottle of water with you next time." Well aware that the uniform sagged the minute his back was turned, Seth rounded the building. After a brief conversation with the duty guard at the rear, he pressed the buzzer beside the reinforced steel door. "Lieutenant Buchanan," he said when Bailey answered through the intercom. "I'd like a few minutes."

It took her some time to get to the door. Seth visualized her coming out of the workroom on the lower level, winding down the short corridor, passing the stairs where she'd hidden from a killer only days before.

He'd been through the building himself twice, top to bottom. He knew that not everyone could have survived what she'd been through in there.

The locks clicked, the door opened. "Lieutenant." She smiled at the guard, silently apologizing for his miserable duty. "Please come in."

She looked neat and tidy, Seth thought, with her trim blouse and slacks, her blond hair scooped back. Only the faint shadows under her eyes spoke of the strain she'd been under.

"I spoke with Dr. Linstrum," Seth began.

"Yes, I expect you did. I'm very grateful for his understanding."

"The stones are back where they started."

She smiled a little. "Well, they're back where they were a few days ago. Who knows if they'll ever see Rome again. Can I get you something cold to drink?" She gestured toward a soft-drink machine standing brightly against a dark wall.

"I'll buy." He plugged in coins. "I'd like to see the diamonds, and have a few words with you."

"All right." She pressed the button for her choice, and retrieved the can that clunked down the shoot. "They're in the vault." She continued to speak as she led the way. "I've arranged to have the security and alarm system beefed up. We've had cameras in the showroom for a number of years, but I'll have them installed at the doors, as well, and for the upper and lower levels. All areas."

"That's wise." He concluded that there was a practical streak of common sense beneath the fragile exterior. "You'll run the business now?"

She opened a door, hesitated. "Yes. My stepfather left it to the three of us, with my stepbrothers sharing eighty percent between them. In the event any of us died without heirs, the shares go to the survivors." She drew in a breath. "I survived."

"That's something to be grateful for, Bailey, not guilty about."

"Yes, that's what Cade says. But you see, I once had

the illusion, at least, that they were family. Have a seat, I'll get the Stars."

He moved into the work area, glanced at the equipment, the long worktable. Intrigued, he stepped closer, examining the glitter of colored stones, the twists of gold. It was going to be a necklace, he realized, running a fingertip over the silky length of a closely linked chain. Something bold, almost pagan.

"I needed to get back to work," she said from behind him. "To do something…different, my own, I suppose, before I faced dealing with these again."

She set down a padded box that held the trio of diamonds.

"Your design?" he asked, gesturing to the piece on the worktable.

"Yes. I see the piece in my head. I can't draw worth a lick, but I can visualize. I wanted to make something for M.J. and for Grace to…" She sighed, sat on the high stool. "Well, let's say to celebrate survival."

"And this is the one for Grace."

"Yes." She smiled, pleased that he'd sensed it. "I see something more streamlined for M.J. But this is Grace." Carefully she set the unfinished work in a tray, slid the padded box containing the Three Stars between them. "They never lose their impact. Each time I see them, it stuns."

"How long before you're finished with them?"

"I'd just begun when—when I had to stop." She cleared her throat. "I've verified their authenticity. They are blue diamonds. Still, both the museum and the insurance carrier prefer more in-depth verification. I'll be running a number of other tests beyond what I've already started or completed. A metallurgist is testing the triangle, but that will be given to me for further study in a day or two. It shouldn't take more than a week altogether before the museum can take possession."

He lifted a stone from the bed, knew as soon as it was in his hand that it was the one Grace had carried with her. He told himself that was impossible. His untrained eye couldn't tell one stone from either of its mates.

Yet he felt her on it. In it.

"Will it be hard to part with them?"

"I should say no, after the past few days. But yes, it will."

Grace's eyes were this color, Seth realized. Not sapphire, but the blue of the rare, powerful diamond.

"Worth killing for," he said quietly, looking at the stone in his hand. "Dying for." Then, annoyed with himself, he set the stone down again. "Your stepbrothers had a client."

"Yes, they spoke of a client, argued about him. Thomas wanted to take the money, the initial deposit, and run."

The money was being checked now, but there wasn't much hope of tracing its source.

"Timothy told Thomas he was a fool, that he'd never be able to run far or fast enough. That he—the client—would find him. He's not even human. Timothy said that, or something like it. They were both afraid, terribly afraid, and terribly desperate."

"Over their heads."

"Yes, I think very much over their heads."

"It would have to be a collector. No one could move these stones for resale." He glanced at the gems sparkling in their trays like pretty stars. "You acquire, buy and sell to collectors of gems."

"Yes—certainly not on a scale like the Three Stars, but yes." She skimmed her fingers absently through her hair. "A client might come to us with a stone, or a request for one. We'd also acquire certain gems on spec, with a particular client in mind."

"You have a client list, then? Names, preferences?"

"Yes, and we have records of what a client had purchased, or sold." She gripped her hands together. "Thomas would have kept it, in his office. Timothy would have copies in his. I'll find them for you."

He touched her shoulder lightly before she could slide from the stool. "I'll get them."

She let out a breath of relief. She had yet to be able to face going upstairs, into the room where she'd seen murder. "Thank you."

He took out his notebook. "If I asked you to name the top gem collectors, your top clients, what names come to mind? Off the top of your head?"

"Oh." Concentrating, she gnawed on her lip. "Peter Morrison in London, Sylvia Smythe-Simmons of New York, Henry and Laura Muller here in D.C., Matthew Wolinski in California. And I suppose Charles Van Horn here in D.C., too, though he's new to it. We sold him three lovely stones over the last two years. One was a spectacular opal I coveted. I'm still hoping he'll let me set it for him. I have this design in my head…."

She shook herself, trailed off when she realized why he was asking. "Lieutenant, I know these people. I've dealt with them personally. The Mullers were friends of my stepfather's. Mrs. Smythe-Simmons is over eighty. None of them are thieves."

He didn't bother to glance up, but continued to write. "Then we'll be able to check them off the list. Taking anything or anyone at face value is a mistake in an investigation, Ms. James. We've had enough mistakes already."

"With mine standing out." Accepting that fact, she nudged her untouched soft drink over the table. "I should have gone to the police right away. I should have turned the information—at the very least, my suspicions—over to the authorities. Several people would still be alive if I had."

"It's possible, but it's not a given." Now he did glance up, noted the haunted look in those soft brown eyes. Compassion stirred. "Did you know your stepbrother was being blackmailed by a second-rate bail bondsman?"

"No," she murmured.

"Did you know that someone was pulling the strings, pulling them hard enough to turn your stepbrother into a killer?"

She shook her head, bit down hard on her lip. "The things I didn't know were the problem, weren't they? I put the two people I love most in terrible danger, then I forgot about them."

"Amnesia isn't a choice, it's a condition. And your friends handled themselves. They still are—in fact, I saw Ms. Fontaine just this morning. She doesn't look any the worse for wear to me."

Bailey caught the disdainful note and turned to face him. "You don't understand her. I would have thought a man who does what you do for a living would be able to see more clearly than that."

He thought he caught a faint hint of pity in her voice, and resented it. "I've always thought of myself as clear-sighted."

"People are rarely clear-sighted when it comes to Grace. They only see what she lets them see—unless they care enough to look deeper. She has the most generous heart of any person I've ever known."

Bailey caught the quick flicker of amused disbelief in his eyes and felt her anger rising against it. Furious, she pushed off the stool. "You don't know anything about her, but you've already dismissed her. Can you conceive of what she's going through right now? Her cousin was murdered—and in her stead."

"She's hardly to blame for that."

"Easy to say. But she'll blame herself, and so will her family. It's easy to blame Grace."

"You don't."

"No, because I know her. And I know she's dealt with perceptions and opinions just like yours most of her life. And her way of dealing with it is to do as she chooses, because whatever she does, those perceptions and opinions rarely change. Right now, she's with her aunt, I imagine, and taking the usual emotional beating."

Her voice heated, became rushed, as emotions swarmed. "Tonight, there'll be a memorial service for Melissa, and the relatives will hammer at her, the way they always do."

"Why should they?"

"Because that's what they do best." Running out of steam she turned her head, looked down at the Three Stars. Love, knowledge, generosity, she thought. Why did it seem there was so little of it in the world? "Maybe you should take another look, Lieutenant Buchanan."

He'd already taken too many, he decided. And he was wasting time. "She certainly inspires loyalty in her friends," he commented. "I'm going to look for those lists."

"You know the way." Dismissing him, Bailey picked up the stones to carry them back to the vault.

Grace was dressed in black, and had never felt less like grieving. It was six in the evening, and a light rain was beginning to fall. It promised to turn the city into a massive steam room instead of cooling it off. The headache that had been slyly brewing for hours snarled at the aspirin she'd already taken and leaped into full, vicious life.

She had an hour before the wake, one she had arranged quickly and alone, because her aunt demanded it. Helen Fontaine was handling grief in her own way—as she did everything else. In this case, it was by meeting Grace with a cold, damning and dry eye. Cutting off any offer of support or sympathy. And demanding that services take place immediately, and at Grace's expense and instigation.

They would be coming from all points, Grace thought as she wandered the large, empty room, with its banks of flowers, thick red drapes, deep pile carpeting. Because such things were expected, such things were reported in the press. And the Fontaines would never give the public media a bone to pick.

Except, of course, for Grace herself.

It hadn't been difficult to arrange for the funeral home, the music, the flowers, the tasteful canapés. Only phone calls and the invocation of the Fontaine name were required. Helen had brought the photograph herself, the large color print in a shining silver frame that now decorated a polished mahogany table and was flanked with red roses in heavy silver vases that Melissa had favored.

There would be no body to view.

Grace had arranged for Melissa's body to be released from the morgue, had already written the check for the cremation and the urn her aunt had chosen.

There had been no thanks, no acknowledgment. None had been expected.

It had been the same from the moment Helen became her legal guardian. She'd been given the necessities of life—Fontaine-style. Gorgeous homes in several countries to live in, perfectly prepared food, tasteful clothing, an excellent education.

And she'd been told, endlessly, how to eat, how to dress, how to behave, who could be selected as a friend and who could not. Reminded, incessantly, of her good fortune—unearned—in having such a family behind her. Tormented, ruthlessly, by the cousin she was there tonight to mourn, for being orphaned, dependent.

For being Grace.

She'd rebelled against all of it, every aspect, every expectation and demand. She'd refused to be malleable, biddable, predictable. The ache for her parents had eventually dimmed, and with it the child's desperate need for love and acceptance.

She'd given the press plenty to report. Wild parties, unwise affairs, unrestricted spending.

When that didn't ease the hurt, she'd found something else. Something that made her feel decent and whole.

And she'd found Grace.

For tonight, she would be just what her family had

come to expect. And she would get through the next endless hours without letting them touch her.

She sat heavily on a sofa with overstuffed velvet seats. Her head pounded, her stomach clutched. Closing her eyes, she willed herself to relax. She would spend this last hour alone, and prepare herself for the rest.

But she'd barely taken the second calming breath when she heard footsteps muffled on the thick patterned carpet. Her shoulders turned to rock, her spine snapped straight. She opened her eyes. And saw Bailey and M.J.

She let her eyes close again, on a pathetic rush of gratitude. "I told you not to come."

"Yeah, like we were going to listen to that." M.J. sat beside her, took her hand.

"Cade and Jack are parking the car." Bailey flanked her other side, took her other hand. "How are you holding up?"

"Better." Tears stung her eyes as she squeezed the hands clasped in hers. "A lot better now."

On a sprawling estate not so many miles from where Grace sat with those who loved her, a man stared out at the hissing rain.

Everyone had failed, he thought. Many had paid for their failures. But retribution was a poor substitute for the Three Stars.

A delay only, he comforted himself. The Stars were his, they were meant to be his. He had dreamed of them, had held them in his hands in those dreams. Sometimes the hands were human, sometimes not, but they were always his hands.

He sipped wine, watched the rain, and considered his options.

His plans had been delayed by three women. That was humiliating, and they would have to be made to pay for that humiliation.

The Salvinis were dead—Bailey James.

The fools he'd hired to retrieve the second Star were dead—M. J. O'Leary.

The man he'd sent with instructions to acquire the third Star at any cost was dead—Grace Fontaine.

And he smiled. That had been indiscreet, as he'd disposed of the lying fool himself. Telling him there'd been an accident, that the woman had fought him, run from him, and fallen to her death. Telling him he'd searched every corner of the house without finding the stone.

That failure had been irritating enough, but then to discover that the wrong woman had died and that the fool had stolen money and jewels without reporting them. Well, such disloyalty in a business associate could hardly be tolerated.

Smiling dreamily, he took a sparkling diamond earring out of his pocket. Grace Fontaine had worn this on her delectable lobe, he mused. He kept it now as a good-luck charm while he considered what steps to take next.

There were only days left before the Stars would be in the museum. Extracting them from those hallowed halls would take months, if not years, of planning. He didn't intend to wait.

Perhaps he had failed because he had been overcautious, had kept his distance from events. Perhaps the gods required a more personal risk. A more intimate involvement.

It was time, he decided, to step out of the shadows, to meet the women who had kept his property from him, face-to-face. He smiled again, excited by the thought, delighted with the possibilities.

When the knock sounded on the door, he answered with great cheer and good humor. "Enter."

The butler, in stern formal black, ventured no farther than the threshold. His voice held no inflection. "I beg your pardon, Ambassador. Your guests are arriving."

"Very well." He sipped the last of his wine, set the empty crystal flute on a table. "I'll be right down."

When the door closed, he moved to the mirror, examined his flawless tuxedo, the wink of diamond studs, the gleam of the thin gold watch at his wrist. Then he examined his face—the smooth contours, the pampered, pale gold skin, the aristocratic nose, the firm, if somewhat thin, mouth. He brushed a hand over the perfectly groomed mane of silver-threaded black hair.

Then, slowly, smilingly, met his own eyes. Pale, almost translucent blue smiled back. His guests would see what he did, a perfectly groomed man of fifty-two, erudite and educated, well mannered and suave. They wouldn't know what plans and plots he held in his heart. They would see no blood on his hands, though it had been only twenty-four short hours since he used them to kill.

He felt only pleasure in the memory, only delight in the knowledge that he would soon dine with the elite and the influential. And he could kill any one of them with a twist of his hands, with perfect immunity.

He chuckled to himself—a low, seductive sound with shuddering undertones. Tucking the earring back in his pocket, he walked from the room.

The ambassador was mad.

Chapter 5

Seth's first thought when he walked into the funeral parlor was that it seemed more like a tedious cocktail party than like a memorial service. People stood or sat in little cliques and groups, many of them nibbling on canapés or sipping wine. Beneath the strains of a muted Chopin étude, voices murmured. There was an occasional roll or tinkle of laughter.

He heard no tears.

Lights were respectfully dimmed, and set off the glitter and gleam of gems and gold. The fragrance of flowers mixed and merged with the scents worn by both men and women. He saw faces, both elegant and bored.

He saw no grief.

But he did see Grace. She stood looking up into the face of a tall, slim man whose golden tan set off his golden hair and bright blue eyes. He held one of her hands in his and smiled winningly. He appeared to be speaking quickly, persuasively. She shook her head once, laid a hand on his chest, then allowed herself to be drawn into an anteroom.

Seth's lip curled in automatic disdain. A funeral was a hell of a place for a flirtation.

"Buchanan." Jack Dakota wandered over. He scanned the room, stuck his hands in the pockets of the suit coat he wished fervently was still in his closet, instead of on his back. "Some party."

Seth watched two women air kiss. "Apparently."

"Doesn't seem like one a sane man would want to crash."

"I have business," he said briefly. Which could have waited until morning, he reminded himself. He should have let it wait. It annoyed him that he'd made the detour, that he'd been thinking of Grace—more, that he'd been unable to lock her out of his head.

He pulled a copy of a mug shot out of his pocket, handed it to Jack. "Recognize him?"

Jack scanned the picture, considered. Slick-looking dude, he thought. Vaguely European in looks, with the sleek black hair, dark eyes and refined features. "Nope. Looks like a poster boy for some wussy cologne."

"You didn't see him during your amazing weekend adventures?"

Jack took one last, harder look, handed the shot back. "Nope. What's his connection?"

"His prints were all over the house in Potomac."

Jack's interest rose. "He the one who killed the cousin?"

Seth met Jack's eyes coolly. "That has yet to be determined."

"Don't give me the cop stand, Buchanan. What'd the guy say? He stopped by to sell vacuum cleaners?"

"He didn't say anything. He was too busy floating facedown in the river."

With an oath, Jack's gaze whipped around the room again. He relaxed fractionally when he spotted M.J. huddled with Cade. "The morgue must be getting crowded. You got a name?"

Seth started to dismiss the question. He didn't care for professions that stood a step back from the police. But there was no denying that the bounty hunter and the private investigator were involved. And there was no avoiding the connection, he told himself.

"Carlo Monturri."

"Doesn't ring a bell either."

Seth hadn't expected it would, but the police—on several continents—knew the name. "He's out of your league, Dakota. His type keeps a fancy lawyer on retainer and doesn't use the local bail bondsman to get sprung."

As he spoke, Seth's eyes moved around the room as a cop's did, sweeping corner to corner, taking in details, body language, atmosphere. "Before he took his last swim, he was expensive hired muscle. He worked alone because he didn't like to share the fun."

"Connections in the area?"

"We're working on it."

Seth saw Grace come out of the anteroom. The man who was with her had his arm draped over her shoulders, pulled her close in an intimate embrace, kissed her. The flare of fury kindled in Seth's gut and bolted up to his heart.

"Excuse me."

Grace saw him the moment he started across the room. She murmured something to the man beside her, dislodged him, then dismissed him. Straightening her spine, she fixed on an easy smile.

"Lieutenant, we didn't expect you."

"I apologize for intruding in your—" he flicked a glance toward the golden boy, who was helping himself to a glass a wine "—grief."

The sarcasm slapped, but she didn't flinch. "I assume you have a reason for coming by."

"I'd like a moment of your time—in private."

"Of course." She turned to lead him out and came face-to-face with her aunt. "Aunt Helen."

"If you could tear yourself away from entertaining your suitors," Helen said coldly, "I want to speak to you."

"Excuse me," Grace said to Seth, and stepped into the anteroom again.

Seth debated moving off, giving them privacy. But he stayed where he was, two paces from the doorway. He told himself murder investigations didn't allow for sensitivity. Though they kept their voices low, he heard both women clearly enough.

"I assume you have Melissa's things at your home," Helen began.

"I don't know. I haven't been able to go through the house thoroughly yet."

Helen said nothing for a moment, simply studied her niece through cold blue eyes. Her face was smooth and showed no ravages of grief in the carefully applied makeup. Her hair was sleek, lightened to a tasteful ash blond. Her hands were freshly manicured and glittered with the diamond wedding band she continued to wear, though she'd shared little but her husband's name in over a decade, and a square-cut sapphire given to her by her latest lover.

"I sincerely doubt Melissa came to your home without a bag. I want her things, Grace. All of her things. You'll have nothing of hers."

"I never wanted anything of hers, Aunt Helen."

"Didn't you?" There was a crackle in the voice—a whip flicking. "Did you think she wouldn't tell me of your affair with her husband?"

Grace merely sighed. It was new ground, but sickeningly familiar. Melissa's marriage had failed, publicly. Therefore, it had to be someone else's fault. It had to be Grace's fault.

"I didn't have an affair with Bobbie. Before, during or after their marriage."

"And whom do you think I would believe? You, or my own daughter?"

Grace tilted her head, twisted a smile on her face. "Why, your own daughter, of course. As always."

"You've always been a liar and a sneak. You've always been ungrateful, a burden I took on out of family duty who never once gave anything back. You were spoiled and willful when I opened my door to you, and you never changed."

Grace's stomach roiled viciously. In defense, she smiled, shrugged. Deliberately careless, she smoothed a hand over the hair sleeked into a coiled twist at the nape of her neck. "No, I suppose I didn't. I'll just have to remain a disappointment to you, Aunt Helen."

"My daughter would be alive if not for you."

Grace willed her heart to go numb. But it ached, and it burned. "Yes, you're right."

"I warned her about you, told her time and again what you were. But you continually lured her back, playing on her affection."

"Affection, Aunt Helen?" With a half laugh, Grace pressed her fingers to the throb in her left temple. "Surely even you don't believe she ever had an ounce of affection for me. She took her cue from you, after all. And she took it well."

"How dare you speak of her in that tone, after you've killed her!" In the pampered face, Helen's eyes burned with loathing. "All of your life you've envied her, used your wiles to influence her. Now your unconscionable life-style has killed her. You've brought scandal and disgrace down on the family name once again."

Grace went stiff. This wasn't grief, she thought. Perhaps grief was there, buried deep, but what was on the surface was venom. And she was weary of being struck by it. "That's the bottom line, isn't it, Aunt Helen? The Fontaine name, the Fontaine reputation. And, of course, the Fontaine stock. Your child is dead, but it's the scandal that infuriates you."

She absorbed the slap without a wince, though the blow printed heat on her cheek, brought blood stinging to the surface. She took one long, deep breath. "That should end things appropriately between the two of us," she said evenly. "I'll have Melissa's things sent to you as soon as possible."

"I want you out of here." Helen's voice shook for the first time—whether in grief or in fury, Grace couldn't have said. "You have no place here."

"You're right again. I don't. I never did."

Grace stepped out of the alcove. The color that had drained out of her face rose slightly when she met Seth's eyes. She couldn't read them in that brief glance, and didn't want to. Without breaking stride, she continued past him and kept walking.

The drizzle that misted the air was a relief. She welcomed the heat after the overchilled, artificial air inside, and the heavy, stifling scent of funeral flowers. Her heels clicked on the wet pavement as she crossed the lot to her car. She was fumbling in her bag for her keys when Seth clamped a hand on her shoulder.

He said nothing at first, just turned her around, studied her face. It was white again—but for the red burn from the slap—the eyes a dark contrast and swimming with emotion. He could feel the tremors of that emotion under the palm of his hand.

"She was wrong."

Humiliation was one more blow to her overwrought system. She jerked her shoulder, but his hand remained in place. "Is that part of your investigative technique, Lieutenant? Eavesdropping on private conversations?"

Did she realize, he wondered, that her voice was raw, her eyes were devastated? He wanted badly to lift a hand to that mark on her face, cool it. Erase it. "She was wrong," he said again. "And she was cruel. You aren't responsible."

"Of course I am." She spun away, jabbing her key at the door lock. After three shaky attempts, she gave up, and they dropped with a jingling splash to the wet pavement as she turned into his arms. "Oh, God." Shuddering, she pressed her face into his chest. "Oh, God."

He didn't want to hold her, wanted to refuse the role of comforter. But his arms came around her before he could stop them, and one hand reached up to brush the smooth twist of her hair. "You didn't deserve that, Grace. You did nothing to deserve that."

"It doesn't matter."

"Yes, it does." He found himself weakening, drawing her closer, trying to will her trembling away. "It always does."

"I'm just tired." She burrowed into him while the rain misted her hair. There was strength here, was all she could think. A haven here. An answer here. "I'm just tired."

Her head lifted, their mouths met, before either of them realized the need was there. The quiet sound in her throat was of relief and gratitude. She opened her battered heart to the kiss, locking her arms around him, urging him to take it.

She had been waiting for him, and, too dazed to question why, she offered herself to him. Surely comfort and pleasure and this all-consuming need were reason enough. His mouth was firm—the one she'd always wanted on hers. His body was hard and solid—a perfect match for hers.

Here he is, she thought with a ragged sigh of joy.

She trembled still, and he could feel his own muscles quiver in response. He wanted to gather her up, carry her out of the rain to someplace quiet and dark where it was only the two of them. To spend years where it would only be the two of them.

His heart pounded in his head, masking the slick sound of traffic over the rain-wet street beyond the lot. Its fast, demanding beat muffled the warning struggling to sound in the corner of his brain, telling him to step back, to break away.

He'd never wanted anything more in his life than to bury himself in her and forget the consequences.

Swamped with emotions and needs, she held him close. "Take me home," she murmured against his mouth. "Seth, take me home, make love with me. I need you to touch me. I want to be with you." Her mouth met his again, in a desperate plea she hadn't known herself capable of.

Every cell in his body burned for her. Every need he'd ever had coalesced into one, and it was only for her. The almost vicious focus of it left him vulnerable and shaky. And furious.

He put his hands on her shoulders, drew her away. "Sex isn't the answer for everyone."

His voice wasn't as cool as he'd wanted, but it was rigid enough to stop her from reaching for him again. Sex? she thought as she struggled to clear her dazzled mind. Did he really believe she'd been speaking about something as simple as sex? Then she focused on his face, the hard set of his mouth, the faint annoyance in his eyes, and realized he did.

Her pride might have been tattered, but she managed to hold on to a few threads. "Well, apparently it's not for you." Reaching up, she smoothed her hair, brushed away rain. "Or if it is, you're the type who insists on being the initiator."

She made her lips curve, though they felt cold now and stiff. "It would have been just fine and dandy if you'd made the move. But when I do, it makes me— what would the term be? Loose?"

"I don't believe it's a term I used."

"No, you're much too controlled for insults." She

bent down, scooped up her wet keys, then stood jingling them in her hand while she studied him. "But you wanted me right back, Seth. You're not quite controlled enough to have masked that little detail."

"I don't believe in taking everything I want."

"Why the hell not?" She gave a short, mirthless laugh. "We're alive, aren't we? And you, of all people, should know how distressingly short life can be."

"I don't have to explain to you how I live my life."

"No, you don't. But it's obvious you're perfectly willing to question how I live mine." Her gaze skimmed past him, back toward the lights glinting in the funeral home. "I'm quite used to that. I do exactly what I choose, without regard for the consequences. I'm selfish and self-involved and careless."

She lifted a shoulder as she turned and unlocked her door. "As for feelings, why should I be entitled to them?"

She slipped into her car, flipped him one last look. Her mouth might have curved with seductive ease, but the sultry smile didn't reach her eyes, or mask the misery in them. "Well, maybe some other time, handsome."

He watched her drive off into the rain. There would be another time, he admitted, if for no other reason than that he hadn't shown her the picture. Hadn't, he thought, had the heart to add to her unhappiness that night.

Feelings, he mused as he headed to his own car. She had them, had plenty of them. He only wished he understood them. He got into his car, wrenched his door shut. He wished to God he understood his own.

For the first time in his life, a woman had reached in and clamped a hand on his heart. And she was squeezing.

* * *

Seth told himself he wasn't postponing meeting with Grace again. The morning after the memorial service had been hellish with work. And when he did carve out time to leave his office, he'd headed toward M.J.'s. It was true he could have assigned this follow-up to one of his men. Despite the fact that the chief of police had ordered him to head the investigation, and give every detail his personal attention, Mick Marshall—the detective who had taken the initial call on the case—could have done this next pass with M. J. O'Leary.

Seth was forced to admit that he wanted to talk to her personally and hoped to slide a few details out of her on Grace Fontaine.

M.J.'s was a cozy, inviting neighborhood pub that ran to dark woods, gleaming brass and thickly padded stools and booths. Business was slow but steady in midafternoon. A couple of men who looked to be college age were sharing a booth, a duet of foamy mugs and an intense game of chess. An older man sat at the bar working a crossword from the morning paper, and a trio of women with department store shopping bags crowding the floor around them huddled over drinks and laughter.

The bartender glanced at Seth's badge and told him he'd find the boss upstairs in her office. He heard her before he saw her.

"Look, pal, if I'd wanted candy mints, I'd have ordered candy mints. I ordered beer nuts. I want them here by six. Yeah, yeah. I know my customers. Get me the damn nuts, pronto."

She sat behind a crowded desk with a battered top. Her short cap of red hair stood up in spikes. Seth watched her rake her fingers through it again as she hung up the phone and pushed a pile of invoices aside. If that was her idea of filing, he thought, it suited the rest of the room.

It was barely big enough to turn around in, crowded with boxes, files, papers, and one ratty chair, on which sat an enormous and overflowing purse.

"Ms. O'Leary?"

She looked up, her brow still creased in annoyance. It didn't clear when she recognized her visitor. "Just what I needed to make my day perfect. A cop. Listen, Buchanan, I'm behind here. As you know, I lost a few days recently."

"Then I'll try to be quick." He stepped inside, pulled the picture out of his pocket and tossed it onto the desk under her nose. "Look familiar?"

She pursed her lips, gave the slickly handsome face a slow, careful study. "Is this the guy Jack told me about? The one who killed Melissa?"

"The Melissa Fontaine case is still open. This man is a possible suspect. Do you recognize him?"

She rolled her eyes, pushed the photo back in Seth's direction. "No. Looks like a creep. Did Grace recognize him?"

He angled his head slightly, his only outward sign of interest. "Does she know many men who look like creeps?"

"Too many," M.J. muttered. "Jack said you came by the memorial service last night to show Grace this picture."

"She was…occupied."

"Yeah, it was a rough night for her." M.J. rubbed her eyes.

"Apparently, though she seemed to have been handling it well enough initially." He glanced down at the photo again, thought of the man he'd seen her kiss. "This looks like her type."

M.J.'s hand dropped, her eyes narrowed. "Meaning?"

"Just that." Seth tucked the photo away. "If one's going by type, this one doesn't appear, on the surface, too far a step from the one she was cozy with at the service."

"Cozy with?" The narrowed eyes went hot, angry green flares. "Grace wasn't cozy with anyone."

"About six-one, a hundred and seventy, blond hair, blue eyes, five-thousand-dollar Italian suit, lots of teeth."

It only took her a moment. At any other time, she would have laughed. But the cool disdain on Seth's face had her snarling. "You stupid son of a bitch, that was her cousin Julian, and he was hitting her up for money, just like he always does."

Seth frowned, backtracked, played the scene through his mind again. "Her cousin…and that would be the victim's…?"

"Stepbrother. Melissa's stepbrother—her father's son from a previous."

"And the deceased's stepbrother was asking Grace for money at his stepsister's memorial?"

This time she appreciated the coating of disgust over his words. "Yeah. He's slime—why should the ambience stop him from shaking her down? Most of them squeeze her for a few bucks now and then." She rose, geared up. "And you've got a hell of a nerve coming in here with your attitude and your superior morals, ace. She wrote that pansy-faced jerk a check for a few thousand to get him off her back, just like she used to pass bucks to Melissa, and some of the others."

"I was under the impression the Fontaines were wealthy."

"Wealth's relative—especially if you live the high life and your allowance from your trust fund is over-drawn, or if you've played too deep in Monte Carlo. And Grace has more of the green stuff than most of them, because her parents didn't blow the bucks. That just burns the relatives," she muttered. "Who do you think paid for that wake last night? It wasn't the dearly departed's mama or papa. Grace's witch of an aunt put the arm on her, then put the blame on her. And she took it, because she thinks it's easier to take it and go her own way. You don't know anything about her."

He thought he did, but the details he was collecting bit by bit weren't adding up very neatly. "I know that she's not to blame for what happened to her cousin."

"Yeah, try telling her that. I know that when we re-alized she'd left and we got back to Cade's, she was in her room crying, and there was nothing any of us could do to help her. And all because those bastards she has the misfortune to be related to go out of their way to make her feel rotten."

Not just her relatives, he thought with a quick twinge of guilt. He'd had a part in that.

"It seems she's more fortunate in her friends than in her family."

"That's because we're not interested in her money, or her name. Because we don't judge her. We just love her. Now, if that's all, I've got work to do."

"I need to speak with Ms. Fontaine." Seth's voice

was as stiff as M.J.'s had been passionate. "Would you know where I might find her?"

Her lips curled. She hesitated a moment, knowing Grace wouldn't appreciate the information being passed along. But the urge to see the cop's preconceptions slapped down was just too tempting. "Sure. Try Saint Agnes's Hospital. Pediatrics or maternity." Her phone rang, so she snatched it up. "You'll find her," she said. "Yeah, O'Leary," she barked into the phone, and turned her back on Seth.

He assumed she was visiting the child of a friend, but when he asked at the nurses' station for Grace Fontaine, faces lit up.

"I think she's in the intensive-care nursery." The nurse on duty checked her watch. "It's her usual time there. Do you know the way?"

Baffled, Seth shook his head. "No." He listened to the directions, while his mind turned over a dozen reasons why Grace Fontaine should have a usual time in a nursery. Since none of them slipped comfortably into a slot, he headed down corridors.

He could hear the high sound of babies crying behind a barrier of glass. And perhaps he stopped for just a moment outside the window of the regular nursery, and his eyes might have softened, just a little, as he scanned the infants in their clear-sided beds. Tiny faces, some slack in sleep, others screwed up into wrinkled balls of fury.

A couple stood beside him, the man with his arm over the woman's robed shoulders. "Ours is third from the left. Joshua Michael Delvecchio. Eight pounds, five ounces. He's one day old."

"He's a beaut," Seth said.

"Which one is yours?" the woman asked.

Seth shook his head, shot one more glance through the glass. "I'm just passing through. Congratulations on your son."

He continued on, resisting the urge to look back at the new parents lost in their own private miracle.

Two turns down the corridor away from the celebration was a smaller nursery. Here machines hummed, and nurses walked quietly. And behind the glass were six empty cribs.

Grace sat beside one, cuddling a tiny, crying baby. She brushed away tears from the pale little cheek, rested her own against the smooth head as she rocked.

It struck him to the core, the picture she made. Her hair was braided back from her face and she wore a shapeless green smock over her suit. Her face was soft as she soothed the restless infant. Her attention was totally focused on the eyes that stared tearfully into hers.

"Excuse me, sir." A nurse hurried up. "This is a restricted area."

Absently, his eyes still on Grace, Seth reached for his badge. "I'm here to speak with Ms. Fontaine."

"I see. I'll tell her you're here, Lieutenant."

"No, don't disturb her." He didn't want anything to spoil that picture. "I can wait. What's wrong with the baby she's holding?"

"Peter's an AIDS baby. Ms. Fontaine arranged for him to have care here."

"Ms. Fontaine?" He felt a fist lodge in his gut. "It's her child?"

"Biologically? No." The nurse's face softened slightly. "I think she considers them all hers. I honestly don't know what we'd do without her help. Not just the foundation, but her."

"The foundation?"

"The Falling Star Foundation. Ms. Fontaine set it up a few years ago to assist critically ill and terminal children and their families. But it's the hands-on that really matters." She gestured back toward the glass with a nod of her head. "No amount of financial generosity can buy a loving touch or sing a lullaby."

He watched the baby calm, drift slowly to sleep in Grace's arms. "She comes here often?"

"As often as she can. She's our angel. You'll have to excuse me, Lieutenant."

"Thank you." As she walked away, he stepped closer to the isolation glass. Grace started toward the crib. It was then that her eyes met his.

He saw the shock come into them first. Even she wasn't skilled enough to disguise the range of emotions that raced over her face. Surprise, embarrassment, annoyance. Then she smoothed the expressions out. Gently, she laid the baby back into the crib, brushed a hand over his cheek. She walked through a side door and disappeared.

It was several minutes before she came out into the corridor. The smock was gone. Now she was a confident woman in a flame-red suit, her mouth carefully tinted to match. "Well, Lieutenant, we meet in the oddest places."

Before she could complete the casual greeting she'd practiced while she tidied her makeup, he took her chin firmly in his hand. His eyes locked intently on hers, probed.

"You're a fake." He said it quietly, stepping closer. "You're a fraud. Who the hell are you?"

"Whatever I like." He unnerved her, that long, intense and all-too-personal study with those golden-brown eyes. "And I don't believe this is the place for an interrogation. I'd like you to let me go now," she said steadily. "I don't want any scenes here."

"I'm not going to cause a scene."

She lifted her brows. "I might." Deliberately she pushed his hand away and started down the corridor. "If you want to discuss the case with me, or have any questions regarding it, we'll do it outside. I won't have it brought in here."

"It was breaking your heart," he murmured. "Holding that baby was breaking your heart."

"It's my heart." Almost viciously, she punched a finger at the button for the elevator. "And it's a tough one, Seth. Ask anyone."

"Your lashes are still wet."

"This is none of your business." Her voice was low and vibrating with fury. "Absolutely none of your business."

She stepped into the crowded elevator, faced front. She wouldn't speak to him about this part of her life, she promised herself. Just the night before, she'd opened herself to him, only to be pushed away, refused. She wouldn't share her feelings again, and certainly not her feelings about something as vital to her as the children.

He was a cop, just a cop. Hadn't she spent several miserable hours the night before convincing herself that was all he was or could be to her? Whatever he stirred in her would have to be stopped—or, if not stopped, at least suppressed.

She would not share with him, she would not trust him, she would not give to him.

By the time she reached the lobby doors, she was steadier. Hoping to shake him quickly, she started toward the lot. Seth merely took her arm, steered her away.

"Over here," he said, and headed toward a grassy area with a pair of benches.

"I don't have time."

"Make time. You're too upset to drive, in any case."

"Don't tell me what I am."

"Apparently that's just what I've been doing. And apparently I've missed several steps. That's not usual for me, and I don't care for it. Sit down."

"I don't want—"

"Sit down, Grace," he repeated. "I apologize."

Annoyed, she sat on the bench, found her sunglasses in her bag and slipped them on. "For?"

He sat beside her, removed the shielding glasses and looked into her eyes. "For not letting myself look beneath the surface. For not wanting to look. And for blaming you because I don't seem able to stop wanting to do this."

He took her face in his hands and captured her mouth with his.

Chapter 6

She didn't move into him. Not this time. Her emotions were simply too raw to risk. Though her mouth yielded beneath his, she lifted a hand and laid it on his chest, as if to keep him at a safe distance.

And still her heart stumbled.

This time she was holding back. He sensed it, felt it in the press of her hand against him. Not refusing, but resisting. And with a knowledge that came from somewhere too deep to measure, he gentled the kiss, seeking not only to seduce, but also to soothe.

And still his heart staggered.

"Don't." It made her throat ache, her mind haze, her body yearn. And it was all too much. She pulled away from him and stood staring out across the little patch of grass until she thought she could breathe again.

"What is it with timing?" Seth wondered aloud. "That makes it so hard to get right?"

"I don't know." She turned then to look at him. He was an attractive man, she decided. The dark hair and hard face, the odd tint of gold in his eyes. But she'd known many attractive men. What was it about this one that changed everything and made her world tilt? "You bother me, Lieutenant Buchanan."

He gave her one of his rare smiles—slow and full and rich. "That's a mutual problem, Ms. Fontaine. You keep me up at night. Like a puzzle where the pieces are all there, but they change shape right before your eyes. And even when you put it all together—or think you have—it doesn't stay the same."

"I'm not a mystery, Seth."

"You are the most fascinating woman I've ever met." His lips curved again when she lifted her brows. "That isn't entirely a compliment. Along with fascination comes frustration." He stood, but didn't step toward her. "Why were you so upset that I found you here, saw you here?"

"It's private." Her tone was stiff again, dismissive. "I go to considerable trouble to keep it private."

"Why?"

"Because I prefer it that way."

"Your family doesn't know about your involvement here?"

The fury that seared through her eyes was burning-cold. "My family has *nothing* to do with this. Nothing. This isn't a Fontaine project, one of their charitable sops for good press and a tax deduction. It's mine."

"Yes, I can see that," he said calmly. Her family had hurt her even more than he'd guessed. And more, he thought, than she had acknowledged. "Why children, Grace?"

"Because they're the innocents." It was out before she realized she meant to say it. Then she closed her eyes and sighed. "Innocence is a precious and perishable commodity."

"Yes, it is. Falling Star? Your foundation. Is that how you see them, stars that burn out and fall too quickly?"

It was her heart he was touching simply by understanding, by seeing what was inside. "It has nothing to do with the case. Why are you pushing me on this?"

"Because I'm interested in you."

She sent him a smile—half inviting, half sarcastic. "Are you? You didn't seem to be when I asked you to bed. But you see me holding a sick baby and you change your tune." She walked toward him slowly, trailed a fingertip down his shirt. "Well, if it's the maternal type that turns you on, Lieutenant—"

"Don't do that to yourself." Again his voice was quiet, controlled. He took her hand, stopped her from backtracking the trail of her finger. "It's foolish. And it's irritating. You weren't playing games in there. You care."

"Yes, I do. I care enormously. And that doesn't make me a hero, and it doesn't make me any different than I was last night." She drew her hand away and stood her ground. "I want you. I want to go to bed with you. That irritates you, Seth. Not the sentiment, but the bluntness of the statement. Isn't it games you'd prefer? That I'd pretend reluctance and let you conquer?"

He only wished it was something just that ordinary. "Maybe I want to know who you are before we end up in bed. I spent a long time looking at your face—that portrait of you in your house. And, looking, I wondered about you. Now, I want you. But I also want all those pieces to fit."

"You might not like the finished product."

"No," he agreed. "I might not."

Then again, she thought… Considering, she angled her head. "I have a thing tonight. A cocktail party hosted by a major contributor to the hospital. I can't afford to skip it. Why don't you take me, then we'll see what happens next?"

He weighed the pros and cons, knew it was a step that would have ramifications he might not be able to handle smoothly. She wasn't simply a woman, and he wasn't simply a man. Whatever was between them had a long reach and a hard grip.

"Do you always think everything through so carefully?" she asked as she watched him.

"Yes." But in her case it didn't seem to matter, he realized. "I can't guarantee my evenings will be free until this case is closed." He shifted times and meetings and paperwork in his head. "But if I can manage it, I'll pick you up."

"Eight's soon enough. If you're not there by quarter after, I'll assume you were tied up."

No complaints, he thought, no demands. Most of the women he'd known shifted to automatic sulk mode when his work took priority. "I'll call if I can't make it."

"Whatever." She sat again, relaxed now. "I don't imagine you came by to see my secret life, or to make a tentative date for a cocktail party." She slipped her sunglasses back on, sat back. "Why are you here?"

He reached inside his jacket for the photo. Grace caught a brief glimpse of his shoulder holster, and the weapon snug inside it. And wondered if he'd ever had occasion to use it.

"I imagine your time is taken up mainly with administration duties." She took the picture from him, but continued to look at Seth's face. "You wouldn't participate in many, what—busts?"

She thought she caught a faint glint of humor in his eyes, but his mouth remained sober. "I like to keep my hand in."

"Yes," she murmured, easily able to imagine him whipping the weapon out. "I suppose you would."

She shifted her gaze, scanned the face in the photo. This time the humor was in her eyes. "Ah, Joe Cool. Or more likely Juan or Jean-Paul Cool."

"You know him?"

"Not personally, but certainly as a type. He likely speaks the right words in three languages, plays a steely game of baccarat, enjoys his brandy and wears black silk underwear. His Rolex, along with his monogrammed gold cufflinks and diamond pinkie ring, would have been gifts from admirers."

Intrigued, Seth sat beside her again. "And what are the right words?"

"You're the most beautiful woman in the room. I adore you. My heart sings when I look into your eyes. Your husband is a fool, and darling, you must stop buying me gifts."

"Been there?"

"With some variations. Only I've never been married and I don't buy trinkets for users. His eyes are cold," she added, "but a lot of women, lonely women, would only see the polish. That's all they want to see." She took a quick, short breath. "This is the man who killed Melissa, isn't it?"

He started to give her the standard response, but she looked up then, and he was close enough to read her eyes through the amber tint of her glasses. "I think it is. His prints were all over the house. Some of the surfaces were wiped, but he missed a lot, which leads me to think he panicked. Either because she fell or because he wasn't able to find what he'd come for."

"And you're leaning toward the second choice, because this isn't the type of man to panic because he'd killed a woman."

"No, he isn't."

"She couldn't have given him what he'd come for. She wouldn't have known what he was talking about."

"No. That doesn't make you responsible. If you indulge yourself by thinking it does, you'd have to blame Bailey, too."

Grace opened her mouth, closed it again, breathed deep. "That's clever logic, Lieutenant," she said after a moment. "So I shed my sackcloth and ashes and blame this man. Have you found him?"

"He's dead." He took the photo back, tucked it away. "And my clever logic leads me to believe that whoever hired him decided to fire him, permanently."

"I see." She felt nothing, no satisfaction, no relief. "So, we're nowhere."

"The Three Stars are under twenty-four-hour guard. You, M.J. and Bailey are safe, and the museum will have its property in a matter of days."

"And a lot of people have died. Sacrifices to the god?"

"From what I've read about Mithra, it isn't blood he wants."

"Love, knowledge and generosity," she said quietly. "Powerful elements. The diamond I held, it has vitality. Maybe that's the same as power. Does he want them because they're beautiful, priceless, ancient, or because he truly believes in the legend? Does he believe that if he has all of them in their triangle, he'll possess the power of the god, and immortality?"

"People believe what they choose to believe. Whatever reason he wants them, he's killed for them." Staring out across the grass, he stepped over one of his own rules and shared his thoughts with her. "Money isn't the driving force. He's laid out more than a million already. He wants to own them, to hold them in his hands, whatever the cost. It's more than coveting," he said quietly, as a murky scene swam into his mind.

A marble altar, a golden triangle with three brilliantly blue points. A dark man with pale eyes and a bloody sword.

"And you don't think he'll stop now. You think he'll try again."

Baffled and uneasy with the image, he shook it off, turned back to logic and instinct. "Oh, yeah." Seth's eyes narrowed, went flat. "He'll try again."

Seth made it to Cade's at 8:14. His final meeting of the day, with the chief of police, had gone past seven, and that had barely given him time to get home, change and drive out again. He'd told himself half a dozen times that he'd be better off staying at home, putting the reports and files away and having a quiet evening to relax his mind.

The press conference set for nine sharp the next morning would be a trial by fire, and he needed to be sharp. Yet here he was, sitting in his car feeling ridiculously nervous and unsettled.

He'd tracked a homicidal junkie through a condemned tenement without breaking a sweat, with a steady pulse he'd interrogated cold, vicious killers— but now, as the white ball of the sun dipped low in the sky, he was as jittery as a schoolboy.

He hated cocktail parties. The inane conversations, the silly food, the buffed faces, all feigning enthusiasm or ennui, depending on their style.

But it wasn't the prospect of a few hours socializing with strangers that unnerved him. It was spending time with Grace without the buffer of the job between them.

He'd never had a woman affect him as she did. And he couldn't deny—at least to himself—that he had been deeply, uniquely affected, from the moment he saw her portrait.

It didn't help to tell himself she was shallow, spoiled, a woman used to men falling at her feet. It hadn't helped before he discovered she was much more than that, and it was certainly no good now.

He couldn't claim to understand her, but he was beginning to uncover all those layers and contrasts that made her who and what she was.

And he knew they would be lovers before the night was over.

He saw her step out of the house, a charge of electric blue from the short strapless dress molded to her body, the long, luxurious fall of ebony hair, the endless and perfect legs.

Did she shock every man's system, Seth wondered, just the look of her? Or was he particularly, specifically vulnerable? He decided either answer would be hard to live with, and got out of his car.

Her head turned at the sound of his door, and that heart-stopping face bloomed with a smile. "I didn't think you were going to make it." She crossed to him, unhurried, and touched her mouth to his. "I'm glad you did."

"I'd said I'd call if I wouldn't be here."

"So you did." But she hadn't counted on it. She'd left the address of the party inside, just in case, but she'd resigned herself to spending the evening without him. She smiled again, smoothed a hand down the lapel of his suit. "I never wait by the phone. We're going to Georgetown. Shall we take my car, or yours?"

"I'll drive." Knowing she expected him to make some comment on her looks, he deliberately kept silent as he walked around the car to open her door.

She slipped in, her legs sliding silkily inside. He wanted his hands there, right there where the abbreviated hem of her dress kissed her thighs. Where the skin would be tender as a ripened peach and smooth as white satin.

He closed the door, walked back around the car and got behind the wheel. "Where in Georgetown?" was all he said.

It was a beautiful old house, with soaring ceilings, heavy antiques and deep, warm colors. The lights blazed down on important people, people of influence and wealth, who carried the scent of power under their perfumes and colognes.

She belonged, Seth thought. She'd melded with the

whole from the moment she stepped through the door to exchange sophisticated cheek brushes with the hostess.

Yet she stood apart. In the midst of all the sleek black, the fussy pastels, she was a bright blue flame daring anyone to touch and be burned.

Like the diamonds, he thought. Unique, potent... irresistible.

"Lieutenant Buchanan, isn't it?"

Seth shifted his gaze from Grace and looked at the short, balding man who was built like a boxer and dressed in Savile Row. "Yes. Mr. Rossi, counsel for the defense. If the defense has deep enough pockets."

Unoffended, Rossi chuckled. "I thought I recognized you. I've crossed you on the stand a few times. You're a tough nut. I've always believed I'd have gotten Tremaine off, or at least hung the jury, if I'd have been able to shake your testimony."

"He was guilty."

"As sin," Rossi agreed readily, "but I'd have hung that jury."

As Rossi started to rehash the trial, Seth resigned himself to talking shop.

Across the room, Grace took a glass from a passing waiter and listened to her hostess's gossip with half an ear. She knew when to chuckle, when to lift a brow, purse her lips, make some interesting comment. It was all routine.

She wanted to leave immediately. She wanted to get Seth out of that dark suit. She wanted her hands on him, all over him. Lust was creeping along her skin like a hot rash. Sips of champagne did nothing to cool her throat, and only added to the bubbling in her blood.

"My dear Sarah."

"Gregor, how lovely to see you."

Grace shifted, sipped, smiled at the sleek, dark man with the creamy voice who bent gallantly over their hostess's hand. Mediterranean, she judged, by the charm of the accent. Fiftyish, but fit.

"You're looking particularly wonderful tonight," he said, lingering over her hand. "And your hospitality, as always, is incomparable. And your guests." He turned smiling pale silvery-blue eyes on Grace. "Perfect."

"Gregor." Sarah simpered, fluttered, then turned to Grace. "I don't believe you've met Gregor, Grace. He's fatally charming, so be very careful. Ambassador DeVane, I'd like to present Grace Fontaine, a dear friend."

"I am honored." He lifted Grace's hand, and his lips were warm and soft. "And enchanted."

"Ambassador?" Grace slipped easily into the role. "I thought ambassadors were old and stodgy. All the ones I've met have been. That is, up until now."

"I'll just leave you with Grace, Gregor. I see we have some late arrivals."

"I'm sure I'm in delightful hands." With obvious reluctance, he released Grace's fingers. "Are you perhaps a connection of Niles Fontaine?"

"He's an uncle, yes."

"Ah. I had the pleasure of meeting your uncle and his charming wife in Capri a few years ago. We have a mutual hobby, coins."

"Yes, Uncle Niles has quite a collection. He's mad for coins." Grace brushed her hair back, lifted it off her bare shoulder. "And where are you from, Ambassador DeVane?"

"Gregor, please, in such friendly surroundings. Then I might be permitted to call you Grace."

"Of course." Her smile warmed to suit the new intimacy.

"I doubt you would have heard of my tiny country. We are only a small dot in the sea, known chiefly for our olive oil and wine."

"Terresa?"

"Now I am flattered again that such a beautiful woman would know my humble country."

"It's a beautiful island. I was there briefly, two years ago, and very much enjoyed it. Terresa is a small jewel in the sea, dramatic cliffs to the west, lush vineyards in the east, and sandy beaches as fine as sugar."

He smiled at her, took her hand again. The connection was as unexpected as the woman, and he found himself compelled to touch. And to keep. "You must promise to return, to allow me to show you the country as it should be seen. I have a small villa in the west, and the view would almost be worthy of you."

"I'd love to see it. How difficult it must be to spend the summer in muggy Washington, when you could be enjoying the sea breezes of Terresa."

"Not at all difficult. Now." He skimmed a thumb over her knuckles. "I find the treasures of your country more and more appealing. Perhaps you would consider joining me one evening. Do you enjoy the opera?"

"Very much."

"Then you must allow me to escort you. Perhaps—" He broke off, a flicker of annoyance marring his smooth features as Seth stepped up to them.

"Ambassador Gregor DeVane of Terresa, allow me to introduce Lieutenant Seth Buchanan."

"You are military," DeVane said, offering a hand.

"Cop," Seth said shortly. He didn't like the ambassador's looks. Not one bit. When he saw DeVane with Grace, he'd had a fast, turbulent impulse to reach for his weapon. But, strangely, his instinctive movement hadn't been up, to his gun, but lower on the side. Where a man would carry a sword.

"Ah, the police." DeVane blinked in surprise, though he already had a full dossier on Seth Buchanan. "How fascinating. I hope you'll forgive me for saying it's my fondest wish never to require your services." Smoothly DeVane slipped a glass from a passing tray, handed it to Seth, then took one for himself. "But perhaps we should drink to crime. Without it, you'd be obsolete."

Seth eyed him levelly. There was recognition, inexplicable, and utterly adversarial, when their eyes locked, pale silver to dark gold. "I prefer drinking to justice."

"Of course. To the scales, shall we say, and their constant need for balancing?" Gregor drank, then inclined his head. "You'll excuse me, Lieutenant Buchanan, I've yet to greet my host. I was—" he turned to Grace and kissed her hand again "—beautifully distracted from my duty."

"It was a pleasure to meet you, Gregor."

"I hope to see you again." He looked deeply into her eyes, held the moment. "Very soon."

The moment he turned away, Grace shivered. There had been something almost possessive in that last, long stare. "What an odd and charming man," she murmured.

Energy was shooting through Seth, the need to do battle. His system sparked with it. "Do you usually let odd and charming men drool over you in public?"

It was small of her, Grace supposed, but she enjoyed a kick of satisfaction at the annoyance in Seth's tone. "Of course. Since I so dislike them drooling over me in private." She turned into him, so that their bodies brushed lightly. Then slanted a look up from under that thick curtain of lashes. "You don't plan to drool, do you?"

He could have damned her for shooting his system from slow burn up to sizzle. "Finish your drink," he said abruptly, "and say your goodbyes. We're going."

Grace gave an exaggerated sigh. "Oh, I do love being dominated by a strong man."

"We're about to put that to the test." He took her half-finished drink, set it aside. "Let's go."

DeVane watched them leave, studied the way Seth pressed a hand to the small of Grace's back to steer her through the crowd. He would have to punish the cop for touching her.

Grace was his property now, DeVane thought as he gritted his teeth painfully tight to suppress the rage. She was meant for him. He'd known it from the moment he took her hand and looked into her eyes. She was perfect, flawless. It wasn't just the Three Stars that were fated for him, but the woman who had held one, perhaps caressed it, as well.

She would understand their power. She would add to it.

Along with the Three Stars of Mithra, DeVane vowed, Grace Fontaine would be the treasure of his collection.

She would bring the Stars to him. And then she would belong to him. Forever.

As she stepped outside, Grace felt another shudder sprint down her spine. She hunched her shoulder blades against it, looked back. Through the tall windows filled with light she could see the guests mingling.

And she saw DeVane, quite clearly. For a moment, she would have sworn their eyes met—but this time there was no charm. An irrational sense of fear lodged in her stomach, had her turning quickly away again.

When Seth pulled open the car door, she got in without complaint or comment. She wanted to go, to get away from those brilliantly lit windows and the man who seemed to watch her from beyond them. Briskly she rubbed the chill from her arms.

"You wouldn't be cold if you'd worn clothes." Seth stuck the key in the ignition.

The single remark, issued with cold and savage control, made her chuckle and chased the chill away. "Why, Lieutenant, and here I was wondering how long you would let me keep on what I am wearing."

"Not a hell of a lot longer," he promised, and pulled out into the street.

"Good." Determined to see that he kept that promise, she squirmed over and began to nibble his ear. "Let's break some laws," she whispered.

"I could already charge myself with intent."

She laughed again, quick, breathless, and had him hard as iron.

He wasn't sure how he managed to handle the car, much less drive it through traffic out of D.C. and back into Maryland. She worked his tie off, undid half the buttons of his shirt. Her hands were everywhere, and her mouth teased his ear, his neck, his jaw, while she murmured husky promises, suggestions.

The fantasies she wove with unerring skill had the blood beating painfully in his loins.

He pulled to a jerky stop in his driveway, then dragged her across the seat. She lost one shoe in the car and the other halfway up the walk as he half carried her. Her laughter, dark, wild, damning, roared in his head. He all but broke his own door down to get her inside. The instant they were, he pushed her back against the wall and savaged her mouth.

He wasn't thinking. Couldn't think. It was all primal, violent need. In the darkened hallway, he hiked up her skirt with impatient hands, found the thin, lacy barrier beneath and ripped it aside. He freed himself, then, gripping her hips, plunged into her where they stood.

She cried out, not in protest, not in shock at the almost brutal treatment. But in pure, overwhelming pleasure. She locked herself around him, let him drive her ruthlessly, crest after torrential crest. And met him thrust for greedy, desperate thrust.

It was mindless and hot and vicious. And it was all that mattered. Sheer animal need. Violent animal release.

Her body shattered, went limp, as she felt him pour into her.

He slapped his hand against the wall to keep his balance, struggled to slow his breathing, clear his fevered brain. They were no more than a step inside his door, he realized, and he'd mounted her like a rutting bull.

There was no point in apologies, he thought. They'd both wanted fast and urgent. No, *wanted* was too tame a word, he decided. They'd craved it, the way starving animals craved meat.

But he'd never treated a woman with less care, or so completely ignored the consequences.

"I meant to get you out of that dress," he managed, and was pleased when she laughed.

"We'll get around to it."

"There's something else I didn't get around to." He eased back, studied her face in the dim light. "Is that going to be a problem?"

She understood. "No." And though it was rash and foolish, she felt a twinge of regret that there would be no quickening of life inside her as a result of their carelessness. "I take care of myself."

"I didn't want this to happen." He took her chin in his hand. "I should have been able to keep my hands off you."

Her eyes glimmered in the dark—confident and amused. "I hope you don't expect me to be sorry you didn't. I want them on me again. I want mine on you."

"While they are." He lifted her chin a little higher. "No one else's are. I don't share."

Her lips curved slowly as she kept his gaze. "Neither do I."

He nodded, accepting. "Let's go upstairs," he said, and swept her into his arms.

Chapter 7

He switched on the light as he carried her into his room. This time he needed to see her, to know when her eyes clouded or darkened, to witness those flickers of pleasure or shock.

This time he would remember man's advantage over the animal, and that the mind and heart could play a part.

She got a sense of a room of average size, simple buff-colored curtains at the windows, clean-lined furniture without color, a large bed with a navy spread tucked in with precise, military tidiness.

There were paintings on the walls that she told herself she would study later, when her heart wasn't skipping. Scenes both urban and rural were depicted in misty, dreamy watercolors that made a personal contrast to the practical room.

But all thoughts of art and decor fled when he set her on her feet beside the bed. She reached out, undid the final buttons of his shirt, while he shrugged out of his jacket. Her brows lifted when she noted he wore his shoulder holster.

"Even to a cocktail party?"

"Habit," he said simply, and took it off, hung it over a chair. He caught the look in her eye. "Is it a problem?"

"No. I was just thinking how it suits you. And wondering if you look as sexy putting it on as you do taking it off." Then she turned, scooped her hair over her shoulder. "I could use some help."

He let his gaze wander over her back. Instead of reaching for the zipper, he drew her against him and lowered his mouth to her bare shoulder. She sighed, tipped her head back.

"That's even better."

"Round one took the edge off," he murmured, then slid his hands around her waist, and up, until they cupped her breasts. "I want you whimpering, wanting, weak."

His thumbs brushed the curves just above the bold blue silk. Focused on the sensation, she reached back, linked her arms around his neck. Her body began to move, timed to his strokes, but when she tried to turn, he held her in place.

She moaned, shifted restlessly, when his fingers curved under her bodice, the backs teasing her nipples, making them heat and ache. "I want to touch you."

"Whimpering," he repeated, and ran his hands down her dress to the hem, then beneath. "Wanting." And cupped her. "Weak." Pierced her.

The orgasm flooded her, one long, slow wave that

swamped the senses. The whimper he'd waited for shuddered through her lips.

He toed off his shoes, then lowered her zipper inch by inch. His fingers barely brushed her skin as he spread the parted material, eased it down her body until it pooled at her feet. He turned her, stepped back.

She wore only a garter, in the same hot blue as the dress, with stockings so sheer they appeared to be little more than mist. Her body was a fantasy of generous curves, and satin skin. Her hair fell like wild black rain over her shoulders.

"Too many men have told you you're beautiful for it to matter that I say it."

"Just tell me you want me. That matters."

"I want you, Grace." He stepped to her again, took her into his arms, but instead of the greedy kiss she'd expected, he gave her one to slowly drown in. Her arms clutched around him, then went limp, at this new assault to the senses.

"Kiss me again," she murmured when his lips wandered to her throat. "Just like that. Again."

So his mouth met hers, let her sink a second time. With a dreamy hum of pleasure, she slipped his shirt away, let her hands explore. It was lovely to be savored, to be given the gift of a slow kindling flame, to feel the control slip out of her hands into his. And to trust.

He let himself learn her body inch by generous inch. Pleasured them both by possessing those full firm breasts, first with hands, then with mouth. He lowered his hands, flicked the hooks of her stockings free one by one—hearing her quick catch of breath each time. Then slid his hands under the filmy fabric to flesh.

Warm, smooth. He lowered her to the bed, felt her

body yield beneath his. Soft, willing. Her lips answered his. Eager, generous.

They watched each other in the light. Moved together. First a sigh, then a groan. She found muscle, the rough skin of an old scar, and the taste of man. Shifting, she drew his slacks down, feasted on his chest as she undressed him. When he took her breasts again, pulled her closer to suckle, her arms quivered and her hair drifted forward to curtain them both.

She felt the heat rising, sliding through her blood like a fever, until her breath was short and shallow. She could hear herself saying his name, over and over, as he patiently built her toward the edge.

Her eyes went cobalt, fascinating him. Her pillowsoft lips trembled, her glorious body quaked. Even as the need for release clawed at him, he continued to savor. Until he finally shifted her to her back and, with his eyes locked on hers, buried himself inside her.

She arched upward, her hands fisting in the sheets, her body stunned with pleasure. "Seth." Her breath expelled in a rush, burned her lungs. "It's never... Not like this. Seth—"

Before she could speak again, he closed her mouth with his and took her.

When sleep came, Grace dreamed she was in her garden in the mountains, with the woods, thick and green and cool, surrounding her. The hollyhocks loomed taller than her head and bloomed in deep, rich reds and clear, shimmering whites. A hummingbird, shimmering sapphire and emerald, drank from a trumpet flower. Cosmos and coneflowers, dahlias and zinnias made a cheerful wave of mixed colors.

Pansies turned their exotic little faces toward the sun and smiled.

Here she was happy, at peace with herself. Alone, but never lonely. Here there was no sound but the song of the breeze through the leaves, the hum of bees, the faint music of the creek bubbling over rocks.

She watched deer walk quietly out of the woods to drink from the slow-moving creek, their hooves lost in the low-lying mist that hugged the ground. The dawn light shimmered like silver, sparkled off the soft dew, caught rainbows in the mist.

Content, she walked through her flowers, fingers brushing blooms, scents rising up to please her senses. She saw the glint among the blossoms, the bright, beckoning blue, and, stooping, plucked the stone from the ground.

Power shimmered in her hand. It was a clean, flowing sensation, pure as water, potent as wine. For a moment, she stood very still, her hand open. The stone resting in her palm danced with the morning light.

Hers to guard, she thought. To protect. And to give.

When she heard the rustle in the woods, she turned, smiling. It would be him, she was certain. She'd waited for him all her life, wanted so desperately to welcome him, to walk into his arms and know they would wrap around her.

She stepped forward, the stone warming her palm, the faint vibrations from it traveling like music up her arm and toward her heart. She would give it to him, she thought. She would give him everything she had, everything she was. For love had no boundaries.

All at once, the light changed, hazed over. The air went cold and whipped with the wind. By the creek, the deer lifted their heads, alert, alarmed, then turned as one and fled into the sheltering trees. The hum of bees died into a rumble of thunder, and lightning snaked over the dingy sky.

There in the darkened wood, close, too close to where her flowers bloomed, something moved stealthily. Her fingers clutched reflexively, closing fast over the stone. And through the leaves she saw eyes, bright, greedy. And watching.

The shadows parted and opened the path to her.

"No." Frantic, Grace pushed at the hands that held her. "I won't give it to you. It's not for you."

"Easy." Seth pulled her up, stroked her hair. "Just a nightmare. Shake it off now."

"Watching me..." She moaned it, pressed her face into his strong, bare shoulder, drew in his scent and was soothed. "He's watching me. In the woods, watching me."

"No, you're here with me." Her heart was pounding hard enough to bring real concern. Seth tightened his grip, as if to slow it and block the tremors that shook her. "It's a dream. There's no one here but me. I've got you."

"Don't let him touch me. I'll die if he touches me."

"I won't." He tipped her face back. "I've got you," he repeated, and warmed her trembling lips with his.

"Seth." Relief shuddered through her as she clutched at him. "I was waiting for you. In the garden, waiting for you."

"Okay. I'm here now." To protect, he thought. And then to cherish. Shaken by the depth of that, he eased her backward, brushed the tumbled hair away from her face. "Must have been a bad one. Do you have a lot of nightmares?"

"What?" Disoriented, trapped between the dream and the present, she only stared at him.

"Do you want the light?" He didn't wait for an answer, but reached around her to switch on the bedside lamp. Grace turned her face away from the glare, pressed her fisted hand against her heart. "Relax now. Come on." He took her hand, started to open her fingers.

"No." She jerked it back. "He wants it."

"Wants what?"

"The Star. He's coming for it, and for me. He's coming."

"Who?"

"I don't…I don't know." Baffled now, she looked down at her hand, slowly opened it. "I was holding the stone." She could still feel the heat, the weight. "I had it. I found it."

"It was a dream. The diamonds are locked in a vault. They're safe." He tipped a finger under her chin until her eyes met his. "You're safe."

"It was a dream." Saying it aloud brought both relief and embarrassment. "I'm sorry."

"It's all right." He studied her, saw that her face was white, her eyes were fragile. Something moved inside him, shifted, urged his hand to reach out, stroke that pale cheek. "You've had a rough few days, haven't you?"

It was just that, the quiet understanding in his voice, that had her eyes filling. She closed them to will back the tears and took careful breaths. The pressure in her chest was unbearable. "I'm going to get some water."

He simply reached out and drew her in. She'd hidden all that fear and grief and weariness inside her very well, he realized. Until now. "Why don't you let it go?"

Her breath hitched, tore. "I just need to—"

"Let it go," he repeated, and settled her head on his shoulder.

She shuddered once, then clung. Then wept.

He offered no words. He just held her.

At eight the next morning, Seth dropped her off at Cade's. She'd protested the hour at which he shook her out of sleep, tried to curl herself into the mattress. He'd dealt with that by simply picking her up, carrying her into the shower and turning it on. Cold.

He'd given her exactly thirty minutes to pull herself together, then packed her into the car.

"The gestapo could have taken lessons from you," she commented as he pulled up behind M.J.'s car. "My hair's still wet."

"I didn't have the hour to spare it must take to dry all that."

"I didn't even have time to put my makeup on."

"You don't need it."

"I suppose that's your idea of a compliment."

"No, it's just a fact."

She turned to him, looking arousing, rumpled and erotic in the strapless dress. "You, on the other hand, look all pressed and tidy."

"I didn't take twenty minutes in the shower." She'd sung in the shower, he remembered. Unbelievably off-key. Thinking of it made him smile. "Go away. I've got work to do."

She pouted, then reached for her purse. "Well, thanks for the lift, Lieutenant." Then laughed when he pushed her back against the seat and gave her the long, thorough kiss she'd been hoping for.

"That almost makes up for the one miserly cup of

coffee you allowed me this morning." She caught his bottom lip between her teeth, and her eyes sparkled into his. "I want to see you tonight."

"I'll come by. If I can."

"I'll be here." She opened the door, shot him a look over her shoulder. "If I can."

Unable to resist, he watched her every sauntering step toward the house. The minute she closed the front door behind her, he shut his eyes.

My God, he thought, he was in love with her. And it was totally impossible.

Inside, Grace all but danced down the hall. She was in love. And it was glorious. It was new and fresh and the first. It was what she'd been waiting for her entire life. Her face glowed as she stepped into the kitchen and found Bailey and Cade at the table, sharing coffee.

"Good morning, troops." She all but sang it as she headed to the coffeepot.

"Good morning to you." Cade tucked his tongue in his cheek. "I like your pajamas."

Laughing, she carried her cup to the table, then leaned down and kissed him full on the mouth. "I just adore you. Bailey, I just adore this man. You'd better snap him up quick, before I get ideas."

Bailey smiled dreamily into her coffee, then looked up, eyes shining and damp. "We're getting married in two weeks."

"What?" Grace bobbled her mug, sloshed coffee dangerously close to the rim. "What?" she repeated, and sat heavily.

"He won't wait."

"Why should I?" Reaching over the table, Cade took Bailey's hand. "I love you."

"Married." Grace looked down at their joined hands. A perfect match, she thought, and let out a shaky sigh. "That's wonderful. That's incredibly wonderful." Laying a hand over theirs, she stared into Cade's eyes. And saw exactly what she needed to see. "You'll be good to her." It wasn't a question, it was acceptance.

After giving his hand a quick squeeze, she sat back. "Well, a wedding to plan, and a whole two weeks to do it. That ought to make us all insane."

"It's just going to be a small ceremony," Bailey began. "Here at the house."

"I'm going to say one word." Cade put a plea in his voice. *"Elopement."*

"No." With a shake of her head, Bailey drew back, picked up her mug. "I'm not going to start our life together by insulting your family."

"They're not human. You can't insult the inhuman. Muffy will bring the beasts with her."

"Don't call your niece and nephew beasts."

"Wait a minute." Grace held up a hand. Her brows knit. "Muffy? Is that Muffy Parris Westlake? She's your sister?"

"Guilty."

Grace managed to suppress most of the snort of laughter. "That would make Doro Parris Lawrence your other sister." She rolled her eyes, picturing the two annoying and self-important Washington hostesses. "Bailey, run for your life. Go to Vegas. You and Cade can get married by a nice Elvis-impersonator judge and have a delightful, quiet life in the desert. Change your names. Never come back."

"See?" Pleased, Cade slapped a hand on the table. "She knows them."

"Stop it, both of you." Bailey refused to laugh, though her voice trembled with it. "We'll have a small, dignified ceremony—with Cade's family." She smiled at Grace. "And mine."

"Keep working on her." Cade rose. "I've got a couple things to do before I go into the office."

Grace picked up her coffee again. "I don't know his family well," she told Bailey. "I've managed to avoid that little pleasure, but I can tell you from what I do know, you've got the cream of the crop."

"I love him so much, Grace. I know it's all happened quickly, but—"

"What does time have to do with it?" Because she knew they were both about to get teary, she leaned forward. "We have to discuss the important, the vital, aspects of this situation, Bailey." She took a deep breath. "When do we go shopping?"

M.J. staggered in to the sound of laughter, and scowled at both of them. "I hate cheerful people in the morning." She poured coffee, tried to inhale it, then turned to study Grace. "Well, well," she said dryly. "Apparently you and the cop got to know each other last night."

"Well enough that I know he's more than a badge and an attitude." Irritated, she pushed her mug aside. "What have you got against him?"

"Other than the fact he's cold and arrogant, superior and stiff, nothing at all. Jack says they call him the Machine. Small wonder."

"I always find it interesting," Grace said coolly, "when people only skim the surface, then judge another human being. All those traits you just listed describe a man you don't know."

"M.J., drink your coffee." Bailey rose to get the cream. "You know you're not fit to be around until you've had a half a gallon."

M.J. shook her head, fisted a hand on a hip covered with a tattered T-shirt and equally tattered shorts. "Just because you slept with him, doesn't mean you know him, either. You're usually a hell of a lot more careful than that, Grace. You might let other people assume you pop into bed with a new guy every other night, but we know better. What the hell were you thinking of?"

"I was thinking of *me,*" she shot back. "I wanted him. I needed him. He's the first man who's ever really touched me. And I'm not going to let you stand there and make something beautiful into something cheap."

No one spoke for a moment. Bailey stood near the table, the creamer in one hand. M.J. slowly straightened from the counter, whistled out a breath. "You're falling for him." Staggered, she raked a hand through her hair. "You're really falling for him."

"I've already hit the ground with a splat. So what?"

"I'm sorry." M.J. struggled to adjust. She didn't have to like the man, she told herself. She just had to love Grace. "There must be something to him, if he got to you. Are you sure you're okay with it?"

"No, I'm not sure I'm okay with it." Temper drained, and doubt snuck in. "I don't know why it's happened or what to do about it. I just know it is. It wasn't just sex." She remembered how he had held her while she cried. How he'd left the light on for her without her having to ask. "I've been waiting for him all my life."

"I know what that means." Bailey set the creamer down, took Grace's hand. "Exactly."

"So do I." With a sigh, M.J. stepped forward. "What's

happening to us? We're three sensible women, and suddenly we're guarding ancient mythical stones, running from bad guys and falling headlong into love with men we've just met. It's crazy."

"It's right," Bailey said quietly. "You know it feels right."

"Yeah." M.J. laid her hand over theirs. "I guess it does."

It wasn't easy for Grace to go back into her house. This time, though, she wasn't alone. M.J. and Jack flanked her like bookends.

"Man." Scanning the wreck of the living area, M.J. hissed out a breath. "I thought they did a number on my place. Of course, you've got a lot more toys to play with."

Then her gaze focused on the splintered railing. And the outline below. "You don't want to do this now, Grace."

"The police cleared the scene. I have to get started on it sometime."

M.J. shook her head. "Where?"

"I'll start in the bedroom." Grace managed a smile. "I'm about to make my dry cleaner a millionaire."

"I'll see what I can do with the railing," Jack told her. "Jury-rig something so it's safe until you have it rebuilt."

"I'd appreciate it."

"Go on up," M.J. suggested. "I'll get a broom. And a bulldozer." She waited until Grace was upstairs before she turned to Jack. "I'm going to do this down here. Get rid of…things." Her gaze wandered to the outline. "She shouldn't have to handle that."

He leaned down to kiss her forehead. "You're a stand-up pal, M.J."

"Yeah, that's me." She inhaled sharply. "Let's see if we can dig up the stereo or the TV out of this mess. I could use some racket in here."

It took most of the afternoon before Grace was satisfied that the house was cleared out enough to call in her cleaning service. She wanted every room scrubbed before she lived there again.

And she was determined to do just that. To live, to be at home, to face whatever ghosts remained. To prove to herself that she could, she separated from M.J. and Jack and went shopping for the first replacements. Then, because the entire day had left her feeling raw, she stopped by Salvini.

She needed to see Bailey.

And she needed to see the Stars.

Once she was buzzed in, she found Bailey up in her office on the phone. With a smile, Bailey gestured her in. "Yes, Dr. Linstrum, I'm faxing the report to you now, and I'll bring you the original personally before five. I can complete the final tests you've ordered tomorrow."

She listened a moment, ran a finger down the soapstone elephant on her desk. "No, I'm fine. I appreciate your concern, and your understanding. The Stars are my priority. I'll have full copies of all the reports for your insurance carrier by end of business day Friday. Yes, thank you. Goodbye."

"You're working very quickly," Grace commented.

"Despite all that happened, hardly any time was lost. And everyone will feel more comfortable when the stones are in the museum."

"I want to see them again, Bailey." She let out a little laugh. "It's silly, but I really need to. I had this dream last night—nightmare, really."

"What kind of dream?"

Grace sat on the edge of the desk and told her. Though her voice was steady, her fingers tapped with nerves.

"I had dreams, too," Bailey murmured. "I'm still having them. So is M.J."

Uneasy, Grace shifted. "Like mine?"

"Similar enough to be more than coincidence." She rose, held out a hand for Grace's. "Let's go take a look."

"You're not breaking any laws, are you?"

As they walked downstairs together, Bailey sent her an amused look. "I think after what I've already done, this is a minor infraction." She tried to block it, but a shudder escaped as they descended the last flight of steps, under which she'd once hidden from a killer.

"Are you going to be all right here?" Instinctively Grace hooked an arm around Bailey's shoulder. "I hate thinking of what happened, and now thinking of you working here, remembering it."

"It's getting better. Grace, I've had my stepbrothers cremated. Or rather, Cade took care of the arrangements. He wouldn't let me handle any of it."

"Good for him. You don't owe them anything, Bailey. You never did. We're your family. We always will be."

"I know."

She passed into the vault room and approached the massive reinforced-steel doors. The security system was complex and intricate, and even with the ease of long practice, it took Bailey three full minutes to disengage.

"Maybe I ought to have one of these installed in my

house," Grace said lightly. "That bastard popped my library safe like it was a gumball machine. He must have fenced the jewelry fast. I hate losing the pieces you made for me."

"I'll make you more. In fact—" Bailey picked up a square velvet box "—let's start now."

Curious, Grace opened the box to a pair of heavy gold earrings. The smooth crescent-shaped gold was studded with stones in deep, dark hues of emerald, ruby and sapphire.

"Bailey, they're beautiful."

"I'd just finished them before…well, before. As soon as I had, I knew they were yours."

"It's not my birthday."

"I thought you were dead." Bailey's voice shook, then strengthened when Grace looked up. "I thought I would never see you again. So let's consider these a celebration of the rest of our lives."

Grace removed the simple studs in her ears, began to replace them with Bailey's gift. "When I'm not wearing them, I'll keep them with my mother's jewelry. The things that matter most."

"They look perfect on you. I knew they would." Bailey turned, took the heavy padded box from its shelf in the vault. Holding it between them, she opened it.

Grace let out a long, uneven sigh. "I honestly thought one would be gone. I would drive up to the mountains and find it in my garden, sitting on the ground beneath the flowers. It was so real, Bailey."

Reaching out, Grace took a stone. Her stone. "I felt it in my hand, just as I do now. It pulsed in my hand like a heart." She laughed a little, but the sound was hollow. "My heart. That's what it seemed like. I didn't realize that until now. It was like holding my own heart."

"There's a link." A little pale, Bailey took another stone from the box. "I don't understand it, but I know it. This is the Star I had. If M.J. was here, she'd have picked hers."

"I never thought I believed in this sort of thing." Grace turned the stone in her hand. "I was wrong. It's incredibly easy to believe it. To know it. Are we protecting them, Bailey, or are they protecting us?"

"I like to think it's both. They brought me Cade." Gently, she replaced her stone, touched a fingertip to the second Star in its hollow. "Brought M.J. Jack." Her face softened. "I opened up the showroom for them a little while ago," she told Grace. "Jack dragged her in and bought her a ring."

"A ring?" Grace lifted a hand to her heart as it swelled. "An engagement ring?"

"An engagement ring. She argued the whole time, kept telling him not to be a jerk. She didn't need any ring. He just ignored her and pointed to this lovely green tourmaline—square-cut, with diamond baguettes. I designed it a few months ago, thinking that it would make a wonderful, nontraditional engagement ring for the right woman. He knew she was the right woman."

"He's perfect for her." Grace brushed a tear from her lashes and beamed. "I knew it as soon as I saw them together."

"I wish you'd seen them today. There she is, grumbling, rolling her eyes, insisting all this fuss is a waste of time and effort. Then he put that ring on her finger. She got this big, sloppy grin on her face. You know the one."

"Yeah." And she could see it, perfectly. "I'm so

happy for her, for you. It's like all that love was there, waiting, and the stones…" She looked down at them again. "They opened the door for it."

"And you, Grace? Have they opened the door for you?"

"I don't know if I'm ready for that." Nerves suddenly sprang to her fingertips. She laid the stone back in its bed. "Seth certainly wouldn't be. I don't think he'd believe in magic of any sort. And as for love…even if that door is wide open and the opportunity is there, he's not a man to fall easily."

"Easy or not—" Bailey closed the lid, replaced the box "—when you're meant to fall, you fall. He's yours, Grace. I saw that in your eyes this morning."

"Well." Grace swallowed the nerves. "I think I may wait awhile to let him in on that."

Chapter 8

There were flowers waiting for her when Grace returned to Cade's. A gorgeous crystal vase was filled with long spears of paper-white long-stemmed roses. Her heart thudded foolishly into her throat as she snatched up the card, tore open the envelope.

Then it deflated and sank.

Not from Seth, she noted. Of course, it had been silly of her to think that he'd have indulged in such a romantic and extravagant gesture. The card read simply:

Until we meet again,

Gregor

The ambassador with the oddly compelling eyes, she mused, and leaned forward to sniff at the tender, just-opening blooms. It had been sweet of him, she told herself. A bit over-the-top, as there were easily three dozen roses in the vase, but sweet.

And she was irritated to realize that if they had been from Seth, she would have mooned over them like a starstruck teenager, would likely have pressed one between the pages of a book, even shed a few tears. She berated herself for being six times a fool.

If these appalling highs and lows were side effects of being in love, Grace thought she could have waited quite a bit longer to experience the sensation. She was just about to toss the card on the table when the phone rang.

She hesitated, as both Cade's and Jack's cars were in the drive, but when the phone rang the third time, she picked it up. "Parris residence."

"Is Grace Fontaine available?" The crisp tones of a well-trained secretary sounded in her ear. "Ambassador DeVane calling."

"Yes, this is she."

"One moment, please, Ms. Fontaine."

Lips pursed thoughtfully, Grace flipped the edge of the card against her palm. The man certainly had had no trouble tracking her down, Grace mused. And just how was she going to handle him?

"Grace." His voice flowed through the phone. "How delightful to speak with you again."

"Gregor." She flipped her hair behind her shoulder, edged a hip onto the table. "How extravagant of you. I've just walked in to your roses." She tipped one down, sniffed again. "They're glorious."

"Merely a token. I was disappointed not to have more time with you last evening. You left so early."

She thought of the wild ride to Seth's, the wilder sex. "I had...a previous engagement."

"Perhaps we can make up for it tomorrow evening. I have a box at the theater. *Tosca.* It's such a beautiful tragedy. There's nothing I would enjoy more than sharing it with you, then a late supper, perhaps."

"It sounds lovely." She rolled her eyes toward the flowers. Oh, dear, she thought. This would never do. "I'm so terribly sorry, Gregor, but I'm not free." With no regret whatsoever, she set the card aside. "Actually, I'm involved with someone, quite seriously."

For me, in any case, she thought. Then she looked through the glass panels of the front door, and her face lit up with surprise and pleasure when she saw Seth's car pull in.

"I see." She was too busy trying to steady her abruptly dancing pulse to notice how his voice had chilled. "Your escort of last evening."

"Yes. I'm terribly flattered, Gregor, and if I were any less involved, I'd leap at the invitation. I hope you'll forgive me, and understand."

Struggling not to squirm with delight, she crooked her finger in invitation as Seth stepped up to the door.

"Of course. If your circumstances change, I hope you'll reconsider."

"I certainly will." With a sultry smile, she walked her fingers up Seth's chest. "And thank you again, Gregor, so much, for the flowers. They're divine."

"It was my pleasure," he said, and his hands balled into bone-white fists as he hung up the receiver.

Humiliated, he thought, snapping his teeth together, grinding them viciously. Rejected for a suitful of muscles and a badge.

She would pay, he promised himself, taking her

photo from his file and gently tapping a well-manicured finger against it. She would pay dearly. And soon.

With the ambassador completely forgotten the moment the connection was broken, Grace tipped her face up to Seth's. "Hello, handsome."

He didn't kiss her, but looked at the flowers, then at the card she'd tossed carelessly beside them. "Another conquest?"

"Apparently." She heard the cold distance in his tone and wasn't certain whether to be flattered or annoyed. She opted for a different tack altogether, and purred. "The ambassador was interested in an evening at the opera and…whatever."

The spurt of jealousy infuriated him. It was a new experience, and one he detested. It left him helpless, made him want to drag her out to his car by the hair, cart her off, lock her up where only he could see and touch and taste.

But more, there was fear, for her. A bone-deep sense of danger.

"It seems the ambassador—and you—move quickly."

No, she realized, the temper was going to come. There was no stopping it. She eased off the table, her smile an icy dare. "I move however it suits me. You should know."

"Yes." He dipped his hands into his pockets to keep them off her. "I should. I do."

Crushed, she angled her chin, aimed those laser blue eyes. "Which am I now, Lieutenant? The whore or the goddess? The ivory princess atop the pedestal, or the tramp? I've been them all—it just depends on the man and how he chooses to look."

"I'm looking at you," he said calmly. "And I don't know what I see."

"Let me know when you make up your mind." She started to move around him, came up short when he took her arm. "Don't push me." She tossed her head so that her hair flew out, settled.

"I could say the same, Grace."

She drew in one hot, deep breath, shoved his hand aside. "If you're interested, I gave the ambassador my regrets and told him I was involved with someone." She flashed a frigid smile and swung toward the stairs. "That, apparently, was my mistake."

He scowled after her, considered striding up the stairs of a house that wasn't his own and finishing the confrontation—one way or the other. Appalled, he pinched the bridge of his nose between his thumb and forefinger and tried to squeeze off the bitter headache plaguing him.

His day had been grueling, and had ended ten long hours after it began, with him staring at the group of photos on his board. Photos of the dead who were waiting for him to find the connection.

And he was already furious with himself because he'd already begun to run a search for data on Gregor DeVane. He couldn't be sure if he had done so due to a basic cop's hunch, or a man's territorial instinct. Or the dreams. It was a question, and a conflict, he'd never had to face before.

But one answer was clear as glass. He'd been out of line with Grace. He was still standing by the foyer table, frowning at the steps and weighing his options, when Cade strolled in from the rear of the house.

"Buchanan." More than a little surprised to see the

homicide lieutenant standing in his foyer scowling, Cade stopped, scratched his jaw. "Ah, I didn't know you were here."

He had no business being there, Seth reminded himself. "Sorry. Grace let me in."

"Oh." After one beat, Cade pinpointed the source of the heat still flashing in the air. "Oh," he said again, and wisely controlled a grin. "Fine. Something I can do for you?"

"No. I'm just leaving."

"Have a spat?"

Seth turned his head, met Cade's obviously amused eyes blandly. "Excuse me?"

"Just a wild stab in the dark. What did you do to tick her off?" Though Seth didn't answer, Cade noted that his gaze shifted briefly to the roses. "Oh, yeah. Guess you didn't send them, huh? If some guy sent Bailey three dozen white roses, I'd probably have to stuff them down his throat, one at a time."

It was the gleam of appreciation that flashed briefly in Seth's eyes that made Cade decide to revise his stance. Maybe he could like Lieutenant Seth Buchanan after all.

"Want a beer?"

The casual and friendly invitation threw Seth off balance. "I— No, I was leaving."

"Come on out back. Jack and I already popped a couple of tops. We're going to fire up the grill and show the women how real men cook." Cade's grin spread charmingly. "Besides, oiling yourself with a couple of brews will make it easier for you to crawl. You're going to crawl anyway, so you might as well be comfortable."

Seth hissed out a breath. "Why the hell not?"

* * *

Grace stayed stubbornly in her room for an hour. She could hear laughter, music, and the silly whack of mallets striking balls as people played an enthusiastic game of croquet. She knew Seth's car was still in the drive, and had promised herself she wouldn't go back down until it was gone.

But she was feeling deprived, and hungry.

Since she'd already changed into shorts and a thin cotton shirt, she paused at the mirror only long enough to freshen her lipstick, spritz on some perfume. Just to make him suffer, she told herself, then sauntered downstairs and out onto the patio.

Steaks were smoking on the grill with Cade at the helm wielding an enormous barbecue fork. Bailey and Jack were arguing over the croquet match, and M.J. was sulking at a picnic table while she nibbled on potato chips.

"Jack knocked me out of the game," she complained, and gestured with her beer. "I still say he cheated."

"Any time you lose," Grace pointed out as she picked up a chip, "it's because someone cheated." Then she slid her gaze to Seth.

He'd taken off his tie, she noted, and his jacket. He still wore his holster. She imagined that was because he didn't feel comfortable hanging his gun over a tree branch. He, too, had a beer in his hand, and was watching the game with apparent interest.

"You still here?"

"Yeah." He'd had two beers, but didn't think crawling was going to be any more comfortable with the lubricant. "I've been invited to dinner."

"Isn't that cozy?" Grace spied what she recognized

as a pitcher of M.J.'s special margaritas and poured herself a glass. The taste was tart, icy, and perfect. In dismissal, she wandered over to the grill to kibitz.

"I know what I'm doing," Cade was saying, and
shifted to guard his territory as Seth joined them. "I
marinated these vegetable kabobs personally. Go away
and leave this to a man."

"I was merely asking if you preferred your mushrooms blackened."

Cade sent her a withering look. "Get her off my back,
Seth. An artist can't work with critics breathing down
his neck and picking on his mushrooms."

"Let's go over here." Seth took her elbow, and was
braced for her jerk. He kept his grip firm and hauled
her away into the rose garden.

"I don't want to talk to you," Grace said furiously.

"You don't have to talk. I'll talk." But it took him
a minute. Apologies didn't come easily to a man who
made it a habit not to make mistakes. "I'm sorry. I over-
reacted."

She said nothing, simply folded her arms and waited.

"You want more?" He nodded, didn't bother to sigh.
"I was jealous, an atypical reaction for me, and I handled it poorly. I apologize."

Grace shook her head. "That's the weakest excuse
for an apology I've ever heard. Not the words, Seth,
the delivery. But fine, I'll accept it in the same spirit
it was offered."

"What do you want from me?" he demanded, frustrated enough to raise his voice and grab her arms.
"What the hell do you want?"

"That." She tossed back her head. "Just that. A little
emotion, a little passion. You can take your cardboard-

stiff apology and stuff it, just like you can stuff the cold, deliberate and dispassionate routine you gave me over the flowers. That icy control doesn't cut it with me. If you feel something—whatever the hell it is—then let me know."

She sucked in her breath, stunned, when he yanked her against him, savaged her mouth with heat and anger and need. She twisted once and was hauled roughly back. Then was left weak and singed and shaken by the time he drew away.

"Is that enough for you?" He hauled her to her toes, his fingers digging in. His eyes weren't dispassionate now, weren't cool, but turbulent. Human. "Enough emotion, enough passion? I don't like to lose control. You can't afford to lose control on the job."

Her breath was heaving. And her heart was flying. "This isn't the job."

"No, but it was supposed to be." He willed his grip to loosen. "You were supposed to be. I can't get you out of my head. Damn it, Grace. I can't get you out."

She laid a hand on his cheek, felt the muscle twitch. "It's the same for me. Maybe the only difference right now is that I want it to be that way."

For how long? he wondered, but he didn't say it. "Come home with me."

"I'd love to." She smiled, stroked her fingers back, into his hair. "But I think we'd better stay for dinner, at least. Otherwise, we'd break Cade's heart."

"After dinner, then." It wasn't difficult at all, he discovered, to bring her hands to his lips, linger over them, then look into her eyes. "I am sorry. But, Grace—?"

"Yes?"

"If DeVane calls you again, or sends flowers?"

Her lips twitched. "Yes?"

"I'll have to kill him."

With a delighted laugh, she threw her arms around Seth's neck. "Now we're talking."

"That was nice." With a satisfied sigh, Grace sank down in the seat of Seth's car and watched the moon shimmer in the sky. "I like seeing the four of them together. But it's funny. It's as if I blinked, and everyone took this huge, giant step forward."

"Red light, green light."

Confused, Grace turned her head to look at him. "What?"

"The game—the kid's game? You know, the person who's it has to say, 'Green light,' turn his back. Everybody can go forward, but then he says, 'Red light' and spins around. If he sees anybody move, they have to go back to the start."

When she gave a baffled laugh, it was his turn to look. "Didn't you ever play games like that when you were a kid?"

"No. I was given the proper lessons, lectured on etiquette and was instructed to take brisk daily walks for exercise. Sometimes I ran," she said softly, remembering. "Fast, and hard, until my heart was bumping in my chest. But I guess I always had to go back to the start."

Annoyed with herself, she shook her shoulders. "My, doesn't that sound pathetic? It wasn't, really. It was just structured." She scooped back her hair, smiled at him. "So what other games did young Seth Buchanan play?"

"The usual." Didn't she know how heartbreaking it was to hear that wistfulness in her voice, then see that quick, careless shrug as she pushed it all aside? "Didn't you have friends?"

"Of course." Then she looked away. "No. It doesn't matter. I have them now. The best of friends."

"Do you know any one of the three of you can start a sentence and either of the other two can finish it?"

"We don't do that."

"Yes, you do. A dozen times tonight, at least. You don't even realize it. And you have this code," he continued. "Little quirks and gestures. M.J.'s half smirk or eye roll, Bailey's downsweep of the lashes or hair-around-the-finger twist. And you lift your left brow, just a fraction, or catch your tongue between your teeth. When you do, you let each other know the joke's your little secret."

She hummed in her throat, not at all sure she liked being deciphered so easily. "Aren't you observant…."

"That's my job." He pulled into his driveway, turned to her. "It shouldn't bother you."

"I haven't decided if it does or not. Did you become a cop because you're observant, or are you observant because you're a cop?"

"Hard to say. I was never really anything else."

"Not even when you were young Seth Buchanan?"

"It was always part of my life. My grandfather was a cop. And my father. My father's brother. Our house was filled with them."

"So it was expected of you?"

"It was understood," he corrected. "If I'd wanted to be a plumber or a mechanic, that would have been fine. But it was what I wanted."

"Why?"

"There's right and there's wrong."

"Just that simple?"

"It should be." He looked at the ring on his finger. "My father was a good cop. Straight. Fair. Solid. You can't ask for more than that."

She laid a hand over his. "You lost him."

"Line of duty. A long time ago." The hurt had passed a long time before, as well, and left room for pride. "He was a good cop, a good father, a good man. He always said there was a choice between doing the right thing or the wrong thing. Either one had a price. But you could pay up on the first and still look yourself in the eye every morning."

Grace leaned over, kissed him lightly. "He did the right thing by you."

"Always. My mother was a cop's wife, steady as a rock. Now she's a cop's mother, and she's still steady. Still there. When I got my gold shield, it meant as much to her as it did to me."

There was a bond, she realized. Deep and true and unquestioned. "But she worries about you."

"Some. But she accepts it. Has to," he added, with the ghost of a smile. "I've got a younger brother and sister. We're all cops."

"It runs through the blood," she murmured. "Are you close?"

"We're family," he said simply, then thought of hers and remembered that such things weren't simple. They were precious. "Yes, we're close."

He was the oldest, she mused. He would have taken his generational placement seriously, and, when his father died, his responsibilities as man of the house with equal weight.

It was hardly a wonder, then, that authority, responsibility, duty, sat so naturally on him. She thought of the weapon he wore, touched a fingertip to the leather strap.

"Have you ever…" She lifted her gaze to his. "Have you ever had to?"

"Yes. But I can still look myself in the eye in the morning."

She accepted that without question. But the next subject was more difficult. "You have a scar, just here." Her memory of it was perfect as she touched her finger just under his right shoulder now. "You were shot?"

"Five years ago. One of those things." There was no point in relaying the details. The bust gone wrong, the shouts and the electric buzz of terror. The insult of the bullet and the bright, stupefying pain. "Most police work is routine—paperwork, tedium, repetition."

"But not all."

"No, not all." He wanted to see her smile again, wanted to prolong what had evolved into a sweet and intimate interlude in a darkened car. Just conversation, without the sizzle of sex. "You've got a tattoo on your incredibly perfect bottom."

She laughed then, and tossed her hair back. "I didn't think you'd noticed."

"I noticed. Why do you have a tattoo of a winged horse on your butt, Grace?"

"It was an impulse, one of those wild-girl things I dragged M.J. and Bailey into."

"They have winged horses on their—"

"No, and what they do have is their little secret. I wanted the winged horse because it was free. You couldn't catch it unless it wanted to be caught." She lifted a hand to his face, changed the mood subtly. "I never wanted to be caught. Before."

He nearly believed her. Lowering his head, he met her lips with his, let the kiss spin out. It was quiet, without urgency. The slow meeting of tongues, the lazy change of angles and depths. Easy sips. Testing nibbles.

Her body shifted fluidly, her hands sliding up his chest to link at the nape of his neck. A purr sounded in her throat. "It's been a long time since I necked in the front seat of a car."

He nudged her hair aside so that his mouth could find that sweet, sensitive curve between neck and shoulder. "Want to try the back seat?"

Her laugh was low and delighted. "Absolutely."

The need had snuck up on him, crept into his bloodstream to stagger his heart. "We'll go inside."

Her breath was a bit unsteady as she leaned back, grinned at him in the shimmer of moonlight. "Chicken."

His eyes narrowed fractionally, making her grin widen. "There's a perfectly good bed in the house."

She made a soft clucking noise, then, chuckling, rubbed her lips over his. "Let's pretend," she whispered, pressing her body to his, sliding it against his. "We're on a dark, deserted road and you've told me the car's broken down."

He said her name, an exasperated sound against her tempting lips. It was only another challenge to her.

"I pretend I believe you, because I want to stay, I want you to…persuade me. You'll say you just want to touch me, and I'll pretend I believe that, too." She took his hand, laid it on her breast and felt the quick thrill when his fingers flexed. "Even though I know that's not all you want. It's not all you want, is it, Seth?"

What he wanted was that dark, slippery slide into her. His hands moved under her shirt, found flesh.

"We're not going to make it into the back seat," he warned her.

She only laughed.

He wasn't sure if he felt smug or stunned by his own behavior when he finally unlocked his front door. Had he been this randy as a teenager? he wondered. That ridiculously reckless. Or was it only Grace who made such things as making desperate love in his own driveway one more adventure?

She stepped inside, lifted the hair off her neck, then let it fall in a gesture that simply stopped his heart. "My place should be ready by tomorrow, the next day at the latest. We'll have to go there. We can skinny-dip in my pool. It's so hot out now."

"You're so beautiful."

She turned, surprised at the mix of resentment and desire in his voice. He stood just inside the door, as if he might turn at any moment and leave her.

"It's a dangerous weapon. Lethal."

She tried to smile. "Arrest me."

"You don't like to be told." He let out a half laugh. "You don't like to be told you're beautiful."

"I didn't do anything to earn how I look."

She said it, he realized, as if beauty were more of a curse than a gift. And in that moment he felt a new level of understanding. He stepped forward, took her face gently in his hands, looked deep and long.

"Well, maybe your eyes are a little too close together."

Her hitch of laughter was pure surprise. "They are not."

"And your mouth, I think it might be just a hair off

center. Let me check." He measured it with his own, lingering over the kiss when her lips curved. "Yeah. Just a hair, but it does throw things off, now that I really look. And let's see…" He turned her head to each side, paused to consider. "Yep. The left profile's weak. Are you getting a double chin there?"

She slapped his hand away, torn between insult and laughter. "I certainly am not."

"I really should check that, too. I don't know if I want to take this whole thing any further if you're getting a double chin."

He grabbed her, tugging her head back gently by the hair so that he could nibble freely under her jaw. She giggled—a young, foolish sound—and squirmed. "Stop that, you idiot." She let out a shriek when he hauled her up into his arms.

"You're no lightweight, either, by the way."

Her eyes went to slits. "Okay, buster, that's all. I'm leaving."

It was a delight to watch him grin—that quick, boyish flash of humor. "I forgot to tell you," he said as he headed for the stairs. "My car's broken down. I'm out of gas. The cat ate my homework. I'm just going to touch you."

He'd made it up two steps when the phone rang. "Damn." He brushed his lips absently over her brow. "I have to get that."

"It's all right. I'll remember where you were." Though he set her down, she didn't think her feet hit the floor. Love was a cushy buffer.

But her smile faded as she saw his eyes change. Suddenly they were flat again, unreadable. She knew as she walked across the room toward him that he'd shifted seamlessly from man to cop.

"Where?" His voice was cool again, controlled. "Is the scene secured?" He swore lightly, barely a whisper under the breath. "Get it secured. I'm on my way." As he hung up, his eyes skimmed over her, focused. "I'm sorry, Grace, I have to go."

She moistened her lips. "Is it bad?"

"I have to go," was all he'd say. "I'll call for a black-and-white to take you back to Cade's."

"Can't I wait here for you?"

"I don't know how long I'll be."

"It doesn't matter." She offered a hand, but wasn't sure she could reach him. "I'd like to wait. I want to wait for you."

No woman ever had. That thought passed quickly through his mind, distracting him. "If you get tired of waiting, call the precinct. I'll leave word there for a uniform to drive you home if you call in."

"All right." But she wouldn't call in. She would wait. "Seth." She moved into him, brushed her lips against his. "I'll see you when you get back."

Chapter 9

Alone, Grace switched on the television, settled on the sofa. Five minutes later, she was up and wandering the house.

He didn't go in for knickknacks, she mused. Probably thought of them as dustcatchers. No plants, no pets. The living room furniture was simple, masculine, and good quality. The sofa was comfortable, of generous size and a deep hunter green. She would have spruced it up with pillows. Burgundy, navy, copper. The coffee table was a square of heavy oak, highly polished and dust-free.

She decided he had a weekly housekeeper. She just couldn't picture Seth wielding a polishing rag. There was a bookcase under the side window and, crouching, she scanned the titles. It pleased her that they had read many of the same books. There was even a gardening book she'd studied herself.

That she could see, she decided. Yes, she could see Seth working out in the yard, turning the earth, planting something that would last.

There was art in this room, as well. She moved closer, certain the watercolor portraits grouped on the wall were the work of the same artist who had done the cityscape and rural scene in his bedroom. She searched for the signature first, and found Marilyn Buchanan looped in the lower corner.

Sister, mother, cousin? she wondered. Someone he loved, and who loved him. She shifted her gaze and studied the first painting.

Seth's father, Grace realized with a jolt. It had to be. The resemblance was there, in the eyes, clear, intense, tawny. The jaw, squared off, almost chiseled. The artist had seen strength, a touch of sadness, and honor. A whisper of humor around the mouth and an innate pride in the set of the head. All were evident in the three-quarter profile view that had the subject staring off at something only he could see.

The next portrait was a woman, perhaps in her forties. It was a pretty face, but the artist hadn't hidden the faint and telltale lines of age, the touches of gray in the dark, curling hair. The hazel eyes looked straight ahead, with humor and with patience. And there was Seth's mouth, Grace thought, smiling easily.

His mother, she concluded. How much strength was contained inside those quiet hazel eyes? Grace wondered. How much was required to stand and accept when everyone you loved faced danger daily?

Whatever the amount, this woman possessed it.

There was another man, young, twenty-something, with a cocky grin and daredevil eyes shades darker than Seth's. Attractive, sexy, with a dark shock of hair falling carelessly over his brow. His brother, certainly.

The last was of a young woman with a shoulder-length sweep of dark hair, the tawny eyes alert, the sculpted mouth just curved in the beginnings of a smile. Lovely, with more of Seth's seriousness about her than the young man. His sister.

She wondered if she would ever meet them, or if she would know them only through their portraits. Seth would take the woman he loved to them, she thought, and let the little slice of hurt pass through her. He would want to—need to—bring her into his mother's home, watch how she melded and mixed with his family.

It was a door he'd have to open on both sides in welcome. Not just because it was traditional, she realized, but because it would matter to him.

But a lover? No, she decided. It wasn't necessary to share a lover with family. He'd never take a woman with whom he shared only sex home to meet his mother.

Grace closed her eyes a moment. Stop feeling sorry for yourself, she ordered briskly. You can't have everything you want or need, so you make the best of what there is.

She opened her eyes again, once more scanned the portraits. Good faces, she thought. A good family.

But where, Grace wondered, was Seth's portrait? There had to be one. What had the artist seen? Had she painted him with that cool cop's stare, that surprisingly beautiful smile, the all-too-rare flash of that grin?

Determined to find out, she left the television blaring and went on the hunt. In the next twenty minutes, she discovered that Seth lived tidily, kept a phone and notepad in every room, used the second bedroom as a combination guest room and office, had turned the tiny third bedroom into a minigym and liked deep colors and comfortable chairs.

She found more watercolors, but no portrait of the man.

She circled the guest room, curious that here, and only here, he'd indulged in some whimsy. Recessed shelves held a collection of figures, some carved in wood, others in stone. Dragons, griffins, sorcerers, unicorns, centaurs. And a single winged horse of alabaster caught soaring in midflight.

Here the paintings reflected the magical—a misty landscape where a turreted castle rose silver into a pale rose-colored sky, a shadow-dappled lake where a single white deer drank.

There were books on Arthur, on Irish legends, the gods of Olympus, and those who had ruled Rome. And there, on the small cherrywood desk, was a globe of blue crystal and a book on Mithra, the god of light.

It made her tremble, clutch her arms. Had he picked up the book because of the case? Or had it already been here? She touched a hand to the slim volume and was certain it was the latter.

One more link between them, she realized, forged before they'd even met. It was so easy for her to accept that, even to be grateful. But she wondered if he felt the same.

She went downstairs, oddly at home after her self-guided tour. It made her smile to see their coffee cups from that morning still in the sink, a little touch of intimacy. She found a bottle of wine in the refrigerator, poured herself a glass and took it with her into the living room.

She went back to the bookcase, thinking of curling up on the couch with the TV for company and a book to pass the time. Then a chill washed over her, so quick, so intense, the wine shook in her hand. She found herself staring out the window, her breath coming short, her other hand clutched on the edge of the bookcase.

Someone watching. It pounded in her brain, a frightened, whispering voice that might have been her own.

Someone watching.

But she saw nothing but the dark, the shimmer of moonlight, the quiet house across the street.

Stop it, she ordered herself. There's no one there. There's nothing there. But she straightened and quickly twitched the curtains closed. Her hands were shaking.

She sipped wine, tried to laugh at herself. The late-breaking bulletin on the television had her turning slowly. A family of four in nearby Bethesda. Murdered.

She knew where Seth had gone now. And could only imagine what he was dealing with.

She was alone. DeVane sat in his treasure room, stroking an ivory statue of the goddess Venus. He'd come to think of it as Grace. As his obsession festered and grew, he imagined Grace and himself together, immortal through time. She would be his most prized possession. His goddess. And the Three Stars would complete his collection of the priceless.

Of course, she would have to be punished first. He knew what had to be done, what would matter most to her. And the other two women were not blameless— they had complicated his plans, caused him to fail. They would have to die, of course.

After he had the Stars, after he had Grace, they would die. And their deaths would be her punishment.

Now she was alone. It would be so easy to take her now. To bring her here. She'd be afraid, at first. He wanted her to be afraid. It was part of her punishment. Eventually he would woo her, win her. Own her. They would have, after all, several lifetimes to be together.

In one of them he would take her back to Terresa. He would make her a queen. A god could settle for no less than a queen.

Take her tonight. The voice that spoke louder and louder in his head every day taunted him. He couldn't trust it. DeVane steadied his breathing, shut his eyes. He would not be rushed. Every detail had to be in place.

Grace would come to him when he was prepared. And she would bring him the Stars.

Seth downed one last cup of sludgy coffee and rubbed at the ache at the back of his neck. His stomach was still raw from what he'd seen in that neat suburban home. He knew civilians and rookie cops believed the vets became immune to the results of violent death— the sights, the smells, the meaningless waste.

It was a lie.

No one could become used to seeing what he'd seen. If they could, they shouldn't wear a badge. The law needed to retain its sense of disgust, of horror, for murder.

What drove a man to take the lives of his own children, of the woman he'd made them with, and then his own? There'd been no one left in that neat suburban home to answer that question. He knew it would haunt him.

Seth scrubbed his hands over his face, felt the knots of tension and fatigue. He rolled his shoulders once, twice, then squared them before cutting through the bull pen, toward the locker room.

Mick Marshall was there, rubbing his sore feet. His wiry red hair stood up like a bush that needed trimming from a face lined with weariness. His eyes were shadowed, his mouth was grim.

"Lieutenant." He pulled his socks back on.

"You didn't have to come in on this, Detective."

"Hell, I heard the gunshots from my own living room." He picked up one of his shoes, but just rested his elbows on his knees. "Two blocks over. Jesus, my kids played with those kids. How the hell am I going to explain this?"

"How well did you know the father?"

"Didn't, really. It's just like they always say, Lieutenant. He was a quiet guy, polite, kept to himself." He gave a short, humorless laugh. "They always do."

"Mulrooney's taking the case. You can assist if you want. Now go home, get some sleep. Go in and kiss your kids."

"Yeah." Mick scraped his fingers through his hair. "Listen, Lieutenant, I got some data on that DeVane guy."

Seth's spine tingled. "Anything interesting?"

"Depends on what floats your boat. He's fifty-two, never married, inherited a big fat pile from his old man, including this big vineyard on that island, that Terresa. Grows olives, too, runs some cattle."

"The gentleman farmer?"

"Oh, he's got more going than that. Lots of interests, spread out all over hell and back. Shipping, communications, import-export. Lots of fingers in lots of pies generating lots of dough. He was made ambassador to the U.S. three years ago. Seems to like it here. He bought some nifty place on Foxhall Road, big mansion, likes to entertain. People don't like to talk about him, though. They get real nervous."

"Money and power make some people nervous."

"Yeah. I haven't gotten a lot of information yet. But there was a woman about five years ago. Opera singer. Pretty big deal, if you're into that sort of thing. Italian lady. Seems like they were pretty tight. Then she disappeared."

"Disappeared." Seth's waning interest snapped back. "How?"

"That's the thing. She just went poof. Italian police can't figure it. She had a place in Milan, left all her things—clothes, jewelry, the works. She was singing at that opera house there, in the middle of a run, you know? Didn't show for the evening performance. She went shopping on that afternoon, had a bunch of things sent back to her place. But she never went back."

"They figure kidnapping?"

"They did. But then there was no ransom call, no body, no sign of her in nearly five years. She was…" Mick screwed up his face in thought. "Thirty, supposed to be at the top of her form, and a hell of a looker. She left a big pile of lire in her accounts. It's still there."

"DeVane was questioned?"

"Yeah. Seems he was on his yacht in the Ionian Sea, soaking up rays and drinking ouzo, when it all went down. A half-dozen guests on board with him. The Italian cop I talked to—big opera fan, by the way—he didn't think DeVane seemed shocked enough, or upset enough. He smelled something, but couldn't make anything stick. Still, the guy offered a reward, five million lire, for her safe return. No one ever collected."

"I'd say that was fairly interesting. Keep digging." And, Seth thought, he'd start doing some digging himself.

"One more thing." Mick cracked his neck from side to side. "And I thought this was interesting too—the guy's a collector. He has a little of everything—coins, stamps, jewelry, art, antiques, statuary. He does it all. But he's also reputed to have a unique and extensive gem collection—rivals the Smithsonian's."

"DeVane likes rocks."

"Oh, yeah. And get this. Two years ago, more or less, he paid three mil for an emerald. Big rock, sure, but its price spiked because it was supposed to be a magic rock." The very idea made Mick's lips curl. "Merlin was supposed to have, you know, conjured it up for Arthur. Seems to me a guy who'd buy into that would be pretty interested in three big blue rocks and all that god and immortality stuff that goes with them."

"I just bet he would." And wasn't it odd, Seth mused, that DeVane's name hadn't been on Bailey's list? A collector whose U.S. residence was only miles from Salvini, yet he'd never done business with them?

No, the lack was too odd to believe.

"Get me what you've got when you go on shift, Mick. I'd like to talk to that Italian cop personally. I appreciate the extra time you put into this."

Mick blinked. Seth never failed to thank his men for good work, but it was generally mechanical. There had been genuine warmth this time, on a personal level. "Sure, no sweat. But you know, Lieutenant, even if you can tie this guy to the case, he'll bounce. Diplomatic immunity. We can't touch him."

"Let's tie him first, then we'll see." Seth glanced over, distracted, when a locker slammed open nearby as a cop was coming on shift. "Get some sleep," he began, then broke off. There, taped to the back of the locker, was Grace, young, laughing and naked.

Her head was tossed back, and that teasing smile, that feminine confidence, that silky power, sparkled in her eyes. Her skin was like polished marble, her curves were generous, with only that rainfall of hair, artfully draped to drive a man insane, covering her.

Mick turned his head, saw the centerfold and winced. Cade had filled him in on the lieutenant's relationship with Grace, and all Mick could think was that someone—very likely the cop currently standing at his locker whistling moronically—was about to die.

"Ah, Lieutenant…" Mick began, with some brave thought of saving his associate's life.

Seth merely held up a hand, cut Mick off and walked to the locker. The cop changing his shirt glanced over. "Lieutenant."

"Bradley," Seth said, and continued to study the glossy photo.

"She's something else, isn't she? One of the guys on day shift said she'd been in and looked just as good in person."

"Did he?"

"You bet. I dug this out of a pile of magazines in my garage. None the worse for wear."

"Bradley." Mick whispered the name and buried his head in his hands. The guy was dead meat.

Seth took a long breath, resisted the urge to rip the

photo down. "Female officers share this locker room, Bradley. This is inappropriate." Where was the tattoo? Seth thought hazily. What had she been when she posed for this? Nineteen, twenty? "Find somewhere else to hang your art."

"Yes, sir."

Seth turned away, then shot one last look over his shoulder. "And she's better in person. Much better."

"Bradley," Mick said as Seth strode out, "you just dodged one major bullet."

Dawn was breaking when Seth let himself into the house. He'd gone by the book on the case in Bethesda. It would close when the forensic and autopsy reports confirmed what he already knew. A man of thirty-six who made a comfortable living as a computer programmer had gotten up from his sofa, where he was watching television, loaded his revolver and ended four lives in the approximate space of ten minutes.

For this crime, Seth could offer no justice.

He could have headed home two hours earlier. But he'd made use of the time difference in Europe to make calls, ask questions, gather data. He was slowly putting together a picture of Gregor DeVane.

A man of wealth he had never sweated for. One who enjoyed prestige and power, who traveled in exalted circles, and had no family.

There was no crime in any of that, Seth thought as he closed his front door behind him.

There was no crime in sending white roses to a beautiful woman.

Or in once being involved with one who'd disappeared. But wasn't it interesting that DeVane had been involved with another woman? A Frenchwoman, a prima ballerina of great beauty who'd been considered the finest dancer of the decade. And who had been found dead of a drug overdose in her Paris home.

The verdict had been suicide, though those closest to her insisted she had never used drugs. She had been fiercely disciplined about her body. DeVane had been questioned in that matter, as well, but only as a matter of form. He had been dining at the White House at the very hour the young dancer slipped into a coma, and then into death.

Still, Seth and the Italian detective agreed it was quite a fascinating coincidence.

A collector, Seth mused, switching off lights automatically. An acquirer of beautiful things, and beautiful women. A man who would pay double the value of an emerald to possess a legend, as well.

He would see how many more threads he could tie, and he would, he decided, have an official chat with the ambassador.

He stepped into the living room, started to hit the next switch, and saw Grace curled upon the couch.

He'd assumed she'd gone home. But there she was, curled into a tight, protective ball on his couch, sleeping. What the hell was she doing here? he wondered.

Waiting for you. Just as she said she would. As no woman had waited before. As he'd wanted no woman to wait.

Emotion thudded into his chest, flooded into his heart. It undid him, he realized, this irrational love. His heart wasn't safe here, wasn't even his own any longer. He wanted it back, wanted desperately to be able to turn away, leave her and go back to his life.

It terrified him that he wouldn't. Couldn't.

She was bound to get bored before too much longer, to lose interest in a relationship he imagined was fueled by impulse and sex on her part. Would she just drift away, he wondered, or end it cleanly? It would be clean, he decided. That would be her way. She wasn't, as he'd once wanted to believe, callous or cold or calculating. She had a very giving heart, but he thought it was also a restless one.

Moving over, he crouched in front of her, studied her face. There was a faint line between her brows. She didn't sleep easily, he realized. What dreams chased her? he asked himself. What worries nagged her?

Poor little rich girl, he thought. Still running until you're out of breath and there's nothing to do but go back to the start.

He stroked a thumb over her brow to smooth it, then slid his arms under her. "Come on, baby," he murmured, "time for bed."

"No." She pushed at him, struggled. "Don't."

More nightmares? Concerned, he gathered her close. "It's Seth. It's all right. I've got you."

"Watching me." She turned her face into his shoulder. "Outside. Everywhere. Watching me."

"Shhh... No one's here." He carried her toward the steps, realizing now why every light in the house had been blazing. She'd been afraid to be alone in the dark. Yet she'd stayed. "No one's going to hurt you, Grace. I promise."

"Seth." She surfaced to the sound of his voice, and her heavy eyes opened and focused on his face. "Seth," she said again. She touched a hand to his cheek, then her lips. "You look so tired."

"We can switch. You can carry me."

She slid her arms around him, pressed her cheek, warm to his. "I heard, on the news. The family in Bethesda."

"You didn't have to wait."

"Seth." She eased back, met his eyes.

"I won't talk about it," he said flatly. "Don't ask."

"You won't talk about it because it troubles you to talk about it, or because you won't share those troubles with me?"

He set her down beside the bed, turned away and peeled off his shirt. "I'm tired, Grace. I have to be back in a few hours. I need to sleep."

"All right." She rubbed the heel of her hand over her heart, where it hurt the most. "I've already had some sleep. I'll go downstairs and call a cab."

He hung his shirt over the back of a chair, sat to take off his shoes. "If that's what you want."

"It's not what I want, but it seems it's what you want." She barely lifted a brow when he heaved his shoe across the room. Then he stared at it as if it had leaped there on its own.

"I don't do things like that," he said between his teeth. "I never do things like that."

"Why not? It always makes me feel better." And because he looked so exhausted, and so baffled by himself, she relented. Walking to him, she stepped in close to where he sat and began to knead the stiff muscles of his shoulders. "You know what you need around here, Lieutenant?" She dipped her head to kiss the top of his. "Besides me, of course. You need to get yourself a bubble tub, something you can sink down into that'll beat all these knots out of you. But for now we'll see what I can do about them."

Her hands felt like glory, smoothing out the knotted muscles in his shoulders. "Why?"

"That's one of your favorite questions, isn't it? Come on, lie down, let me work on this rock you call a back."

"I just need to sleep."

"Um-hmm." Taking charge, she nudged him back, climbed onto the bed to kneel beside him. "Roll over, handsome."

"I like this view better." He managed a half smile, toyed with the ends of her hair. "Why don't you come here? I'm too tired to fight you off."

"I'll keep that in mind." She gave him a push. "Roll over, big boy."

With a grunt, he rolled over on his stomach, then let out a second grunt when she straddled him and those wonderful hands began to press and stroke and knead.

"You, being you, would consider a regular massage an indulgence. But that's where you're wrong." She pressed down with the heels of her hands, worked forward to knead with her fingertips. "You give your body relief, it works better for you. I get one every week at the club. Stefan could do wonders for you."

"Stefan." He closed his eyes and tried not to think about another man with his hands all over her. "Figures."

"He's a professional," she said dryly. "And his wife is a pediatric therapist. She's wonderful with the children at the hospital."

He thought of the children, and that was what weakened him. That, and her soothing hands, her quiet voice.

Sunlight filtered, a warm red, through his closed lids, but he could still see.

"The kids were in bed."

Her hands froze for a moment. Then, with a long, quiet breath, she moved them again, up and down his spine, over his shoulder blades, up to the tight length of his neck. And she waited.

"The youngest girl had a doll—one of those Raggedy Anns. An old one. She was still holding it. There were Disney posters all over the walls. All those fairy tales and happy endings. The way it's supposed to be when you're a kid. The older girl had one of those teen magazines beside the bed—the kind ten-year-olds read because they can't wait to be sixteen. They never woke up. Never knew neither one of them would get to be sixteen."

She said nothing. There was nothing that could be said. But, leaning down, she touched her lips to the back of his shoulder and felt him let loose a long, ragged breath.

"It twists you when it's kids. I don't know a cop who can deal with it without having it twist his guts. The mother was on the stairs. Looks like she heard the shots, starting running up to her kids. After, he went back to the living room, sat down on the sofa and finished it."

She curled herself into him, hugged herself to his back and just held on. "Try to sleep," she murmured.

"Stay. Please."

"I will." She closed her eyes, listened to his breathing deepen. "I'll stay."

But he woke alone. As sleep was clearing, he wondered if he'd dreamed the meeting at dawn. Yet he could smell her—on the air, on his own skin where she'd curled close. He was still stretched crosswise over the bed, and he tilted his wrist to check the watch he'd neglected to take off.

Whatever else was going on inside him, his internal clock was still in working order.

He gave himself an extra two minutes under the shower to beat back fatigue, and when shaving promised himself to do nothing more than vegetate on his next personal day. He pretended it wasn't going to be another hot, humid, hazy day while he knotted his tie.

Then he swore, scooped fingers though his just-combed hair, remembering he'd neglected to set the timer on his coffeemaker. The minutes it would take to brew it would not only set his teeth on edge, they would eat into his schedule.

But the one thing he categorically refused to do was start the day with the poison that simmered at the cop shop.

His mind was so focused on coffee that when the scent of it wafted like a siren's call as he came down the stairs, he thought it was an illusion.

Not only was the pot full of gloriously rich black liquid, Grace was sitting at his kitchen table, reading the morning paper and nibbling on a bagel. Her hair was scooped back from her face, and she appeared to be wearing nothing more than one of his shirts.

"Good morning." She smiled up at him, then shook her head. "Are you human? How can you look so official and intimidating on less than three hours' sleep?"

"Practice. I thought you'd gone."

"I told you I'd stay. Coffee's hot. I hope you don't mind that I helped myself."

"No." He stood exactly where he was. "I don't mind."

"If it's all right with you, I'll just loiter over coffee awhile before I get dressed. I'll get myself back to Cade's and change. I want to drop by the hospital later this morning, then I'm going home. It's time I did. The cleaning crew should be finished by this afternoon, so I thought..." She trailed off as he just continued to stare at her.

"What is it?" She gave an uncertain smile and rubbed at her nose.

Keeping his eyes on hers, he took the phone from the wall and punched in a number on memory. "This is Buchanan," he said. "I won't be in for a couple hours. I'm taking personal time." He hung up, held out a hand. "Come back to bed. Please."

She rose, and put her hand in his.

When clothes were scattered carelessly on the floor, the sheets turned back, the shades pulled to filter the beat of the sun, he covered her.

He needed to hold, to touch, to indulge himself for one hour with the flow of emotion she caused in him. Only an hour, yet he didn't hurry. Instead, he lingered over slow, deep, drugging kisses that lasted eons, loitered over long, smooth, soft caresses that stretched into forever.

She was there for him. Simply there. Open, giving, offering a seemingly endless supply of warmth.

She sighed, shakily, as he stroked her to helpless response, moving over her tenderly, his patience infinite. Each time their mouths met, with that slow slide of tongue, her heart shuddered in her breast.

There were the soft, slippery sounds of intimacy, the quiet murmurs of lovers, drifting into sighs and moans.

Both of them were lost, mired in thick layers of sensation, the air around them like syrup, causing movement to slow and pleasure to last.

Her breath sighed out as he trailed lazily down her body with hands and mouth, as her own hands stroked over his back, then his shoulders. She opened for him, arching up in welcome, then shuddering as his tongue brought on a long, rolling climax.

And because he needed it as much as she, she let her hands fall limply, let him take her wherever he chose. Her blood beat hot and the heat brought a dew of roused passion to her skin. His hands slicked over her skin like silk.

"Tell me you want me." He trailed slow, open-mouthed kisses up her torso.

"Yes." She gripped his hips, urged him. "I want you."

"Tell me you need me." His tongue slid over her nipple.

"Yes." She moaned again when he suckled gently. "I need you."

Tell me you love me. But that he demanded only in his mind as he brought his mouth to hers again, sank into that wet, willing promise.

"Now." He kept his eyes open and on hers.

"Yes." She rose to meet him. "Now."

He glided inside her, filling her so slowly, so achingly, that they both trembled. He saw her eyes swim with tears and found the urge for tenderness stronger than any other. He kissed her again, softly, moved inside her one slow beat at a time.

The sweetness of it had a tear spilling over, trailing down her glowing cheek. Her lips trembled, and he felt her muscles contract and clutch him. "Don't close your eyes." He whispered it, sipped the tear from her cheek. "I want to see your eyes when I take you over."

She couldn't stop it. The tenderness stripped her. Her vision blurred with tears, and the blue of her eyes deepened to midnight. She said his name, then murmured it again against his lips. And her body quivered as the next long, undulating wave swamped her.

"I can't—"

"Let me have you." He was falling, falling, falling, and he buried his face in her hair. "Let me have all of you."

Chapter 10

In the nursery, Grace was rocking an infant. The baby girl was barely big enough to fill the crook of her arm from elbow to wrist, but the tiny infant watched her steadily with the deeply blue eyes of a newborn.

The hole in her heart had been repaired, and her prognosis was good.

"You're going to be fine, Carrie. Your mama and papa are so worried about you, but you're going to be just fine. She stroked the baby's cheek and thought—hoped—Carrie smiled a little.

Grace was tempted to sing her to sleep, but knew the nursing staff rolled their eyes and snickered whenever she tried a lullaby. Still, the babies were rarely critical of her admittedly poor singing voice, so she half sang, half murmured, until Carrie's baby owl's eyes grew heavy.

Even when she slept, Grace continued to rock. It

was self-serving now, she knew. Anyone who had ever rocked a baby understood that it soothed the adult, as well as the child. And here, with an infant dozing in her arms, and her own eyes heavy, she could admit her deepest secret.

She pined for children of her own. She longed to carry them inside her, to feel the weight, the movement within, to push them into life with that last sharp pang of childbirth, to hold them to her breast and feel them drink from her.

She wanted to walk the floor with them when they were fretful, to watch them sleep. To raise them and watch them grow, she thought, closing her eyes as she rocked. To care for them, to comfort them in the night, even to watch them take that first wrenching step away from her.

Motherhood was her greatest wish and her most secret desire.

When she first involved herself with the pediatric wing, she'd worried that she was doing so to assuage that gnawing ache inside her. But she knew it wasn't true. The first time she held a sick child in her arms and gave comfort, she'd understood that her commitment encompassed so much more.

She had so much to give, such an abundance of love that needed to be offered. And here it could be accepted without question, without judgment. Here, at least, she could do something worthwhile, something that mattered.

"Carrie matters," she murmured, kissing the top of the sleeping baby's head before she rose to settle her in her crib. "And one day soon you'll go home, strong and healthy. You won't remember that I once rocked you to sleep when your mama couldn't be here. But I will."

She smiled at the nurse who came in, stepped back. "She seems so much better."

"She's a tough little fighter. You've got a wonderful touch with the babies, Ms. Fontaine." The nurse picked up charts, began to make notes.

"I'll try to give you an hour or so in a couple of days. And you'll be able to reach me at home again, if you need to."

"Oh?" The nurse looked up, peered over the top of wire-framed glasses. The murder at Grace's home, and the ensuing investigation, were hot topics at the hospital. "Are you sure you'll be... comfortable at home?"

"I'm going to make sure I'm comfortable." Grace gave Carrie a final look, then stepped out into the hall.

She just had time, she decided, to stop by the pediatric ward and visit the older children. Then she could call Seth's office and see if he was interested in a little dinner for two at her place.

She turned and nearly walked into DeVane.

"Gregor?" She fixed a smile on her face to mask the sudden odd bumping of her heart. "What a surprise. Is someone ill?"

He stared at her, unblinking. "Ill?"

What was wrong with his eyes? she wondered, that they seemed so pale and unfocused. "We are in the hospital," she said, keeping the smile on her face, and, vaguely concerned, she laid a hand on his arm. "Are you all right?"

He snapped back, appalled. For a moment, his mind seemed to have switched off. He'd only been able to see her, to smell her. "Quite well," he assured her. "Momentarily distracted. I didn't expect to see you, either."

Of course, that was a lie, he'd planned the meeting meticulously. He took her hand, bowed over it, kissed her fingers.

"It is, of course, a pleasure to see you anywhere. I've come by here as our mutual friends interested me in the care children receive here. Children and their welfare are a particular interest of mine."

"Really?" Her smile warmed immediately. "Mine, too. Would you like a quick tour?"

"With you as my guide, how could I not?" He turned, signaled to two men who stood stiffly several paces back. "Bodyguards," he told Grace, tucking her hand into the crook of his arm and patting it. "Distressingly necessary in today's climate. Tell me, why am I so fortunate as to find you here today?"

As she usually did, she covered the truth and kept her privacy. "The Fontaines donated significantly to this particular wing. I like to stop in from time to time to see what the hospital's doing with it." She flashed a twinkling look. "And you just never know when you might run into a handsome doctor—or ambassador."

She strolled along, explaining various sections and wondering how much she might, with a little time and charm, wheedle out of him for the children. "General pediatrics is on the floor above. Since this section houses maternity, they wouldn't want kids zooming down the corridors while mothers are in labor or resting."

"Yes, children can be quite boisterous." He detested them. "It's one of my deepest regrets that I have none of my own. But having never found the right woman…"

He gestured with his free hand. "As I grow older, I'm resigned to having no one to carry on my name."

"Gregor, you're in your prime. A strong, vital man who can have as many children as he likes for years yet."

"Ah." He looked into her eyes again. "But there is still the right woman to be found."

She felt a shiver of discomfort at his pointed statement and intense gaze. "I'm sure you'll find her. We have some preemies here." She stepped closer to the glass. "So tiny," she said softly. "So defenseless."

"It's a pity when they're flawed."

She frowned at his choice of words. "Some of them need more time under controlled conditions and medical care to fully develop. But I wouldn't call them flawed."

Another error, he thought with an inner sense of irritation. He could not seem to keep his mind sharp with her scent invading his senses. "Ah, my English is sometimes awkward. You must forgive me."

She smiled again, wanting to ease his obvious discomfort. "Your English is wonderful."

"Is it clever enough to convince you to share a quiet lunch with me? As friends," he said, lacing his smile with regret. "With similar interests."

She glanced, as he did, at the babies. It was tempting, she admitted. He was a charming man—a wealthy and influential one. She might, with careful campaigning, persuade him to assist her in setting up an international branch of Falling Star, an ambition that had been growing in her lately.

"I would love to, Gregor, but right now I'm simply swamped. I was just on my way home when I ran into you. I have to check on some…repairs." That seemed the simplest way to explain it. "But I'd love to have a rain check. One I'd hope to cash in very soon. There's something concerning our similar interests that I'd love to have your advice on, and your input."

"I would love to be of any service whatsoever." He kissed her hand again. Tonight, he thought. He would have her tonight, and there would be no more need for this charade.

"That's so kind of you." Because she felt guilty for her disinterest and coolness in the face of his interest, she kissed his cheek. "I really must run. Do call me about that rain check. Next week, perhaps, for lunch." With a final, flashing smile, she dashed off.

As he watched her, his fisted fingers dug crescents into his palms. Fighting for control, he nodded to one of the silent men who waited for him. "Follow her only," he ordered. "And wait for instructions."

Cade didn't think of himself as a whiner—and, considering how well he tolerated his own family, he believed himself one of the most patient, most amiable, of men. But he was certain that if Grace had him shift one more piece of furniture from one end of her enormous living area to the other, he would break down and weep.

"It looks great."

"Hmm…" She stood, one hand on her hip, the fingers of the other tapping against her lip.

The gleam in her eye was enough to strike terror in Cade's heart and had his already aching muscles crying out in protest. "Really, fabulous. A hundred percent. Get the camera. I see a cover of *House and Garden* here."

"You're wheedling, Cade," she said absently. "Maybe the conversation pit did look better facing the other way." His moan was pitiful, and only made her lips twitch. "Of course, that would mean the coffee table and those two accent pieces would have to shift. And the palm tree—isn't it a beauty?—would have to go there."

The beauty weighed fifty pounds if it weighed an ounce. Cade abandoned pride and whined. "I still have stitches," he reminded her.

"Ah, what's a few stitches to a big, strong man like you?" She fluttered at him, patted his cheek and watched his ego war with his sore back. Giving in, she let loose a long, rolling laugh. "Gotcha. It's fine, darling, absolutely fine. You don't have to carry another cushion."

"You mean it?" His eyes went puppylike with hope. "It's done?"

"Not only is it done, but you're going to sit down, put up your feet, while I go get you an icy beer that I stocked in my fridge just for tall, handsome private investigators."

"You're a goddess."

"So I've been told. Make yourself at home. I'll be right back."

When Grace came back bearing a tray, she saw that Cade had taken her invitation to heart. He sat back on the thick cobalt-blue cushions of her new U-shaped sofa arrangement, his feet propped on the mirror-bright surface of the ebony coffee table, his eyes shut.

"I really did wear you out, didn't I?"

He grunted, opened one eye. Then both popped open in appreciation when she set the loaded tray on the table. "Food," he said, and sprang for it.

She had to laugh as he dived into her offer of glossy green grapes, Brie and crackers, the heap of caviar on ice with toast points. "It's the least I can do for such an attractive moving man." Settling beside him, she picked up the glass of wine she'd poured for herself. "I owe you, Cade."

With his mouth half-full, he scanned the living room, nodded. "Damn straight."

"I don't just mean the manual labor. You gave me a safe haven when I needed one. And most of all, I owe you for Bailey."

"You don't owe me for Bailey. I love her."

"I know. So do I. I've never seen her happier. She was just waiting for you." Leaning over, Grace kissed his cheek. "I always wanted a brother. Now, with you and Jack, I have two. Instant family. They fit, too, don't they?" she commented. "M.J. and Jack. As if they've always been a team."

"They keep each other on their toes. It's fun to watch."

"It is. And speaking of Jack, I thought he was going to give you a hand with our little redecorating project."

Cade scooped caviar onto a piece of toast. "He had a skip to trace."

"A what?"

"A bail jumper to bring in. He didn't think it was going to take him long." Cade swallowed, sighed. "He doesn't know what he's missing."

"I'll give him the chance to find out." She smiled. "I still have plans for a couple of the rooms upstairs."

It gave Cade his opening. "You know, Grace, I wonder if you're rushing this a little. It's going to take some time to put a house this size back in shape. Bailey and I would like you to stay at our place for a while."

Their place, Grace mused. Already it was their place.

"It's more than livable here, Cade. M.J. and I talked about it," she continued. "She and Jack are going to her apartment. It's time we all got back to our routines."

But M.J. wasn't going to be alone, Cade thought, and thoughtfully sipped his beer. "There's still somebody pulling the strings out there. Somebody who wants the Three Stars."

"I don't have them," Grace reminded him. "I can't get them. There's no reason to bother with me at this point."

"I don't know how much reason has to do with it, Grace. I don't like you being here alone."

"Just like a brother." Delighted with him, she gave his arm a squeeze. "Listen, Cade, I've got a new alarm system, and I'm considering buying a big, mean, ugly dog." She started to mention the pistol she had in her nightstand, and the fact that she knew how to use it, but thought that would only worry him more. "I'll be fine."

"What does Buchanan think?"

"I haven't asked him. He's going to come by later— so I won't really be alone."

Satisfied with that, Cade handed her a grape. "You've got him worried."

Her lips curved as she popped the grape into her mouth. "Do I?"

"I don't know him well—I don't think anyone does. He's…I guess *self-contained* would be the word. Doesn't let a lot show on the surface. But when I walked in yesterday, after you'd gone upstairs, he was just standing there, looking up after you." Now Cade grinned. "There was plenty on the surface then. It was pretty illuminating. Seth Buchanan, human being." Then he winced, tipped back his beer. "Sorry, I didn't mean to—"

"It's all right. I know exactly what you mean. He's

got an almost terrifying self control, and that impenetrable aura of authority."

"It seems to me that you've managed to dent the armor. In my opinion, that's just what he needed. You're just what he needed."

"I hope he thinks so. It turns out he's just what I needed. I'm in love with him." With a half laugh, she shook her head and sipped her wine. "I can't believe I told you that. I rarely tell men my secrets."

"Brothers are different."

She smiled at him. "Yes, they are."

"I hope Seth appreciates just how lucky he is."

"I don't think Seth believes in luck."

She suspected Seth didn't believe in the Three Stars of Mithra, either. And she had discovered that she did. In a very short time, she'd simply opened her mind, stretched her imagination and accepted. They had magic, and they had power. She had been touched by both—as had Bailey and M.J. and the men who were linked to them.

Grace had no doubt that whoever wanted that magic, that power, would stop at nothing to gain them. It wouldn't matter when they were in the museum. He would still crave them, still plot to possess them.

But he could no longer reach the stones through her. That part of her connection, she thought with relief, was over. She was safe in her own home, and would learn to live there again. Starting now.

She dressed carefully in a long white dress of thin watered silk that left her shoulders bare and flirted with her ankles. Beneath the flowing silk she wore only skin, creamed and scented.

She left her hair loose, scooped back at the sides with silver combs, her mother's sapphire drops at her ears, gleaming like twin stars. On impulse, she'd clasped a thick silver bracelet high on her forearm—a touch of pagan.

When she looked into the mirror after dressing, she'd felt an odd jolt—as if she could see herself in the glass, with the faint ghost of someone else merged with her.

But she'd laughed it off, chalked it up to nerves and anticipation, and busied herself completing her preparations.

She filled the rooms she'd redone with candles and flowers, pleased with the welcome they offered. On the table by the window facing her side garden she arranged the china and crystal for her meticulously plotted dinner for two.

The champagne was iced, the music was on low and the lights were romantically dimmed. All she needed was the man.

Seth saw the candles in the windows when he pulled up in the drive. Fatigue layered over frustration and had him, in the dim light of the car, rubbing gritty eyes.

And there were candles in the windows.

He was forced to admit that for the first time in his adult life he didn't have a handle on himself, or on the world around him. He certainly didn't have a handle on the woman who had lit those candles, and who was waiting in that soft, flickering light.

He'd moved on DeVane on pure instinct—and part of that instinct, he knew, was territorial. Nothing could have been more out of character for him. Perhaps that was why he was feeling slightly...out of himself. Out of control. Grace had become a center, a focal point.

Or was it an obsession?

Hadn't he come here because he couldn't keep away? Just as he had dug into DeVane's background because the man roused some primal defense mechanism.

Maybe that was how it started, Seth admitted, but his cop's instincts were still honed. DeVane was dirty. And with a little more time, a little more digging, he would link the man with the deaths surrounding the diamonds.

Without the diplomatic block, Seth thought, he had enough already to bring the man in for questioning. DeVane liked to collect—and he collected the rare, the precious, and frequently those items that held some whiff of magic.

And Gregor DeVane had financed an expedition the year before to search for the legendary Stars. A rival archaeologist had found them first, and the Washington museum had acquired them.

DeVane had lost more than two million dollars on the hunt and the Stars had slipped through his fingers.

And the rival archaeologist had met with a tragic and fatal accident three months after the find, in the jungles of Costa Rica.

Seth didn't believe in coincidence. The man who had kept DeVane from possessing the diamonds was dead. And so, Seth had discovered, was the head of the expedition DeVane had put together.

No, he didn't believe in coincidence.

DeVane had been a resident of D.C. for nearly two years, on and off, without ever meeting Grace. Now, directly after Grace's connection with the Stars, the man was not only at the same social function, but happened to make a play for her?

Life simply wasn't that tidy.

A little more time, Seth promised himself, rubbing his temples to clear the headache. He'd find the solid connection—link DeVane to the Salvinis, to the bail bondsman, to the men who had died in a crashed van, to Carlo Monturri. He needed only one link, and then the rest of the chain would fall into place.

But at the moment, he needed to get out of the stuffy car, go inside and face what was happening to his personal life.

With a short laugh, Seth climbed out of the car. A personal life. Wasn't that part of the problem? He'd never had one, hadn't allowed himself one. Now, a matter of days after he'd met Grace, it was threatening to swallow him.

He needed time there, too, he told himself. Time to step back, gain some distance for a more objective look. He'd allowed things to move too fast, to get out of control. That would have to be fixed. A man who fell in love overnight couldn't trust himself. It was time to reassert some logic.

They were dynamically different—in backgrounds, in life-styles and in goals. Physical attraction was bound to fade, or certainly stabilize. He could already foresee her easing back once the initial excitement peaked. She'd grow restless, certainly annoyed with the demands on his work. He would be neither willing nor able to spin her through the social whirl that was such an intricate part of her life.

She was bound to look toward someone else who would. A beautiful woman, vital, sought-after, flattered at every turn, wouldn't be content to light a candle in the window for many nights.

He'd be doing them both a favor by slowing down, stepping back. As he lifted a hand to the gleaming brass knocker, he refused to hear the mocking voice inside his head that called him a liar—and a coward.

She answered the knock quickly, as if she'd only been waiting for it. She stood in the doorway, soft light filtering through the long flow of white silk. The power of her, pure and pagan, stopped his breath.

Though he kept his arms at his sides, she moved into him, and ripped at his heart with a welcoming kiss.

"It's good to see you." Grace skimmed her fingers along his cheekbones, under his shadowed eyes. "You've had a long one, Lieutenant. Come in and relax."

"I haven't got a lot of time. I've got work." He waited, saw the flicker of disappointment in her eyes. It helped justify what he was determined to do. But then she smiled, took his hand.

"Well, let's not waste what time you've got standing in the foyer. You haven't eaten, have you?"

Why didn't she ask him why he couldn't stay? he wondered, irrationally irritated. Why wasn't she complaining? "No."

"Good. Sit down and have a drink. Can you have a drink, or are you officially on duty?" She walked into the living area as she spoke, then drew the chilling champagne from its silver bucket. "I don't suppose one glass would matter, in any case. And I won't tell." She released the cork with an expert's twist and a muffled, celebratory pop. "I've just put the canapés out, so help yourself."

She gestured toward the silver tray on the coffee

table before moving off with a quiet, slippery rustle of silk to pour two flutes.

"Tell me what you think. I worked poor Cade to death pushing things around in here, but I wanted to get at least the living space in order again quickly."

It looked as if it had been clipped from a glossy magazine on perfect living. Nothing was out of place, everything was gleaming and lovely. Bold colors mixed with whites and blacks, tasteful knickknacks, and artwork that appeared to have been selected with incredible care over a long period of time.

Yet she'd done it in days—or hours. That, Seth supposed, was the power of wealth and breeding.

Yet the room didn't look calculated or cold. It looked generous and welcoming. Soft surfaces, soft edges, with touches that were so Grace everywhere. Antique bottles in jewel tones, a china cat curled up for a nap, a lush, thriving fern in a copper pot.

And flowers, candlelight.

He looked up, noted the unbroken gleam of wood circling the balcony. "I see you've had it repaired."

Something's wrong, was all she could think as she stepped forward and handed him his glass. "Yes, I wanted that done as soon as possible. That, and the new security system. I think you'll approve."

"I'll take a look at it, if you like."

"I'd like it better if you'd relax while you can. Why don't I bring dinner in?"

"You cooked?"

Now she laughed. "I wouldn't do that to you, but I'm an expert at ordering in—and at presentation. Try to unwind. I'll be right back."

As she glided out, he looked down at the tray. A sil-

ver bowl of glossy black caviar, little fancy bites of elegant finger foods. He turned his back on them and,
carrying his glass, walked over to study her portrait.

When she came back, wheeling an antique cart, he
continued to look at her painted face. "He was in love
with you, wasn't he? The artist?"

Grace drew a careful breath at that cool tone. "Yes,
he was. He knew I didn't love him. I often wished I
could have. Charles is one of the kindest, gentlest men
I know."

"Did you sleep with him?"

A chill snaked up her spine, but she kept her hands
steady as she set plates on the candle-and-flower-decked
table. "No. It wouldn't have been fair, and I care about
him too much."

"You'd rather sleep with men you don't care about."

She hadn't seen it coming, Grace realized. How foolish of her not to have seen this coming. "No, but I won't
sleep with men who I could hurt like that. I would have
hurt Charles by being his lover, so I stayed his friend."

"And the wives?" He did turn now, eyes narrowed as
he studied the woman instead of the portrait. "Like the
woman who was married to that earl you were mixed
up with? Didn't you worry about hurting her?"

Grace picked up her wine again, quite deliberately
cocked her head. She had never slept with the earl he'd
mentioned, or with any other married man. But she had
never bothered to argue with public perception. Nor
would she bother to deny it now.

"Why would I? I wasn't married to her."

"And the guy who tried to kill himself after you
broke your engagement?"

She touched the glass to her lips, swallowed frothy

wine that burned like shards of glass in her throat. "Overly dramatic of him, wasn't it? I don't think you're in the mood for Caesar salad and steak Diane, are you, Lieutenant? Rich food doesn't set well during interrogations."

"No one's interrogating you, Grace."

"Oh, yes, you are. But you neglected to read me my rights."

Her frigid anger helped justify his own. It wasn't the men—he knew it wasn't the men he'd very deliberately tossed in her face that scraped at him. It was the fact that they didn't matter to him, that somehow nothing seemed to matter but her.

"It's odd you're so sensitive about answering questions about men, Grace. You hadn't troubled to hide your...track record."

"I expected better from you." She said it softly, so he barely heard, then shook her head, smiled coolly. "Foolish of me. No, I've never troubled to hide anything—unless it mattered. The men didn't matter, for the most part. Do you want me to tell you that you're different? Would you believe me if I did?"

He was afraid he would. Terrified he would. "It isn't necessary. We've moved too fast, Grace. I'm not comfortable with it."

"I see." She thought she did now, perfectly. "You'd like to slow things down." She set her glass aside, knowing her hand would start to shake. "It appears you've taken a couple of those giant steps while I've had my back turned. I really should have played that game as a child, so I'd be more alert for sudden moves."

"This isn't a game."

"No, I suppose it isn't." She had her pride, but she

also had her heart. And she had to know. "How could you have made love with me like that this morning, Seth, and do this tonight? How could you have touched me the way you have—the way no one ever has—and hurt me like this?"

It was because of what had swamped him that morning, he realized. The helplessness of his need. "I'm not trying to hurt you."

"No, that only makes it worse. You're doing both of us a favor, aren't you? Isn't that how you've worked it out? Break things off before they get too messy? Too late." Her voice broke, but she managed to shore it up again. "It's already messy."

"Damn it." He took a step toward her, then stopped dead when her head whipped up, and those hot blue eyes scorched him.

"Don't even think about touching me now, when those thoughts are still in your head. You go your tidy way, Lieutenant, and I'll go mine. I don't believe in slowing down. You either go forward, or you stop."

Furious with herself, she lifted a hand and flicked a tear off her cheek. "Apparently, we've stopped."

Chapter 11

He stood there wondering what in the hell he was doing. Here was the woman he loved, who—by some wild twist of fate—might actually love him. Here was a chance for that life he'd never allowed himself, the family, the home, the woman. He was pushing them all away, with both hands, and couldn't seem to stop.

"Grace...I want to give us both time to consider what we're doing, where this is going."

"No, you don't." She tossed back her hair with one angry jerk of her head. "Do you think because I've only known you a matter of days that I don't understand how your head works? I've been more intimate with you than I've been with anyone in my life. I *know* you." She managed a deep, ragged breath. "What you want is to get that wheel back under your hands, that control button back under your thumb. This whole thing has run away from you, and you just can't let that happen."

"That may be true." Was true, he realized. Was absolutely, mortifyingly true. "But it doesn't change the point. I'm in the middle of an investigation, and I'm not as objective as I need to be, because I'm involved with you. After it's done—"

"After it's done, what?" she demanded. "We pick up where you left off? I don't think so, Lieutenant. What happens when you're in the middle of the next investigation? And the next? Do I strike you as someone who's going to wait around until you have the time, and the room, to continue an on-again, off-again relationship with me?"

"No." His spine stiffened. "I'm a cop, and my work takes priority."

"I don't believe I've ever asked you to change that. In fact, I found your dedication to your work admirable, attractive. Even heroic." Her smile was thin and brief. "But that's irrelevant, and so is this conversation." She turned away, picked up her wine again. "You know the way out."

No, she'd never asked him to change anything. Never questioned his work. What the hell had he done? "This needs to be discussed."

"That's your style, not mine. Do you actually think you can stand here, in my home..." Her voice began to hitch and jerk. "In my home, and break my heart, dump me and expect a civilized conversation? I want you *out*." She slammed her glass down, snapping the fragile stem of the glass, splattering wine. "Right now."

Where had the panic come from? he wondered. His beeper went off and was ignored. "We're not leaving it this way."

"Exactly this way," she corrected. "Do you think

I'm stupid? Do you think I don't see that you walked in here tonight looking to pick a fight so that it would end exactly this way? Do you think I don't know now that no matter how much I gave you, you'd hold back from me, question, analyze, dissect everything? Well, analyze this. I was willing to give more, whatever you wanted to take. Now you can spend the rest of your life wondering just what you lost here tonight."

As his beeper sounded again, she swept by him, wrenched open the front door. "You'll have to answer that call of duty elsewhere, Lieutenant."

He stepped to her, but, though his arms ached, he resisted the need to reach out. "When I'm done with this, I'm coming back."

"You won't be welcome."

He could feel himself step up to a line he'd never crossed. "That isn't going to matter. I'm coming back."

She said nothing at all, simply shut the door in his face and turned the lock with a hard, audible click.

She leaned back against the door, her breath shallow now, and hot, as pain swept through her. It was worse now that the door was closed, now that she had shut him out. And the candles still flickered, the flowers still bloomed.

She saw that every step she'd taken that day, and the day before, all they way back to the moment she'd walked into her own home and seen him coming down the stairs toward her, had been leading to this moment of blind grief and loss.

She'd been powerless to stop it, she thought, to change what she was, what had come before or what would come after. It was only fools who believed they controlled their own destiny as she'd once believed she controlled hers.

And she'd been a fool to indulge in those pathetic fantasies, dreams where they had belonged together, where they'd made a life together, a home and children together. Where she'd believed she was only waiting for him to finally make all those longings that had always, always, been one handspan out of her reach, come true.

The mythical power of the stones, she thought with a half laugh. Love, knowledge and generosity. Their magic had been cruel to her, giving her that tantalizing glimpse of her every desire, then wrenching it away again and leaving her alone.

The knock on the door had her closing her eyes. How dare he come back, she thought. How dare he, after he'd smashed all her dreams, her hopes, her needs. And how dare she still love him in spite of it.

Well, he wouldn't see her cry, she promised herself, and straightened to scrub her hands over her damp cheeks. He wouldn't see her crawl. He wouldn't see her at all, because she wouldn't let him in.

Resolutely she headed for the phone. He wouldn't be pleased when she called 911 and reported an intruder, she mused. But it would make her point. She picked up the receiver just as the sound of shattering glass had her whirling toward her terrace doors.

She had time to see the man burst through them, time to hear her alarm scream in warning. She even had time to struggle as thick arms grabbed her. Then the cloth was over her face, smelling sickeningly of chloroform.

And she had time only to think of Seth before her world spun and went black.

* * *

Seth was barely three miles away when the next call came through. He jerked up his phone, snarled into it. "Buchanan."

"Lieutenant, Detective Marshall again. I just heard an automatic come through on dispatch. Suspected break-in, 2918 East Lark Lane, Potomac."

"What?" For one stunning moment, his mind went blank. "Grace?"

"I recognized the address from the homicide. Her alarm system's been triggered, she didn't answer the check-in call."

"I'm five minutes from there." He was already swinging around in a fast, tire-squealing turn. "Get the two closest black-and-whites on the scene. Now."

"I'm already on it. Lieutenant—"

But Seth had already tossed the phone aside.

It was a new system, Seth told himself, fighting for calm and logic. New systems often had glitches.

She was upset, not answering her phone, ignoring the confusion. It would be just like her. She was even now defiantly pouring herself another glass of champagne, cursing him.

Maybe she'd even set off the alarm herself, just so he'd come streaking back with his stomach encased in ice and his heart paralyzed. It would be just like her.

And that was one more lie, he thought as he careened around a corner. It was nothing like her at all.

The candles were still burning in her windows. He tried to be relieved by that as he stood on the brakes in her driveway and bolted out of his car. Dinner would still be warm, the music would still be playing, and Grace would be there, standing under her portrait, furious with him.

He beat on the door foolishly, wildly, before he snapped himself back. She wouldn't answer. She was too angry to answer. When the first patrol car pulled up, he turned, flashed his badge.

"Check the east side," he ordered. "I'll take the west."

He turned on his heel, started around the side. He caught the glimmer of the blue water in her pool in the moonlight, and the thought slid in and out of his mind that they'd never used it together, never slipped into that cool water naked.

Then he saw the broken glass. His heart simply stopped. His weapon was in his hand and he was through the shattered door, with no thought to procedure. Someone was shouting her name, racing from room to room in blind panic. It couldn't be him, yet he found himself on the stairs, short of breath, ice cold, dizzy with fear and watching a uniformed cop bend to pick up a scrap of cloth.

"Smells like chloroform, Lieutenant." The officer hesitated, took a step toward the man clinging to the banister. "Lieutenant?"

He couldn't speak. His voice was gone, and every sweaty hour of training with it. Seth's dulled gaze shifted, focused on the face, the portrait. Slowly, and with great effort, he widened his vision again, pulled on the mask of control.

"Search the house. Every inch of it." His eyes locked on the second uniform. "Call in for backup. Now. Then make a sweep of the grounds. Move."

Grace came to slowly, with a roll of nausea and a blinding headache. A nightmare, still black at the edges, circled dully, like a vulture patiently waiting to drop.

She squeezed her eyes tighter, rolled her head on the pillow, then cautiously opened them.

Where? The thought was dull, foolish. Not my room, she realized, and struggled to fight off the clinging mists that clouded her brain.

It was satin beneath her cheek. She knew the cool, slippery feel of satin against the skin. White satin, like a bride's dress. Baffled, she skimmed her hand over the thick, luxurious spread of the huge canopied bed.

She could smell jasmine, and roses, and vanilla. All white scents, cool white scents. The walls of the room were ivory and had a sheen like silk. For a moment, she thought she was in a coffin, a huge, elaborate coffin, and her heart beat thick and fast.

She made herself sit up, almost afraid that her head would hit the lid and she would find herself screaming and clawing for freedom as she smothered. But there was nothing, only that fragrant air, and she took a long, unsteady breath of it.

She remembered now—the crash of glass, the big man in black with thick arms. She wanted to panic and forced herself to take another of those jerky breaths. Carefully, hampered by her spinning head, she slid her legs over the edge of the bed until her feet sank into thick, virginal white carpet. She swayed, nearly retched, then forced her feet over that sea of white to the door.

She went slippery with panic when the knob resisted her. Her breath came in ragged gulps as she fought and tugged on the knob of faceted crystal. Then she turned her back, leaned against it and made herself survey what she understood now was her prison.

White on white on white, blinding to the eye. A dainty Queen Anne chair brocaded in white, filmy lace curtains hung like ghosts, heaps of white pillows on a curved white chaise. There were edges of gold that only enhanced the avalanche of white, elegant furniture in pale wood smothered in that snowfall.

She went to the windows first, shuddered when she found them barred, the slices of night beyond them silvered by the moon. She saw nothing familiar—a long roll of lawn, meticulously planted flowers and shrubs, tall, shielding trees.

Wheeling, she saw another door, bolted for it, nearly wept when the knob turned easily. But beyond was a lustrous bath, white-tiled, the frosted-glass windows barred, the angled skylight a soaring ten feet above the floor.

And on the long gleaming counter were jars, bottles, creams, powders. All her own preferences, her scents, her lotions. Her stomach knotted greasily.

Ransom, she told herself. It was a kidnapping, someone who believed her family could be forced to pay for her safe return.

But she knew that was a lie.

The Stars. She leaned weakly against the jamb, pressed her lips together to keep the whimper silent. She'd been taken because of the Three Stars. They would be her ransom.

Her knees trembled as she turned away, ordered herself to calm down, to think clearly. There had to be a way out. There always was.

Her alarm had gone off, she remembered. Seth couldn't have been far away. Would he have gotten the report, come back? It didn't matter. He would have gotten it soon enough. Whatever had happened between them, he would do everything in his power to find her. From duty, if nothing else.

In the meantime, she was on her own. But that didn't mean she was defenseless.

She took two stumbling steps back when the lock on her door clicked, then forced herself to stop, straighten. The door opened, and two men stepped inside. One she recognized quickly enough as her abductor. The other was smaller, wiry, dressed in formal black, with a face as giving as rock.

"Ms. Fontaine," he said in a voice both British and cultured. "If you'd come with me, please."

A butler, she realized, and had to swallow a bubble of hysteria. She knew the type too well, and she assumed an amused and annoyed expression. "Why?"

"He's ready to see you now."

When she made no move to obey, the bigger man stepped in, towering over her, then jerked a thumb toward the doorway.

"Charming," she said dryly. She took a step forward, calculating how quickly she would have to move. The butler inclined his head impassively.

"You're on the third floor," he told her. "Even if you could somehow reach the main level on your own, there are guards. They are under order not to harm you, unless it's unavoidable. If you'll pardon me, I would advise against risking it."

She would risk it, she thought, and a great deal more. But not until she had at least an even chance of success. Without so much as a flick of a glance at the man beside her, she followed the butler out of the room and down a gently lit corridor.

The house was old, she calculated, but beautifully restored. At least three stories, so it was large. A glimpse at her watch told her it had been less than two hours since she was drugged. Time enough to drive some distance, she imagined.

But the view through the bars hadn't been countryside. She'd seen lights—city lights, houses through the trees. A neighborhood, she decided. Exclusive, wealthy, but a neighborhood.

Where there were houses, there were people. And where there were people, there was help.

She was led down a wide, curving staircase of gleaming oak. And saw the guard at the landing, his gun holstered but visible.

Down another hallway. Antiques, paintings, artwork. Her eye was expert enough to recognize the Monet on the wall, the porcelain vase from the Han dynasty on a pedestal, the Nok terra-cotta head from Nigeria.

Her host, she thought, had excellent and eclectic taste. The treasures she saw, small and large, spanned continents and centuries.

A collector, she realized with a chill. Now he had her, and was hoping to trade her for the Three Stars of Mithra.

With what Grace considered absurd formality, under the circumstances, the butler approached tall double doors, opened them, and with seamless expertise bowed slightly from the waist.

"Miss Grace Fontaine."

Seeing no immediate alternative, she stepped through the open doors into an enormous dining room with a frescoed ceiling and a dazzling trio of chandeliers. She scanned the long mahogany table, the Georgian candelabra gaily lit and spaced at precise intervals down its length, and focused on the man who rose and smiled charmingly.

Her worlds overlapped—reality and fear. "Gregor."

"Grace." Elegant in his tux, diamonds winking, he crossed to her, took her numb hand in his. "How delightful to see you." He tucked her arm through his, patted it affectionately. "I don't believe you've dined."

He knew where she was. Seth had no doubt of it, but his first fiery urge to rush to the elegant estate in D.C. and tear it apart single-handedly had to be suppressed.

He could get her killed.

He was certain Ambassador Gregor DeVane had killed before.

The call that interrupted his scene with Grace had been confirmation of yet another woman who had once been linked to the ambassador, a beautiful German scientist who had been found murdered in her home in Berlin, the apparent victim of a bungled burglary.

The dead woman had been an anthropologist who had a keen interest in Mithraism. For six months during the previous year, she had been romantically linked with Gregor DeVane. Then she was dead, and none of her research notes on the Three Stars of Mithra had been recovered.

He knew DeVane was responsible, just as he knew DeVane had Grace. But he couldn't prove it, and he didn't have probable cause to sway any judge to issue a search warrant into the home of a foreign ambassador.

Once more he stood in Grace's living room. Once more he stared up at her portrait and imagined her dead. But this time, he wasn't thinking like a cop.

He turned as Mick Marshall stepped beside him. "We won't find anything here to link him. In twelve hours, the diamonds will be turned over to the museum. He's going to use her to see that doesn't happen. I'm going to stop him."

Mick looked up at the portrait. "What do you need?"

"No. No cops."

"Lieutenant…Seth, if you're right, and he's got her, you're not going to get her out alone. You need to put together a team. You need a hostage negotiator."

"There's no time. We both know that." His eyes weren't flat and cool now, weren't cop's eyes. They were full of storms and passions. "He'll kill her."

His heart was coated with a sheet of ice, but it beat with fiery heat inside the casing. "She's smart. She'll play whatever game she needs to in order to stay alive, but if she makes the wrong move he'll kill her. I don't need a psychiatric profile to see into his head. He's a sociopath with a god complex and an obsession. He wants those diamonds and what he believes they represent. Right now he wants Grace, but if she doesn't serve his purpose, she'll end up like the others. That's not going to happen, Mick."

He reached into his pocket, took out his badge and held it out. This time he wouldn't go by the book, couldn't afford to play by the rules. "You take this for me, hang on to it. I may want it back."

"You're going to need help," Mick insisted. "You're going to need men."

"No cops," Seth repeated, and pushed his badge into Mick's reluctant hand. "Not this time."

"You can't go in solo. It's suicide, professional and literal."

Seth cast one last glance at the portrait. "I won't be alone."

She wouldn't tremble, Grace promised herself. She wouldn't show him how frightened she was. Instead, she brushed her hair from her shoulder with a careless hand.

"Do you always have your dinner companions abducted from their homes and drugged, Ambassador?"

"You must forgive the clumsiness." Considerately he drew out a chair for her. "It was necessary to be quick. I trust you're suffering no ill effects."

"Other than great annoyance, no." She sat, skimmed her gaze over the dish of marinated mushrooms a silent servant placed before her. They reminded her, painfully, of the noise-filled cookout at Cade's. "And a loss of appetite."

"Oh, you must at least sample the food." He sat at the head of the table, picked up his fork. It was gold and heavy and had once slipped between the lips of an emperor. "I've gone to considerable trouble to have your favorites prepared." His smile remained genial, but his eyes went cold. "Eat, Grace. I detest waste."

"Since you've gone to such lengths." She forced down a bite, ordered her hand not to shake, her stomach not to revolt.

"I hope your room is comfortable. I had to have it prepared for you rather quickly. You'll find appropriate clothing in the armoire and bureau. You've only to ask if there's something else you wish."

"I prefer windows without bars, and doors without locks."

"Temporary precautions, I promise you. Once you're at home here…" His hand covered hers, the grip tightening cruelly when she attempted to pull away. "…and I do very much want you to be at home here, such measures won't be necessary."

She didn't wince as the bones in her hand ground together. When she stopped the resistance, his fingers relaxed, stroked once, then slid away.

"And just how long do you intend to keep me here?"

He smiled, picked up her wineglass, held it out to her. "Eternity. You and I, Grace, are destined to share eternity."

Under the table, her aching hand shook and went clammy. "That's quite some time." She started to set her wine down, untouched, then caught the hard glint in his eye and sipped. "I'm flattered, but confused."

"It's pointless to pretend you don't understand. You held the Star in your hand. You survived death, and you came to me. I've seen your face in my dreams."

"Yes." She could feel her blood drain slowly, as if leeched out of her veins. Looking into his eyes she remembered the nightmares—the shadow in the woods. Watching. "I've seen you in mine."

"You'll bring me the Stars, Grace, and the power. I understand why I failed now. Every step was simply another on the path that brought us here. Together we'll possess the Stars. And I will possess you. Don't worry," he said when she flinched. "You'll come to me a willing bride. But my patience has limits. Beauty is my weakness," he continued, and skimmed a fingertip down her bare arm, toyed idly with the thick silver bracelet she wore. "And perfection my greatest delight. You, my dear, have both. Understand, you'll have no choice should my patience run out. My household staff is…well trained."

Fear was a bright, icy flash, but her voice was steady with disgust. "And would turn a deaf ear and blind eye to rape?"

"I don't enjoy that word during dinner." He gave a sulky little shrug and signaled for the next course. "A woman of your appetites will grow hungry soon enough. And one of your intelligence will undoubtedly see the wisdom of an amiable partnership."

"It's not sex you want, Gregor." She couldn't bear to look down at the tender pink salmon on her plate. "It's subjugation. I'm so poor at subjugation."

"You misunderstand me." He forked up fish and ate with enjoyment. "I intend to make you a goddess, and subject to no one. And I will have everything. No mortal man will come between us." He smiled again. "Certainly not Lieutenant Buchanan. The man is becoming a nuisance. He's probing into my affairs, where he has no business probing. I've seen him…"

DeVane's voice trailed off to a whisper, and there was a hint of fear in it. "In the night. In my dreams. He comes back. He always comes back. No matter how often I kill him." Then his eyes cleared, and he sipped wine the color of melted gold. "Now he's stirring up old business and looking for new."

She could feel the alarming beat of her pulse in her throat, at her wrists, in her temples. "He'll be looking for me, very soon now."

"Possibly. I'll deal with him, when and if the time comes. That could have been tonight, had he not left you so abruptly. Oh, I have considered just what will be done about the lieutenant. But I prefer to wait until I have the Stars. It's possible…" Thoughtfully DeVane picked up his napkin, dabbed at his lips. "I may spare him once I have what belongs to me. If you wish it. I can be magnanimous…under the right circumstances."

Her heart was in her throat now, filling it, blocking it. "If I do what you want, you'll leave him alone?"

"It's possible. We'll discuss it. But I'm afraid I developed an immediate dislike for the man. And I am still annoyed with you, dear Grace, for rejecting my own invitation for such an ordinary man."

She didn't hesitate, couldn't afford to, while her mind whirled with fear for Seth. She made her lips curve silkily. "Gregor, surely you forgive me for that. I was so… crushed when you didn't press your case. A woman, after all, enjoys a more determined pursuit."

"I don't pursue. I take."

"Obviously." She pouted. "It was horrid of you to have manhandled me that way, and frightened me half to death. I may not forgive you for it."

"Be careful how deep you play the game." His voice was low with warning and, she thought, with interest. "I'm not green."

"No." She skimmed a hand over his cheek before she rose. "But maturity has so many advantages."

Her legs were watery, but she roamed the cavernous room, her gaze traveling quickly toward windows, exits. Escape. "You have such a beautiful home. So many treasures." She angled her head, hoped the challenge she issued was worth the risk. "I do love…things. But I warn you, Gregor, I won't be any man's pretty toy."

She walked to him slowly, skimming a fingertip down her throat, between her breasts, while the silk she wore whispered around her. "And when I'm backed into a corner…I scratch."

Seductively she laid a hand on the table, leaned toward him. "You want me?" she breathed it, purred it, watching his eyes darken, sliding her fingers toward the knife beside his plate. "To touch me? To have me?" Her fingers closed over the handle, gripped hard.

"Not in a hundred lifetimes," she said as she struck. She was fast, and she was desperate. But he'd shifted to draw her to him, and the knife struck his shoulder instead of his heart. As he cried out in shock and rage, she whirled. Grabbing one of the heavy chairs, she smashed the long window and sent glass raining out. But when she leaped forward, strong arms grabbed her from behind.

She fought viciously, her breath panting out. The fragile silk she wore ripped. Then she froze when the knife she had used was pressed against her throat. She didn't bother to struggle against the arms that held her as DeVane leaned his face close to hers. His eyes were mad with fury.

"I could kill you for that. But it would be too little and too quick. I would have made you my equal. I would have shared that with you. Now I'll just take what I choose from you. Until I tire of you."

"You'll never get the Stars," she said steadily. "And you'll never get Seth."

"I'll have exactly what I choose. And you'll help me."

She started to shake her head, flinched as the blade nicked. "I'll do nothing to help you."

"But you will. If you don't do exactly as I tell you, I will pick up the phone. With one single word from me, Bailey James and M. J. O'Leary will die tonight. It will only take a word."

He saw the wild fear come into her eyes, the helpless terror that hadn't been there for her own life. "I have men waiting for that word. If I give it, there will be a terrible and tragic explosion in the night at Cade Parris's home. Another at a small neighborhood pub, just before closing. And as one last twist, a third explosion will destroy the home, and the single occupant, of a certain Lieutenant Buchanan's residence. Their fate is in your hands, Grace. And the choice is yours."

She wanted to call his bluff, but, staring into his eyes, she understood that he wouldn't hesitate to do as he threatened. No, he longed to do it. Their lives meant nothing to him. And everything to her.

"What do you want me to do?"

Bailey was fighting against panic when the phone rang. She stared at it as if it were a snake that had rattled into life. With a silent prayer, she lifted the receiver. "Hello?"

"Bailey."

"Grace." Her fingers went white-knuckled as she whirled. Seth shook his head, held up a hand in caution. "Are you all right?"

"For the moment. Listen very carefully, Bailey, my life depends on it. Do you understand?"

"No. Yes." Stall, she knew she'd been ordered to stall. "Grace, I'm so frightened for you. What happened? Where are you?"

"I can't go into that now. You have to be calm, Bailey. You have to be strong. You were always the calm one. Like when we took that art history exam in college and I was so intimidated by Professor Greenbalm, and you were so cool. You have to be cool now, Bailey, and you have to follow my instructions."

"I will. I'll try." She looked helplessly at Seth as he signaled her to stretch it out. "Just tell me if you're hurt."

"Not yet. But he will hurt me. He'll kill me, Bailey, if you don't do what he wants. Get him what he wants. I know I'm asking a great deal. He wants the stones.

You have to go get them. You can't take Cade. You can't call…the police."

String it out, Bailey reminded herself. Keep Grace talking. "You don't want me to call Seth?"

"No. He isn't important. He's just another cop. You know he doesn't matter. You're to wait until 1:30 exactly, then you're to leave the house. Go to Salvini, Bailey. You've got to go to Salvini. Leave M.J. out of it, just like we used to. Understand?"

Bailey nodded, kept her eyes on Seth's. "Yes, I understand."

"Once you get to Salvini, put the stones in a briefcase. Wait there. You'll get a call with the next set of instructions. You'll be all right. You know how you used to like to sneak out of the dorm at night and go out driving alone after curfew? Just think of it that way. Exactly that way, Bailey, and you'll be fine. If you don't, he'll take everything away from me. Do you understand?"

"Yes. Grace—"

"I love you," she managed before the phone went dead.

"Nothing," Cade said tightly as he stared down at the tracing equipment. "He's got it jammed. The signal's all over the board. It wouldn't home in."

"She wants me to go to Salvini," Bailey said quietly.

"You're not going anywhere," Cade said, interrupting her, but Bailey laid a hand on his arm, looked toward M.J.

"No, she meant that part. You understood?"

"Yeah." M.J. pressed her fingers to her eyes, tried to think past the terror. "She was pumping in as much as she could. Bailey and Grace never left me out of anything, so she wanted me along. She wants us out of here, but she was stringing him about the stones. Bailey never jumped curfew."

"She was giving you signals," Jack said. "Trying to punch in what she could manage."

"She knew we'd understand. He must have told her something would happen to us if she didn't cooperate." Bailey reached out for M.J.'s hand. "She wanted us to contact Seth. That's why she said you didn't matter—because we know you do."

Seth dragged a hand through his hair—a rare wasted motion. He had no choice but to trust their instincts. No choice but to trust Grace's sense of survival. "All right. She wants me to know what's happening, and wants you out of the house."

"Yes. She wants us out of the house, thinks we'll be safer at Salvini."

"You'll be safer at the precinct," Seth told her. "And that's where both of you are going."

"No." Bailey's voice remained calm. "She wants us at Salvini. She made a point of it."

Seth studied her, and gauged his options. He could have them taken into protective custody. That was the logical step. Or he could let the game play out. That was a risk. But it was the risk that fit.

"Salvini, then. But Detective Marshall will arrange for guards. You'll stay put until you hear differently."

M.J. bristled. "You expect us to just sit around and wait while Grace is in trouble?"

"That's exactly what you're going to do," Seth said coolly. "She's risking her life to see that you're safe. I'm not going to disappoint her."

"He's right, M.J." Jack lifted a brow as she snarled

at him. "Go ahead and fume. But you're outnumbered here. You and Bailey follow instructions."

Seth noted with some surprise that M.J. closed her mouth, gave one brisk nod in assent. "What was the business about the art history exam, Bailey?"

Bailey sucked in air. "Professor Greenbalm's first name was Gregory."

"Gregory." *Gregor.* "Close enough." Seth looked at the two men he needed. "We don't have a lot of time."

Chapter 12

Grace doubted very much that she would live through the night. There were so many things she hadn't done. She had never shown Bailey and M.J. Paris, as they had always planned. She would never see the willow she'd planted on her country hillside grow tall and bend gracefully over her tiny pond. She had never had a child.

The unfairness clawed at her, along with the fear. She was only twenty-six years old, and she was going to die.

She'd seen her sentence in DeVane's eyes. And she knew he intended to kill those she loved, as well. He wouldn't be satisfied with anything less than erasing all the lives that had touched what his obsessed mind considered his.

All she could hang on to now was the hope that Bailey had understood her.

"I'm going to show you what you could have had." His arm bandaged, a fresh tuxedo covering the damage,

DeVane led her through a concealed panel, and down a well-lit set of stone stairs that were polished like ebony. He'd taken a painkiller. His eyes were glassy with it, and vicious.

They were the eyes that had stared out of the woods in her nightmares. And as he walked down the curve of those glossy black stairs, she felt the tug of some deep memory.

By torchlight then, she thought hazily. Down and down, with the torches flickering and the Stars glittering in their home of gold, on a white stone. And death waiting.

The harsh breathing of the man beside her. DeVane's? Someone else's? It was a hot, secret sound that chilled the skin. A room, she thought, struggling to grip the slippery chain of memories. A secret room of white and gold. And she had been locked in it for eternity.

She stopped at the last curve, not so much in fear as in shock. Not here, she thought frantically, but somewhere else. Not her, but part of her. Not him, but someone like him.

DeVane's fingers dug into her arm, but she barely felt the pain. Seth—the man with Seth's eyes, dressed as a warrior, coated with dust and the dents of battle. He'd come for her, and for the Stars.

And died for it.

"No." The stairway spun, and she gripped the cool wall for balance. "Not again. Not this time."

"There's little choice." DeVane jerked her forward, pulled her down the remaining steps. He stopped at a thick door, gestured impatiently for his guard to step back. Holding Grace's arm in a bruising grip, he drew out a heavy key, fit it in an old lock that for reasons Grace couldn't fathom made her think of Alice's rabbit hole.

"I want you to see what could have been yours. What I would have shared with you."

At his rough shove, she stumbled inside and stood blinking in shock.

No, not the rabbit hole, she realized, her dazzled eyes wide and stunned. Ali Baba's cave. Gold gleamed in mountains, jewels winked in rivers. Paintings she recognized as works of the masters crowded together on the walls. Statues and sculpture, some as small as the Fabergé eggs perched on gold stands, others soaring to the ceiling, were jammed inside.

Furs and sweeps of silk, ropes of pearls, carvings and crowns, were jammed into every available space. Mozart played brilliantly on hidden speakers.

It was, she realized, not a fairy-tale cave at all. It was merely a spoiled boy's elaborate and greedy clubhouse. Here he could hide his possessions from the world, keep them all to himself and chortle over them, she imagined.

And how many of these toys had he stolen? she wondered. How many had he killed for?

She wouldn't die here, she promised herself. And neither would Seth. If this was indeed history overlapping, she wouldn't allow it to repeat itself. She would fight with whatever weapons she had.

"You have quite a collection, Gregor, but your presentation could use some work." The first weapon was mild disdain, laced with amusement. "Even the precious loses impact when crammed together in such a disorganized manner."

"It's mine. All of it. A lifetime's work. Here." Like that spoiled boy, he snatched up a goblet of gold, thrust it out to her for admiration. "Queen Guinevere sipped from this before she cuckolded Arthur. He should have cut out her heart for that."

Grace turned the cup in her hand and felt nothing. It was empty not only of wine, she mused, but of magic.

"And here." He grabbed a pair of ornate diamond earrings, thrust them into Grace's face. "Another queen—Marie Antoinette—wore these while her country plotted her death. You might have worn them."

"While you plotted mine." With deliberate scorn, she dismissed the offering and turned away. "No, thank you."

"I have an arrow the goddess Diana hunted with. The girdle worn by Juno."

Her heart thrummed like a harp, but she only chuckled. "Do you really believe that?"

"They're mine." Furious with her reaction, he pushed his way through his collection, laid a hand over the cold marble slab he'd had built. "I'll have the Stars soon. They will be the apex of my collection. I'll set them here, with my own hands. And I'll have everything."

"They won't help you. They won't change you." She didn't know where the words came from, or the knowledge behind them, but she saw his eyes flicker in surprise. "Your fate's already sealed. They'll never be yours. It's not meant, not this time. They're for the light, and for the good. You'll never see them here in the dark."

His stomach jittered. There was power in her words, in her eyes, when she should have been cowed and frightened. It unnerved him. "By sunrise I'll have them here. I'll show them to you." His breath was short and shallow as he approached her. "And I'll have you. I'll keep you as long as I wish. Do with you what I wish."

The hand against her cheek was cold, made her think wildly of a snake, but she didn't cringe away. "You'll never have the Stars, and you'll never have me. Even if you hold us, you'll never have us. That was true before, but it's only more true now. And that will eat away at you, day after day, until there's nothing left of you but madness."

He struck her, hard enough to knock her back against the wall, to have pain spinning in her head. "Your friends will die tonight." He smiled at her, as if he were discussing a small mutual interest. "You've already sent them to oblivion. I'm going to let you live a long time knowing that."

He took her by the arm and, pulling open the door, dragged her from the room.

"He'll have surveillance cameras," Seth said as they prepared to scale the wall at the rear of DeVane's D.C. estate. "He's bound to have guards patrolling the grounds."

"So we'll be careful." Jack checked the point of his knife, stuck it in his boot, then examined the pistol he'd tucked in his belt. "And we'll be quiet."

"We stick together until we reach the house." Cade went over the plan in his head. "I find security, disarm it."

"Failing that, set the whole damn business off. We could get lucky in the confusion. It'll bring the cops. If things don't go well, you could be dealing with a lot more than a bust for a B-and-E."

Jack issued a pithy one-word opinion on that. "Let's go get her out." He shot Seth one quick grin as he boosted himself up. "Man, I hope he doesn't have dogs. I really hate when they have dogs."

They landed on the soft grass on the other side. It was possible their presence was detected from that moment. It was a risk they were willing to take. Like shadows, they moved through the starstruck night, slipping through the heavy dark amid the sheltering trees.

Before, on his quest for the Stars and the woman, he'd come alone, and perhaps that arrogance had been his defeat. Baffled by the sudden thought, the quick spurt of what some might have called vision, Seth pushed the feeling aside.

He could see the house through the trees, the glimmer of lights in windows. Which room was she in? How badly was she frightened? Was she hurt? Had he touched her?

Baring his teeth, he bit off the thoughts. He had to focus only on getting inside, finding her. For the first time in years, he felt the weight of his weapon at his side. Knew he intended to use it.

He gave no thought to rules, to his career, to the life he'd built step by deliberate step.

He saw the guard pass by, only a yard beyond the verge of the grove. When Jack tapped his shoulder and signaled, Seth met his eyes, nodded.

Seconds later, Jack sprang at the man from behind, and with a quick twist, rammed his head into the trunk of an oak and then dragged the unconscious body into the shadows.

"One down," he breathed and tucked his newly acquired weapon away.

"They'll have regular check-in," Cade murmured. "We can't know how soon they'll miss his contact."

"Then let's move." Seth signaled Jack to the north, Cade to the south. Staying low, they rushed those gleaming lights.

The guard who escorted Grace back to her room was silent. At least two hundred and fifty pounds of muscle, she calculated. But she'd seen his eyes flicker down over her bodice, scan the ripped silk that exposed flesh at her side.

She knew how to use her looks as a weapon. Deliberately she tipped her face up to his, let her eyes fill helplessly. "I'm so frightened. So alone." She risked touching a hand to his arm. "You won't hurt me, will you? Please don't hurt me. I'll do anything you want."

He said nothing, but his eyes were keen on her face when she moistened her lips with the tip of her tongue, keeping the movement slow and provocative. "Anything," she repeated, her voice husky, intimate. "You're so strong, so…in charge." Did he even speak English? she wondered. What did it matter? The communication was clear enough.

At the door to her prison, she turned, flashed a smoldering look, sighed deeply. "Don't leave me alone," she murmured. "I'm so afraid of being alone. I need… someone." Taking a chance, she lifted a fingertip, rubbed it over his lips. "He doesn't have to know," she whispered. "No one has to know. It's our secret."

Though it revolted her, she took his hand, placed it on her breast. The flex of his fingers chilled her skin, but she made herself smile invitingly as he lowered his head and crushed her mouth.

Don't think of it, don't think, she warned herself as his hands roamed her. It's not you. He's not touching you.

"Inside." She hoped he interpreted her quick shudder as desire. "Come inside with me. We'll be alone."

He opened the door, his eyes still hungry on her face, on her body. She would either win here, she thought, or lose everything. She let out a teasing laugh as he grabbed for her the moment the door was locked behind him.

"Oh, there's no hurry now, handsome." She tossed her hair back, glided out of his reach. "No need to rush such a lovely friendship. I want to freshen up for you."

Still he said nothing, but his eyes were narrowing with impatience, suspicion. Still smiling, she reached for the heavy cut-crystal atomizer on the bureau. A woman's weapon, she thought coldly as she gently spritzed her skin, the air. "I prefer using all of my senses." Her fingers tightened convulsively on the bottle as she swayed toward him.

She jerked the bottle up and sprayed perfume directly into his leering eyes. He hissed in shock, grabbed instinctively for his stinging eyes. Putting all her strength behind it, she smashed the crystal into his face, and her knee into his groin.

He staggered, but didn't go down. There was blood on his face, and beneath it, his skin had gone a pasty shade of white. He was fumbling for his gun and, frantic, she kicked out, aiming low again. This time he went to his knees, but his hands were still reaching for the gun snapped to his side.

Sobbing now, she heaved up a footstool, upholstered in white, tasseled in gold. She rammed it into his already bleeding face, then, lifting it high, crashed it onto his head. Desperately she scrabbled to unstrap his gun, her clammy hands slipping off leather and steel. When she held it in two shaking hands, prepared to do whatever was necessary, she saw that he was unconscious.

Her breath tore out of her lungs in a wild laugh. "I guess I'm just not that kind of girl." Too frightened for caution, she yanked the keys free of his clip, stabbed one after the other at the lock until it gave. And raced like a deer fleeing wolves, down the corridor, through the golden light.

A shadow moved at the head of the stairs, and with a low, keening moan, she lifted the gun.

"That's the second time you've pointed a weapon in my direction."

Her vision grayed at the sound of Seth's voice. Clamping down hard on her lip, she cleared it as he stepped out of the shadows and into the light. "You. You came."

It wasn't armor he wore, she thought dizzily. But black—shirt, slacks, shoes. It wasn't a sword he carried, but a gun.

It wasn't a memory. It was real.

Her dress was torn, bloody. Her face was bruised, her eyes were glassy with shock. He'd killed two men to get this far. And seeing her this way, he thought it hadn't been enough. Not nearly enough.

"It's all right now." He resisted the urge to rush to her, grab her close. She looked as though she might shatter at a touch. "We're going to get you out. No one's going to hurt you."

"He's going to kill them." She forced air in and out of her lungs. "He's going to kill them no matter what I do. He's insane. They're not safe from him. We're none of us safe from him. He killed you before," she ended on a whisper. "He'll try again."

He took her arm to steady her, gently slipped the gun from her hand. "Where is he, Grace?"

"There's a room, through a panel in the library, down the stairs. Just like before…lifetimes ago. Do you remember?" Spinning between images, she pressed a hand to her head. "He's there with his toys, all the glittering toys. I stabbed him with a dinner knife."

"Good girl." How much of the blood was hers? He

could detect no wound other than the bruises on her face
and arms. "Come on now, come with me."

He led her down the stairs. There was the guard
she'd seen before. But he wasn't standing now. Averting
her eyes, she stepped around him, gestured. She was
steadier now. The past didn't always run in a loop, she
knew. Sometimes it changed. People made it change.

"It's back there, the third door down on the left." She
cringed when she caught a movement. But it was Jack,
melting out of a doorway.

"It's clear," he said to Seth.

"Take her out." His eyes said everything as he nudged
her into Jack's arms. *Take care of her. I'm trusting you.*

Jack hitched her against his side to keep his weapon
hand free. "You're okay, honey."

"No." She shook her head. "He's going to kill them.
He has explosives, something, at the house, at the pub.
You have to stop him. The panel. I'll show you."

She wrenched away from Jack, staggered like a
drunk toward the library. "Here." She turned a rosette
in the carving of the chair rail. "I watched him." The
panel slid smoothly open.

"Jack, get her out. Call in a 911. I'll deal with him."

She was floating, just under the surface of thick,
warm water. "He'll have to kill him," she said faintly
as Seth disappeared into the opening. "This time he
can't fail."

"He knows what he has to do."

"Yes, he always does." And the room spun once,
wildly. "Jack, I'm sorry," she managed before she spun
with it.

He hadn't locked the door, Seth noted. Arrogant
bastard, so sure no one would trespass on his sacred

ground. With his weapon lifted, Seth eased the heavy door open, blinked once at the bright gleam of gold.

He stepped inside, focused on the man sitting in a thronelike chair in the center of all the glory. "It's done, DeVane."

DeVane wasn't surprised. He'd known the man would come. "You risk a great deal." His smile was cold as a snake's, his eyes mad as a hatter's. "You did before. You remember, don't you? Dreamed of it, didn't you? You came to steal from me before, to take the Stars and the woman. You had a sword then, heavy and unjeweled."

Something vague and quick passed through Seth's mind. A stone castle, a stormy sky, a room of great wealth. A woman beloved. On an altar, a triangle wrenched from the hands of the god, adorned with diamonds as blue as stars.

"I killed you." DeVane laughed softly. "Left your body for the crows."

"That was then." Seth stepped forward. "This is now."

DeVane's smile spread. "I am beyond you." He lifted his hand, and the gun he held in it.

Two shots were fired, so close together they sounded as one. The room shook, echoed, settled, and went back to gleaming. Slowly Seth stepped closer, looked down at the man who lay facedown on a hill of gold.

"Now you are," Seth murmured. "You're beyond me now."

She heard the shots. For one unspeakable moment everything inside her stopped. Heart, mind, breath, blood. Then it started again, a tidal wave of feeling that had her springing off the bench where Jack had put her, the air heaving in and out of her lungs.

And she knew, because she felt, because her heart could beat, that it hadn't been Seth who'd met the bullet. If he had died, she would have known. Some piece of her heart would have broken off from the whole and shattered.

Still, she waited, her eyes on the house, because she had to see.

The stars wheeled overhead, the moon shot light through the trees. Somewhere in the distance, a night bird began to call out, with hope and joy.

Then he walked out of the house. Whole. Tears clogged her throat and were swallowed. They stung her eyes and were willed away. She had to see him clearly, the man she had accepted that she loved, and couldn't have.

He walked to her, his eyes dark and cool, his gait steady.

He'd already regained control, she realized. Already tucked whatever he'd had to do away in some compartment where it wouldn't interfere with what had to be done next.

She wrapped her arms around herself, hands clamped tight on her forearms. She'd never know that one gesture, that turning into herself and not him, was what stopped him from reaching for her.

So he stood, with an armspan of distance between them and looked at the woman he accepted that he loved, and had pushed away.

She was pale, and even now he could see the quick trembles that ripped through her. But he wouldn't have said she was fragile. Even now, with death shimmering between them, she wasn't fragile.

Her voice was strong and steady. "It's over?"

"Yeah, it's over."

"He was going to kill them."

"That's over, too." His need to touch her, to hold on, was overwhelming. He felt that his knees were about to give way. But she turned, shifted her body away, and looked out into the dark.

"I need to see them. Bailey and M.J."

"I know."

"You need my statement."

God. His control wavered enough for him to press his fingers against burning eyes. "It can wait."

"Why? I want it over. I need to put it behind me." She steadied herself again, then turned slowly. And when she faced him, his hands were at his sides and his eyes clear. "I need to put it all behind me."

Her meaning was clear enough, Seth thought. He was part of that all.

"Grace, you're hurt and you're in shock. An ambulance is on the way."

"I don't need an ambulance."

"Don't tell me what the hell you need." Fury swarmed through him, buzzed in his head like a nest of mad hornets. "I said the damn statement can wait. You're shaking. For God's sake, sit down."

When he reached out to take her arm, she jerked back, her chin snapping up, her shoulders hunching. "Don't touch me. Just…don't." If he touched her, she might break. If she broke she would weep. And weeping, she would beg.

The words were a knife in the gut, the deep and desperate blue of her eyes a blow to the face. Because he felt his fingers tremble, he stuffed them into his pockets, took a step back. "All right. Sit down. Please."

Had he thought she wasn't fragile? She looked as if

she would shatter into pieces with one hard thought. She was sheet pale, her eyes enormous. Blood and bruises marked her face.

And there was nothing he could do. Nothing she would let him do.

He heard the distant wail of sirens, and footsteps from behind him. Cade, his face grim, walked to Grace, tucked a blanket he'd brought from the house over her shoulders.

Seth watched as she turned into him, how her body seemed to go fluid and flow into the arms Cade offered her. He heard the fractured sob even as she muffled it against Cade's shoulder.

"Get her out of here." His fingers burned to reach out, stroke her hair, to take something away with him. "Get her the hell out of here."

He walked back into the house to do what needed to be done.

The birds sang their morning song as Grace stepped out into her garden. The woods were quiet and green. And safe. She'd needed to come here, to her country escape. To come alone. To be alone.

Bailey and M.J. had understood. In a few days, she thought, she would go into town, call, see if they'd like to come up, bring Jack and Cade. She would need to see them soon. But she couldn't bear to go back yet. Not yet.

She could still hear the shots, the quick jolt of them shuddering through her as Jack had taken her outside. She'd known it was DeVane and not Seth who had met the bullet. She'd simply known.

She hadn't seen Seth again that night. It had been easy to avoid him in the confusion that followed. She'd answered all the questions the local police had asked, made statements to the government officials. She'd stood up to it, then quietly demanded that Cade or Jack take her to Salvini, take her to Bailey and M.J.

And the Three Stars.

Stepping down onto her blooming terraces, she brought it back into her head, and her heart. The three of them standing in the near dark of a near-empty room, she with her torn and bloody dress.

Each of them had taken a point of the triangle, had felt the sing of power, seen the flicker of impossible light. And had known it was done.

"It's as if we've done this before," Bailey had murmured. "But it wasn't enough then. It was lost, and so were we."

"It's enough now." M.J. had looked up, met each of their eyes in turn. "Like a cycle, complete. A chain, with the links forged. It's weird, but it's right."

"A museum instead of a temple this time." Regret and relief had mixed within Grace as they set the Stars down again. "A promise kept, and, I suppose, destinies fulfilled."

She'd turned to both of them, embraced them. Another triangle. "I've always loved you both, needed you both. Can we go somewhere? The three of us." The tears had come then, flooding. "I need to talk."

She'd told them everything, poured out heart and soul, hurt and terror, until she was empty. And she supposed, because it was them, she'd healed a little.

Now she would heal on her own.

She could do it here, Grace knew, and, closing her eyes, she just breathed. Then, because it always soothed, she set down her gardening basket, and began to tend her blooms.

She heard the car coming, the rumble of wheels on

gravel, and her brow creased in mild irritation. Her neighbors were few and far between and rarely intruded. She wanted no company but her plants, and she stood, her flowers flowing at her feet, determined to politely and firmly send the visitor away again.

Her heart kicked once, hard, when she saw that the car was Seth's. She watched in silence as it stopped in the middle of her lane and he got out and started toward her.

She looked like something out of a misty legend herself, he thought. Her hair blowing in the breeze, the long, loose skirt of her dress fluttering, and flowers in a sea around her. His nerves jangled.

And his stomach clutched when he saw the bruise marring her cheek.

"You're a long way from home, Seth." She spoke without expression as he stopped two steps beneath her.

"You're a hard woman to find, Grace."

"That's the way I prefer it. I don't care for company here."

"Obviously." Both to give himself time to settle and because he was curious, he scanned the land, the house perched on the hill, the deep secrets of the woods. "It's a beautiful spot."

"Yes."

"Remote." His gaze shifted back to hers so quickly, so intensely, he nearly made her jolt. "Peaceful. You've earned some peace."

"That's why I'm here." She lifted a brow. "And why are you here?"

"I needed to talk to you. Grace—"

"I intended to see you when I came back," she said quickly. "We didn't talk much that night. I suppose

I was more shaken up than I realized. I never even thanked you."

It was worse, he realized, that cool, polite voice was worse than a shouted curse. "You don't have anything to thank me for."

"You saved my life and, I believe, the lives of the people I love. I know you broke rules, even the law, to find me, to get me away from him. I'm grateful."

The palms of his hands went clammy. She was making him see it again, feel it again. All that rage and terror. "I'd have done anything to get you away from him."

"Yes, I think I know that." She had to look away. It hurt too much to look into his eyes. She'd promised herself, sworn to herself she wouldn't be hurt again. "And I wonder if any of us had a choice in what happened over that short, intense period of time. Or," she added with a ghost of a smile, "if you choose to believe what happened, over centuries. I hope you haven't—that your career won't suffer because of what you did for me."

His eyes went dark, flat. "The job's secure, Grace."

"I'm glad." He had to leave, she thought. He had to leave now, before she crumbled. "I still intend to write a letter to your superiors. And you might know I have an uncle in the Senate. I wouldn't be surprised, when the smoke clears, if you got a promotion out of it."

His throat was raw. He couldn't clear it. "Look at me, damn it." When her gaze shot back to his face, he curled his hands into fists to keep from touching her. "Do you think that matters?"

"Yes, I do. It matters, Seth, certainly to me. But for now, I'm taking a few days, so if you'll excuse me, I want to get to my gardening before the heat of the day."

"Do you think this ends it?"

She leaned over, took up her clippers and snipped off wilted blooms. They faded all too quickly, she thought. And that left an ache in the heart. "I think you already ended it."

"Don't turn away from me." He took her arm, hauled her toward him, as panic and fury spiraled through him. "You can't just turn away. I can't—" He broke off, his hand lifting to lie on the bruise on her cheek. "Oh, God, Grace. He hurt you."

"It's nothing." She stepped back quickly, nearly flinching, and his hand fell heavily to his side. "Bruises fade. And he's gone. You saw to that. He's gone, and it's over. The Three Stars are where they belong, and everything's back in its place. Everything's as it was meant to be."

"Is it?" He didn't step to her, couldn't bear to see her shrink back from him again. "I hurt you, and you won't forgive me for it."

"Not entirely," she agreed, fighting to keep it light. "But saving my life goes a long way to—"

"Stop it," he said in a voice both ragged and quiet. "Just stop it." Undone, he whirled away, pacing, nearly trampling her bedding plants. He hadn't known he could suffer like this—the ice in the belly, the heat in the brain.

He spoke, looking out into her woods, into shadows and cool green shade. "Do you know what it did to me, knowing he had you? Knowing it. Hearing your voice on the phone, the fear in it?"

"I don't want to think about it. I don't want to think about any of that."

"I can't do anything but think of it. And see you— every time I close my eyes, I see you the way you stood there in that hallway, blood on your dress, marks on your skin. Not knowing—not knowing what he'd done to you. And remembering—half remembering some other time when I couldn't stop him."

"It's over," she said again, because her legs were turning to water. "Leave it alone."

"You might have gotten away without me," he continued. "You took out a guard twice your size. You might have pulled it off without any help from me. You might not have needed me at all. And I realized that was part of my problem all along. Believing, being certain, I needed you so much more than you could possibly need me. Being afraid of that. Stupid to be afraid of that," he said as he came up the steps again. "Once you understand real fear, the fear of knowing you could lose the most important thing in your life in one single heartbeat, nothing else can touch you."

He gathered her to him, too desperate to heed her resistance. And, with a shuddering gulp of air, buried his face in her hair. "Don't push me away, don't send me away."

"This isn't any good." It hurt to be held by him, yet she wished she could go on being held just like this, with the sun warm on her skin and his face pressed into her hair.

"I need you. I need you," he repeated, and turned his urgent mouth to hers.

The hammer blow of emotion struck and she buckled. It swirled from one of them to the other in an unbridled storm, left her heart shaken and weak. She closed her eyes, slid her arms around him. Need would be enough, she promised herself. She would make it enough for both of them. There was too much inside her that she ached to give for her to turn him away.

"I won't send you away." Her hands stroked over his back, soothed the tension. "I'm glad you're here. I want you here." She drew back, brought his hand to her cheek. "Come inside, Seth. Come to bed."

His fingers tightened on hers. Then gently lifted her head up. It made him ache to realize she believed there was only that he wanted from her. That he'd let her think it.

"Grace, I didn't come here to take you to bed. I didn't come here to start where we left off."

Why had he been so resistant to seeing what was in her eyes? he wondered. Why had he refused to believe what was so blatantly real, so generously offered to him.

"I came here to beg. The third Star is generosity," he said, almost to himself. "You didn't make me beg. I didn't come here for sex, Grace. Or for gratitude."

Confused, she shook her head. "What do you want, Seth? Why did you come?"

He wasn't sure he'd fully realized why until just now. "To hear you tell me what you want. What you need."

"Peace." She gestured. "I have that here. Friendship. I have that, too."

"And that's it? That's enough?"

"It's been enough all my life."

He caught her face in his hands before she could step away. "If you could have more? What do you want, Grace?"

"Wanting what you can't have only makes you unhappy."

"Tell me." He kept his eyes focussed on hers. "Straight out, for once. Just say what you want."

"Family. Children. I want children and a man who loves me—who wants to make that family with me." Her lips curved slowly, but the smile didn't reach her eyes. "Surprised I'd want to spoil my figure? Spend a few years of my life changing diapers?"

"No." He slid his hands down to her shoulders, firming his grip. She was poised to move, he noted. To run. "No, I'm not surprised."

"Really? Well." She moved her shoulders as if to shrug off the weight of his touch. "If you're going to stay, let's go inside. I'm thirsty."

"Grace, I love you." He watched her smile slide away from her face, felt her body go absolutely still.

"What? What did you say to me?"

"I love you." Saying it, he realized, was power. True power. "I fell in love with you before I'd seen you. Fell in love with an image, a memory, a wish. I can't be sure which it is, or if it was all of them. I don't know if it was fate, or choice, or luck. But it was so fast, so hard, so deep, I wouldn't let myself believe, and I wouldn't let myself trust. And I turned you away because you let yourself do both. I came here to tell you that." His hands slid down her arms and clasped hers.

"Grace, I'm asking you to believe in us again, to trust in us again. And to marry me."

"You—" She had to take a step back, had to press a hand to her heart. "You want to marry me."

"I'm asking you to come back with me today. I know it's old-fashioned, but I want you to meet my family."

The pressure in her chest all but burst her heart. "You want me to meet your family."

"I want them to meet the woman I love, the woman I want to have a life with. The life I've been waiting to start—waiting for her to start." He brought her hand to his cheek, held it there while his eyes looked deep into hers. "The woman I want to make children with."

"Oh." The weight on her chest released in a flood, poured out of her...until her heart was in her swimming eyes.

"Don't cry." It seemed he would beg after all. "Grace, please, don't. Don't tell me I left it too late." Awkwardly he brushed at her tears with his thumbs. "Don't tell me I ruined it."

"I love you so much." She closed her fingers around his wrists, watched the emotion leap into his eyes. "I've been so unhappy waiting for you. I was so sure I'd missed you. Again. Somehow."

"Not this time." He kept his hands on her face, kissed her gently. "Not ever again."

"No, not ever again," she murmured against his lips.

"Say yes," he asked her. "I want to hear you say yes."

"Yes. To everything."

She held him close in the flower-scented morning where the stars slept behind the sky. And felt the last link of an endless chain fall into place.

"Seth."

He kept his eyes shut, his cheek on her hair. And his smile bloomed slow and easy. "Grace."

"We're where we're supposed to be. Can you feel it?" She drew a deep breath. "All of us are where we belong now."

She lifted her face, found his mouth waiting. "And now," he said quietly, "it begins."

* * * * *

THE LAW IS A LADY

To all the experts at R&R Lighting Company

Chapter 1

Merle T. Johnson sat on the ripped vinyl seat of a stool in Annie's Cafe, five miles north of Friendly. He lingered over a lukewarm root beer, half listening to the scratchy country number piping out from Annie's portable radio. *"A woman was born to be hurt"* was the lament of Nashville's latest hopeful. Merle didn't know enough about women to disagree.

He was on his way back to Friendly after checking out a complaint on one of the neighboring ranches. Sheep-stealing, he thought as he chugged down more root beer. Might've been exciting if there'd been anything to it. Potts was getting too old to know how many sheep he had in the first place. Sheriff knew there was nothing to it, Merle thought glumly. Sitting in the dingy little cafe with the smell of fried hamburgers and onions clinging to the air, Merle bemoaned the injustice of it.

There was nothing more exciting in Friendly, New

Mexico, than hauling in old Silas when he got drunk and disorderly on Saturday nights. Merle T. Johnson had been born too late. If it had been the 1880s instead of the 1980s, he'd have had a chance to face desperados, ride in a posse, face off a gunslinger—the things deputies were supposed to do. And here he was, he told himself fatalistically, nearly twenty-four years old, and the biggest arrest he had made was pulling in the Kramer twins for busting up the local pool hall.

Merle scratched his upper lip where he was trying, without much success, to grow a respectable mustache. The best part of his life was behind him, he decided, and he'd never be more than a deputy in a forgotten little town, chasing imaginary sheep thieves.

If just *once* somebody'd rob the bank. He dreamed over this a minute, picturing himself in a high-speed chase and shoot-out. That would be something, yessiree. He'd have his picture in the paper, maybe a flesh wound in the shoulder. The idea became more appealing. He could wear a sling for a few days. Now, if the sheriff would only let him carry a gun...

"Merle T., you gonna pay for that drink or sit there dreaming all day?"

Merle snapped back to reality and got hastily to his feet. Annie stood watching him with her hands on her ample hips. She had small, dark eyes, florid skin and an amazing thatch of strawberry-colored hair. Merle was never at his best with women.

"Gotta get back," he muttered, fumbling for his wallet. "Sheriff needs my report."

Annie gave a quick snort and held out her hand, damp palm up. After she snatched the crumpled bill, Merle headed out without asking for his change.

The sun was blinding and brilliant. Merle automatically narrowed his eyes against it. It bounced off the road surface in waves that shimmered almost like liquid. But the day was hot and dusty. On both sides of the ribbon of road stretched nothing but rock and sand and a few tough patches of grass. There was no cloud to break the strong, hard blue of the sky or filter the streaming white light of the sun. He pulled the rim of his hat down over his brow as he headed for his car, wishing he'd had the nerve to ask Annie for his change. His shirt was damp and sticky before he reached for the door handle.

Merle saw the sun radiate off the windshield and chrome of an oncoming car. It was still a mile away, he judged idly as he watched it tool up the long, straight road. He continued to watch its progress with absent-minded interest, digging in his pocket for his keys. As it drew closer his hand remained in his pocket. His eyes grew wide.

That's some car! he thought in stunned admiration.

One of the fancy foreign jobs, all red and flashy. It whizzed by without pausing, and Merle's head whipped around to stare after it. *Oo-wee!* he thought with a grin. *Some* car. Must have been doing seventy easy. Probably has one of those fancy dashboards with— Seventy!

Springing into his car, Merle managed to get the keys out of his pocket and into the ignition. He flipped on his siren and peeled out, spitting gravel and smoking rubber. He was in heaven.

Phil had been driving more than eighty miles non-stop. During the early part of the journey, he'd held an involved conversation on the car phone with his producer in L.A. He was annoyed and tired. The dust-colored scenery and endless flat road only annoyed him further. Thus far, the trip had been a total waste. He'd checked out five different towns in southwest New Mexico, and none of them had suited his needs. If his luck didn't change, they were going to have to use a set after all. It wasn't his style. When Phillip Kincaid directed a film, he was a stickler for authenticity. Now he was looking for a tough, dusty little town that showed wear around the edges. He wanted peeling paint and some grime. He was looking for the kind of place everyone planned to leave and no one much wanted to come back to.

Phil had spent three long hot days looking, and nothing had satisfied him. True, he'd found a couple of sand-colored towns, a little faded, a little worse for wear, but they hadn't had the right feel. As a director—a highly successful director of American films—Phillip Kincaid relied on gut reaction before he settled down to refining angles. He needed a town that gave him a kick in the stomach. And he was running short on time.

Already Huffman, the producer, was getting antsy, pushing to start the studio scenes. Phil was cursing himself again for not producing the film himself when he cruised by Annie's Cafe. He had stalled Huffman for another week, but if he didn't find the right town to represent New Chance, he would have to trust his location manager to find it. Phil scowled down the endless stretch of road. He didn't trust details to anyone but himself. That, and his undeniable talent, were the reasons for his success at the age of thirty-four. He was tough, critical and volatile, but he treated each of his films as though it were a child requiring endless care and patience. He wasn't always so understanding with his actors.

He heard the wail of the siren with mild curiosity. Glancing in the mirror, Phil saw a dirty, dented police car that might have been white at one time. It was bearing down on him enthusiastically. Phil swore, gave momentary consideration to hitting the gas and leaving the annoyance with his dust, then resignedly pulled over. The blast of heat that greeted him when he let down the window did nothing to improve his mood. Filthy place, he thought, cutting the engine. Grimy dust hole. He wished for his own lagoonlike pool and a long, cold drink.

Elated, Merle climbed out of his car, ticket book in hand. Yessiree, he thought again, this was some machine. About the fanciest piece he'd seen outside the TV. Mercedes, he noted, turning the sound of it over in his mind. French, he decided with admiration. Holy cow, he'd stopped himself a French car not two miles out of town. He'd have a story to tell over a beer that night.

The driver disappointed him a bit at first. He didn't look foreign or even rich. Merle's glance passed ignorantly over the gold Swiss watch to take in the T-shirt and jeans. Must be one of those eccentrics, he concluded. Or maybe the car was stolen. Merle's blood began to pound excitedly. He looked at the man's face.

It was lean and faintly aristocratic, with well-defined bones and a long, straight nose. The mouth was unsmiling, even bored. He was clean shaven with the suggestion of creases in his cheeks. His hair seemed a modest brown; it was a bit long and curled over his ears. In the tanned face the eyes were an arresting clear water-blue. They were both bored and annoyed and, if Merle had been able to latch on the word, aloof. He wasn't Merle's image of a desperate foreign-car thief.

"Yes?"

The single frosty syllable brought Merle back to business. "In a hurry?" he asked, adopting what the sheriff would have called his tough-cop stance.

"Yes."

The answer made Merle shift his feet. "License and registration," he said briskly, then leaned closer to the window as Phil reached in the glove compartment. "Glory be, look at the dash! It's got everything and then some. A phone, a phone right there in the car. Those French guys are something."

Phil sent him a mild glance. "German," he corrected, handing Merle the registration.

"German?" Merle frowned doubtfully. "You sure?"

"Yes." Slipping his license out of his wallet, Phil passed it through the open window. The heat was pouring in.

Merle accepted the registration. He was downright sure Mercedes was a French name. "This your car?" he asked suspiciously.

"As you can see by the name on the registration," Phil returned coolly, a sure sign that his temper was frayed around the edges.

Merle was reading the registration at his usual plodding speed. "You streaked by Annie's like a bat out of—" He broke off, remembering that the sheriff didn't hold with swearing on the job. "I stopped you for excessive speed. Clocked you at seventy-two. I bet this baby rides so smooth you never noticed."

"As a matter of fact, I didn't." Perhaps if he hadn't been angry to begin with, perhaps if the heat hadn't been rolling unmercifully into the car, Phil might have played his hand differently. As Merle began to write up the ticket Phil narrowed his eyes. "Just how do I know you clocked me at all?"

"I was just coming out of Annie's when you breezed by," Merle said genially. His forehead creased as he formed the letters. "If I'd waited for my change, I wouldn't have seen you." He grinned, pleased with the hand of fate. "You just sign this," he said as he ripped the ticket from the pad. "You can stop off in town and pay the fine."

Slowly, Phil climbed out of the car. When the sun hit his hair, deep streaks of red shot through it. Merle was reminded of his mother's mahogany server. For a moment they stood eye to eye, both tall men. But one was lanky and tended to slouch, the other lean, muscular and erect.

"No," Phil said flatly.

"No?" Merle blinked against the direct blue gaze. "No what?"

"No, I'm not signing it."

"Not signing?" Merle looked down at the ticket still in his hand. "But you have to."

"No, I don't." Phil felt a trickle of sweat roll down his back. Inexplicably it infuriated him. "I'm not signing, and I'm not paying a penny to some two-bit judge who's feeding his bank account from this speed trap."

"Speed trap!" Merle was more astonished than insulted. "Mister, you were doing better'n seventy, and the road's marked clear—fifty-five. Everybody knows you can't do more than fifty-five."

"Who says I was?"

"I clocked you."

"Your word against mine," Phil returned coolly. "Got a witness?"

Merle's mouth fell open. "Well, no, but…" He pushed back his hat. "Look, I don't need no witness, I'm the deputy. Just sign the ticket."

It was pure perversity. Phil hadn't the least idea how fast he'd been going and didn't particularly care. The road had been long and deserted; his mind had been in L.A. But knowing this wasn't going to make him take the cracked ballpoint the deputy offered him.

"No."

"Look, mister, I already wrote up the ticket." Merle read refusal in Phil's face and set his chin. After all, he was the law. "Then I'm going to have to take you in," he said dangerously. "The sheriff's not going to like it."

Phil gave him a quick smirk and held out his hands, wrists close. Merle stared at them a moment, then looked helplessly from car to car. Beneath the anger, Phil felt a stir of sympathy.

"You'll have to follow me in," Merle told him as he pocketed Phil's license.

"And if I refuse?"

Merle wasn't a complete fool. "Well, then," he said amiably, "I'll have to take you in and leave this fancy car sitting here. It might be all in one piece when the tow truck gets here. Then again…"

Phil acknowledged the point with a slight nod, then climbed back into his car. Merle sauntered to his, thinking how fine he was going to look bringing in that fancy red machine.

They drove into Friendly at a sedate pace. Merle nodded occasionally to people who stopped their business to eye the small procession. He stuck his hand out the window to signal a halt, then braked in front of the sheriff's office.

"Okay, inside." Abruptly official, Merle stood straight. "The sheriff'll want to talk to you." But the icy gleam in the man's eye kept Merle from taking his arm. Instead he opened the door and waited for his prisoner to walk through.

Phil glimpsed a small room with two cells, a bulletin board, a couple of spindly chairs and a battered desk. An overhead fan churned the steamy air and whined. On the floor lay a large mound of mud-colored fur that turned out to be a dog. The desk was covered with books and papers and two half-filled cups of coffee. A dark-haired woman bent over all this, scratching industriously on a yellow legal pad. She glanced up as they entered.

Phil forgot his annoyance long enough to cast her in three different films. Her face was classically oval, with a hint of cheekbone under honey-toned skin. Her nose was small and delicate, her mouth just short of wide, with a fullness that was instantly sensual. Her hair was black, left to fall loosely past her shoulders in carelessly sweeping waves. Her brows arched in question. Beneath them her eyes were thickly lashed, darkly green and faintly amused.

"Merle?"

The single syllable was full throated, as lazy and sexy as black silk. Phil knew actresses who would kill for a voice like that one. If she didn't stiffen up in front of a camera, he thought, and if the rest of her went with the face… He let his eyes sweep down. Pinned to her left breast was a small tin badge. Fascinated, Phil stared at it.

"Excess of speed on Seventeen, Sheriff."

"Oh?" With a slight smile on her face, she waited for Phil's eyes to come back to hers. She had recognized the appraisal when he had first walked in, just as she recognized the suspicion now. "Didn't you have a pen, Merle?"

"A pen?" Baffled, he checked his pockets.

"I wouldn't sign the ticket." Phil walked to the desk to get a closer look at her face. "Sheriff," he added. She could be shot from any imaginable angle, he concluded, and still look wonderful. He wanted to hear her speak again.

She met his assessing stare straight on. "I see. What was his speed, Merle?"

"Seventy-two. Tory, you should see his car!" Merle exclaimed, forgetting himself.

"I imagine I will," she murmured. She held out her hand, her eyes still on Phil's. Quickly, Merle gave her the paperwork.

Phil noted that her hands were long, narrow and elegant. The tips were painted in shell-pink. What the hell is she doing here? he wondered, more easily visualizing her in Beverly Hills.

"Well, everything seems to be in order, Mr.... Kincaid." Her eyes came back to his. A little mascara, he noticed, a touch of eyeliner. The color's hers. No powder, no lipstick. He wished fleetingly for a camera and a couple of hand-held lights. "The fine's forty dollars," she said lazily. "Cash."

"I'm not paying it."

Her lips pursed briefly, causing him to speculate on their taste. "Or forty days," she said without batting an eye. "I think you'd find it less…inconvenient to pay the fine. Our accommodations won't suit you."

The cool amusement in her tone irritated him. "I'm not paying any fine." Placing his palms on the desk, he leaned toward her, catching the faint drift of a subtle, sophisticated scent. "Do you really expect me to believe you're the sheriff? What kind of scam are you and this character running?"

Merle opened his mouth to speak, glanced at Tory, then shut it again. She rose slowly. Phil found himself surprised that she was tall and as lean as a whippet. A model's body, he thought, long and willowy—the kind that made you wonder what was underneath those clothes. This one made jeans and a plaid shirt look like a million dollars.

"I never argue with beliefs, Mr. Kincaid. You'll have to empty your pockets."

"I will not," he began furiously.

"Resisting arrest." Tory lifted a brow. "We'll have to make it sixty days." Phil said something quick and rude. Instead of being offended, Tory smiled. "Lock him up, Merle."

"Now, just a damn minute—"

"You don't want to make her mad," Merle whispered, urging Phil back toward the cells. "She can be mean as a cat."

"Unless you want us to tow your car…and charge you for that as well," she added, "you'll give Merle your keys." She flicked her eyes over his furious face. "Read him his rights, Merle."

"I know my rights, damn it." Contemptuously he shrugged off Merle's hand. "I want to make a phone call."

"Of course." Tory sent him another charming smile. "As soon as you give Merle your keys."

"Now, look—" Phil glanced down at her badge again "—Sheriff," he added curtly. "You don't expect me to fall for an old game. This one—" he jerked a thumb at Merle "—waits for an out-of-towner to come by, then tries to hustle him out of a quick forty bucks. There's a law against speed traps."

Tory listened with apparent interest. "Are you going to sign the ticket, Mr. Kincaid?"

Phil narrowed his eyes. "No."

"Then you'll be our guest for a while."

"You can't sentence me," Phil began heatedly. "A judge—"

"Justice of the peace," Tory interrupted, then tapped a tinted nail against a small framed certificate. Phil saw the name Victoria L. Ashton.

He gave her a long, dry look. "You?"

"Yes, handy, isn't it?" She cocked her head to the side. "Sixty days, Mr. Kincaid, or two hundred and fifty dollars."

"Two-fifty!"

"Bail's set at five hundred. Would you care to post it?"

"The phone call," he said through clenched teeth.

"The keys," she countered affably.

Swearing under his breath, Phil pulled the keys from his pocket and tossed them to her. Tory caught them neatly. "You're entitled to one local call, Mr. Kincaid."

"It's long distance," he muttered. "I'll use my credit card."

After indicating the phone on her desk, Tory took the

keys to Merle. "Two-fifty!" he said in an avid whisper. "Aren't you being a little rough on him?"

Tory gave a quick, unladylike snort. "Mr. Hollywood Kincaid needs a good kick in the ego," she mumbled. "It'll do him a world of good to stew in a cell for a while. Take the car to Bestler's Garage, Merle."

"Me? *Drive* it?" He looked down at the keys in his hand.

"Lock it up and bring back the keys," Tory added. "And don't play with any of the buttons."

"Aw, Tory."

"Aw, Merle," she responded, then sent him on his way with an affectionate look.

Phil waited impatiently as the phone rang. Someone picked up. "Answering for Sherman, Miller and Stein." He swore.

"Where the hell's Lou?" he demanded.

"Mr. Sherman is out of the office until Monday," the operator told him primly. "Would you care to leave your name?"

"This is Phillip Kincaid. You get Lou now, tell him I'm in—" He turned to cast a dark look at Tory.

"Welcome to Friendly, New Mexico," she said obligingly.

Phil's opinion was a concise four-letter word. "Friendly, New Mexico. In jail, damn it, on some trumped-up charge. Tell him to get his briefcase on a plane, pronto."

"Yes, Mr. Kincaid, I'll try to reach him."

"You reach him," he said tightly and hung up. When he started to dial again, Tory walked over and calmly disconnected him.

"One call," she reminded him.

"I got a damn answering service."

"Tough break." She gave him the dashing smile that both attracted and infuriated him. "Your room's ready, Mr. Kincaid."

Phil hung up the phone to face her squarely. "You're not putting me in that cell."

She looked up with a guileless flutter of lashes. "No?"

"No."

Tory looked confused for a moment. Her sigh was an appealingly feminine sound as she wandered around the desk. "You're making this difficult for me, Mr. Kincaid. You must know I can't manhandle you into a cell. You're bigger than I am."

Her abrupt change of tone caused him to feel more reasonable. "Ms. Ashton..." he began.

"Sheriff Ashton," Tory corrected and drew a .45 out of the desk drawer. Her smile never wavered as Phil gaped at the large gun in her elegant hand. "Now, unless you want another count of resisting arrest on your record, you'll go quietly into that first cell over there. The linen's just been changed."

Phil wavered between astonishment and amusement. "You don't expect me to believe you'd use that thing."

"I told you I don't argue with beliefs." Though she kept the barrel lowered, Tory quite deliberately cocked the gun.

He studied her for one full minute. Her eyes were too direct and entirely too calm. Phil had no doubt she'd put a hole in him—in some part of his anatomy that she considered unimportant. He had a healthy respect for his body.

"I'll get you for this," he muttered as he headed for the cell.

Her laugh was rich and attractive enough to make him turn in front of the bars. Good God, he thought, he'd like to tangle with her when she didn't have a pistol in her hand. Furious with himself, Phil stalked into the cell.

"Doesn't that line go something like, 'When I break outta this joint, you're gonna get yours'?" Tory pulled the keys from a peg, then locked the cell door with a jingle and snap. Struggling not to smile, Phil paced the cell.

"Would you like a harmonica and a tin cup?"

He grinned, but luckily his back was to her. Dropping onto the bunk, he sent her a fulminating glance. "I'll take the tin cup if it has coffee in it."

"Comes with the service, Kincaid. You've got free room and board in Friendly." He watched her walk back to the desk to replace the pistol. Something in the lazy, leggy gait affected his blood pressure pleasantly. "Cream and sugar?" she asked politely.

"Black."

Tory poured the coffee, aware that his eyes were on her. She was partly amused by him, partly intrigued. She knew exactly who he was. Over her basic disdain for what she considered a spoiled, tinsel-town playboy was a trace of respect. He hadn't attempted to influence her with his name or his reputation. He'd relied on his temper. And it was his temper, she knew, that had landed him in the cell in the first place.

Too rich, she decided, too successful, too attractive. And perhaps, she mused as she poured herself a cup, too talented. His movies were undeniably brilliant. She

wondered what made him tick. His movies seemed to
state one image, the glossies another. With a quiet laugh
she thought she might find out for herself while he was
her "guest."

"Black," she stated, carrying both cups across the
room. "Made to order."

He was watching the way she moved; fluidly, with
just a hint of hip. It was those long legs, he decided, and
some innate confidence. Under different circumstances
he would have considered her quite a woman. At the
moment he considered her an outrageous annoyance.
Silently he unfolded himself from the bunk and went
to accept the coffee she held between the bars. Their
fingers brushed briefly.

"You're a beautiful woman, Victoria L. Ashton," he
muttered. "And a pain in the neck."

She smiled. "Yes."

That drew a laugh from him. "What the hell are you
doing here, playing sheriff?"

"What the hell are you doing here, playing criminal?"

Merle burst in the door, grinning from ear to ear.
"Holy cow, Mr. Kincaid, that's *some* car!" He dropped
the keys in Tory's hand, then leaned against the bars.
"I swear, I could've just sat in it all day. Bestler's eyes
just about popped out when I drove it in."

Making a low sound in his throat, Phil turned away
to stare through the small barred window at the rear
of the cell. He scowled at his view of the town. Look
at this place! he thought in frustration. Dusty little nowhere. Looks like all the color was washed away twenty
years ago. Baked away, he corrected himself as sweat
ran uncomfortably down his back. There seemed to be

nothing but brown—dry, sparse mesa in the distance and parched sand. All the buildings, such as they were, were different dull shades of brown, all stripped bare by the unrelenting sun. Damn place still had wooden sidewalks, he mused, sipping at the strong coffee. There wasn't a coat of paint on a storefront that wasn't cracked and peeling. The whole town looked as though it had drawn one long, tired communal breath and settled down to wait until it was all over.

It was a gritty, hopeless-looking place with a sad sort of character under a film of dust and lethargy. People stayed in a town like this when they had no place else to go or nothing to do. Came back when they'd lost hope for anything better. And here he was, stuck in some steamy little cell....

His mind sharpened.

Staring at the tired storefronts and sagging wood, Phil saw it all through the lens of a camera. His fingers wrapped around a window bar as he began to plot out scene after scene. If he hadn't been furious, he'd have seen it from the first moment.

This was Next Chance.

Chapter 2

For the next twenty minutes Tory paid little attention to her prisoner. He seemed content to stare out of the window with the coffee growing cold in his hand. After dispatching Merle, Tory settled down to work.

She was blessed with a sharp, practical and stubborn mind. These traits had made her education extensive. Academically she'd excelled, but she hadn't always endeared herself to her instructors. *Why?* had always been her favorite question. In addition her temperament, which ranged from placid to explosive, had made her a difficult student. Some of her associates called her a tedious annoyance—usually when they were on the opposing side. At twenty-seven Victoria L. Ashton was a very shrewd, very accomplished attorney.

In Albuquerque she kept a small, unpretentious office in an enormous old house with bad plumbing. She shared it with an accountant, a real-estate broker and a private investigator. For nearly five years she had lived on the third floor in two barnlike rooms while keeping her office below. It was a comfortable arrangement that Tory had had no inclination to alter even when she'd been able to afford to.

Professionally she liked challenges and dealing with finite details. In her personal life she was more lacka-daisical. No one would call her lazy, but she saw more virtue in a nap than a brisk jog. Her energies poured out in the office or courtroom—and temporarily in her position as sheriff of Friendly, New Mexico.

She had grown up in Friendly and had been content with its yawning pace. The sense of justice she had in-herited from her father had driven her to law school. Still, she had had no desire to join a swank firm on ei-ther coast, or in any big city in between. Her independ-ence had caused her to risk starting her own practice. Fat fees were no motivation for Tory. She'd learned early how to stretch a dollar when it suited her—an ability she got from her mother. People, and the way the law could be made to work to their advantage or disadvan-tage, interested her.

Now Tory settled behind her desk and continued drafting out a partnership agreement for a pair of fledg-ling songwriters. It wasn't always simple to handle cases long distance, but she'd given her word. Absentmind-edly she sipped her coffee. By fall she would be back in Albuquerque, filling her caseload again and trading her badge for a briefcase. In the meantime the weekend was looming. Payday. Tory smiled a little as she wrote. Friendly livened up a bit on Saturday nights. People tended to have an extra beer. And there was a poker game scheduled at Bestler's Garage that she wasn't supposed to know about. Tory knew when it was advantageous to look the other way. Her father would have said people need their little entertainments.

Leaning back to study what she had written, Tory propped one booted foot on the desk and twirled a raven lock around her finger. Abruptly coming out of his reverie, Phil whirled to the door of the cell.

"I have to make a phone call!" His tone was urgent and excited. Everything he had seen from the cell window had convinced him that fate had brought him to Friendly.

Tory finished reading a paragraph, then looked up languidly. "You've had your phone call, Mr. Kincaid. Why don't you relax? Take a tip from Dynamite there," she suggested, wiggling her fingers toward the mound of dog. "Take a nap."

Phil curled his hands around the bars and shook them. "Woman, I have to use the phone. It's important."

"It always is," Tory murmured before she lowered her eyes to the paper again.

Ready to sacrifice principle for expediency, Phil growled at her. "Look, I'll sign the ticket. Just let me out of here."

"You're welcome to sign the ticket," she returned pleasantly, "but it won't get you out. There's also the charge of resisting arrest."

"Of all the phony, trumped-up—"

"I could add creating a public nuisance," she considered, then glanced over the top of her papers with a smile. He was furious. It showed in the rigid stance of his hard body, in the grim mouth and fiery eyes. Tory felt a small twinge in the nether regions of her stomach. Oh, yes, she could clearly see why his name was linked with dozens of attractive women. He was easily the most beautiful male animal she'd ever seen. It was that trace of aristocratic aloofness, she mused, coupled with the really extraordinary physique and explosive temper. He was like some sleek, undomesticated cat.

Their eyes warred with each other for a long, silent moment. His were stony; hers were calm.

"All right," he muttered, "how much?"

Tory lifted a brow. "A bribe, Kincaid?"

He knew his quarry too well by this time. "No. How much is my fine…Sheriff?"

"Two hundred and fifty dollars." She sent her hair over her shoulder with a quick toss of her head. "Or you can post bail for five hundred."

Scowling at her, Phil reached for his wallet. *When I get out of here,* he thought dangerously, *I'm going to make that tasty little morsel pay for this.* A glance in his wallet found him more than a hundred dollars short of bond. Phil swore, then looked back at Tory. She still had the gently patient smile on her face. He could cheerfully strangle her. Instead he tried another tack. Charm had always brought him success with women.

"I lost my temper before, Sheriff," he began, sending her the slightly off-center smile for which he was known. "I apologize. I've been on the road for several days and your deputy got under my skin." Tory went on smiling. "If I said anything out of line to you, it was because you just don't fit the image of small-town peace officer." He grinned and became boyishly appealing— Tom Sawyer caught with his hand in the sugar bowl.

Tory lifted one long, slim leg and crossed it over the other on the desk. "A little short, are you, Kincaid?"

Phil clenched his teeth on a furious retort. "I don't like to carry a lot of cash on the road."

"Very wise," she agreed with a nod. "But we don't accept credit cards."

"Damn it, I have to get out of here!"

Tory studied him dispassionately. "I can't buy claustrophobia," she said. "Not when I read you crawled into a two-foot pipe to check camera angles on *Night of Desperation*."

"It's not—" Phil broke off. His eyes narrowed. "You know who I am?"

"Oh, I make it to the movies a couple of times a year," she said blithely.

The narrowed eyes grew hard. "If this is some kind of shakedown—"

Her throaty laughter cut him off. "Your self-importance is showing." His expression grew so incredulous, she laughed again before she rose. "Kincaid, I don't care who you are or what you do for a living, you're a bad-tempered man who refused to accept the law and got obnoxious." She sauntered over to the cell. Again he caught the hint of a subtle perfume that suited French silk, more than faded denim. "I'm obliged to rehabilitate you."

He forgot his anger in simple appreciation of blatant beauty. "God, you've got a face," he muttered. "I could work a whole damn film around that face."

The words surprised her. Tory was perfectly aware that she was physically attractive. She would have been a fool to think otherwise, and she'd heard men offer countless homages to her looks. This was hardly a homage. But something in his tone, in his eyes, made a tremor skip up her spine. She made no protest when he reached a hand through the bars to touch her hair. He let it fall through his fingers while his eyes stayed on hers.

Tory felt a heat to which she had thought herself immune. It flashed through her as though she had stepped into the sun from out of a cool, dim room. It was the kind of heat that buckled your knees and made you gasp out loud in astonished wonder. She stood straight and absorbed it.

A dangerous man, she concluded, surprised. A very dangerous man. She saw a flicker of desire in his eyes, then a flash of amusement. As she watched, his mouth curved up at the corners.

"Baby," he said, then grinned, "I could make you a star."

The purposely trite words dissolved the tension and made her laugh. "Oh, Mr. Kincaid," she said in a breathy whisper, "can I really have a screen test?" A startled Phil could only watch as she flung herself against the bars of the cell dramatically. "I'll wait for you, Johnny," she said huskily as tears shimmered in her eyes and her soft lips trembled. "No matter how long it takes." Reaching through the bars, she clutched at him. "I'll write you every day," she promised brokenly. "And dream of you every night. Oh, Johnny—" her lashes fluttered down "—kiss me goodbye!"

Fascinated, Phil moved to oblige her, but just before his lips brushed hers, she stepped back, laughing. "How'd I do, Hollywood? Do I get the part?"

Phil studied her in amused annoyance. It was a pity, he thought, that he hadn't at least gotten a taste of that beautiful mouth. "A little overdone," he stated with more asperity than truth. "But not bad for an amateur."

Tory chuckled and leaned companionably against the bars. "You're just mad."

"Mad?" he tossed back in exasperation. "Have you ever spent any time in one of these cages?"

"As a matter of fact I have." She gave him an easy grin. "Under less auspicious circumstances. Relax, Kincaid, your friend will come bail you out."

"The mayor," Phil said on sudden inspiration. "I want to see the mayor. I have a business proposition," he added.

"Oh." Tory mulled this over. "Well, I doubt I can oblige you on a Saturday. The mayor mostly fishes on Saturday. Want to tell me about it?"

"No."

"Okay. By the way, your last film should've taken the Oscar. It was the most beautiful movie I've ever seen."

Her sudden change of attitude disconcerted him. Cautiously, Phil studied her face but saw nothing but simple sincerity. "Thanks."

"You don't look like the type who could make a film with intelligence, integrity and emotion."

With a half laugh he dragged a hand through his hair. "Am I supposed to thank you for that too?"

"Not necessarily. It's just that you really do look like the type who squires all those busty celebrities around. When do you find time to work?"

He shook his head. "I…manage," he said grimly.

"Takes a lot of stamina," Tory agreed.

He grinned. "Which? The work or the busty celebrities?"

"I guess you know the answer to that. By the way," she continued before he could formulate a reasonable response, "don't tell Merle T. you make movies." Tory gave him the swift, dashing grin. "He'll start walking like John Wayne and drive us both crazy."

When he smiled back at her, both of them studied each other in wary silence. There was an attraction on both sides that pleased neither of them.

"Sheriff," Phil said in a friendly tone, "a phone call. Remember the line about the quality of mercy?"

Her lips curved, but before she could agree, the door to the office burst in.

"Sheriff!"

"Right here, Mr. Hollister," she said mildly. Tory glanced from the burly, irate man to the skinny, terrified teenager he pulled in with him. "What's the problem?" Without hurry she crossed back to her desk, stepping over the dog automatically.

"Those punks," he began, puffing with the exertion of running. "I warned you about them!"

"The Kramer twins?" Tory sat on the corner of her desk. Her eyes flickered down to the beefy hand that gripped a skinny arm. "Why don't you sit down, Mr. Hollister. You—" she looked directly at the boy "—it's Tod, isn't it?"

He swallowed rapidly. "Yes, ma'am—Sheriff. Tod Swanson."

"Get Mr. Hollister a glass of water, Tod. Right through there."

"He'll be out the back door before you can spit," Hollister began, then took a plaid handkerchief out of his pocket to wipe at his brow.

"No, he won't," Tory said calmly. She jerked her head at the boy as she pulled up a chair for Hollister. "Sit down, now, you'll make yourself sick."

"Sick!" Hollister dropped into a chair as the boy scrambled off. "I'm already sick. Those—those punks."

"Yes, the Kramer twins."

She waited patiently while he completed a lengthy, sometimes incoherent dissertation on the youth of today. Phil had the opportunity to do what he did best: watch and absorb.

Hollister, he noticed, was a hotheaded old bigot with a trace of fear for the younger generation. He was sweating profusely, dabbing at his brow and the back of his neck with the checkered handkerchief. His shirt was wilted and patched with dark splotches. He was flushed, overweight and tiresome. Tory listened to him with every appearance of respect, but Phil noticed the gentle tap of her forefinger against her knee as she sat on the edge of the desk.

The boy came in with the water, two high spots of color on his cheeks. Phil concluded he'd had a difficult time not slipping out the back door. He judged the boy to be about thirteen and scared right down to the bone. He had a smooth, attractive face, with a mop of dark hair and huge brown eyes that wanted to look everywhere at once. He was too thin; his jeans and grubby shirt were nearly in tatters. He handed Tory the water with a hand that shook. Phil saw that when she took it from him, she gave his hand a quick, reassuring squeeze. Phillip began to like her.

"Here." Tory handed Hollister the glass. "Drink this, then tell me what happened."

Hollister drained the glass in two huge gulps. "Those punks, messing around out back of my store. I've chased 'em off a dozen times. They come in and steal anything they can get their hands on. I've told you."

"Yes, Mr. Hollister. What happened this time?"

"Heaved a rock through the window." He reddened alarmingly again. "This one was with 'em. Didn't run fast enough."

"I see." She glanced at Tod, whose eyes were glued to the toes of his sneakers. "Which one threw the rock?"

"Didn't see which one, but I caught this one." Hollister rose, stuffing his damp handkerchief back in his pocket. "I'm going to press charges."

Phil saw the boy blanch. Though Tory continued to look at Hollister, she laid a hand on Tod's arm. "Go sit down in the back room, Tod." She waited until he was out of earshot. "You did the right thing to bring him in, Mr. Hollister." She smiled. "And to scare the pants off him."

"He should be locked up," the man began.

"Oh, that won't get your window fixed," she said reasonably. "And it would only make the boy look like a hero to the twins."

"In my day—"

"I guess you and my father never broke a window," she mused, smiling at him with wide eyes. Hollister blustered, then snorted.

"Now, look here, Tory..."

"Let me handle it, Mr. Hollister. This kid must be three years younger than the Kramer twins." She lowered her voice so that Phil strained to hear. "He could have gotten away."

Hollister shifted from foot to foot. "He didn't try," he mumbled. "Just stood there. But my window—"

"How much to replace it?"

He lowered his brows and puffed for a minute. "Twenty-five dollars should cover it."

Tory walked around the desk and opened a drawer. After counting out bills, she handed them over. "You have my word, I'll deal with him—and with the twins."

"Just like your old man," he muttered, then awkwardly patted her head. "I don't want those Kramers hanging around my store."

"I'll see to it."

With a nod he left.

Tory sat on her desk again and frowned at her left boot. She wasn't just like her old man, she thought. He'd always been sure and she was guessing. Phil heard her quiet, troubled sigh and wondered at it.

"Tod," she called, then waited for him to come to her. As he walked in his eyes darted in search of Hollister before they focused, terrified, on Tory. When he stood in front of her, she studied his white, strained face. Her heart melted, but her voice was brisk.

"I won't ask you who threw the rock." Tod opened his mouth, closed it resolutely and shook his head. "Why didn't you run?"

"I didn't—I couldn't…." He bit his lip. "I guess I was too scared."

"How old are you, Tod?" She wanted to brush at the hair that tumbled over his forehead. Instead she kept her hands loosely folded in her lap.

"Fourteen, Sheriff. Honest." His eyes darted up to hers, then flew away like a small, frightened bird. "Just last month."

"The Kramer twins are sixteen," she pointed out gently. "Don't you have friends your own age?"

He gave a shrug of his shoulders that could have meant anything.

"I'll have to take you home and talk to your father, Tod."

He'd been frightened before, but now he looked up at her with naked terror in his eyes. It wiped the lecture she had intended to give him out of her mind. "Please." It came out in a whisper, as though he could say nothing more. Even the whisper was hopeless.

"Tod, are you afraid of your father?" He swallowed and said nothing. "Does he hurt you?" He moistened his lips as his breath began to shake. "Tod." Tory's voice became very soft. "You can tell me. I'm here to help you."

"He…" Tod choked, then shook his head swiftly. "No, ma'am."

Frustrated, Tory looked at the plea in his eyes. "Well, then, perhaps since this is a first offense, we can keep it between us."

"M-ma'am?"

"Tod Swanson, you were detained for malicious mischief. Do you understand the charge?"

"Yes, Sheriff." His Adam's apple began to tremble.

"You owe the court twenty-five dollars in damages, which you'll work off after school and on weekends at a rate of two dollars an hour. You're sentenced to six months probation, during which time you're to keep away from loose women, hard liquor and the Kramer twins. Once a week you're to file a report with me, as I'll be serving as your probation officer."

Tod stared at her as he tried to take it in. "You're not…you're not going to tell my father?"

Slowly, Tory rose. He was a few inches shorter, so that he looked up at her with his eyes full of confused hope. "No." She placed her hands on his shoulders. "Don't let me down."

His eyes brimmed with tears, which he blinked back furiously. Tory wanted badly to hold him, but knew better. "Be here tomorrow morning. I'll have some work for you."

"Yes, yes, ma'am—Sheriff." He backed away warily, waiting for her to change her mind. "I'll be here, Sheriff." He was fumbling for the doorknob, still watching her. "Thank you." Like a shot, he was out of the office, leaving Tory staring at the closed door.

"Well, Sheriff," Phil said quietly, "you're quite a lady."

Tory whirled to see Phil eyeing her oddly. For the first time she felt the full impact of the clear blue gaze. Disconcerted, she went back to her desk. "Did you enjoy seeing the wheels of justice turn, Kincaid?" she asked.

"As a matter of fact, I did." His tone was grave enough to cause her to look back at him. "You did the right thing by that boy."

Tory studied him a moment, then let out a long sigh. "Did I? We'll see, won't we? Ever seen an abused kid, Kincaid? I'd bet that fifteen-hundred-dollar watch you're wearing one just walked out of here. There isn't a damn thing I can do about it."

"There are laws," he said, fretting against the bars. Quite suddenly he wanted to touch her.

"And laws," she murmured. When the door swung open, she glanced up. "Merle. Good. Take over here. I have to run out to the Kramer place."

"The twins?"

"Who else?" Tory shot back as she plucked a black flat-brimmed hat from a peg. "I'll grab dinner while I'm out and pick up something for our guest. How do you feel about stew, Kincaid?"

"Steak, medium rare," he tossed back. "Chef's salad, oil and vinegar and a good Bordeaux."

"Don't let him intimidate you, Merle," Tory warned as she headed for the door. "He's a cream puff."

"Sheriff, the phone call!" Phil shouted after her as she started to close the door.

With a heavy sigh Tory stuck her head back in. "Merle T., let the poor guy use the phone. Once," she added firmly, then shut the door.

Ninety minutes later Tory sauntered back in with a wicker hamper over her arm. Phil was sitting on his bunk, smoking quietly. Merle sat at the desk, his feet propped up, his hat over his face. He was snoring gently.

"Is the party over?" Tory asked. Phil shot her a silent glare. Chuckling, she went to Merle and gave him a jab in the shoulder. He scrambled up like a shot, scraping his boot heels over the desk surface.

"Aw, Tory," he muttered, bending to retrieve his hat from the floor.

"Any trouble with the desperate character?" she wanted to know.

Merle gave her a blank look, then grinned sheepishly. "Come on, Tory."

"Go get something to eat. You can wander down to Hernandez's Bar and the pool hall before you go off duty."

Merle placed his hat back on his head. "Want me to check Bestler's Garage?"

"No," she said, remembering the poker game. Merle would figure it his bound duty to break it up if he happened in on it. "I checked in earlier."

"Well, okay..." He shuffled his feet and cast a sidelong glance at Phil. "One of us should stay here tonight."

"I'm staying." Plucking up the keys, she headed for the cell. "I've got some extra clothes in the back room."

"Yeah, but, Tory..." He wanted to point out that she was a woman, after all, and the prisoner had given her a couple of long looks.

"Yes?" Tory paused in front of Phil's cell.

"Nothin'," he muttered, reminded that Tory could handle herself and always had. He blushed before he headed for the door.

"Wasn't that sweet?" she murmured. "He was worried about my virtue." At Phil's snort of laughter she lifted a wry brow.

"Doesn't he know about the large gun in the desk drawer?"

"Of course he does." Tory unlocked the cell. "I told him if he played with it, I'd break all his fingers. Hungry?"

Phil gave the hamper a dubious smile. "Maybe."

"Oh, come on, cheer up," Tory ordered. "Didn't you get to make your phone call?"

She spoke as though appeasing a little boy. It drew a reluctant grin from Phil. "Yes, I made my phone call." Because the discussion with his producer had gone well, Phil was willing to be marginally friendly. Besides, he was starving. "What's in there?"

"T-bone, medium rare, salad, roasted potato—"

"You're kidding!" He was up and dipping into the basket himself.

"I don't kid a man about food, Kincaid, I'm a humanitarian."

"I'll tell you exactly what I think you are—after I've eaten." Phil pulled foil off a plate and uncovered the steak. The scent went straight to his stomach. Dragging over a shaky wooden chair, he settled down to devour his free meal.

"You didn't specify dessert, so I went for apple pie." Tory drew a thick slice out of the hamper.

"I might just modify my opinion of you," Phil told her over a mouthful of steak.

"Don't do anything hasty," she suggested.

"Tell me something, Sheriff." He swallowed, then indicated the still-sleeping dog with his fork. "Doesn't that thing ever move?"

"Not if he can help it."

"Is it alive?"

"The last time I looked," she muttered. "Sorry about the Bordeaux," she continued. "Against regulations. I got you a Dr Pepper."

"A what?"

Tory pulled out a bottle of soda. "Take it or leave it."

After a moment's consideration Phil held out his hand. "What about the mayor?"

"I left him a message. He'll probably see you tomorrow."

Phil unscrewed the top off the bottle, frowning at her. "You're not actually going to make me sleep in this place."

Cocking her head, Tory met his glance. "You have a strange view of the law, Kincaid. Do you think I should book you a room at the hotel?"

He washed down the steak with the soda, then grimaced. "You're a tough guy, Sheriff."

"Yeah." Grinning, she perched on the edge of the bunk. "How's your dinner?"

"It's good. Want some?"

"No. I've eaten." They studied each other with the

same wary speculation. Tory spoke first. "What is Phillip C. Kincaid, boy wonder, doing in Friendly, New Mexico?"

"I was passing through," he said warily. He wasn't going to discuss his plans with her. Something warned him he would meet solid opposition.

"At seventy-two miles per hour," she reminded him.

"Maybe."

With a laugh she leaned back against the brick wall. He watched the way her hair settled lazily over her breasts. A man would be crazy to tangle with that lady, he told himself. Phillip Kincaid was perfectly sane.

"And what is Victoria L. Ashton doing wearing a badge in Friendly, New Mexico?"

She gazed past him for a moment with an odd look in her eyes. "Fulfilling an obligation," she said softly.

"You don't fit the part." Phil contemplated her over another swig from the bottle. "I'm an expert on who fits and who doesn't."

"Why not?" Lifting her knee, Tory laced her fingers around it.

"Your hands are too soft." Thoughtfully, Phil cut another bite of steak. "Not as soft as I expected when I saw that face, but too soft. You don't pamper them, but you don't work with them either."

"A sheriff doesn't work with her hands," Tory pointed out.

"A sheriff doesn't wear perfume that costs a hundred and fifty an ounce that was designed to drive men wild either."

Both brows shot up. Her full bottom lip pushed forward in thought. "Is that what it was designed for?"

"A sheriff," he went on, "doesn't usually look like she

just walked off the cover of *Harper's Bazaar,* treat her deputy like he was her kid brother or pay some boy's fine out of her own pocket."

"My, my," Tory said slowly, "you are observant." He shrugged, continuing with his meal. "Well, then, what part would you cast me in?"

"I had several in mind the minute I saw you." Phil shook his head as he finished off his steak. "Now I'm not so sure. You're no fragile desert blossom." When her smile widened, he went on. "You could be if you wanted to, but you don't. You're no glossy sophisticate either. But that's a choice too." Taking the pie, he rose to join her on the bunk. "You know, there are a number of people out in this strange world who would love to have me as a captive audience while they recited their life's story."

"At least three of four," Tory agreed dryly.

"You're rough on my ego, Sheriff." He tasted the pie, approved, then offered her the next bite. Tory opened her mouth, allowing herself to be fed. It was tangy, spicy and still warm.

"What do you want to know?" she asked, then swallowed.

"Why you're tossing men in jail instead of breaking their hearts."

Her laugh was full of appreciation as she leaned her head back against the wall. Still, she wavered a moment. It had been so long, she mused, since she'd been able just to talk to someone—to a man. He was interesting and, she thought, at the moment harmless.

"I grew up here," she said simply.

"But you didn't stay." When she sent him a quizzical look, he fed her another bite of pie. It occurred to him that it had been a long time since he'd been with a woman who didn't want or even expect anything from him. "You've got too much polish, Victoria," he said, finding her name flowed well on his tongue. "You didn't acquire it in Friendly."

"Harvard," she told him, rounding her tones. "Law."

"Ah." Phil sent her an approving nod. "That fits. I can see you with a leather briefcase and a pin-striped suit. Why aren't you practicing?"

"I am. I have an office in Albuquerque." Her brows drew together. "A pin-striped suit?"

"Gray, very discreet. How can you practice law in Albuquerque and uphold it in Friendly?" He pushed the hair from her shoulder in a casual gesture that neither of them noticed.

"I'm not taking any new cases for a while, so my workload's fairly light." She shrugged it off. "I handle what I can on paper and make a quick trip back when I have to."

"Are you a good lawyer?"

Tory grinned. "I'm a terrific lawyer, Kincaid, but I can't represent you—unethical."

He shoved another bite of pie at her. "So what are you doing back in Friendly?"

"You really are nosy, aren't you?"

"Yes."

She laughed. "My father was sheriff here for years and years." A sadness flickered briefly into her eyes and was controlled. "I suppose in his own quiet way he held the town together—such as it is. When he died, nobody knew just what to do. It sounds strange, but in a town this size, one person can make quite a difference, and he was…a special kind of man."

The wound hasn't healed yet, he thought, watching her steadily. He wondered, but didn't ask, how long ago her father had died.

"Anyway, the mayor asked me to fill in until things settled down again, and since I had to stay around to straighten a few things out anyway, I agreed. Nobody wanted the job except Merle, and he's…" She gave a quick, warm laugh. "Well, he's not ready. I know the law, I know the town. In a few months they'll hold an election. My name won't be on the ballot." She shot him a look. "Did I satisfy your curiosity?"

Under the harsh overhead lights, her skin was flawless, her eyes sharply green. Phil found himself reaching for her hair again. "No," he murmured. Though his eyes never left hers, Tory felt as though he looked at all of her—slowly and with great care. Quite unexpectedly her mouth went dry. She rose.

"It should have," she said lightly as she began to pack up the dirty dishes. "Next time we have dinner, I'll expect your life story." When she felt his hand on her arm, she stopped. Tory glanced down at the fingers curled around her arm, then slowly lifted her eyes to his. "Kincaid," she said softly, "you're in enough trouble."

"I'm already in jail," he pointed out as he turned her to face him.

"The term of your stay can easily be lengthened."

Knowing he should resist and that he couldn't, Phil drew her into his arms. "How much time can I get for making love to the sheriff?"

"What you're going to get is a broken rib if you don't let me go." *Miscalculation,* her mind stated bluntly. This man is never harmless. On the tail of that came the thought of how wonderful it felt to be held against him.

His mouth was very close and very tempting. And it simply wasn't possible to forget their positions.

"Tory," he murmured. "I like the way that sounds." Running his fingers up her spine, he caught them in her hair. With her pressed tight against him, he could feel her faint quiver of response. "I think I'm going to have to have you."

A struggle wasn't going to work, she decided, any more than threats. As her own blood began to heat, Tory knew she had to act quickly. Tilting her head back slightly, she lifted a disdainful brow. "Hasn't a woman ever turned you down before, Kincaid?"

She saw his eyes flash in anger, felt the fingers in her hair tighten. Tory forced herself to remain still and relaxed. Excitement shivered through her, and resolutely she ignored it. His thighs were pressed hard against hers; the arms wrapped around her waist were tense with muscle. The firm male feel of him appealed to her, while the temper in his eyes warned her not to miscalculate again. They remained close for one long throbbing moment.

Phil's fingers relaxed before he stepped back to measure her. "There'll be another time," he said quietly. "Another place."

With apparent calm, Tory began gathering the dishes again. Her heart was thudding at the base of her throat. "You'll get the same answer."

"The hell I will."

Annoyed, she turned to see him watching her. With his hands in his pockets he rocked back gently on his heels. His eyes belied the casual stance. "Stick with your bubbleheaded blondes," she advised coolly. "They photograph so well, clinging to your arm."

She was angry, he realized suddenly, and much more moved by him than she had pretended. Seeing his advantage, Phil approached her again. "You ever take off that badge, Sheriff?"

Tory kept her eyes level. "Occasionally."

Phil lowered his gaze, letting it linger on the small star. "When?"

Sensing that she was being outmaneuvered, Tory answered cautiously. "That's irrelevant."

When he lifted his eyes back to hers, he was smiling. "It won't be." He touched a finger to her full bottom lip. "I'm going to spend a lot of time tasting that beautiful mouth of yours."

Disturbed, Tory stepped back. "I'm afraid you won't have the opportunity or the time."

"I'm going to find the opportunity and the time to make love with you several times—" he sent her a mocking grin "—Sheriff."

As he had anticipated, her eyes lit with fury. "You conceited fool," she said in a low voice. "You really think you're irresistible."

"Sure I do." He continued to grin maddeningly. "Don't you?"

"I think you're a spoiled, egotistical ass."

His temper rose, but Phil controlled it. If he lost it, he'd lose his advantage. He stepped closer, keeping a bland smile on his face. "Do you? Is that a legal opinion or a personal one?"

Tory tossed back her head, fuming. "My personal opinion is—"

He cut her off with a hard, bruising kiss.

Taken completely by surprise, Tory didn't struggle. By the time she had gathered her wits, she was too involved to attempt it. His mouth seduced hers expertly, parting her lips so that he could explore deeply and at his leisure. She responded out of pure pleasure. His mouth was hard, then soft—gentle, then demanding. He took her on a brisk roller coaster of sensation. Before she could recover from the first breathtaking plunge, they were climbing again. She held on to him, waiting for the next burst of speed.

He took his tongue lightly over hers, then withdrew it, tempting her to follow. Recklessly, she did, learning the secrets and dark tastes of his mouth. For a moment he allowed her to take the lead; then, cupping the back of her head in his hand, he crushed her lips with one last driving force. He wanted her weak and limp and totally conquered.

When he released her, Tory stood perfectly still, trying to remember what had happened. The confusion in her eyes gave him enormous pleasure. "I plead guilty, Your Honor," he drawled as he dropped back onto the bunk. "And it was worth it."

Hot, raging fury replaced every other emotion. Storming over to him, she grabbed him by the shirt front. Phil didn't resist, but grinned.

"Police brutality," he reminded her. She cursed him fluently, and with such effortless style, he was unable to conceal his admiration. "Did you learn that at Harvard?" he asked when she paused for breath.

Tory released him with a jerk and whirled to scoop up the hamper. The cell door shut behind her with a furious clang. Without pausing, she stormed out of the office.

Still grinning, Phil lay back on the bunk and pulled

out a cigarette. She'd won round one, he told himself. But he'd taken round two. Blowing out a lazy stream of smoke, he began to speculate on the rematch.

Chapter 3

When the alarm shrilled, Tory knocked it off the small table impatiently. It clattered to the floor and continued to shrill. She buried her head under the pillow. She wasn't at her best in the morning. The noisy alarm vibrated against the floor until she reached down in disgust and slammed it off. After a good night's sleep she was inclined to be cranky. After a poor one she was dangerous.

Most of the past night had been spent tossing and turning. The scene with Phil had infuriated her, not only because he had won, but because she had fully enjoyed that one moment of mindless pleasure. Rolling onto her back, Tory kept the pillow over her face to block out the sunlight. The worst part was, she mused, he was going to get away with it. She couldn't in all conscience use the law to punish him for something that had been strictly personal. It had been her own fault for lowering her guard and inviting the consequences. And she had enjoyed talking with him, sparring with someone quick with words. She missed matching wits with a man.

But that was no excuse, she reminded herself. He'd made her forget her duty…and he'd enjoyed it. Disgusted, Tory tossed the pillow aside, then winced at the brilliant sunlight. She'd learned how to evade an advance as a teenager. What had caused her to slip up this time? She didn't want to dwell on it. Grumpily she dragged herself from the cot and prepared to dress.

Every muscle in his body ached. Phil stretched out his legs to their full length and gave a low groan. He was willing to swear Tory had put the lumps in the mattress for his benefit. Cautiously opening one eye, he stared at the man in the next cell. The man slept on, as he had from the moment Tory had dumped him on the bunk the night before. He snored outrageously. When she had dragged him in, Phil had been amused. The man was twice her weight and had been blissfully drunk. He'd called her "good old Tory," and she had cursed him halfheartedly as she had maneuvered him into the cell. Thirty minutes after hearing the steady snoring, Phil had lost his sense of humor.

She hadn't spoken a word to him. With a detached interest Phil had watched her struggle with the drunk. It had pleased him to observe that she was still fuming. She'd been in and out of the office several times before midnight, then had locked up in the same frigid silence. He'd enjoyed that, but then had made a fatal error: When she had gone into the back room to bed, he had tortured himself by watching her shadow play on the wall as she had undressed. That, combined with an impossible mattress and a snoring drunk-and-disorderly, had led to an uneasy night. He hadn't awakened in the best of moods.

Sitting up with a wince, he glared at the unconscious man in the next cell. His wide, flushed face was cherubic, ringed with a curling blond circle of hair. Ruefully, Phil rubbed a hand over his own chin and felt the rough stubble. A fastidious man, he was annoyed at not having a razor, a hot shower or a fresh set of clothes. Rising, he determined to gain access to all three immediately.

"Tory!" His voice was curt, one of a man accustomed to being listened to. He received no response. "Damn it, Tory, get out here!" He rattled the bars, wishing belligerently that he'd kept the tin cup. He could have made enough noise with it to wake even the stuporous man in the next cell. "Tory, get out of that bed and come here." He swore, promising himself he'd never allow anyone to lock him in anything again. "When I get out…" he began.

Tory came shuffling in, carrying a pot of water. "Button up, Kincaid."

"You listen to me," he retorted. "I want a shower and a razor and my clothes. And if—"

"If you don't shut up until I've had my coffee, you're going to take your shower where you stand." She lifted the pot of water meaningfully. "You can get cleaned up as soon as Merle gets in." She went to the coffeepot and began to clatter.

"You're an arrogant wretch when you've got a man caged," he said darkly.

"I'm an arrogant wretch anyway. Do yourself a favor,

Kincaid, don't start a fight until I've had two cups. I'm not a nice person in the morning."

"I'm warning you." His voice was as low and dangerous as his mood. "You're going to regret locking me in here."

Turning, she looked at him for the first time that morning. His clothes and hair were disheveled. The clean lines of his aristocratic face were shadowed by the night's growth of beard. Fury was in his stance and in the cool water-blue of his eyes. He looked outrageously attractive.

"I think I'm going to regret letting you out," she muttered before she turned back to the coffee. "Do you want some of this, or are you just going to throw it at me?"

The idea was tempting, but so was the scent of the coffee. "Black," he reminded her shortly.

Tory drained half a cup, ignoring her scalded tongue before she went to Phil. "What do you want for breakfast?" she asked as she passed the cup through the bars.

He scowled at her. "A shower, and a sledgehammer for your friend over there."

Tory cast an eye in the next cell. "Silas'll wake up in an hour, fresh as a daisy." She swallowed more coffee. "Keep you up?"

"Him and the feather bed you provided."

She shrugged. "Crime doesn't pay."

"I'm going to strangle you when I get out of here," he promised over the rim of his cup. "Slowly and with great pleasure."

"That isn't the way to get your shower." She turned as the door opened and Tod came in. He stood hesitantly at the door, jamming his hands in his pockets. "Good morning." She smiled and beckoned him in. "You're early."

"You didn't say what time." He came warily, shifting his eyes from Phil to Silas and back to Phil again. "You got prisoners."

"Yes, I do." Catching her tongue between her teeth, she jerked a thumb at Phil. "This one's a nasty character."

"What's he in for?"

"Insufferable arrogance."

"He didn't kill anybody, did he?"

"Not yet," Phil muttered, then added, unable to resist the eager gleam in the boy's eyes, "I was framed."

"They all say that, don't they, Sheriff?"

"Absolutely." She lifted a hand to ruffle the boy's hair. Startled, he jerked and stared at her. Ignoring his reaction, she left her hand on his shoulder. "Well, I'll put you to work, then. There's a broom in the back room. You can start sweeping up. Have you had breakfast?"

"No, but—"

"I'll bring you something when I take care of this guy. Think you can keep an eye on things for me for a few minutes?"

His mouth fell open in astonishment. "Yes, ma'am!"

"Okay, you're in charge." She headed for the door, grabbing her hat on the way. "If Silas wakes up, you can let him out. The other guy stays where he is. Got it?"

"Sure thing, Sheriff." He sent Phil a cool look. "He won't pull nothing on me."

Stifling a laugh, Tory walked outside.

Resigned to the wait, Phil leaned against the bars and drank his coffee while the boy went to work with the broom. He worked industriously, casting furtive glances over his shoulder at Phil from time to time. He's a good-looking boy, Phil mused. He brooded over his reaction to Tory's friendly gesture, wondering how he would react to a man.

"Live in town?" Phil ventured.

Tod paused, eyeing him warily. "Outside."

"On a ranch?"

He began to sweep again, but more slowly. "Yeah."

"Got any horses?"

The boy shrugged. "Couple." He was working his way cautiously over to the cell. "You're not from around here," he said.

"No, I'm from California."

"No, kidding?" Impressed, Tod sized him up again. "You don't look like such a bad guy," he decided.

"Thanks." Phil grinned into his cup.

"How come you're in jail, then?"

Phil pondered over the answer and settled for the unvarnished truth. "I lost my temper."

Tod gave a snort of laughter and continued sweeping. "You can't go to jail for that. My pa loses his all the time."

"Sometimes you can." He studied the boy's profile. "Especially if you hurt someone."

The boy passed the broom over the floor without much regard for dust. "Did you?"

"Just myself," Phil admitted ruefully. "I got the sheriff mad at me."

"Zac Kramer said he don't hold with no woman sheriff."

Phil laughed at that, recalling how easily a woman sheriff had gotten him locked in a cell. "Zac Kramer doesn't sound very smart to me."

Tod sent Phil a swift, appealing grin. "I heard she went to their place yesterday. The twins have to wash all Old Man Hollister's windows, inside and out. For free."

Tory breezed back in with two covered plates. "Breakfast," she announced. "He give you any trouble?" she asked Tod as she set a plate on her desk.

"No, ma'am." The scent of food made his mouth water, but he bent back to his task.

"Okay, sit down and eat."

He shot her a doubtful look. "Me?"

"Yes, you." Carrying the other plate, she walked over to get the keys. "When you and Mr. Kincaid have finished, run the dishes back to the hotel." Without waiting for a response, she unlocked Phil's cell. But Phil watched the expression on Tod's face as he started at his breakfast.

"Sheriff," Phil murmured, taking her hand, rather than the plate she held out to him, "you're a very classy lady." Lifting her hand, he kissed her fingers lightly.

Unable to resist, she allowed her hand to rest in his a moment. "Phil," she said on a sigh, "don't be disarming—you'll complicate things."

His brow lifted in surprise as he studied her. "You know," he said slowly, "I think it's already too late."

Tory shook her head, denying it. "Eat your breakfast," she ordered briskly. "Merle will be coming by with your clothes soon."

When she turned to leave, he held her hand another moment. "Tory," he said quietly, "you and I aren't finished yet."

Carefully she took her hand from his. "You and I never started," she corrected, then closed the door of the cell with a resolute clang. As she headed back to the coffeepot she glanced at Tod. The boy was making his way through bacon and eggs without any trouble.

"Aren't you eating?" Phil asked her as he settled down to his own breakfast.

"I'll never understand how anyone can eat at this hour," Tory muttered, fortifying herself on coffee. "Tod, the sheriff's car could use a wash. Can you handle it?"

"Sure thing, Sheriff." He was half out of the chair before Tory put a restraining hand on his shoulder.

"Eat first," she told him with a chuckle. "If you finish up the sweeping and the car, that should do it for today." She sat on the corner of the desk, enjoying his appetite. "Your parents know where you are?" she asked casually.

"I finished my chores before I left," he mumbled with a full mouth.

"Hmmm." She said nothing more, sipping instead at her coffee. When the door opened, she glanced over, expecting to see Merle. Instead she was struck dumb.

"Lou!" Phil was up and holding on to the bars. "It's about time."

"Well, Phil, you look very natural."

Lou Sherman, Tory thought, sincerely awed. One of the top attorneys in the country. She'd followed his cases, studied his style, used his precedents. He looked just as commanding in person as in any newspaper or magazine picture she'd ever seen of him. He was a huge man, six foot four, with a stocky frame and a wild thatch of white hair. His voice had resonated in courtrooms for more than forty years. He was tenacious, flamboyant and feared. For the moment Tory could only stare at the figure striding into her office in a magnificent pearl-gray suit and baby-pink shirt.

Phil called him an uncomplimentary name, which

made him laugh loudly. "You'd better have some respect if you want me to get you out of there, son." His eyes slid to Phil's half-eaten breakfast. "Finish eating," he advised, "while I talk to the sheriff." Turning, he gazed solemnly from Tory to Tod. "One of you the sheriff?"

Tory hadn't found her voice yet. Tod jerked his head at her. "She is," he stated with his mouth still full.

Lou let his eyes drift down to her badge. "Well, so she is," he said genially. "Best-looking law person I've seen... No offense," he added with a wide grin.

Remembering herself, Tory rose and extended her hand. "Victoria Ashton, Mr. Sherman. It's a pleasure to meet you."

"My pleasure, Sheriff Ashton," he corrected with a great deal of charm. "Tell me, what's the kid done now?"

"Lou—" Phil began, and got an absent wave of the hand from his attorney.

"Finish your eggs," he ordered. "I gave up a perfectly good golf date to fly over here. Sheriff?" he added with a questioning lift of brow.

"Mr. Kincaid was stopped for speeding on Highway Seventeen," Tory began. "When he refused to sign the ticket, my deputy brought him in." After Lou's heavy sigh she continued. "I'm afraid Mr. Kincaid wasn't co-operative."

"Never is," Lou agreed apologetically.

"Damn it, Lou, would you just get me out of here?"

"All in good time," he promised without looking at him. "Are there any other charges, Sheriff?"

"Resisting arrest," she stated, not quite disguising a grin. "The fine is two hundred and fifty, bail set at five hundred. Mr. Kincaid, when he decided to…cooperate, was a bit short of funds."

Lou rubbed a hand over his chin. The large ruby on his pinky glinted dully. "Wouldn't be the first time," he mused.

Incensed at being ignored and defamed at the same time, Phil interrupted tersely. "She pulled a gun on me."

This information was met with another burst of loud laughter from his attorney. "Damn, I wish I'd been here to see his face."

"It was worth the price of a ticket," Tory admitted.

Phil started to launch into a stream of curses, remembered the boy—who was listening avidly—and ground his teeth instead. "Lou," he said slowly, "are you going to get me out or stand around exchanging small talk all day? I haven't had a shower since yesterday."

"Very fastidious," Lou told Tory. "Gets it from his father. I got him out of a tight squeeze or two as I recall. There was this little town in New Jersey… Ah, well, that's another story. I'd like to consult with my client, Sheriff Ashton."

"Of course." Tory retrieved the keys.

"Ashton," Lou murmured, closing his eyes for a moment. "Victoria Ashton. There's something about that name." He stroked his chin. "Been sheriff here long?"

Tory shook her head as she started to unlock Phil's cell. "No, actually I'm just filling in for a while."

"She's a lawyer," Phil said disgustedly.

"That's it!" Lou gave her a pleased look. "I knew the name was familiar. The Dunbarton case. You did a remarkable job."

"Thank you."

"Had your troubles with Judge Withers," he recalled,

flipping through his memory file. "Contempt of court. What was it you called him?"

"A supercilious humbug," Tory said with a wince.

Lou chuckled delightedly. "Wonderful choice of words."

"It cost me a night in jail," she recalled.

"Still, you won the case."

"Luckily the judge didn't hold a grudge."

"Skill and hard work won you that one," Lou disagreed. "Where did you study?"

"Harvard."

"Look," Phil interrupted testily. "You two can discuss this over drinks later."

"Manners, Phil, you've always had a problem with manners." Lou smiled at Tory again. "Excuse me, Sheriff. Well, Phil, give me one of those corn muffins there and tell me your troubles."

Tory left them in privacy just as Merle walked in, carrying Phil's suitcase. Dynamite wandered in behind him, found his spot on the floor and instantly went to sleep. "Just leave that by the desk," Tory told Merle. "After Kincaid's taken care of, I'm going out to the house for a while. You won't be able to reach me for two hours."

"Okay." He glanced at the still-snoring Silas. "Should I kick him out?"

"When he wakes up." She looked over at Tod. "Tod's going to wash my car."

Stuffing in the last bite, Tod scrambled up. "I'll do it now." He dashed out the front door.

Tory frowned after him. "Merle, what do you know about Tod's father?"

He shrugged and scratched at his mustache. "Swanson keeps to himself, raises some cattle couple miles north of town. Been in a couple of brawls, but nothing important."

"His mother?"

"Quiet lady. Does some cleaning work over at the hotel now and again. You remember the older brother, don't you? He lit out a couple years ago. Never heard from him since."

Tory absorbed this with a thoughtful nod. "Keep an eye out for the boy when I'm not around, okay?"

"Sure. He in trouble?"

"I'm not certain." She frowned a moment, then her expression relaxed again. "Just keep your eyes open, Merle T.," she said, smiling at him affectionately. "Why don't you go see if the kid's found a bucket? I don't think it would take much persuasion to get him to wash your car too."

Pleased with the notion, Merle strode out again.

"Sheriff—" Tory turned back to the cell as Lou came out "—my client tells me you also serve as justice of the peace?"

"That's right, Mr. Sherman."

"In that case, I'd like to plead temporary insanity on the part of my client."

"You're cute, Lou," Phil muttered from the cell door. "Can I take that shower now?" he demanded, indicating his suitcase.

"In the back," Tory told him. "You need a shave," she added sweetly.

He picked up the case, giving her a long look. "Sheriff, when this is all over, you and I have some personal business."

Tory lifted her half-finished coffee. "Don't cut your throat, Kincaid."

Lou waited until Phil had disappeared into the back room. "He's a good boy," he said with a paternal sigh. Tory burst out laughing.

"Oh, no," she said definitely, "he's not."

"Well, it was worth a try." He shrugged it off and settled his enormous bulk into a chair. "About the charge of resisting arrest," he began. "I'd really hate for it to go on his record. A night in jail was quite a culture shock for our Phillip, Victoria."

"Agreed." She smiled. "I believe that charge could be dropped if Mr. Kincaid pays the speeding fine."

"I've advised him to do so," Lou told her, pulling out a thick cigar. "He doesn't like it, but I'm…" He studied the cigar like a lover. "Persuasive," he decided. He shot her an admiring look. "So are you. What kind of a gun?"

Tory folded her hands primly. "A .45."

Lou laughed heartily as he lit his cigar. "Now, tell me about the Dunbarton case, Victoria."

The horse kicked up a cloud of brown dust. Responding to Tory's command, he broke into an easy gallop. Air, as dry as the land around them, whipped by them in a warm rush. The hat Tory had worn to shield herself from the sun lay on the back of her neck, forgotten. Her movements were so attuned to the horse, she was barely conscious of his movements beneath her. Tory wanted to think, but first she wanted to clear her mind. Since childhood, riding had been her one sure way of doing so.

Sports had no appeal for her. She saw no sense in

hitting or chasing a ball around some court or course. It took too much energy. She might swim a few laps now and again, but found it much more agreeable to float on a raft. Sweating in a gym was laughable. But riding was a different category. Tory didn't consider it exercise or effort. She used it now, as she had over the years, as a way to escape from her thoughts for a short time.

For thirty minutes she rode without any thought of destination. Gradually she slowed the horse to a walk, letting her hands relax on the reins. He would turn, she knew, and head back to the ranch.

Phillip Kincaid. He shot back into her brain. A nuisance, Tory decided. One that should be over. At the moment he should already be back on his way to L.A. Tory dearly hoped so. She didn't like to admit that he had gotten to her. It was unfortunate that despite their clash, despite his undeniable arrogance, she had liked him. He was interesting and funny and sharp. It was difficult to dislike someone who could laugh at himself. There would be no problem if it ended there.

Feeling the insistent beat of the sun on her head, Tory absently replaced her hat. It hadn't ended there because there had been that persistent attraction. That was strictly man to woman, and she hadn't counted on it when she had tossed him in jail. He'd outmaneuvered her once. That was annoying, but the result had been much deeper. When was the last time she had completely forgotten herself in a man's arms? When was the last time she had spent most of the night thinking about a man? Had she ever? Tory let out a deep breath, then frowned at the barren, stone-colored landscape.

No, her reaction had been too strong for comfort— and the fact that she was still thinking about him disturbed her. A woman her age didn't dwell on one kiss that way. Yet, she could still remember exactly how his mouth had molded to hers, how the dark, male taste of him had seeped into her. With no effort at all, she could feel the way his body had fit against hers, strong and hard. It didn't please her.

There were enough problems to be dealt with during her stay in Friendly, Tory reminded herself, without dwelling on a chance encounter with some bad-tempered Hollywood type. She'd promised to ease the town through its transition to a new sheriff; there was the boy, Tod, on her mind. And her mother. Tory closed her eyes for a moment. She had yet to come to terms with her mother.

So many things had been said after her father's death. So many things had been left unsaid. For a woman who was rarely confused, Tory found herself in a turmoil whenever she dealt with her mother. As long as her father had been alive, he'd been the buffer between them. Now, with him gone, they were faced with each other. With a wry laugh Tory decided her mother was just as baffled as she was. The strain between them wasn't lessening, and the distance was growing. With a shake of her head she decided to let it lie. In a few months Tory would be back in Albuquerque and that would be that. She had her life to live, her mother had hers.

The wise thing to do, she mused, was to develop the same attitude toward Phil Kincaid. Their paths weren't likely to cross again. She had purposely absented herself from town for a few hours to avoid him. Tory made a face at the admission. No, she didn't want to see him again. He was trouble. It was entirely too easy for him to be charming when he put his mind to it. And she was wise enough to recognize determination when she saw it. For whatever reason—pique or attraction—he wanted her. He wouldn't be an easy man to handle. Under most circumstances Tory might have enjoyed pitting her will against his, but something warned her not to press her luck.

"The sooner he's back in Tinsel Town, the better," she muttered, then pressed her heels against the horse's sides. They were off at a full gallop.

Phil pulled his car to a halt beside the corral and glanced around. A short distance to the right was a small white-framed house. It was a very simple structure, two stories high, with a wide wooden porch. On the side was a clothesline with a few things baking dry in the sun. There were a few spots of color from flowers in pottery pots on either side of the steps. The grass was short and parched. One of the window screens was torn. In the background he could see a few outbuildings and what appeared to be the beginnings of a vegetable garden. Tory's sheriff's car was parked in front, freshly washed but already coated with a thin film of dust.

Something about the place appealed to him. It was isolated and quiet. Without the car in front, it might fit into any time frame in the past century. There had been some efforts to keep it neat, but it would never be prosperous. He would consider it more a homestead than a ranch. With the right lighting, he mused, it could be very effective. Climbing out of the car, Phil moved to the right to study it from a different angle. When he heard the low drum of hoofs, he turned and watched Tory approach.

He forgot the house immediately and swore at his

lack of a camera. She was perfect. Under the merciless
sun she rode a palamino the shade of new gold. Nothing could have been a better contrast for a woman of
her coloring. With her hat again at her back, her hair
flew freely. She sat straight, her movements in perfect
timing with the horse's. Phil narrowed his eyes and
saw them in slow motion. That was how he would film
it—with her hair lifting, holding for a moment before it
fell again. The dust would hang in the air behind them.
The horse's strong legs would fold and unfold so that the
viewer could see each muscle work. This was strength
and beauty and a mastery of rider over horse. He wished
he could see her hands holding the reins.

He knew the moment she became aware of him.
The rhythm never faltered, but there was a sudden
tension in the set of her shoulders. It made him smile.
No, we're not through yet, he thought to himself. Not
nearly through. Leaning against the corral fence, he
waited for her.

Tory brought the palamino to a stop with a quick
tug of reins. Remaining in the saddle, she gave Phil a
long, silent look. Casually he took sunglasses out of his
pocket and slipped them on. The gesture annoyed her.
"Kincaid," she said coolly.

"Sheriff," he returned.

"Is there a problem?"

He smiled slowly. "I don't think so."

Tory tossed her hair behind her shoulder, trying to
disguise the annoyance she felt at finding him there. "I
thought you'd be halfway to L.A. by now."

"Did you?"

With a sound of impatience she dismounted. The
saddle creaked with the movement as she brought one

slim leg over it, then vaulted lightly to the ground. Keeping the reins in her hand, she studied him a moment. "I assume your fine's been paid. You know the other charges were dropped."

"Yes."

She tilted her head. "Well?"

"Well," he returned amiably, amused at the temper that shot into her eyes. *Yes, I'm getting to you, Victoria, he thought, and I haven't even started yet.*

Deliberately she turned away to uncinch the saddle. "Has Mr. Sherman gone?"

"No, he's discussing flies and lures with the mayor." Phil grinned. "Lou found a fishing soulmate."

"I see." Tory hefted the saddle from the palamino, then set it on the fence. "Then you discussed your business with the mayor this morning."

"We came to an amicable agreement," Phil replied, watching as she slipped the bit from the horse's mouth. "He'll give you the details."

Without speaking, Tory gave the horse a slap on the flank, sending him inside the corral. The gate gave a long creak as she shut it. She turned then to face Phil directly. "Why should he?"

"You'll want to know the schedule and so forth before the filming starts."

Her brows drew together. "I beg your pardon."

"I came to New Mexico scouting out a location for my new movie. I needed a tired little town in the middle of nowhere."

Tory studied him for a full ten seconds. "And you found it," she said flatly.

"Thanks to you." He smiled, appreciating the irony. "We'll start next month."

Sticking her hands in her back pockets, Tory turned to walk a short distance away. "Wouldn't it be simpler to shoot in a studio or in a lot?"

"No."

At his flat answer she turned back again. "I don't like it."

"I didn't think you would." He moved over to join her. "But you're going to live with it for the better part of the summer."

"You're going to bring your cameras and your people and your confusion into town," she began angrily. "Friendly runs at its own pace. Now you want to bring in a lifestyle most of these people can't even imagine."

"We'll give very sedate orgies, Sheriff," he promised with a grin. He laughed at the fury that leaped to her eyes. "Tory, you're not a fool. We're not coming to party, we're coming to work. Keep an actor out in this sun for ten takes, he's not going to be disturbing the peace at night. He's going to be unconscious." He caught a strand of her hair and twisted it around his finger. "Or do you believe everything you read in *Inside Scoop?*"

She swiped his hand away in an irritated gesture. "I know more about Hollywood than you know about Friendly," she retorted. "I've spent some time in L.A., represented a screenwriter in an assault case. Got him off," she added wryly. "A few years ago I dated an actor, went to a few parties when I was on the coast." She shook her head. "The gossip magazines might exaggerate, Phil, but the values and lifestyle come through loud and clear."

He lifted a brow. "Judgmental, Tory?"

"Maybe," she agreed. "But this is my town. I'm responsible for the people and for the peace. If you go ahead with this, I warn you, one of your people gets out of line, he goes to jail."

His eyes narrowed. "We have our own security."

"Your security answers to me in my town," she tossed back. "Remember it."

"Not going to cooperate, are you?"

"Not any more than I have to."

For a moment they stood measuring each other in silence. Behind them the palamino paced restlessly around the corral. A fleeting, precious breeze came up to stir the heat and dust. "All right," Phil said at length, "let's say you stay out of my way, I'll stay out of yours."

"Perfect," Tory agreed, and started to walk away. Phil caught her arm.

"That's professionally," he added.

As she had in his cell, Tory gave the hand on her arm a long look before she raised her eyes to his. This time Phil smiled.

"You're not wearing your badge now, Tory." Reaching up, he drew off his sunglasses, then hooked them over the corral fence. "And we're not finished."

"Kincaid—"

"Phil," he corrected, drawing her deliberately into his arms. "I thought of you last night when I was lying in that damned cell. I promised myself something."

Tory stiffened. Her palms pressed against his chest, but she didn't struggle. Physically he was stronger, she reasoned. She had to rely on her wits. "Your thoughts and your promises aren't my problem," she replied coolly. "Whether I'm wearing my badge or not, I'm still sheriff, and you're annoying me. I can be mean when I'm annoyed."

"I'll just bet you can be," he murmured. Even had he wanted to, he couldn't prevent his eyes from lingering on her mouth. "I'm going to have you, Victoria," he said softly. "Sooner or later." Slowly he brought his eyes back to hers. "I always keep my promises."

"I believe I have something to say about this one."

His smile was confident. "Say no," he whispered before his mouth touched hers. She started to jerk back, but he was quick. His hand cupped the back of her head and kept her still. His mouth was soft and persuasive. Long before the stiffness left her, he felt the pounding of her heart against his. Patiently he rubbed his lips over hers, teasing, nibbling. Tory let out an unsteady breath as her fingers curled into his shirt.

He smelled of soap, a fragrance that was clean and sharp. Unconsciously she breathed it in as he drew her closer. Her arms had found their way around his neck. Her body was straining against his, no longer stiff but eager. The mindless pleasure was back, and she surrendered to it. She heard his quiet moan before his lips left hers, but before she could protest, he pressed them to her throat. He was murmuring something neither of them understood as his mouth began to explore. The desperation came suddenly, as if it had been waiting to take them both unaware. His mouth was back on hers with a quick savageness that she anticipated.

She felt the scrape of his teeth and answered by nipping into his bottom lip. The hands at her hips dragged her closer, tormenting both of them. Passion flowed between them so acutely that avid, seeking lips weren't enough. He ran his hands up her sides, letting his thumbs find their way between their clinging bodies to stroke her breasts. She responded by diving deep into his mouth and demanding more.

Tory felt everything with impossible clarity: the soft, thin material of her shirt rubbing against the straining points of her breasts as his thumbs pressed against her; the heat of his mouth as it roamed wildly over her face, then back to hers; the vibration of two heartbeats.

He hadn't expected to feel this degree of need. Attraction and challenge, but not pain. It wasn't what he had planned—it wasn't what he wanted, and yet, he couldn't stop. She was filling his mind, crowding his senses. Her hair was too soft, her scent too alluring. And her taste…her taste too exotic. Greedily, he devoured her while her passion drove him farther into her.

He knew he had to back away, but he lingered a moment longer. Her body was so sleek and lean, her mouth so incredibly agile. Phil allowed himself to stroke her once more, one last bruising contact of lips before he dragged himself away.

They were both shaken and both equally determined not to admit it. Tory felt her pulse hammering at every point in her body. Because her knees were trembling, she stood very straight. Phil waited a moment, wanting to be certain he could speak. Reaching over, he retrieved his sunglasses and put them back on. They were some defense; a better one was to put some distance between them until he found his control.

"You didn't say no," he commented.

Tory stared at him, warning herself not to think until later. "I didn't say yes," she countered.

He smiled. "Oh, yes," he corrected, "you did. I'll be back," he added before he strode to his car.

Driving away, he glanced in his rearview mirror to

see her standing where he had left her. As he punched in his cigarette lighter he saw his hand was shaking. Round three, he thought on a long breath, was a draw.

Chapter 4

Tory stood exactly where she was until even the dust kicked up by Phil's tires had settled. She had thought she knew the meaning of passion, need, excitement. Suddenly the words had taken on a new meaning. For the first time in her life she had been seized by something that her mind couldn't control. The hunger had been so acute, so unexpected. It throbbed through her still, like an ache, as she stared down the long flat road, which was now deserted. How was it possible to need so badly, so quickly? And how was it, she wondered, that a woman who had always handled men with such casual ease could be completely undone by a kiss?

Tory shook her head and made herself turn away from the road Phil had taken. None of it was characteristic. It was almost as if she had been someone else for a moment—someone whose strength and weakness could be drawn out and manipulated. And yet, even now, when she had herself under control, there was something inside her fighting to be recognized. She was going to have to take some time and think about this carefully.

Hoisting the saddle, Tory carried it toward the barn. *I'll be back.* Phil's last words echoed in her ears and sent an odd thrill over her skin. Scowling, Tory pushed open the barn door. It was cooler inside, permeated with the pungent scent of animals and hay. It was a scent of her childhood, one she barely noticed even when returning after months away from it. It never occurred to her to puzzle over why she was as completely at home there as she was in a tense courtroom or at a sophisticated party. After replacing the tack, she paced the concrete floor a moment and began to dissect the problem.

Phil Kincaid was the problem; the offshoots were her strong attraction to him, his effect on her and the fact that he was coming back. The attraction, Tory decided, was unprecedented but not astonishing. He was appealing, intelligent, fun. Even his faults had a certain charm. If they had met under different circumstances, she could imagine them getting to know each other slowly, dating perhaps, enjoying a congenial relationship. Part of the spark, she mused, was due to the way they had met, and the fact that each was determined not to be outdone by the other. That made sense, she concluded, feeling better.

And if that made sense, she went on, it followed that his effect on her was intensified by circumstances. Logic was comfortable, so Tory pursued it. There was something undeniably attractive about a man who wouldn't take no for an answer. It might be annoying, even infuriating, but it was still exciting. Beneath the sheriff's badge and behind the Harvard diploma, Tory was a woman first and last. It didn't hurt when a man knew how to kiss the way Phil Kincaid knew how to kiss, she added wryly. Unable to resist, Tory ran the tip of her tongue over her lips. Oh, yes, she thought with a quick smile, the man was some terrific kisser.

Vaguely annoyed with herself, Tory wandered from the barn. The sun made her wince in defense as she headed for the house. Unconsciously killing time, she poked inside the henhouse. The hens were sleeping in the heat of the afternoon, their heads tucked under their wings. Tory left them alone, knowing her mother had gathered the eggs that morning.

The problem now was that he was coming back. She was going to have to deal with him—and with his own little slice of Hollywood, she added with a frown. At the moment Tory wasn't certain which disturbed her more. Damn, but she wished she'd known of Phil's plans. If she could have gotten to the mayor first… Tory stopped herself with a self-deprecating laugh. She would have changed absolutely nothing. As mayor, Bud Toomey would eat up the prestige of having a major film shot in his town. And as the owner of the one and only hotel, he must have heard the dollars clinking in his cash register.

Who could blame him? Tory asked herself. Her objections were probably more personal than professional in any case. The actor she had dated had been successful and slick, an experienced womanizer and hedonist. She knew too many of her prejudices lay at his feet. She'd been very young when he'd shown her Hollywood from his vantage point. But even without that, she reasoned, there was the disruption the filming would bring to Friendly, the effect on the townspeople and the very real possibility of property damage. As sheriff, all of it fell to her jurisdiction.

What would her father have done? she wondered as she stepped into the house. As always, the moment she was inside, memories of him assailed her—his big, booming voice, his laughter, his simple, man-of-the-earth logic. To Tory his presence was an intimate part of everything in the house, down to the hassock where he had habitually rested his feet after a long day.

The house was her mother's doing. There were the clean white walls in the living room, the sofa that had been re-covered again and again—this time it wore a tidy floral print. The rugs were straight and clean, the pictures carefully aligned. Even they had been chosen to blend in rather than to accent. Her mother's collection of cacti sat on the windowsill. The fragrance of a potpourri, her mother's mixture, wafted comfortably in the air. The floors and furniture were painstakingly clean, magazines neatly tucked away. A single geranium stood in a slender vase on a crocheted doily. All her mother's doing; yet, it was her father Tory thought of when she entered her childhood home. It always was.

But her father wouldn't come striding down the steps again. He wouldn't catch her to him for one of his bear hugs and noisy kisses. He'd been too young to die, Tory thought as she gazed around the room as though she were a stranger. Strokes were for old men, feeble men, not strapping men in their prime. There was no justice to it, she thought with the same impotent fury that hit her each time she came back. No justice for a man who had dedicated his life to justice. He should have had more time, might have had more time, if... Her thoughts broke off as she heard the quiet sounds coming from the kitchen.

Tory pushed away the pain. It was difficult enough to see her mother without remembering that last night in the hospital. She gave herself an extra moment to settle before she crossed to the kitchen.

Standing in the doorway, she watched as Helen relined the shelves in the kitchen cabinets. Her mother's consistent tidiness had been a sore point between them since Tory had been a girl. The woman she watched was tiny and blond, a youthful-looking fifty, with ladylike hands and a trim pink housedress. Tory knew the dress had been pressed and lightly starched. Her mother would smell faintly of soap and nothing else. Even physically Tory felt remote from her. Her looks, her temperament, had all come from her father. Tory could see nothing of herself in the woman who patiently lined shelves with dainty striped paper. They'd never been more than careful strangers to each other, more careful as the years passed. Tory kept a room at the hotel rather than at home for the same reason she kept her visits with her mother brief. Invariably their encounters ended badly.

"Mother."

Surprised, Helen turned. She didn't gasp or whirl at the intrusion, but simply faced Tory with one brow slightly lifted. "Tory. I thought I heard a car drive away."

"It was someone else."

"I saw you ride out." Helen straightened the paper meticulously. "There's lemonade in the refrigerator. It's a dry day." Without speaking, Tory fetched two glasses and added ice. "How are you, Tory?"

"Very well." She hated the stiffness but could do

nothing about it. So much stood between them. Even as she poured the fresh lemonade from her mother's marigold-trimmed glass pitcher, she could remember the night of her father's death, the ugly words she had spoken, the ugly feelings she had not quite put to rest. They had never understood each other, never been close, but that night had brought a gap between them that neither knew how to bridge. It only seemed to grow wider with time.

Needing to break the silence, Tory spoke as she replaced the pitcher in the refrigerator. "Do you know anything about the Swansons?"

"The Swansons?" The question in Helen's voice was mild. She would never have asked directly. "They've lived outside of town for twenty years. They keep to themselves, though she's come to church a few times. I believe he has a difficult time making his ranch pay. The oldest son was a good-looking boy, about sixteen when he left." Helen replaced her everyday dishes on the shelf in tidy stacks, then closed the cupboard door. "That would have been about four years ago. The younger one seems rather sweet and painfully shy."

"Tod," Tory murmured.

"Yes." Helen read the concern but knew nothing about drawing people out, particularly her daughter. "I heard about Mr. Hollister's window."

Tory lifted her eyes briefly. Her mother's were a calm, deep brown. "The Kramer twins."

A suggestion of a smile flickered on her mother's lips. "Yes, of course."

"Do you know why the older Swanson boy left home?"

Helen picked up the drink Tory had poured her. But

she didn't sit. "Rumor is that Mr. Swanson has a temper. Gossip is never reliable," she added before she drank.

"And often based in fact," Tory countered.

They fell into one of the stretches of silence that characteristically occurred during their visits. The refrigerator gave a loud click and began to hum. Helen carefully wiped away the ring of moisture her glass had made on the countertop.

"It seems Friendly is about to be immortalized on film," Tory began. At her mother's puzzled look she continued. "I had Phillip C. Kincaid in a cell overnight. Now it appears he's going to use Friendly as one of the location shoots for his latest film."

"Kincaid," Helen repeated, searching her mind slowly. "Oh, Marshall Kincaid's son."

Tory grinned despite herself. She didn't think Phil would appreciate that sort of recognition; it occurred to her simultaneously that it was a tag he must have fought all of his professional career. "Yes," she agreed thoughtfully. "He's a very successful director," she found herself saying, almost in defense, "with an impressive string of hits. He's been nominated for an Oscar three times."

Though Helen digested this, her thoughts were still on Tory's original statement. "Did you say you had him in jail?"

Tory shook off the mood and smiled a little. "Yes, I did. Traffic violation," she added with a shrug. "It got a little complicated...." Her voice trailed off as she remembered that stunning moment in his cell when his mouth had taken hers. "He's coming back," she murmured.

"To make a film?" Helen prompted, puzzled by her daughter's bemused expression.

"What? Yes," Tory said quickly. "Yes, he's going to do some filming here, I don't have the details yet. It seems he cleared it with the mayor this morning."

But not with you, Helen thought, but didn't say so. "How interesting."

"We'll see," Tory muttered. Suddenly restless, she rose to pace to the sink. The view from the window was simply a long stretch of barren ground that was somehow fascinating. Her father had loved it for what it was—stark and desolate.

Watching her daughter, Helen could remember her husband standing exactly the same way, looking out with exactly the same expression. She felt an intolerable wave of grief and controlled it. "Friendly will be buzzing about this for quite some time," she said briskly.

"It'll buzz all right," Tory muttered. But no one will think of the complications, she added to herself.

"Do you expect trouble?" her mother asked.

"I'll handle it."

"Always so sure of yourself, Tory."

Tory's shoulders stiffened automatically. "Am I, Mother?" Turning, she found her mother's eyes, calm and direct, on her. They had been just that calm, and just that direct, when she had told Tory she had requested her father's regulator be unplugged. Tory had seen no sorrow, no regret or indecision. There had been only the passive face and the matter-of-fact words. For that, more than anything else, Tory had never forgiven her.

As they watched each other in the sun-washed kitchen, each remembered clearly the garishly lit waiting room that smelled of old cigarettes and sweat. Each remembered the monotonous hum of the air conditioner and the click of feet on tile in the corridor outside....

"No!" Tory had whispered the word, then shouted it. "No, you can't! You can't just let him die!"

"He's already gone, Tory," Helen had said flatly. "You have to accept it."

"No!" After weeks of seeing her father lying motionless with a machine pumping oxygen into his body, Tory had been crazy with grief and fear. She had been a long, long way from acceptance. She'd watched her mother sit calmly while she had paced—watched her sip tea while her own stomach had revolted at the thought of food. *Brain-dead.* The phrase had made her violently ill. It was she who had wept uncontrollably at her father's bedside while Helen had stood dry-eyed.

"You don't care," Tory had accused. "It's easier for you this way. You can go back to your precious routine and not be disturbed."

Helen had looked at her daughter's ravaged face and nodded. "It is easier this way."

"I won't let you." Desperate, Tory had pushed her hands through her hair and tried to think. "There are ways to stop you. I'll get a court order, and—"

"It's already done," Helen had told her quietly.

All the color had drained from Tory's face, just as she had felt all the strength drain from her body. Her father was dead. At the flick of a switch he was dead. Her mother had flicked the switch. "You killed him."

Helen hadn't winced or shrunk from the words. "You know better than that, Tory."

"If you'd loved him—if you'd loved him, you couldn't have done this."

"And your kind of love would have him strapped to that machine, helpless and empty."

"Alive!" Tory had tossed back, letting hate wash over the unbearable grief. "Damn you, he was still alive."

"Gone," Helen had countered, never raising her voice. "He'd been gone for days. For weeks, really. It's time you dealt with it."

"It's so easy for you, isn't it?" Tory had forced back the tears because she had wanted—needed—to meet her mother on her own terms. "Nothing—no one—has ever managed to make you *feel*. Not even him."

"There are different kinds of love, Tory," Helen returned stiffly. "You've never understood anything but your own way."

"Love?" Tory had gripped her hands tightly together to keep from striking out. "I've never seen you show anyone love. Now Dad's gone, but you don't cry. You don't mourn. You'll go home and hang out the wash because nothing—by God, nothing—can interfere with your precious routine."

Helen's shoulders had been very straight as she faced her daughter. "I won't apologize for being what I am," she had said. "Any more than I expect you to defend yourself to me. But I do say you loved your father too much, Victoria. For that I'm sorry."

Tory had wrapped her arms around herself tightly, unconsciously rocking. "Oh, you're so cold," she had whispered. "So cold. You have no feelings." She had badly needed comfort then, a word, an arm around her. But Helen was unable to offer, Tory unable to ask. "You did this," she had said in a strained, husky voice. "You took him from me. I'll never forgive you for it."

"No." Helen had nodded slightly. "I don't expect you will. You're always so sure of yourself, Tory."

Now the two women watched each other across a new grave: dry-eyed, expressionless. A man who had been husband and father stood between them still. Words threatened to pour out again—harsh, bitter words. Each swallowed them.

"I have to get back to town," Tory told her. She walked from the room and from the house. After standing in the silence a moment, Helen turned back to her shelves.

The pool was shaped like a crescent and its water was deep, deep blue. There were palm trees swaying gently in the night air. The scent of flowers was strong, almost tropical. It was a cool spot, secluded by trees, banked with blossoming bushes. A narrow terrace outlined the pool with mosaic tile that glimmered in the moonlight. Speakers had been craftily camouflaged so that the strains of Debussy seemed to float out of the air. A tall iced drink laced with Jamaican rum sat on a glass-topped patio table beside a telephone.

Still wet from his swim, Phil lounged on a chaise. Once again he tried to discipline his mind. He'd spent the entire day filming two key scenes in the studio. He'd had a little trouble with Sam Dressler, the leading man. It wasn't surprising. Dressler didn't have a reputation for being congenial or cooperative, just for being good. Phil wasn't looking to make a lifelong friendship, just a film. Still, when the clashes began this early in a production, it wasn't a good omen of things to come. He was going to have to use some strategy in handling Dressler.

At least, Phil mused as he absently picked up his

drink, he'd have no trouble with the crew. He'd hand-picked them and had worked with each and every one of them before. Bicks, his cinematographer, was the best in the business—creative enough to be innovative and practical enough not to insist on making a statement with each frame. His assistant director was a workhorse who knew the way Phil's mind worked. Phil knew his crew down to the last gaffer and grip. When they went on location...

Phil's thoughts drifted back to Tory, as they had insisted on doing for days. She was going to be pretty stiff-necked about having her town invaded, he reflected. She'd hang over his shoulder with that tin badge pinned to her shirt. Phil hated to admit that the idea appealed to him. With a little pre-planning, he could find a number of ways to put himself in her path. Oh, yes, he intended to spend quite a bit of time getting under Sheriff Ashton's skin.

Soft, smooth skin, Phil remembered, that smelled faintly of something that a man might find in a harem. Dark, dusky and titillating. He could picture her in silk, something chic and vivid, with nothing underneath but that long, lean body of hers.

The quick flash of desire annoyed him enough to cause him to toss back half his drink. He intended to get under her skin, but he didn't intend for it to work the other way around. He knew women, how to please them, charm them. He also knew how to avoid the complication of *one* woman. There was safety in numbers; using that maxim, Phil had enjoyed his share of women.

He liked them not only sexually but as companions. A great many of the women whose names he had been romantically linked with were simply friends. The number of women he had been credited with conquering amused him. He could hardly have worked the kind of schedule he imposed on himself if he spent all his time in the bedroom. Still, he had enjoyed perhaps a bit more than his share of romances, always careful to keep the tone light and the rules plain. He intended to do exactly the same thing with Tory.

It might be true that she was on his mind a great deal more often than any other woman in his memory. It might be true that he had been affected more deeply by her than anyone else. But...

Phil frowned over the *but* a moment. But, he re-affirmed, it was just because their meeting had been unique. The memory of his night in the steamy little cell caused him to grimace. He hadn't paid her back for that yet, and he was determined to. He hadn't cared for being under someone else's control. He'd grown used to deference in his life, a respect that had come first through his parents and then through his own talent. He never thought much about money. The fact that he hadn't been able to buy himself out of the cell was infuriating. Though more often than not he did for himself, he was accustomed to servants—perhaps more to having his word obeyed. Tory hadn't done what he ordered, and had done what he asked only when it had suited her.

It didn't matter that Phil was annoyed when people fawned over him or catered to him. That was what he was used to. Instead of fawning, Tory had been lightly disdainful, had tossed out a compliment on his work, then laughed at him. And had made him laugh, he remembered.

He wanted to know more about her. For days he had toyed with the notion of having someone check into

Victoria L. Ashton, Attorney. What had stopped him had not been a respect for privacy so much as a desire to make the discoveries himself. Who was a woman who had a face like a madonna, a voice like whiskey and honey and handled a .45? Phil was going to find out if it took all of the dry, dusty summer. He'd find the time, he mused, although the shooting schedule was backbreaking.

Leaning back against the cushion of the chaise, Phil looked up at the sky. He'd refused the invitation to a party on the excuse that he had work and a scene to shoot early in the morning. Now he was thinking of Tory instead of the film, and he no longer had any sense of time. He knew he should work her out of his system so that he could give the film his full attention, without distractions. He knew he wouldn't. Since he'd returned from Friendly, he hadn't had the least inclination to pick up the phone and call any of the women he knew. He could pacify friends and acquaintances by using the excuse of his work schedule, but he knew. There was only one companion he wanted at the moment, one woman. One lover.

He wanted to kiss her again to be certain he hadn't imagined the emotions he had felt. And the sense of *rightness*. Oddly, he found he didn't want to dilute the sensation with the taste or feel of another woman. It worried him but he brushed it off, telling himself that the obsession would fade once he had Tory where he wanted her. What worried him more was the fact that he wanted to talk to her. Just talk.

Vaguely disturbed, Phil rose. He was tired, that was all. And there was that new script to read before he went to bed. The house was silent when he entered through the glass terrace doors. Even the music had stopped without his noticing. He stepped down into the sunken living room, the glass still in his hand.

The room smelled very faintly of the lemon oil the maid had used that morning. The maroon floor tiles shone. On the deep, plump cushions of the sofa a dozen pillows were tossed with a carelessness that was both inviting and lush. He himself had chosen the tones of blue and green and ivory that dominated the room, as well as the Impressionist painting on the wall, the only artwork in the room. There were mirrors and large expanses of windows that gave the room openness. It held nothing of the opulence of the houses he had grown up in, yet maintained the same ambience of money and success. Phil was easy with it, as he was with his life, himself and his views on his future.

Crossing the room, he walked toward the curving open staircase that led to the second floor. The treads were uncarpeted. His bare feet slapped the wood gently. He was thinking that he had been pleased with the rushes. He and Huffman had watched them together. Now that the filming was progressing, his producer was more amiable. There were fewer mutterings about guarantors and cost overruns. And Huffman had been pleased with the idea of shooting the bulk of the film on location. Financially the deal with Friendly had been advantageous. Nothing put a smile on a producer's face quicker, Phil thought wryly. He went to shower.

The bath was enormous. Even more than the secluded location, it had been Phil's main incentive for buying the house high in the hills. The shower ran along one wall, with the spray shooting from both sides. He switched it on, stripping out of his trunks while the bathroom grew steamy. Even as he stepped inside, he remembered the cramped little stall he had showered in that stifling morning in Friendly.

The soap had still been wet, he recalled, from Tory. It had been a curiously intimate feeling to rub the small cake along his own skin and imagine it sliding over hers. Then he had run out of hot water while he was still covered with lather. He'd cursed her fluently and wanted her outrageously. Standing between the hot crisscrossing sprays, Phil knew he still did. On impulse he reached out and grabbed the phone that hung on the wall beside the shower.

"I want to place a call to Friendly, New Mexico," he told the operator. Ignoring the time, he decided to take a chance. "The sheriff's office." Phil waited while steam rose from the shower. The phone clicked and hummed then rang.

"Sheriff's office."

The sound of her voice made him grin. "Sheriff."

Tory frowned, setting down the coffee that was keeping her awake over the brief she was drafting. "Yes?"

"Phil Kincaid."

There was complete silence as Tory's mouth opened and closed. She felt a thrill she considered ridiculously juvenile and straightened at her desk. "Well," she said lightly, "did you forget your toothbrush?"

"No." He was at a loss for a moment, struggling to formulate a reasonable excuse for the call. He wasn't a love-struck teenager who called his girl just to hear her voice. "The shooting's on schedule," he told her, thinking fast. "We'll be in Friendly next week. I wanted to be certain there were no problems."

Tory glanced over at the cell, remembering how he

had looked standing there. "Your location manager has been in touch with me and the mayor," she said, deliberately turning her eyes away from the cell. "You have all the necessary permits. The hotel's booked for you. I had to fight to keep my own room. Several people are making arrangements to rent out rooms in their homes to accommodate you." She didn't have to add that the idea didn't appeal to her. Her tone told him everything. Again he found himself grinning.

"Still afraid we're going to corrupt your town, Sheriff?"

"You and your people will stay in line, Kincaid," she returned, "or you'll have your old room back."

"It's comforting to know you have it waiting for me. Are you?"

"Waiting for you?" She gave a quick snort of laughter. "Just like the Egyptians waited for the next plague."

"Ah, Victoria, you've a unique way of putting things."

Tory frowned, listening to the odd hissing on the line. "What's that noise?"

"Noise?"

"It sounds like water running."

"It is," he told her. "I'm in the shower."

For a full ten seconds Tory said nothing, then she burst out laughing. "Phil, why did you call me from the shower?"

Something about her laughter and the way she said his name had him struggling against a fresh torrent of needs. "Because it reminded me of you."

Tory propped her feet on the desk, forgetting her brief. Something in her was softening. "Oh?" was all she said.

"I remembered running out of hot water halfway through my shower in your guest room." He pushed wet hair out of his eyes. "At the time I wasn't in the mood to lodge a formal complaint."

"I'll take it up with the management." She caught her tongue between her teeth for a moment. "I wouldn't expect deluxe accommodations in the hotel, Kincaid. There's no room service or phones in the bathroom."

"We'll survive."

"That's yet to be seen," she said dryly. "Your group may undergo culture shock when they find themselves without a Jacuzzi."

"You really think we're a soft bunch, don't you?" Annoyed, Phil switched the phone to his other hand. It nearly slid out of his wet palm. "You may learn a few things about the people in the business this summer, Victoria. I'm going to enjoy teaching you."

"There's nothing I want to learn from you," she said quietly.

"*Want* and *need* are entirely different words," he pointed out. He could almost see the flash of temper leap into her eyes. It gave him a curious pleasure.

"As long as you play by the rules, there won't be any trouble."

"There'll be a time, Tory," he murmured into the receiver, "that you and I will play by my rules. I still have a promise to keep."

Tory pulled her legs from the desk so that her boots hit the floor with a clatter. "Don't forget to wash behind your ears," she ordered, then hung up with a bang.

Chapter 5

Tory was in her office when they arrived. The rumble of cars outside could mean only one thing. She forced herself to complete the form she was filling out before she rose from her desk. Of course she wasn't in any hurry to see him again, but it was her duty to be certain the town remained orderly during the arrival of the people from Hollywood. Still, she hesitated a moment, absently fingering her badge. She hadn't yet resolved how she was going to handle Phil. She knew the law clearly enough, but the law wouldn't help when she had to deal with him without her badge. Tod burst through the door, his eyes wide, his face flushed.

"Tory, they're here! A whole bunch of them in front of the hotel. There're vans and cars and everything!"

Though she felt more like swearing, she had to smile at him. He only forgot himself and called her Tory when he was desperately excited. And he was such a sweet boy, she mused, so full of dreams. Crossing to him, she dropped an arm over his shoulder. He no longer cringed.

"Let's go see," she said simply.

"Tory—Sheriff," Tod corrected himself, although the words all but tumbled over each other, "do you think that guy'll let me watch him make the movie? You know, the guy you had in jail."

"I know," Tory murmured as they stepped outside. "I imagine so," she answered absentmindedly.

The scene outside was so out of place in Friendly, it almost made Tory laugh. There were several vehicles in front of the hotel, and crowds of people. The mayor stood on the sidewalk, talking to everyone at once. Several of the people from California were looking around the town with expressions of curiosity and astonishment. They were being looked over with the same expressions by people from Friendly.

Different planets, Tory mused with a slight smile. Take me to your leader. When she spotted Phil, the smile faded.

He was dressed casually, as he had been on his first visit to town—no different than the members of his crew. And yet, there was a difference. He held the authority; there was no mistaking it. Even while apparently listening to the mayor, he was giving orders. And, Tory added thoughtfully, being obeyed. There seemed to be a certain friendliness between him and his crew, as well as an underlying respect. There was some laughter and a couple of shouts as equipment was unloaded, but the procedure was meticulously orderly. He watched over every detail.

"Wow," Tod said under his breath. "Look at all that

stuff. I bet they've got cameras in those boxes. Maybe I'll get a chance to look through one."

"Mmm." Tory saw Phil laugh and heard the sound of it drift to her across the street. Then he saw her.

His smile didn't fade but altered subtly. They assessed each other while his people milled and hers whispered. The assessment became a challenge with no words spoken. She stood very straight, her arm still casually draped around the boy's shoulders. Phil noticed the gesture even as he felt a stir that wasn't wholly pleasant. He ached, he discovered, baffled. Just looking at her made him ache. She looked cool, even remote, but her eyes were directed at his. He could see the small badge pinned to the gentle sweep of her breast. On the dry, sweltering day she was wine, potent and irresistible—and perhaps unwise. One of his crew addressed him twice before Phil heard him.

"What?" His eyes never left Tory's.

"Huffman's on the phone."

"I'll get back to him." Phil started across the street.

When Tory's arm stiffened, Tod glanced up at her in question. He saw that her eyes were fixed on the man walking toward them. He frowned, but when Tory's arm relaxed, so did he.

Phil stopped just short of the sidewalk so that their eyes were at the same level. "Sheriff."

"Kincaid," she said coolly.

Briefly he turned to the boy and smiled. "Hello, Tod. How are you?"

"Fine." The boy stared at him from under a thatch of tumbled hair. The fact that Phil had spoken to him, and remembered his name, made something move inside Tory. She pushed it away, reminding herself she couldn't afford too many good feelings toward Phil Kincaid. "Can I…" Tod began. He shifted nervously, then drew up his courage. "Do you think I could see some of that stuff?"

A grin flashed on Phil's face. "Sure. Go over and ask for Bicks. Tell him I said to show you a camera."

"Yeah?" Thrilled, he stared at Phil for a moment, then glanced up at Tory in question. When she smiled down at him, Phil watched the boy's heart leap to his eyes.

Uh-oh, he thought, seeing the slight flush creep into the boy's cheeks. Tory gave him a quick squeeze and the color deepened.

"Go ahead," she told him.

Phil watched the boy dash across the street before he turned his gaze back to Tory. "It seems you have another conquest. I have to admire his taste." When she stared at him blankly, he shook his head. "Good God, Tory, the kid's in love with you."

"Don't be ridiculous," she retorted. "He's a child."

"Not quite," he countered. "And certainly old enough to be infatuated with a beautiful woman." He grinned again, seeing her distress as her eyes darted after Tod. "I was a fourteen-year-old boy once myself."

Annoyed that he had pointed out something she'd been oblivious to, Tory glared at him. "But never as innocent as that one."

"No," he agreed easily, and stepped up on the sidewalk. She had to shift the angle of her chin to keep her eyes in line with his. "It's good to see you, Sheriff."

"Is it?" she returned lazily as she studied his face.

"Yes, I wondered if I'd imagined just how beautiful you were."

"You've brought quite a group with you," she commented, ignoring his statement. "There'll be more, I imagine."

"Some. I need some footage of the town, the countryside. The actors will be here in a couple of days."

Nodding, she leaned against a post. "You'll have to store your vehicles at Bestler's. If you have any plans to use a private residence or a store for filming, you'll have to make the arrangements individually. Hernandez's Bar is open until eleven on weeknights, one on Saturday. Consumption of alcohol on the streets is subject to a fifty-dollar fine. You're liable for any damage to private property. Whatever alterations you make for the filming will again have to be cleared individually. Anyone causing a disturbance in the hotel or on the streets after midnight will be fined and sentenced. As this is your show, Kincaid, I'll hold you personally responsible for keeping your people in line."

He listened to her rundown of the rules with the appearance of careful interest. "Have dinner with me."

She very nearly smiled. "Forget it." When she started to walk by him, he took her arm.

"Neither of us is likely to do that, are we?"

Tory didn't shake off his arm. It felt too good to be touched by him again. She did, however, give him a long, lazy look. "Phil, both of us have a job to do. Let's keep it simple."

"By all means." He wondered what would happen if he kissed her right then and there. It was what he wanted, he discovered, more than anything he had wanted in quite some time. It would also be unwise. "What if we call it a business dinner?"

Tory laughed. "Why don't we call it what it is?"

"Because then you wouldn't come, and I do want to talk to you."

The simplicity of his answer disconcerted her. "About what?"

"Several things." His fingers itched to move to her face, to feel the soft, satiny texture of her skin. He kept them loosely hooked around her arm. "Among them, my show and your town. Wouldn't it simplify matters for both of us if we understood each other and came to a few basic agreements?"

"Maybe."

"Have dinner with me in my room." When her brow arched, he continued lazily. "It's also my office for the time being," he reminded her. "I'd like to clear the air regarding my film. If we're going to argue, Sheriff, let's do it privately."

The *Sheriff* did it. It was both her title and her job. "All right," she agreed. "Seven o'clock."

"Fine." When she started to walk away, he stopped her. "Sheriff," he said with a quick grin, "leave the gun in the desk, okay? It'll kill my appetite."

She gave a snort of laughter. "I can handle you without it, Kincaid."

Tory frowned at the clothes hanging inside her closet. Even while she had been showering, she had considered putting on work clothes—and her badge—for her dinner with Phil. But that would have been petty, and pettiness wasn't her style. She ran a fingertip over an emerald-green silk dress. It was very simply cut, narrow, with a high neck that buttoned to the waist. Serviceable and attractive, she decided, slipping it off the hanger. Laying it across the bed, she shrugged out of her robe.

Outside, the streets were quiet. She hoped they stayed that way, as she'd put Merle in charge for the evening. People would be gathered in their homes, at the drugstore, at the bar, discussing the filming. That had been the main topic of the town for weeks, over-riding the heat, the lack of rain and the Kramer twins. Tory smiled as she laced the front of her teddy. Yes, people needed their little entertainments, and this was the biggest thing to happen in Friendly in years. She was going to have to roll with it. To a point.

She slipped the dress over her head, feeling the silk slither on her skin. It had been a long time, she realized, since she had bothered about clothes. In Albuquerque she took a great deal of care about her appearance. A courtroom image was as important as an opening state-ment, particularly in a jury trial. People judged. Still, she was a woman who knew how to incorporate style with comfort.

The dress flattered her figure while giving her com-plete freedom of movement. Tory looked in the bureau-top mirror to study her appearance. The mirror cut her off at just above the waist. She rose on her toes and turned to the side but was still frustrated with a partial view of herself. Well, she decided, letting her feet go flat again, it would just have to do.

She sprayed on her scent automatically, remember-ing too late Phil's comment on it. Tory frowned at the delicate bottle as she replaced it on the dresser. She could hardly go and scrub the perfume off now. With a shrug she sat on the bed to put on her shoes. The mat-tress creaked alarmingly. Handling Phil Kincaid was no problem, she told herself. That was half the reason she had agreed to have dinner with him. It was a matter of principle. She wasn't a woman to be seduced or charmed into submission, particularly by a man of Kincaid's reputation. Spoiled, she thought again, but with a tad too much affection for her liking. He'd grown up privileged, in a world of glitter and glamour. He expected everything to come his way, women included.

Tory had grown up respecting the value of a dollar in a world of ordinary people and day-to-day struggles. She, too, expected everything to come her way—after she'd arranged it. She left the room determined to come out on top in the anticipated encounter. She even began to look forward to it.

Phil's room was right next door. Though she knew he had seen to that small detail himself, Tory planned to make no mention of it. She gave a brisk knock and waited.

When he opened the door, the glib remark Phil had intended to make vanished from his brain. He remembered his own thoughts about seeing her in something silk and vivid and could only stare. *Exquisite.* It was the word that hammered inside his brain, but even that wouldn't come through his lips. He knew at that moment he'd have to have her or go through his life obsessed with the need to.

"Victoria," he managed after a long moment.

Though her pulse had begun to pound at the look in his eyes, at the husky way he had said her name, she gave him a brisk smile. "Phillip," she said very formally. "Shall I come in or eat out here?"

Phil snapped back. Stammering and staring wasn't going to get him very far. He took her hand to draw her inside, then locked the door, uncertain whether he was locking her in or the world out.

Tory glanced around the small, haphazardly furnished room. Phil had already managed to leave his mark on it. The bureau was stacked with papers. There was a notepad, scrawled in from margin to margin, a few stubby pencils and a two-way radio. The shades were drawn and the room was lit with candles. Tory lifted her brows at this, glancing toward the folding card table covered with the hotel's best linen. Two dishes were covered to keep in the heat while a bottle of wine was open. Strolling over, Tory lifted it to study the label.

"Château Haut-Brion Blanc," she murmured with a perfect accent. Still holding the bottle, she sent Phil a look. "You didn't pick this up at Mendleson's Liquors."

"I always take a few…amenities when I go on location."

Tilting her head, Tory set down the bottle. "And the candles?"

"Local drugstore," he told her blandly.

"Wine and candlelight," she mused. "For a business dinner?"

"Humor the director," he suggested, crossing over to pour out two glasses of wine. "We're always setting scenes. It's uncontrollable." Handing her a glass, he touched it with the rim of his own. "Sheriff, to a comfortable relationship."

"Association," she corrected, then drank. "Very nice," she approved. She let her eyes skim over him briefly. He wore casual slacks, impeccably tailored, with an open-collared cream-colored shirt that accented his lean torso. The candlelight picked up the deep tones of red in his hair. "You look more suited to your profession than when I first saw you," she commented.

"And you less to yours," he countered.

"Really?" Turning away, she wandered the tiny room. The small throw rug was worn thin in patches, the headboard of the bed scarred, the nightstand a bit unsteady. "How do you like the accommodations, Kincaid?"

"They'll do."

She laughed into her wine. "Wait until it gets hot."

"Isn't it?"

"Do the immortal words 'You ain't seen nothing yet' mean anything to you?"

He forced himself to keep his eyes from the movements of her body under the silk. "Want to see all the Hollywood riffraff melt away, Tory?"

Turning, she disconcerted him by giving him her dashing smile. "No, I'll wish you luck instead. After all, I invariably admire your finished product."

"If not what goes into making it."

"Perhaps not," she agreed. "What are you feeding me?"

He was silent for a moment, studying the eyes that laughed at him over the rim of a wineglass. "The menu is rather limited."

"Meat loaf?" she asked dubiously, knowing it was the hotel's specialty.

"God forbid. Chicken and dumplings."

Tory walked back to him. "In that case I'll stay." They sat, facing each other across the folding table. "Shall we get business out of the way, Kincaid, or will it interfere with your digestion?"

He laughed, then surprised her by reaching out to take one of her hands in both of his. "You're a hell of a woman, Tory. Why are you afraid to use my first name?"

She faltered a moment, but let her hand lay unresisting in his. Because it's too personal, she thought. "Afraid?" she countered.

"Reluctant?" he suggested, allowing his fingertip to trace the back of her hand.

"Immaterial." Gently she removed her hand from his. "I was told you'd be shooting here for about six weeks." She lifted the cover from her plate and set it aside. "Is that firm?"

"According to the guarantors," Phil muttered, taking another sip of wine.

"Guarantors?"

"Tyco, Inc., completion-bond company."

"Oh, yes." Tory toyed with her chicken. "I'd heard that was a new wave in Hollywood. They guarantee that the movie will be completed on time and within budget—or else they pay the overbudget costs. They can fire you, can't they?"

"Me, the producer, the stars, anyone," Phil agreed.

"Practical."

"Stifling," he returned, and stabbed into his chicken.

"From your viewpoint, I imagine," Tory reflected. "Still, as a business, it makes sense. Creative people often have to be shown certain...boundaries. Such as," she continued, "the ones I outlined this morning."

"And boundaries often have to be flexible. Such as," he said with a smile, "some night scenes we'll be shooting. I'm going to need your cooperation. The townspeople are welcome to watch any phase of the shoot, as long as they don't interfere, interrupt or get in the way. Also, some of the equipment being brought in is very expensive and very sensitive. We have security, but as sheriff, you may want to spread the word that it's off limits."

"Your equipment is your responsibility," she reminded him. "But I will issue a statement. Before you shoot your night scenes, you'll have to clear it through my office."

He gave her a long, hard look. "Why?"

"If you're planning on working in the middle of the night in the middle of town, I'll need prior confirmation. In that way I can keep disorder to a minimum."

"There'll be times I'll need the streets blocked off and cleared."

"Send me a memo," she said. "Dates, times. Friendly can't come to a stop to accommodate you."

"It's nearly there in any case."

"We don't have a fast lane." Irresistibly she sent him a grin. "As you discovered."

He gave her a mild glance. "I'd also like to use some of the locals for extras and walk-ons."

Tory rolled her eyes. "God, you are looking for trouble. Go ahead," she said with a shrug, "send out your casting call, but you'd better use everyone that answers it, one way or another."

As he'd already figured that one out for himself, Phil was unperturbed. "Interested?" he asked casually.

"Hmm?"

"Are you interested?"

Tory laughed as she held out her glass for more wine. "No."

Phil let the bottle hover a moment. "I'm serious, Tory. I'd like to put you on film."

"I haven't got the time or the inclination."

"You've got the looks and, I think, the talent."

She smiled, more amused than flattered. "Phil, I'm a lawyer. That's exactly what I want to be."

"Why?"

He saw immediately that the question had thrown her off balance. She stared at him a moment with the glass to her lips. "Because the law fascinates me," she said after a pause. "Because I respect it. Because I like to think that occasionally I have something to do with the process of justice. I worked hard to get into Harvard, and harder when I got there. It means something to me."

"Yet, you've given it up for six months."

"Not completely." She frowned at the steady flame of the candle. "Regardless, it's necessary. There'll still be cases to try when I go back."

"I'd like to see you in the courtroom," he murmured, watching the quiet light flicker in her eyes. "I bet you're fabulous."

"Outstanding," she agreed, smiling again. "The assistant D.A. hates me." She took another bite of chicken. "What about you? Why directing instead of acting?"

"It never appealed to me." Leaning back, Phil found himself curiously relaxed and stimulated. He felt he could look at her forever. Her fragrance, mixed with the scent of hot wax, was erotic, her voice soothing. "And I suppose I liked the idea of giving orders rather than taking them. With directing you can alter a scene, change a tone, set the pace for an entire story. An actor can only work with one character, no matter how complex it may be."

"You've never directed either of your parents." Tory let the words hang so that he could take them either as a statement or a question. When he smiled, the creases in his cheeks deepened so that she wondered how it would feel to run her fingers along them.

"No." He tipped more wine into his glass. "It might make quite a splash, don't you think? The three of us together on one film. Even though they've been divorced for over twenty-five years, they'd send the glossies into a frenzy."

"You could do two separate films," she pointed out.

"True." He pondered over it a moment. "If the right scripts came along…" Abruptly he shook his head. "I've thought of it, even been approached a couple of times, but I'm not sure it would be a wise move professionally or personally. They're quite a pair," he stated with a grin. "Temperamental, explosive and probably two of the best dramatic actors in the last fifty years. Both of them wring the last drop of blood from a character."

"I've always admired them," Tory agreed. "Especially in the movies they made together. They put a lot of chemistry on the screen."

"And off it," Phil murmured. "It always amazed me that they managed to stay together for almost ten years. Neither of them had that kind of longevity in their other marriages. The problem was that they never stopped competing. It gave them the spark on the screen and a lot of problems at home. It's difficult to live with someone when you're afraid he or she might be just a little better than you are."

"But you're very fond of them, aren't you?" She watched his mobile brow lift in question. "It shows," she told him. "It's rather nice."

"Fond," he agreed. "Maybe a little wary. They're formidable people, together or separately. I grew up listening to lines being cued over breakfast and hearing producers torn to shreds at dinner. My father lived each role. If he was playing a psychotic, I could expect to find a crazed man in the bathroom."

"Obsession," Tory recalled, delighted. "1957."

"Very good," Phil approved. "Are you a fan?"

"Naturally. I got my first kiss watching Marshall Kincaid in *Endless Journey.*" She gave a throaty laugh. "The movie was the more memorable of the two."

"You were in diapers when that movie was made," Phil calculated.

"Ever heard of the late show?"

"Young girls," he stated, "should be in bed at that hour."

Tory suppressed a laugh. Resting her elbows on the table, she set her chin on cupped hands. "And young boys?"

"Would stay out of trouble," he finished.

"The hell they would," Tory countered, chuckling. "As I recall, your...exploits started at a tender age. What was the name of that actress you were involved with when you were sixteen? She was in her twenties as I remember, and—"

"More wine?" Phil interrupted, filling her glass before she could answer.

"Then there was the daughter of that comedian."

"We were like cousins."

"Really?" Tory drew out the word with a doubtful look. "And the dancer...ah, Nicki Clark."

"Great moves," Phil remembered, then grinned at her. "You seem to be more up on my...exploits than I am. Did you spend all your free time at Harvard reading movie magazines?"

"My roommate did," Tory confessed. "She was a

drama major. I see her on a commercial now and again. And then I knew someone in the business. Your name's dropped quite a bit at parties."

"The actor you dated."

"Total recall," Tory murmured, a bit uncomfortable. "You amaze me."

"Tool of the trade. What was his name?"

Tory picked up her wine, studying it for a moment. "Chad Billings."

"Billings?" Surprised and not altogether pleased, Phil frowned at her. "A second-rate leech, Tory. I wouldn't think him your style."

"No?" She shot him a direct look. "He was diverting and…educational."

"And married."

"Judgmental, Phil?" she countered, then gave a shrug. "He was in between victims at the time."

"Aptly put," Phil murmured. "If you got your view of the industry through him, I'm surprised you didn't put up roadblocks to keep us out."

"It was a thought," she told him, but smiled again. "I'm not a complete fool, you know."

But Phil continued to frown at her, studying her intensely. He was more upset at thinking of her with Billings than he should have been. "Did he hurt you?" he demanded abruptly.

Surprised, Tory stared at him. "No," she said slowly. "Although I suppose he might have if I'd allowed it. We didn't see each other exclusively or for very long. I was in L.A. on a case at the time."

"Why Albuquerque?" Phil wondered aloud. "Lou was impressed with you, and he's not easily impressed.

Why aren't you in some glass and leather office in New York?"

"I hate traffic." Tory sat back now, swirling the wine and relaxing. "And I don't rush."

"L.A.?"

"I don't play tennis."

He laughed, appreciating her more each moment. "I love the way you boil things down, Tory. What do you do when you're not upholding the law?"

"As I please, mostly. Sports and hobbies are too demanding." She tossed back her hair. "I like to sleep."

"You forget, I've seen you ride."

"That's different." The wine had mellowed her mood. She didn't notice that the candles were growing low and the hour late. "It relaxes me. Clears my head."

"Why do you live in a room in the hotel when you have a house right outside of town?" Her fingers tightened on the stem of the wineglass only slightly: He was an observant man.

"It's simpler."

Leave this one alone for a while, he warned himself. It's a very tender spot.

"And what do you do when you're not making a major statement on film?" she asked, forcing her hand to relax.

Phil accepted her change of subject without question. "Read scripts…watch movies."

"Go to parties," Tory added sagely.

"That too. It's all part of the game."

"Isn't it difficult sometimes, living in a town where so much is pretense? Even considering the business end of your profession, you have to deal with the lunacy, the make-believe, even the desperation. How do you separate the truth from the fantasy?"

"How do you in your profession?" he countered.

Tory thought for a moment, then nodded. "Touché." Rising, she wandered to the window. She pushed aside the shade, surprised to see that the sun had gone down. A few red streaks hovered over the horizon, but in the east the sky was dark. A few early stars were already out. Phil sat where he was, watched her and wanted her.

"There's Merle making his rounds," Tory said with a smile in her voice. "He's got his official expression on. I imagine he's hoping to be discovered. If he can't be a tough lawman from the nineteenth century, he'd settle for playing one." A car pulled into town, stopping in front of the pool hall with a sharp squeal of brakes. "Oh, God, it's the twins." She sighed, watching Merle turn and stride in their direction. "There's been no peace in town since that pair got their licenses. I suppose I'd better go down and see that they stay in line."

"Can't Merle handle a couple of kids?"

Tory's laugh was full of wicked appreciation. "You don't know the Kramers. There's Merle," she went on, "giving them basic lecture number twenty-two."

"Did they wash all of Hollister's windows?" Phil asked as he rose to join her.

Tory turned her head, surprised. "How did you know about that?"

"Tod told me." He peeked through the window, finding he wanted a look at the infamous twins. They seemed harmless enough from a distance, and disconcertingly alike. "Which one's Zac?"

"Ah…on the right, I think. Maybe," she added with a shake of her head. "Why?"

"'Zac Kramer don't hold with no woman sheriff,'" he quoted.

Tory grinned up at him. "Is that so?"

"Just so." Hardly aware he did so, Phil reached for her hair. "Obviously he's not a very perceptive boy."

"Perceptive enough to wash Mr. Hollister's windows," Tory corrected, amused by the memory. "And to call me a foxy chick only under his breath when he thought I couldn't hear. Of course, that could have been Zeke."

"'Foxy chick'?" Phil repeated.

"Yes," Tory returned with mock hauteur. "'A *very* foxy chick.' It was his ultimate compliment."

"Your head's easily turned," he decided. "What if I told you that you had a face that belongs in a Raphael painting?"

Tory's eyes lit with humor. "I'd say you're reaching."

"And hair," he said with a subtle change in his voice. "Hair that reminds me of night…a hot summer night that keeps you awake, and thinking, and wanting." He plunged both hands into it, letting his fingers tangle. The shade snapped back into place, cutting them off from the outside.

"Phil," Tory began, unprepared for the suddenness of desire that rose in both of them.

"And skin," he murmured, not even hearing her, "that makes me think of satin sheets and tastes like something forbidden." He touched his mouth to her cheek, allowing the tip of his tongue to brush over her. "Tory." She felt her name whisper along her skin and thrilled to it. She had her hands curled tightly around his arms, but not in protest. "Do you know how often I've thought of you these past weeks?"

"No." She didn't want to resist. She wanted to feel

that wild sweep of pleasure that came from the press of his mouth on hers. "No," she said again, and slid her arms around his neck.

"Too much," he murmured, then swore. "Too damn much." And his mouth took her waiting one.

The passion was immediate, frenetic. It ruled both of them. Each of them sought the mindless excitement they had known briefly weeks before. Tory had thought she had intensified the sensation in her mind as the days had passed. Now she realized she had lessened it. This sort of fervor couldn't be imagined or described. It had to be experienced. Everything inside her seemed to speed up—her blood, her heart, her brain. And all sensation, all emotion, seemed to be centered in her mouth. The taste of him exploded on her tongue, shooting through her until she was so full of him, she could no longer separate herself. With a moan she tilted her head back, inviting him to plunge deeper into her mouth. But he wanted more.

Her hair fell straight behind her, leaving her neck vulnerable. Surrendering to a desperate hunger, he savaged it with kisses. Tory made a sound that was mixed pain and pleasure. Her scent seemed focused there, heated by the pulse at her throat. It drove him nearer the edge. He dragged at the silk-covered buttons, impatient to find the hidden skin, the secret skin that had preyed on his mind. The groan sounded in his throat as he slipped his hand beneath the thin teddy and found her.

She was firm, and slender enough to fit his palm. Her heartbeat pounded against it. Tory turned her head, but only to urge him to give the neglected side of her neck attention. With her hands in his hair she pulled him back to her. His hands searched everywhere with a sort of wild reverence, exploring, lingering, possessing. She could feel his murmurs as his lips played over her skin, although she could barely hear them and understood them not at all. The room seemed to grow closer and hotter, so that she longed to be rid of her clothes and find relief...and delight.

Then he pulled her close so that their bodies pressed urgently. Their mouths met with fiery demand. It seemed the storm had just begun. Again and again they drew from each other until they were both breathless. Though he had fully intended to end the evening with Tory in his bed, Phil hadn't expected to be desperate. He hadn't known that all control could be so easily lost. The warm curves of a woman should bring easy pleasure, not this trembling pain. A kiss was a prelude, not an all-consuming force. He knew only that all of him, much more than his body, was crying out for her. Whatever was happening to him was beyond his power to stop. And she was the only answer he had.

"God, Tory." He took his mouth on a wild journey of her face, then returned to her lips. "Come to bed. For God's sake, come to bed. I want you."

She felt as though she were standing on the edge of a cliff. The plunge had never seemed more tempting— or more dangerous. It would be so easy, so easy, just to lean forward and fly. But the fall... She fought for sanity through a brain clouded with the knowledge of one man. It was much too soon to take the step.

"Phil." Shaken, she drew away from him to lean against the windowsill. "I... No," she managed, lifting both hands to her temples. He drew her back against him.

"Yes," he corrected, then crushed his lips to hers

again. Her mouth yielded irresistibly. "You can't pretend you don't want me as much as I want you."

"No." She let her head rest on his shoulder a moment before she pushed out of his arms. "I can't," she agreed in a voice thickened with passion. "But I don't do everything I want. That's one of the basic differences between us."

His eyes flicked briefly down to the unbuttoned dress. "We also seem to have something important in common. This doesn't happen every time—between every man and woman."

"No." Carefully she began to do up her buttons. "It shouldn't have happened between us. I didn't intend it to."

"I did," he admitted. "But not quite this way."

Her eyes lifted to his. She understood perfectly. This had been more intense than either of them had bargained for. "It's going to be a long summer, Phil," she murmured.

"We're going to be together sooner or later, Tory. We both know it." He needed something to balance him. Going to the table, he poured out another glass of wine. He drank, drank again, then looked at her. "I have no intention of backing off."

She nodded, accepting. But she didn't like the way her hands were shaking. "I'm not ready."

"I can be a patient man when necessary." He wanted nothing more than to pull her to the bed and take what they both needed. Instead he took out a cigarette and reminded himself he was a civilized man.

Tory drew herself up straight. "Let's both concentrate on our jobs, shall we?" she said coolly. She wanted to get out, but she didn't want to retreat. "I'll see you around, Kincaid."

"Damn right you will," he murmured as she headed for the door.

She flicked the lock off, then turned to him with a half smile. "Keep out of trouble," she ordered, closing the door behind her.

Chapter 6

Phil sat beside the cameraman on the Tulip crane. "Boom up." At his order the crane operator took them seventeen feet above the town of Friendly. It was just dawn. He'd arranged to have everyone off the streets, although there was a crowd of onlookers behind the crane and equipment. All entrances to town had been blocked off on the off chance that someone might drive through. He wanted desolation and the tired beginning of a new day.

Glancing down, he saw that Bicks was checking the lighting and angles. Brutes, the big spotlights, were set to give daylight balance. He knew, to an inch, where he wanted the shadows to fall. For this shot Phil would act as assistant cameraman, pulling the focus himself.

Phil turned his attention back to the street. He knew what he wanted, and he wanted to capture it as the sun rose, with as much natural light as possible. He looked through the lens and set the shot himself. The crane was set on tracks. He would have the cameraman begin with a wide shot of the horizon and the rising sun, then dolly back to take in the entire main street of Friendly. No soft focus there, just harsh reality. He wanted to pick up the dust on the storefront windows. Satisfied with what he saw through the camera lens, Phil marked the angle with tape, then nodded to his assistant director.

"Quiet on the set."

"New Chance, scene three, take one."

"Roll it," Phil ordered, then waited. With his eyes narrowed, he could visualize what his cameraman saw through the lens. The light was good. Perfect. They'd have to get it in three takes or less or else they'd have to beef it up with gels and filters. That wasn't what he wanted here. He felt the crane roll backward slowly on cue. A straight shot, no panning right to left. They'd take in the heart of the town in one long shot. Chipped paint, sagging wood, torn screens. Later they'd cut in the scene of the leading man walking in from the train station. He was coming home, Phil mused, because there was no place else to go. And he found it, exactly as he had left it twenty years before.

"Cut." The noise on the ground started immediately. "I want another take. Same speed."

At the back of the crowd Tory watched. She wasn't thrilled with being up at dawn. Both her sense of duty and her curiosity had brought her. Phil had been perfectly clear about anyone peeking through windows during this shot. He wanted emptiness. She told herself she'd come to keep her people out of mischief, but when it was all said and done, she had wanted to see Phil at work.

He was very commanding and totally at ease with it, but, she reasoned as she stuck her hands in her back pockets, it didn't seem so hard. Moving a little to the side, she tried to see the scene he was imagining. The town looked tired, she decided, and a little reluctant to face the new day. Though the horizon was touched with golds and pinks, a gray haze lay over the street and buildings.

It was the first time he had shot anything there. For the past week he had been filming landscapes. Tory had stayed in Friendly, sending Merle out occasionally to check on things. It had kept him happy and had given Tory the distance she wanted. As her deputy came back brimming with reports and enthusiasm, she was kept abreast in any case.

But today the urge to see for herself had been too strong to resist. It had been several days—and several long nights—since their evening together. She had managed to keep herself busier than necessary in order to avoid him. But Tory wasn't a woman to avoid a problem for long. Phil Kincaid was still a problem.

Apparently satisfied, Phil ordered the operator to lower the crane. People buzzed around Tory like bees. A few children complained about being sent off to school. Spotting Tod, Tory smiled and waved him over.

"Isn't it neat?" he demanded the moment he was beside her. "I wanted to go up in it," he continued, indicating the crane, "but Mr. Kincaid said something about insurance. Steve let me see his camera though, even let me take some pictures. It's a thirty-five millimeter with all kinds of lenses."

"Steve?"

"The guy who was sitting next to Mr. Kincaid. He's the cameraman." Tod glanced over, watching Phil in a discussion with his cameraman and several members of the crew. "Isn't he something?"

"Steve?" Tory repeated, smiling at Tod's pleasure.

"Well, yeah, but I meant Mr. Kincaid." Shaking his head, he let out a long breath. "He's awful smart. You should hear some of the words he uses. And boy, when he says so, everybody jumps."

"Do they?" Tory murmured, frowning over at the man under discussion.

"You bet," Tod confirmed. "And I heard Mr. Bicks say to Steve that he'd rather work with Mr. Kincaid than anybody. He's a tough sonofa—" Catching himself, Tod broke off and flushed. "I mean, he said he was tough, but the best there was."

As she watched, Phil was pointing, using one hand and then the other as he outlined his needs for the next shot. It was very clear that he knew what he wanted and that he'd get it. She could study him now. He was too involved to notice her or the crowd of people who stared and mumbled behind the barrier of equipment.

He wore jeans and a pale blue T-shirt with scuffed sneakers. Hanging from his belt was a case that held sunglasses and another for a two-way radio. He was very intense, she noted, when working. There was none of the careless humor in his eyes. He talked quickly, punctuating the words with hand gestures. Once or twice he interrupted what he was saying to call out another order to the grips who were setting up light stands.

A perfectionist, she concluded, and realized it shouldn't surprise her. His movies projected the intimate care she was now seeing firsthand. A stocky man in a fielder's cap lumbered up to him, talking over an enormous wad of gum.

"That's Mr. Bicks," Tod murmured reverently. "The cinematographer. He's got two Oscars and owns part of a boxer."

Whatever he was saying, Phil listened carefully, then simply shook his head. Bicks argued another moment, shrugged, then gave Phil what appeared to be a solid punch on the shoulder before he walked away. A tough sonofabitch, Tory mused. Apparently so.

Turning to Tod, she mussed his hair absently. "You'd better get to school."

"Aw, but..."

She lifted her brow, effectively cutting off his excuse. "It's nearly time for summer vacation. They'll still be here."

He mumbled a protest, but she caught the look in his eye as he gazed up at her. Uh-oh, she thought, just as Phil had. Why hadn't she seen this coming? She was going to have to be careful to be gentle while pointing the boy in another direction. A teenage crush was nothing to smile at and brush away.

"I'll come by after school," he said, beaming up at her. Before she could respond, he was dashing off, leaving her gnawing on her bottom lip and worrying about him.

"Sheriff."

Tory whirled sharply and found herself facing Phil. He smiled slowly, setting the sunglasses in front of his eyes. It annoyed her that she had to strain to see his expression through the tinted glass. "Kincaid," she responded. "How's it going?"

"Good. Your people are very cooperative."

"And yours," she said. "So far."

He grinned at that. "We're expecting the cast this afternoon. The location manager's cleared it with you about parking the trailers and so forth?"

"She's very efficient," Tory agreed. "Are you getting what you want?"

He took a moment to answer. "With regard to the film, yes, so far." Casually he reached down to run a finger over her badge. "You've been busy the last few days."

"So have you."

"Not that busy. I've left messages for you."

"I know."

"When are you going to see me?"

She lifted both brows. "I'm seeing you right now." He took a step closer and cupped the back of her neck in his hand. "Phil—"

"Soon," he said quietly.

Though she could feel the texture of each of his fingers on the back of her neck, she gave him a cool look. "Kincaid, create your scenes on the other side of the camera. Accosting a peace officer will land you back in that cell. You'll find it difficult to direct from there."

"Oh, I'm going to accost you," he warned under his breath. "With or without that damn badge, Victoria. Think about it."

She didn't step back or remove his hand, although she knew several pair of curious eyes were on them. "I'll give it a few minutes," she promised dryly.

Only the tensing of his fingers on her neck revealed his annoyance. She thought he was about to release her and relaxed. His mouth was on hers so quickly, she could only stand in shock. Before she could think to push him away, he set her free. Her eyes were sharply green and furious when he grinned down at her.

"See you, Sheriff," he said cheerfully, and sauntered back to his crew.

For the better part of the day Tory stayed in her office and fumed. Now and again Phil's voice carried through her open window as he called out instructions. She knew they were doing pans of the town and stayed away from the window. She had work to do, she reminded herself. And in any case she had no interest in the filming. It was understandable that the townspeople would stand around and gawk, but she had better things to do.

I should have hauled him in, she thought, scowling down at her legal pad. I should have hauled him in then and there. And she would have if it wouldn't have given him too much importance. He'd better watch his step, Tory decided. One wrong move and she was going to come down on him hard. She picked up her coffee and gulped it down with a grimace. It was cold. Swearing, she rose to pour a fresh cup.

Through the screen in the window she could see quite a bit of activity and hear a flood of conversation interrupted when the filming was in progress. It was past noon and hot as the devil. Phil had been working straight through for hours. With a grudging respect she admitted that he didn't take his job lightly. Going back to her desk, Tory concentrated on her own.

She hardly noticed that two hours had passed when Merle came bursting into the office. Hot, tired and annoyed with having her concentration broken, she opened her mouth to snap at him, but he exploded with enthusiasm before she had the chance.

"Tory, they're here!"

"Terrific," she mumbled, turning to her notes again. "Who?"

"The actors. Came from the airport in limousines. Long, black limousines. There are a half dozen of those Winnebagos set up outside of town for dressing rooms and stuff. You should see inside them. They've got telephones and TVs and everything."

She lifted her head. "Been busy, Merle T.?" she asked languidly, but he was too excited to notice.

"Sam Dressler," he went on, pacing back and forth with a clatter of boots. "Sam Dressler, right here in Friendly. I guess I've seen every movie he's ever made. He shook my hand," he added, staring down at his own palm, awed. "Thought I was the sheriff." He sent Tory a quick look. "'Course I told him I was the deputy."

"Of course," she agreed, amused now. It was never possible for her to stay annoyed with Merle. "How'd he look?"

"Just like you'd think," he told her with a puzzled shake of his head. "All tanned and tough, with a diamond on his finger fit to blind you. Signed autographs for everybody who wanted one."

Unable to resist, Tory asked, "Did you get one?"

"Sure I did." He grinned and pulled out his ticket book. "It was the only thing I had handy."

"Very resourceful." She glanced at the bold signature Merle held out for her. At the other end of the page were some elegant looping lines. "Marlie Summers," Tory read. She recalled a film from the year before, and the actress's pouting sexuality.

"She's about the prettiest thing I ever saw," Merle murmured.

Coming from anyone else, Tory would have given

the remark no notice. In this case, however, her eyes shot up and locked on Merle's. What she saw evoked in her a feeling of distress similar to what she had experienced with Tod. "Really?" she said carefully.

"She's just a little thing," Merle continued, gazing down at the autograph. "All pink and blond. Just like something in a store window. She's got big blue eyes and the longest lashes…" He trailed off, tucking the book back in his pocket.

Growing more disturbed, Tory told herself not to be silly. No Hollywood princess was going to look twice at Merle T. Johnson. "Well," she began casually, "I wonder what her part is."

"She's going to tell me all about it tonight," Merle stated, adjusting the brim of his hat.

"What?" It came out in a quick squeak.

Grinning, Merle gave his hat a final pat, then stroked his struggling mustache. "We've got a date." He strode out jauntily, leaving Tory staring with her mouth open.

"A date?" she asked the empty office. Before she could react, the phone beside her shrilled. Picking it up, she barked into it, "What is it?"

A bit flustered by the greeting, the mayor stammered. "Tory—Sheriff Ashton, this is Mayor Toomey."

"Yes, Bud." Her tone was still brusque as she stared at the door Merle had shut behind him.

"I'd like you to come over to the office, Sheriff. I have several members of the cast here." His voice rang with importance again. "Mr. Kincaid thought it might be a good idea for you to meet them."

"Members of the cast," she repeated, thinking of Marlie Summers. "I'd love to," she said dangerously, then hung up on the mayor's reply.

Her thoughts were dark as she crossed the street. No Hollywood tootsie was going to break Merle's heart while she was around. She was going to make that clear as soon as possible. She breezed into the hotel, giving several members of Phil's crew a potent stare as they loitered in the lobby. Bicks doffed his fielder's cap and grinned at her.

"Sheriff."

Tory sent him a mild glance and a nod as she sauntered through to the office. Behind her back he rolled his eyes to the ceiling, placing the cap over his heart. A few remarks were made about the advantages of breaking the law in Friendly while Tory disappeared into a side door.

The tiny office was packed, the window air-conditioning unit spitting hopefully. Eyes turned to her. Tory gave the group a brief scan. Marlie was sitting on the arm of Phil's chair, dressed in pink slacks and a frilled halter. Her enviable curves were displayed to perfection. Her hair was tousled appealingly around a piquant face accented with mink lashes and candy-pink lipstick. She looked younger than Tory had expected, almost like a high school girl ready to be taken out for an ice-cream soda. Tory met the baby-blue eyes directly, and with an expression that made Phil grin. He thought mistakenly that she might be a bit jealous.

"Sheriff." The mayor bustled over to her, prepared to act as host. "This is quite an honor for Friendly," he began, in his best politician's voice. "I'm sure you recognize Mr. Dressler."

Tory extended her hand to the man who approached her. "Sheriff." His voice was rich, the cadence mellow as he clasped her hand in both of his. She was a bit surprised to find them callused. "This is unexpected," he murmured while his eyes roamed her face thoroughly. "And delightful."

"Mr. Dressler, I admire your work." The smile was easy because the words were true.

"Sam, please." His brandy voice had only darkened attractively with age, losing none of its resonance. "We get to be a close little family on location shoots. Victoria, isn't it?"

"Yes." She found herself inclined to like him and gave him another smile.

"Bud, here, is making us all quite comfortable," he went on, clapping the mayor on the shoulder. "Will you join us in a drink?"

"Ginger ale's fine, Bud."

"The sheriff's on duty." Hearing Phil's voice, Tory turned, her head only, and glanced at him. "You'll find she takes her work very seriously." He touched Marlie's creamy bare shoulder. "Victoria Ashton, Marlie Summers."

"Sheriff." Marlie smiled her dazzling smile. The tiniest hint of a dimple peeked at the corner of her mouth. "Phil said you were unusual. It looks like he's right again."

"Really?" Accepting the cold drink Bud handed her, Tory assessed the actress over the rim. Marlie, accustomed to long looks and feminine coolness, met the stare straight on.

"Really," Marlie agreed. "I met your deputy a little while ago."

"So I heard."

So the wind blows in that direction, Marlie mused as she sipped from her own iced sangria. Sensing tension and wanting to keep things smooth, Bud hurried on with the rest of the introductions.

The cast ranged from ingenues to veterans—a girl Tory recognized from a few commercials; an ancient-looking man she remembered from the vague black-and-white movies on late-night television; a glitzy actor in his twenties, suited for heartthrobs and posters. Tory managed to be pleasant, stayed long enough to satisfy the mayor, then slipped away. She'd no more than stepped outside when she felt an arm on her shoulder.

"Don't you like parties, Sheriff?"

Taking her time, she turned to face Phil. "Not when I'm on duty." Though she knew he'd worked in the sun all day, he didn't look tired but exhilarated. His shirt was streaked with sweat, his hair curling damply over his ears, but there was no sign of fatigue on his face. It's the pressure that feeds him, she realized. Again she was drawn to him, no less than when they had been alone in his room. "You've put in a long day," she murmured.

He caught her hair in his hand. "So have you. Why don't we go for a drive?"

Tory shook her head. "No, I have things to do." Wanting to steer away from the subject, she turned to what had been uppermost on her mind. "Your Marlie made quite an impression on Merle."

Phil gave a quick laugh. "Marlie usually does."

"Not on Merle," Tory said so seriously that he sobered.

"He's a big boy, Tory."

"A boy," she agreed significantly. "He's never seen anything like your friend in there. I won't let him get hurt."

Phil let out a deep breath. "Your duties as sheriff include advice to the lovelorn? Leave him alone," he ordered before she could retort. "You treat him as though he were a silly puppy who doesn't respond to training."

She took a step back at that. "No, I don't," she disagreed, sincerely shaken by the idea. "He's a sweet boy who—"

"Man," Phil corrected quietly. "He's a man, Tory. Cut the apron strings."

"I don't know what you're talking about," she snapped.

"You damn well do," he corrected. "You can't keep him under your wing the way you do with Tod."

"I've known Merle all my life," she said in a low voice. "Just keep Cotton Candy in line, Kincaid."

"Always so sure of yourself, aren't you?"

Her color drained instantly, alarmingly. For a moment Phil stared at her in speechless wonder. He'd never expected to see that kind of pain in her eyes. Instinctively he reached out for her. "Tory?"

"No." She lifted a hand to ward him off. "Just—leave me alone." Turning away, she walked across the street and climbed into her car. With an oath Phil started to go back into the hotel, then swore again and backtracked. Tory was already on her way north.

Her thoughts were in turmoil as she drove. Too much was happening. She squeezed her eyes shut briefly. Why should that throw her now? she wondered. She'd always been able to take things in stride, handle them at her own pace. Now she had a deep-seated urge just to keep driving, just to keep going. So many people wanted things from her, expected things. Including, she admitted, herself. It was all closing in suddenly. She needed someone to talk to. But the only one who had ever fit that job was gone.

God, she wasn't sure of herself. Why did everyone say so? Sometimes it was so hard to be responsible, to *feel* responsible. Tod, Merle, the mayor, the Kramers, Mr. Hollister. Her mother. She just wanted peace—enough time to work out what was happening in her own life. Her feelings for Phil were closing in on her. Pulling the car to a halt, Tory realized it was those feelings that were causing her—a woman who had always considered herself calm—to be tense. Piled on top of it were problems that had to come first. She'd learned that from her father.

Glancing up, she saw she had driven to the cemetery without even being aware of it. She let out a long breath, resting her forehead against the steering wheel. It was time she went there, time she came to terms with what she had closed her mind to since that night in the hospital. Climbing out of the car, Tory walked across the dry grass to her father's grave.

Odd that there'd been a breeze here, she mused, looking at the sky, the distant mountains, the long stretches of nothing. She looked at anything but what was at her feet. There should be some shade, she thought, and cupped her elbows in her palms. Someone should plant some trees. I should have brought some flowers, she thought suddenly, then looked down.

WILLIAM H. ASHTON

She hadn't seen the gravestone before—hadn't been back to the cemetery since the day of the funeral. Now a quiet moan slipped through her lips. "Oh, Dad."

It isn't right, she thought with a furious shake of her head. It just isn't right. How can he be down there in the dark when he always loved the sun? "Oh, no," she murmured again. I don't know what to do, she thought silently, pleading with him. I don't know how to deal with it all. I still need you. Pressing a palm on her forehead, she fought back tears.

Phil pulled up behind her car, then got out quietly. She looked very alone and lost standing among the headstones. His first instinct was to go to her, but he suppressed it. This was private for her. Her father, he thought, looking toward the grave at which Tory stared. He stood by a low wrought-iron gate at the edge of the cemetery and waited.

There was so much she needed to talk about, so much she still needed to say. But there was no more time. He'd been taken too suddenly. Unfair, she thought again on a wave of desolate fury. He had been so young and so good.

"I miss you so much," she whispered. "All those long talks and quiet evenings on the porch. You'd smoke those awful cigars outside so that the smell wouldn't get in the curtains and irritate Mother. I was always so proud of you. This badge doesn't suit me," she continued softly, lifting her hand to it. "It's the law books and the courtroom that I understand. I don't want to make a mistake while I'm wearing it, because it's yours." Her fingers tightened around it. All at once she felt painfully alone, helpless, empty. Even the anger had slipped away unnoticed. And yet the acceptance she tried to feel was blocked behind a grief she refused to release. If she cried, didn't it mean she'd taken the first step away?

Wearily she stared down at the name carved into the

granite. "I don't want you to be dead," she whispered. "And I hate it because I can't change it."

When she turned away from the grave, her face was grim. She walked slowly but was halfway across the small cemetery before she saw Phil. Tory stopped and stared at him. Her mind went blank, leaving her with only feelings. He went to her.

For a moment they stood face-to-face. He saw her lips tremble open as if she were about to speak, but she only shook her head helplessly. Without a word he gathered her close. The shock of grief that hit her was stronger than anything that had come before. She trembled first, then clutched at him.

"Oh, Phil, I can't bear it." Burying her face against his shoulder, Tory wept for the first time since her father's death.

In silence he held her, overwhelmed with a tenderness he'd felt for no one before. Her sobbing was raw and passionate. He stroked her hair, offering comfort without words. Her grief poured out in waves that seemed to stagger her and made him hurt for her to a degree that was oddly intimate. He thought he could feel what she felt, and held her tighter, waiting for the first throes to pass.

At length her weeping quieted, lessening to trembles that were somehow more poignant than the passion. She kept her face pressed against his shoulder, relying on his strength when her own evaporated. Light-headed and curiously relieved, she allowed him to lead her to a small stone bench. He kept her close to his side when they sat, his arm protectively around her.

"Can you talk about it?" he asked softly.

Tory let out a long, shuddering sigh. From where they

sat she could see the headstone clearly. "I loved him," she murmured. "My mother says too much." Her throat felt dry and abused when she swallowed. "He was everything good. He taught me not just right and wrong but all the shades in between." Closing her eyes, she let her head rest on Phil's shoulder. "He always knew the right thing. It was something innate and effortless. People knew they could depend on him, that he'd make it right. I depended on him, even in college, in Albuquerque—I knew he was there if I needed him."

He kissed her temple in a gesture of simple understanding. "How did he die?"

Feeling a shudder run through her, Phil drew her closer still. "He had a massive stroke. There was no warning. He'd never even been sick that I can remember. When I got here, he was in a coma. Everything..." She faltered, searching for the strength to continue. With his free hand Phil covered hers. "Everything seemed to go wrong at once. His heart just...stopped." She ended in a whisper, lacing her fingers through his. "They put him on a respirator. For weeks there was nothing but that damn machine. Then my mother told them to turn it off."

Phil let the silence grow, following her gaze toward the headstone. "It must have been hard for her."

"No." The word was low and flat. "She never wavered, never cried. My mother's a very decisive woman," she added bitterly. "And she made the decision alone. She told me after it was already done."

"Tory." Phil turned her to face him. She looked pale, bright-eyed and achingly weary. Something seemed to tear inside him. "I can't tell you the right or wrong of it, because there really isn't any. But I do know there comes a time when everyone has to face something that seems impossible to accept."

"If only I could have seen it was done for love and not…expediency." Shutting her eyes, she shook her head. "Hold me again." He drew her gently into his arms. "That last night at the hospital was so ugly between my mother and me. He would have hated that. I couldn't stop it," she said with a sigh. "I still can't."

"Time." He kissed the top of her head. "I know how trite that sounds, but there's nothing else but time."

She remained silent, accepting his comfort, drawing strength from it. If she had been able to think logically, Tory would have found it inconsistent with their relationship thus far that she could share her intimate feelings with him. At the moment she trusted Phil implicitly.

"Once in a while, back there," she murmured, "I panic."

It surprised him enough to draw her back and study her face again. "You?"

"Everyone thinks because I'm Will Ashton's daughter, I'll take care of whatever comes up. There're so many variables to right and wrong."

"You're very good at your job."

"I'm a good lawyer," she began.

"And a good sheriff," he interrupted. Tilting her chin up, he smiled at her. "That's from someone who's been on the wrong side of your bars." Gently he brushed the hair from her cheeks. They were warm and still damp. "And don't expect to hear me say it in public."

Laughing, she pressed her cheek to his. "Phil, you can be a very nice man."

"Surprised?"

"Maybe," she murmured. With a sigh she gave him one last squeeze, then drew away. "I've got work to do."

He stopped her from rising by taking her hands again. "Tory, do you know how little space you give yourself?"

"Yes." She disconcerted him by bringing his hand to her lips. "These six months are for him. It's very important to me."

Standing as she did, Phil cupped her face in his hands. She seemed to him very fragile, very vulnerable, suddenly. His need to look out for her was strong. "Let me drive you back. We can send someone for your car."

"No, I'm all right. Better." She brushed her lips over his. "I appreciate this. There hasn't been anyone I could talk to."

His eyes became very intense. "Would you come to me if you needed me?"

She didn't answer immediately, knowing the question was more complex than the simple words. "I don't know," she said at length.

Phil let her go, then watched her walk away.

Chapter 7

The camera came in tight on Sam and Marlie. Phil wanted the contrast of youth and age, of dissatisfaction and acceptance. It was a key scene, loaded with tension and restrained sexuality. They were using Hernandez's Bar, where the character Marlie portrayed worked as a waitress. Phil had made almost no alterations in the room. The bar was scarred, the mirror behind it cracked near the bottom. It smelled of sweat and stale liquor. He intended to transmit the scent itself onto film.

The windows were covered with neutral-density paper to block off the stream of the sun. It trapped the stale air in the room. The lights were almost unbearably hot, so that he needed no assistance from makeup to add beads of sweat to Sam's face. It was the sixth take, and the mood was growing edgy.

Sam blew his lines and swore ripely.

"Cut." Struggling with his temper, Phil wiped his forearm over his brow. With some actors a few furious words worked wonders. With Dressler, Phil knew, they would only cause more delays.

"Look, Phil—" Sam tore off the battered Stetson he wore and tossed it aside "—this isn't working."

"I know. Cut the lights," he ordered. "Get Mr. Dressler a beer." He addressed this to the man he had hired to see to Sam's needs on the location shoot. The individual attention had been Phil's way of handling Dressler and thus far had had its benefits. "Sit down for a while, Sam," he suggested. "We'll cool off." He waited until Sam was seated at a rear table with a portable fan and a beer before he plucked a can from the cooler himself.

"Hot work," Marlie commented, leaning against the bar.

Glancing over, Phil noted the line of sweat that ran down the front of her snug blouse. He passed her the can of beer. "You're doing fine."

"It's a hell of a part," she said before she took a deep drink. "I've been waiting for one like this for a long time."

"The next take," Phil began, narrowing his eyes, "when you say the bit about sweat and dust, I want you to grab his shirt and pull him to you."

Marlie thought it over, then set the can on the bar. "Like this…? *There's nothing,*" she spat out, grabbing Phil's damp shirt, *"nothing in this town but sweat and dust."* She put her other hand to his shirt and pulled him closer. *"Even the dreams have dust on them."*

"Good."

Marlie flashed a smile before she picked up the beer

again. "Better warn Sam," she suggested, offering Phil the can. "He doesn't like improvising."

"Hey, Phil." Phil glanced over to see Steve with his hand on the doorknob. "That kid's outside with the sheriff. Wants to know if they can watch."

Phil took a long, slow drink. "They can sit in the back of the room." His eyes met Tory's as she entered. It had been two days since their meeting in the cemetery. Since then there had been no opportunity—or she'd seen to it that there'd been none—for any private conversation. She met the look, nodded to him, then urged Tod back to a rear table.

"The law of the land," Marlie murmured, causing Phil to look at her in question. "She's quite a woman, isn't she?"

"Yes."

Marlie grinned before she commandeered the beer again. "Merle thinks she's the greatest thing to come along since sliced bread."

Phil pulled out a cigarette. "You're seeing quite a bit of the deputy, aren't you? Doesn't seem your style."

"He's a nice guy," she said simply, then laughed. "His boss would like me run out of town on a rail."

"She's protective."

With an unintelligible murmur that could have meant anything, Marlie ran her fingers through her disordered cap of curls. "At first I thought she had something going with him." In response to Phil's quick laugh she lifted a thin, penciled brow. "Of course, that was before I saw the way you looked at her." It was her turn to laugh when Phil's expression became aloof. "Damn, Phil, you can look like your father sometimes." After handing him the empty can of beer, she turned away. "Makeup!" she demanded.

"Those are 4Ks," Tod was telling Tory, pointing to lights. "They have to put that stuff over the windows so the sun doesn't screw things up. On an inside shoot like this, they have to have something like 175-foot candles."

"You're getting pretty technical, aren't you?"

Tod shifted a bit in his chair, but his eyes were excited when they met Tory's. "Mr. Kincaid had them develop the film I shot in the portable lab. He said it was good. He said there were schools I could go to to learn about cinematography."

She cast a look in Phil's direction, watching him discuss something in undertones with Steve. "You're spending quite a lot of time with him," she commented.

"Well, when he's not busy… He doesn't mind."

"No, I'm sure he doesn't." She gave his hand a squeeze.

Tod returned the pressure boldly. "I'd rather spend time with you," he murmured.

Tory glanced down at their joined hands, wishing she knew how to begin. "Tod…"

"Quiet on the set!"

With a sigh Tory turned her attention to the scene in front of the bar. She'd come because Tod had been so pitifully eager that she share his enthusiasm. And she felt it was good for him to take such an avid interest in the technical aspects of the production. Unobtrusively she had kept her eye on him over the past days, watching him with members of the film crew. Thus far, no one appeared to object to his presence or his questions. In fact, Tory mused, he was becoming a kind of mascot. More and more his conversations were accented with the jargon of the industry. His mind seemed to soak up the terms, and his understanding was almost intuitive. He didn't appear to be interested in the glamorous end of it.

And what was so glamorous about it? she asked herself. The room was airless and steaming. It smelled, none too pleasantly, of old beer. The lights had the already unmerciful temperature rising. The two people in position by the bar were circled by equipment. How could they be so intense with each other, she wondered, when lights and cameras were all but on top of them? Yet, despite herself, Tory became engrossed with the drama of the scene.

Marlie's character was tormenting Sam's, ridiculing him for coming back a loser, taunting him. But somehow a rather abrasive strength came through in her character. She seemed a woman trapped by circumstances who was determined to fight her way out. Somehow she made the differences in their ages inconsequential. As the scene unfolded, an objective viewer would develop a respect for her, perhaps a cautious sympathy. Before long the viewer would be rooting for her. Tory wondered if Dressler realized, for all his reputation and skill, who would be the real star of this scene.

She's very good, Tory admitted silently. Marlie Summers wasn't the pampered, glittery Tinsel Town cutie Tory had been ready to believe her to be. Tory recognized strength when she saw it. Marlie infused both a grit and a vulnerability into the character that was instantly admirable. And the sweat, Tory continued, was her own.

"Cut!" Phil's voice jolted her in her chair. "That's it." Tory saw Marlie exhale a long breath. She won-

dered if there was some similarity in finishing a tense
scene such as that one and winding up a difficult cross-
examination. She decided that the emotion might be
very much the same.

"Let's get some reaction shots, Marlie." Painstakingly he arranged for the change in angles and lighting.
When the camera was in position, he checked through
the lens himself, repositioned Marlie, then checked
again. "Roll it…. Cue."

They worked for another thirty minutes, perfecting
the shot. It was more than creativity, more than talent. The nuts and bolts end of the filming were tough,
technical and wearily repetitious. No one complained,
no one questioned, when told to change or to do over.
There was an unspoken bond: the film. Perhaps, she
reflected, it was because they knew it would outlast all
of them. Their small slice of immortality. Tory found
herself developing a respect for these people who took
such an intense pride in their work.

"Cut. That's a wrap." Tory could almost feel the communal sigh of relief. "Set up for scene fifty-three in…"
Phil checked his watch. "Two hours." The moment the
lights shut down, the temperature dropped.

"I'm going to see what Mr. Bicks is doing," Tod announced, scrambling up. Tory remained sitting where
she was a moment, watching Phil answer questions and
give instructions. He never stops, she realized. One
might be an actor, another a lighting expert or a cinematographer, but he touches every aspect. Rich and privileged, yes, she reflected, but not afraid of hard work.

"Sheriff."

Tory turned her head to see Marlie standing beside
her. "Ms. Summers. You were very impressive."

"Thanks." Without waiting for an invitation, Marlie took a chair. "What I need now is a three-hour shower." She took a long pull from the glass of ice water she held in her hand as the two women studied each other in silence. "You've got an incredible face," Marlie said at length. "If I'd had one like that, I wouldn't have had to fight for a part with some meat on it. Mine's like a sugarplum."

Tory found herself laughing. Leaning back, she hooked her arm over the back of her chair. "Ms. Summers, as sheriff, I should warn you that stealing's a crime. You stole that scene from Sam very smoothly."

Tilting her head, Marlie studied her from a new angle. "You're very sharp."

"On occasion."

"I can see why Merle thinks you hold the answer to the mysteries of the universe."

Tory sent her a long, cool look. "Merle is a very naive, very vulnerable young man."

"Yes." Marlie set down her glass. "I like him." They gave each other another measuring look. "Look, let me ask you something, from one attractive woman to another. Did you ever find it pleasant to be with a man who liked to talk to you, to listen to you?"

"Yes, of course." Tory frowned. "Perhaps it's that I can't imagine what Merle would say to interest you."

Marlie gave a quick laugh, then cupped her chin on her palm. "You're too used to him. I've been scrambling my way up the ladder since I was eighteen. There's nothing I want more than to be on top. Along the way, I've met a lot of men. Merle's different."

"If he falls in love with you, he'll be hurt," Tory

pointed out. "I've looked out for him on and off since we were kids."

Marlie paused a moment. Idly she drew patterns through the condensation on the outside of her water glass. "He's not going to fall in love with me," she said slowly. "Not really. We're just giving each other a bit of the other's world for a few weeks. When it's over, we'll both have something nice to remember." She glanced over her shoulder and spotted Phil. "We all need someone now and again, don't we, Sheriff?"

Tory followed the direction of Marlie's gaze. At that moment Phil's eyes lifted to hers. "Yes," she murmured, watching him steadily. "I suppose we do."

"I'm going to get that shower now." Marlie rose. "He's a good man," she added. Tory looked back at her, knowing who she referred to now.

"Yes, I think you're right." Deep in thought, Tory sat a moment longer. Then, standing, she glanced around for Tod.

"Tory." Phil laid a hand on her arm. "How are you?"

"Fine." She smiled, letting him know she hadn't forgotten the last time they had been together. "You're tougher than I thought, Kincaid, working in this oven all day."

He grinned. "That, assuredly, is a compliment."

"Don't let it go to your head. You're sweating like a pig."

"Really," he said dryly. "I hadn't noticed."

She spotted a towel hung over the back of a chair and plucked it up. "You know," she said as she wiped off his face, "I imagined directors would do more delegating than you do."

"My film," he said simply, stirred by the way she

brushed the cloth over his face. "Tory." He captured her free hand. "I want to see you—alone."

She dropped the towel back on the table. "Your film," she reminded him. "And there's something I have to do." Her eyes darted past him, again in search of Tod.

"Tonight," he insisted. He'd gone beyond the point of patience. "Take the evening off, Tory."

She brought her eyes back to his. She'd gone beyond the point of excuses. "If I can," she agreed. "There's a place I know," she added with a slow smile. "South of town, about a mile. We used it as a swimming hole when I was a kid. You can't miss it—it's the only water around."

"Sunset?" He would have lifted her hand to his lips, but she drew it away.

"I can't promise." Before he could say anything else, she stepped past him, then called for Tod.

Even as she drew the boy back outside, he was expounding. "Tory, it's great, isn't it? About the greatest thing to happen in town in forever! If I could, I'd go with them when they leave." He sent her a look from under his tumbled hair. "Wouldn't you like to go, Tory?"

"To Hollywood?" she replied lightly. "Oh, I don't think it's my style. Besides, I'll be going back to Albuquerque soon."

"I want to come with you," he blurted out.

They were just outside her office door. Tory turned and looked down at him. Unable to resist, she placed her hand on his cheek. "Tod," she said softly.

"I love you, Tory," he began quickly. "I could—"

"Tod, come inside." For days she had been working out what she would say to him and how to say it. Now, as they walked together into her office, she felt completely inadequate. Carefully she sat on the edge of her desk and faced him. "Tod—" She broke off and shook her head. "Oh, I wish I were smarter."

"You're the smartest person I know," he said swiftly. "And so beautiful, and I love you, Tory, more than anything."

Her heart reached out for him even as she took his hands. "I love you, too, Tod." As he started to speak she shook her head again. "But there are different kinds of love, different ways of feeling."

"I only know how I feel about you." His eyes were very intense and just above hers as she sat on the desk. Phil had been right, she realized. He wasn't quite a child.

"Tod, I know this won't be easy for you to understand. Sometimes people aren't right for each other."

"Just because I'm younger," he began heatedly.

"That's part of it," Tory agreed, keeping her voice quiet. "It's hard to accept, when you feel like a man, that you're still a boy. There's so much you have to experience yet, and to learn."

"But when I do..." he began.

"When you do," she interrupted, "you won't feel the same way about me."

"Yes, I will!" he insisted. He surprised both of them by grabbing her arms. "It won't change because I don't want it to. And I'll wait if I have to. I love you, Tory."

"I know you do. I know it's very real." She lifted her hands to cover his. "Age doesn't mean anything to the heart, Tod. You're very special to me, a very important part of my life."

"But you don't love me." The words trembled out with anger and frustration.

"Not in the way you mean." She kept her hands firm on his when he would have jerked away.

"You think it's funny."

"No," she said sharply, rising. "No, I think it's lovely. And I wish things could be different because I know the kind of man you'll be. It hurts—for me too."

He was breathing quickly, struggling with tears and a sharp sense of betrayal. "You don't understand," he accused, pulling away from her. "You don't care."

"I do. Tod, please—"

"No." He stopped her with one ravaged look. "You don't." With a dignity that tore at Tory's heart, he walked out of the office.

She leaned back against the desk, overcome by a sense of failure.

The sun was just setting when Tory dropped down on the short, prickly grass by the water. Pulling her knees to her chest, she watched the flaming globe sink toward the horizon. There was an intensity of color against the darkening blue of the sky. Nothing soft or mellow. It was a vivid and demanding prelude to night.

Tory watched the sky with mixed emotions. The day as a whole was the kind she would have liked to wrap up and ship off to oblivion. The situation with Tod had left her emotionally wrung out and edgy. As a result she had handled a couple of routine calls with less finesse than was her habit. She'd even managed to snarl at Merle before she had gone off duty. Glancing down at the badge on her breast, she considered tossing it into the water.

A beautiful mess you've made of things, Sheriff, she told herself. Ah, the hell with it, she decided, resting her chin on her knees. She was taking the night off. Tomorrow she would straighten everything out, one disaster at a time.

The trouble was, she thought with a half smile, she'd forgotten the art of relaxation over the past few weeks. It was time to reacquaint herself with laziness. Lying back, Tory shut her eyes and went instantly to sleep.

Drifting slowly awake with the feather-light touch of fingers on her cheek, Tory gave a sleepy sigh and debated whether she should open her eyes. There was another touch—a tracing of her lips this time. Enjoying the sensation, she made a quiet sound of pleasure and let her lashes flutter up.

The light was dim, deep, deep dusk. Her eyes focused gradually on the sky above her. No clouds, no stars, just a mellow expanse of blue. Taking a deep breath, she lifted her arms to stretch. Her hand was captured and kissed. Tory turned her head and saw Phil sitting beside her.

"Hello."

"Watching you wake up is enough to drive a man crazy," he murmured, keeping her hand in his. "You're sexier sleeping than most women are wide awake."

She gave a lazy laugh. "Sleeping's always been one of my best things. Have you been here long?"

"Not long. The filming ran a bit over schedule." He flexed his back muscles, then smiled down at her. "How was your day?"

"Rotten." Tory blew out a breath and struggled to sit up. "I talked with Tod this afternoon. I didn't handle it well. Damn." Tory rested her forehead on her knees again. "I didn't want to hurt that boy."

"Tory—" Phil stroked a hand down her hair "—there

was no way he wouldn't be hurt some. Kids are resilient. He'll bounce back."

"I know." She turned her head to look at him, keeping her cheeks on her knees. "But he's so fragile. Love's fragile, isn't it? So easily shattered. I suppose it's best that he hate me for a while."

"He won't," Phil disagreed. "You mean too much to him. After a while his feelings will slip into perspective. I imagine he'll always think of you as his first real love."

"It makes me feel very special, but I don't think I made him believe that. Anyway," she continued, "after I'd made a mess out of that, I snarled at one of the town fathers, bit off the head of a rancher and took a few swipes at Merle." She swore with the expertise he had admired before. "Sitting here, I knew I was in danger of having a major pity party, so I went to sleep instead."

"Wise choice. I came near to choking my overseer."

"Overseer? Oh, the guarantor." Tory laughed, shaking back her hair. "So we both had a lovely day."

"Let's drink to it." Phil picked up a bottle of champagne from beside him.

"Well, how about that." Tory glanced at the label and pursed her lips. "You always go first-class, Kincaid."

"Absolutely," he agreed, opening the bottle with a pop and fizz. He poured the brimming wine into a glass. Tory took it, watching the bubbles explode as he filled his own. "To the end of the day."

"To the end of the day!" she agreed, clinking her glass against his. The ice-cold champagne ran excitedly over her tongue. "Nice," she murmured, shutting her eyes and savoring. "Very nice."

They drank in companionable silence as the darkness deepened. Overhead a few stars flickered hesitantly while the moon started its slow rise. The night was as hot and dry as the afternoon and completely still. There wasn't even a whisper of breeze to ripple the water. Phil leaned back on an elbow, studying Tory's profile.

"What are you thinking?"

"That I'm glad I took the night off." Smiling, she turned her head so she faced him fully. The pale light of the moon fell over her features, accenting them.

"Good God, Tory," he breathed. "I've got to get that face on film."

She threw back her head and laughed with a freedom she hadn't felt in days. "So take a home movie, Kincaid."

"Would you let me?" he countered immediately.

She merely filled both glasses again. "You're obsessed," she told him.

"More than's comfortable, yes," he murmured. He sipped, enjoying the taste, but thinking of her. "I wasn't sure you'd come."

"Neither was I." She studied the wine in her glass with apparent concentration. "Another glass of this and I might admit I enjoy being with you."

"We've half a bottle left."

Tory lifted one shoulder in a shrug before she drank again. "One step at a time," she told him. "But then," she murmured, "I suppose we've come a few steps already, haven't we?"

"A few." His fingers ran over the back of her hand. "Does it worry you?"

She gave a quick, rueful laugh. "More than's comfortable, yes."

Sitting up, he draped a casual arm around her shoulders. "I like the night best. I have the chance to think."

He sensed her complete relaxation, feeling a pleasant stir as she let her head rest on his shoulder. "During the day, with all the pressure, the demands, when I think, I think on my feet."

"That's funny." She lifted a hand across her body to lace her fingers with his. "In Albuquerque I did some of my best planning in bed the night before a court date. It's easier to let things come and go in your head at night." Tilting her face, Tory brushed his lips with hers. "I do enjoy being with you."

He returned the kiss, but with equal lightness. "I didn't need the champagne?"

"Well...it didn't hurt." When he chuckled, she settled her head in the crook of his shoulder again. It felt right there, as if it belonged. "I've always loved this spot," Tory said quietly. "Water's precious around here, and this has always been like a little mirage. It's not very big, but it's pretty deep in places. The townspeople enjoy calling it a lake." She laughed suddenly. "When we were kids, we'd troop out here sometimes on an unbearably hot day. We'd strip and jump in. Of course, it was frowned on when we were teenagers, but we still managed."

"Our decadent youth."

"Good, clean fun, Kincaid," she disagreed.

"Oh, yeah? Why don't you show me?"

Tory turned to him with a half smile. When he only lifted a brow in challenge, she grinned. A small pulse of excitement beat deep inside her. "You're on." Pushing him away, she tugged off her shoes. "The name of the game is to get in first."

As he stripped off his shirt it occurred to him that he'd never seen her move quickly before. He was still

pulling off his shoes when she was naked and racing
for the water. The moonlight danced over her skin, over
the hair that streamed behind her back, causing him to
stop and stare after her. She was even more exquisite
than he had imagined. Then she was splashing up to
her waist and diving under. Shaking himself out of the
trance, Phil stripped and followed her.

The water was beautifully cool. It shocked his heated
skin on contact, then caressed it. Phil gave a moan of
pure pleasure as he sank to his shoulders. The small
swimming hole in the middle of nowhere gave him just
as much relief as his custom-made pool. More, he realized, glancing around for Tory. She surfaced, face lifted,
hair slicked back. The moonlight caught the glisten of
water on her face. A naiad, he thought. She opened her
eyes. They glimmered green, like a cat's.

"You're slow, Kincaid."

He struggled against an almost painful flood of desire. This wasn't the moment to rush. They both knew
this was their time, and there were hours yet to fill.
"I've never seen you move fast before," he commented,
treading water.

"I save it up." The bottom was just below her toes.
Tory kicked lazily to keep afloat. "Conserving energy
is one of my personal campaigns."

"I guess that means you don't want to race."

She gave him a long look. "You've got to be kidding."

"Guess you wouldn't be too hard to beat," he considered. "Skinny," he added.

"I am not." Tory put the heel of her hand into the
water, sending a spray into his face.

"Couple of months in a good gym might build you

up a bit." He smiled, calmly wiping the water from his eyes.

"I'm built up just fine," she returned. "Is this amateur psychology, Kincaid?"

"Did it work?" he countered.

In answer she twisted and struck out, kicking up a curtain of water into his face as she headed for the far side of the pool. Phil grinned, observing that she could move like lightning when she put her mind to it, then started after her.

She beat him by two full strokes, then waited, laughing, while she shook back her hair. "Better keep up your membership to that gym, Kincaid."

"You cheated," he pointed out.

"I won. That's what counts."

He lifted a brow, amused and intrigued that she wasn't even winded. Apparently her statement about strong energy was perfectly true. "And that from an officer of the law."

"I'm not wearing my badge."

"I noticed."

Tory laughed again, moving out in a gentle sidestroke toward the middle of the pool. "I guess you're in pretty good shape...for a Hollywood director."

"Is that so?" He swam alongside of her, matching her languid movements.

"You don't have a paunch—yet," she added, grinning. Gently but firmly, Phil pushed her head under. "So you want to play dirty," she murmured when she surfaced. In a quick move she had his legs scissored between hers, then gave his chest a firm shove. Off guard, Phil went over backward and submerged. He came up, giving his head a toss to free his eyes of dripping hair. Tory was already a few yards away, treading water and chuckling.

"Basic Self-Defense 101," she informed him. "Though you have to make allowances for buoyancy in the water."

This time Phil put more effort into his strokes. Before Tory had reached the other side, he had a firm grip on her ankle. With a tug he took her under the water and back to him. Sputtering, she found herself caught in his arms.

"Want to try a few free throws?" he invited.

A cautious woman, Tory measured her opponent and the odds. "I'll pass. Water isn't my element."

Her arms were trapped between their bodies, but when she tried to free them, he only brought her closer. His smile faded into a look of understanding. She felt her heart begin a slow, dull thud.

He took her mouth with infinite care, wanting to savor the moment. Her lips were wet and cool. With no hesitation her tongue sought his. The kiss deepened slowly, luxuriously while he supported her, keeping her feet just above the sandy bottom. The feeling of weightlessness aroused her and she allowed herself to float, holding on to him as though he were an anchor. Their lips warmed from an intimate heat before they began to search for new tastes.

Without hurry they roamed each other's faces, running moist kisses over moist skin. With quiet whispers the water lapped around them as they shifted and searched.

Finding her arms free at last, Tory wrapped them about his neck, pressing her body against his. She heard Phil suck in his breath at the contact, felt the shudder race through him before his mouth crushed down on hers. The time had passed for slow loving. Passion too long suppressed exploded as mouth sought eager mouth. Keeping one arm firm at her waist, he began to explore her as he had longed to do. His fingers slid over her wet skin.

Tory moved against him, weakening them both so that they submerged, locked together. Streaming wet, they surfaced with their lips still fused, then gasped for air. Her hands ran over him, drawing him closer, then away, to seek more of him. Unable to bear the hunger, she thrust her fingers into his hair and pulled his lips back to hers. With a sudden violence he bent her back until her hair streamed behind her on the surface of the water. His mouth rushed over her face, refusing her efforts to halt it with hers while he found her breast with his palm.

The throaty moan that wrenched from her evoked a new wave of passion. Phil lifted her so he could draw her hot, wet nipple into his mouth. His tongue tormented them both until her hands fell into the pool in a submission he hadn't expected. Drunk on power, he took his mouth over her trembling skin, down to where the water separated him from her. Frustrated with the barrier, he let his mouth race up again to her breast until Tory clutched at his shoulders, shuddering.

Her head fell back as he lowered her so that her neck was vulnerable and glistening in the moonlight. He kissed it hungrily, hearing her cry with anguished delight.

Cool, cool water, but she was so hot that his legs nearly buckled at the feel of her. Tory was beyond all but dark, vivid sensations. To her the water felt steamy, heated by her own body. Her breathing seemed to echo in the empty night, then shudder back to her. She would have shouted for him to take her, but his name would only come as a gasp through her lips. She couldn't bear it; the need was unreasonable. With a strength conceived in passion she locked her legs tightly around his waist and lowered herself to him.

They swayed for a moment, equally stunned. Then he gripped her legs, letting her take him on a wild, impossible journey. There was a rushing, like the sound of the wind inside her head. Trembling, they slid down into the water.

With some vague recollection of where they were, Phil caught Tory against him again. "We'd better get out of here," he managed. "We'll drown."

Tory let her head fall on his shoulder. "I don't mind."

With a low, shaky laugh, Phil lifted her into his arms and carried her from the pond.

Chapter 8

He laid her down, then dropped on his back on the grass beside her. For some time the only sound in the night was their mixed breathing. The stars were brilliant now, the moon nearly full. Both of them stared up.

"You were saying something," Phil began in a voice that still wasn't steady, "about water not being your element."

Tory gave a choke of laughter that turned into a bubble, then a burst of pure appreciation. "I guess I could be wrong."

Phil closed his eyes, the better to enjoy the heavy weakness that flowed through his system.

Tory sighed and stretched. "That was wonderful."

He drew her closer against his side. "Cold?"

"No."

"This grass—"

"Terrible, isn't it?" With another laugh Tory twisted

so that she lay over his chest. Her wet skin slid over his. Lazily he ran a hand down the length of her back as she smiled back at him. Her hair was slicked close to her head, her skin as pale and exquisite as marble in the moonlight. A few small drops of water clung to her lashes.

"You're beautiful when you're wet," he told her, drawing her down for a slow, lingering kiss.

"So are you." When he grinned, she ran both thumbs from his jaw to his cheekbones. "I like your face," she decided, tilting her head as she studied it. "That aristocratic bone structure you get from your father. It's no wonder he was so effective playing those swashbuckling roles early in his career." She narrowed her eyes as if seeking a different perspective. "Of course," she continued thoughtfully, "I rather like it when yours takes on that aloof expression."

"Aloof?" He shifted a bit as the grass scratched his bare skin.

"You do it very well. Your eyes have a terrific way of saying 'I beg your pardon' and meaning 'Go to hell.' I've noticed it, especially when you talk to that short man with the little glasses."

"Tremaine," Phil muttered. "Associate producer and general pain in the neck."

Tory chuckled and kissed his chin. "Don't like anyone else's hands on your movie, do you?"

"I'm very selfish with what belongs to me." He took her mouth again with more fervor than he had intended. As the kiss lengthened and deepened he gave a quick sound of pleasure and pressed her closer. When their lips parted, their eyes met. Both of them knew they were heading for dangerous ground. Both of them treaded carefully. Tory lowered her head to his chest, trying to think logically.

"I suppose we knew this was going to happen sooner or later."

"I suppose we did."

She caught her bottom lip between her teeth a moment. "The important thing is not to let it get complicated."

"No." He frowned up at the stars. "We both want to avoid complications."

"In a few weeks we'll both be leaving town." They were unaware that they had tightened their holds on the other. "I have to pick up my caseload again."

"I have to finish the studio scenes," he murmured.

"It's a good thing we understand each other right from the beginning." She closed her eyes, drawing in his scent as though she were afraid she might forget it. "We can be together like this, knowing no one will be hurt when it's over."

"Yeah."

They lay in silence, dealing with a mutual and unstated sense of depression and loss. We're adults, Tory thought, struggling against the mood. Attracted to each other. It isn't any more than that. Can't be any more than that. But she wasn't as sure of herself as she wanted to be.

"Well," she said brightly, lifting her head again. "So tell me how the filming's going? That scene today seemed to click perfectly."

Phil forced himself to match her mood, ignoring the doubts forming in his own head. "You came in on the last take," he said dryly. "It was like pulling teeth."

Tory reached across him for the bottle of champagne.

The glass was covered with beads of sweat. "It looked to me like Marlie Summers came out on top," she commented as she poured.

"She's very good."

Resting her arm on his chest, Tory drank. The wine still fizzled cold. "Yes, I thought so, too, but I wish she'd steer away from Merle."

"Worried about his virtue, Tory?" he asked dryly.

She shot him an annoyed look. "He's going to get hurt."

"Why?" he countered. "Because a beautiful woman's interested enough to spend some time with him? Now, look," he continued before she could retort, "you have your own view of him. It's possible someone else might have another."

Frowning, she drank again. "How's he going to feel when she leaves?"

"That's something he'll have to deal with," Phil said quietly. "He already knows she's going to."

Again their eyes met in quick, almost frightened recognition. Tory looked away to study the remaining wine in her glass. It was different, she told herself. She and Phil both had certain priorities. When they parted, it would be without regret or pain. It had to be.

"It might not be easy to accept," she murmured, wanting to believe she still spoke of Merle.

"On either side," he replied after a long pause.

Tory turned her head to find his eyes on hers, light and clear and very intense. The ground was getting shaky again. "I suppose it'll work out for the best... for everyone." Determined to lighten the mood, she smiled down at him. "You know, the whole town's excited about those scenes you're shooting with them as extras. The Kramer twins haven't gotten out of line for an entire week."

"One of them asked me if he could have a close-up."

"Which one?"

"Who the hell can tell?" Phil demanded. "This one tried to hustle a date with Marlie."

Tory laughed, pressing the back of her wrist to her mouth to hold in a swallow of champagne. "Had to be Zac. He's impossible. Are you going to give him his close-up?"

"I'll give him a swift kick in the pants if he messes around the crane again," Phil returned.

"Uh-oh, I didn't hear about that."

Phil shrugged. "It didn't seem necessary to call the law on him."

"Tempting as it might be," she returned. "I wouldn't have thrown him in the penitentiary. Handling the Kramers has become an art."

"I had one of my security guards put the fear of God into him," Phil told her easily. "It seemed to do the trick."

"Listen, Phil, if any of my people need restraining, I expect to be informed."

With a sigh, he plucked the glass from her hand, tossed it aside, then rolled on top of her. "You've got the night off, Sheriff. We're not going to talk about it."

"Really." Her arms were already linked around his neck. "Just what are we going to talk about, then?"

"Not a damn thing," he muttered and pressed his mouth to hers.

Her response was a muffled sound of agreement. He could taste the champagne on her tongue and lingered over it. The heat of the night had already dried their skin, but he ran his hands through the cool dampness of her hair. He could feel her nipples harden against the pressure of his chest. This time, he thought, there would be no desperation. He could enjoy her slowly— the long, lean lines of her body, the silken texture of her skin, the varied, heady tastes of her.

From the wine-flavored lips he took an unhurried journey to the warmer taste of her throat. But his hands were already roaming demandingly. Tory moved under him with uncontrollable urgency as his thumb found the peak of her breast, intensifying her pleasure. To his amazement Phil found he could have taken her immediately. He banked the need. There was still so much of her to learn of, so much to experience. Allowing the tip of his tongue to skim along her skin, he moved down to her breast.

Tory arched, pressing him down. His slow, teasing kisses made her moan in delighted frustration. Beneath the swell of her breast, his mouth lingered to send shivers and more shivers of pleasure through her. His tongue flicked lazily over her nipple, then retreated to soft flesh. She moaned his name, urging him back. He circled slowly, mouth on one breast, palm on the other, thrilling to her mindless murmurs and convulsive movements beneath him. Taking exquisite care, he captured a straining peak between his teeth. Leaving it moist and wanting, he journeyed to her other breast to savor, to linger, then to devour.

His hands had moved lower, so that desire throbbed over her at so many points, she was delirious for fulfillment. Anxious to discover all she could about his body, Tory ran her fingertips over the taut muscles of his shoulders, down the strong back. Through a haze of sensation she felt him shudder at her touch. With delicious slowness she skimmed her fingers up his rib cage. She heard him groan before his teeth nipped into her tender flesh. Open and hungry, his mouth came swiftly back to hers.

When she reached for him, he drew in a sharp breath at the contact. Burying his face in her neck, Phil felt himself drowning in pleasure. The need grew huge, but again he refused it.

"Not yet," he murmured to himself and to her. "Not yet."

He passed down the valley between her breasts, wallowing in the hot scent that clung to her skin. Her stomach quivered under his lips. Tory no longer felt the rough carpet of grass under her back, only Phil's seeking mouth and caressing hands. His mouth slipped lower and she moaned, arching—willing, wanting. His tongue was quick and greedy, shooting pleasure from the core of her out even to her fingertips. Her body was heavy with it, her head light. He brought her to a shuddering crest, but relentlessly allowed no time for recovery. His fingers sought her even as his mouth found fresh delight in the taste of her thigh.

She shook her head, unable to believe she could be so helpless. Her fingers clutched at the dry grass while her lips responded to the dizzying pace he set. Her skin was damp again, quivering in the hot night air. Again and again he drove her up, never letting her settle, never allowing her complete release.

"Phil," she moaned between harsh, shallow breaths. "I need…"

He'd driven himself to the verge of madness. His body throbbed in one solid ache for her. Wildly he took his mouth on a frantic journey up her body. "What?" he demanded. "What do you need?"

"You," she breathed, no longer aware of words or meanings. "You."

With a groan of triumph he thrust into her, catapulting them both closer to what they insisted on denying.

She'd warned him about the heat. Still, Phil found himself cursing the unrelenting sun as he set up for another outdoor shot. The grips had set up stands with butterflies—long black pieces of cloth—to give shade between takes. The cameraman stood under a huge orange-and-white umbrella and sweated profusely. The actors at least could spend a few moments in the shade provided while Phil worked almost exclusively in the streaming sun, checking angles, lighting, shadows. Reflectors were used to bounce the sunlight and carbon arcs balanced the back lighting. A gaffer, stripped to the waist, adjusted a final piece of blue gel over a bulb. The harsh, glaring day was precisely what Phil wanted, but it didn't make the work any more pleasant.

Forcing down more salt tablets, he ordered the next take. Oddly, Dressler seemed to have adjusted to the heat more easily than the younger members of the cast and crew. Or, Phil mused as he watched him come slowly down the street with the fledgling actor who played his alter ego, he's determined not to be outdone. As time went on, he became more competitive—and the more competitive he became, particularly with Marlie, the more Phil was able to draw out of him.

Yeah, Phil thought as Dressler turned to the younger actor with a look of world-weariness. He ran through his dialogue slowly, keeping the pace just short of dragging. He was a man giving advice reluctantly, without any confidence that it was viable or would be listened to in any case. He talked almost to himself. For a moment Phil forgot his own discomfort in simple admiration for a pro who had found the heart of his character. He was growing old and didn't give a damn—wanted to be left alone, but had no hope that his wishes would be respected. Once he had found his moment of glory, then had lost it. He saw himself in the younger man and felt a bitter pity. Ultimately he turned and walked slowly away. The camera stayed on him for a silent thirty seconds.

"Cut. Perfect," Phil announced in a rare show of unconditional approval. "Lunch," he said dropping a hand on the younger actor's shoulder. "Get out of the sun for a while. I'll need you for reaction shots in thirty minutes." He walked over to meet Sam. "That was a hell of a job."

Grinning, Sam swiped at his brow. "Somebody's got to show these kids how it's done. That love scene with Marlie's going to be interesting," he added a bit ruefully. "I keep remembering she's my daughter's age."

"That should keep you in character."

Sam laughed, running his fingers through his thick salt-and-pepper hair. "Well, the girl's a pro," he said after a moment. "This movie's going to shoot her into the fast lane quick." He sent Phil a long, steady look. "And you and I," he added, "are going to win each other an Oscar." When Phil only lifted a brow, Sam slapped him on the back. "Don't give me that look, boy," he said, amused. "You're talking to one who's been passed over a few times himself. You can be lofty and say awards don't mean a damn...but they do." Again his eyes met Phil's. "I want this one just as much as you do." He ran a hand over his stomach. "Now I'm going to get myself a beer and put my feet up."

He sauntered off, leaving Phil looking after him. He didn't want to admit, even to himself, that he desired his profession's ultimate accolade. In a few short words Dressler had boiled it all down. Yes, he wanted to direct outstanding films—critically and financially successful, lasting, important. But he wanted that little gold statue. With a wry grin Phil swiped at his brow with his forearm. It seemed that the need to win, and to be acknowledged, didn't fade with years. Dressler had been in the business longer than Phil had been alive; yet, he was still waiting for the pot at the end of the rainbow. Phil adjusted his sunglasses, admitting he wasn't willing to wait thirty-five years.

"Hey, Phil." Bicks lumbered over to him, mopping his face. "Look, you've got to do something about that woman."

Phil pulled out a cigarette. "Which?"

"That sheriff." Bicks popped another piece of gum into his mouth. "Great looker," he added. "Got a way of walking that makes a man home right in on her..." He trailed off, observing the look in Phil's eyes. "Just an observation," he muttered.

"What do you expect me to do about the way Sheriff Ashton walks, Bicks?"

Catching the amusement in Phil's tone, Bicks grinned. "Nothing, please. A man's got to have something pleasant to look at in this place. But damn it, Phil, she gave me a ticket and slapped a two-hundred-and-fifty-dollar fine on me."

Phil pushed his glasses up on his head with a weary

sigh. He'd wanted to catch a quick shower before re-
suming the shoot. "What for?"

"Littering."

"Littering?" Phil repeated over a snort of laughter.

"Two hundred and fifty bucks for dropping gum
wrappers in the street," Bicks returned, not seeing the
humor. "Wouldn't listen to reason either. I'd have picked
'em up and apologized. Two hundred and fifty bucks
for a gum wrapper, Phil. Jeez."

"All right, all right, I'll talk to her." After checking
his watch, Phil started up the street. "Set up for the next
scene in twenty minutes."

Tory sat with her feet propped up on the desk as she
struggled to decipher Merle's report on a feud between
two neighboring ranches. It seemed that a dispute over
a line of fence was becoming more heated. It was going
to require her attention. So was the letter she had just
received from one of her clients in Albuquerque. When
Phil walked in, she glanced up from the scrawled pad
and smiled.

"You look hot," she commented.

"Am hot," he countered, giving the squeaking fan
above their heads a glance. "Why don't you get that
thing fixed?"

"And spoil the atmosphere?"

Phil stepped over the sleeping dog, taking a seat on
the corner of her desk. "We're going to be shooting one
of the scenes with the townspeople milling around later.
Are you going to watch?"

"Sure."

"Want to do a cameo?" he asked with a grin.

"No, thanks."

Leaning over, he pressed his lips to hers. "Dinner in my room tonight?"

Tory smiled. "You still have those candles?"

"All you want," he agreed.

"You talked me into it," she murmured, drawing his face back for a second kiss.

"Tory, if I brought a camera out to your ranch one day, would you let me film you riding that palomino?"

"Phil, for heaven's sake—"

"Home movies?" he interrupted, twirling her hair around his finger.

She gave a capitulating sigh. "If it's important to you."

"It is." He straightened, checked his watch, then pulled out a cigarette. "Listen, Tory, Bicks tells me you fined him for littering."

"That's right." The phone rang, and Phil waited while she took the call. After a moment he realized her tone was slightly different. With interest he listened to the legal jargon roll off her tongue. It must be Albuquerque, he realized. He watched her carefully, discovering this was a part of her life he knew nothing of. She'd be tough in court, he mused. There was an intensity under that languid exterior that slipped out at unexpected moments. And what did she do after a day in court or a day in the office?

There'd be men, he thought, instantly disliking the image. A woman like Tory would only spend evenings alone, nights alone, if she chose to. He looked away, taking a deep drag on his cigarette. He couldn't start thinking along those lines, he reminded himself. They were both free agents. That was the first rule.

"Phil?"

He turned back to see that she had replaced the receiver. "What?"

"You were saying?"

"Ah…" He struggled to remember the point of his visit. "Bicks," he continued.

"Yes, what about him?"

"A two-hundred-and-fifty-dollar fine for littering," Phil stated, not quite erasing the frown that had formed between his brows.

"Yes, that's the amount of the fine."

"Tory, be reasonable."

Her brow lifted. "Reasonable, Kincaid?"

Her use of his surname told him what level they were dealing on. "It's certainly extreme for a gum wrapper."

"We don't vary the fine according to the style of trash," she replied with an easy shrug. "A tin of caviar would have cost him the same amount."

Goaded, Phil rose. "Listen, Sheriff—"

"And while we're on the subject," she interrupted, "you can tell your people that if they don't start picking up after themselves more carefully, they're all going to be slapped with fines." She gave him a mild smile. "Let's keep Friendly clean, Kincaid."

He took a slow drag. "You're not going to hassle my people."

"You're not going to litter my town."

He swore, coming around the desk when the door opened. Pleased to see Tod, Tory swung her legs to the floor and started to stand. It was then that she saw the dull bruise on the side of his face. Fury swept through her so quickly, she was forced to clench her hands into fists to control it. Slowly she walked to him and took his face in her hands.

"How did you get this?"

He shrugged, avoiding her eyes. "It's nothing."

Fighting for calm, Tory lifted his hands, examining the knuckles carefully. There was no sign that he'd been fighting. "Your father?"

He shook his head briskly. "I came to do the sweeping up," he told her, and tried to move away.

Tory took him firmly by the shoulders. "Tod, look at me."

Reluctantly he lifted his eyes. "I've still got five dollars to work off," he said tightly.

"Did your father put this bruise on your face?" she demanded. When he started to drop his eyes again, she gave him a quick shake. "You answer me."

"He was just mad because—" He broke off, observing the rage that lit her face. Instinctively he cringed away from it. Tory set him aside and started for the door.

"Where are you going?" Moving quickly, Phil was at the door with her, his hand over hers on the knob.

"To see Swanson."

"No!" They both turned to see Tod standing rigid in the center of the room. "No, you can't. He won't like it. He'll get awful mad at you."

"I'm going to talk to your father, Tod," Tory said in a careful voice, "to explain to him why it's wrong for him to hurt you this way."

"Only when he loses his temper." Tod dashed across the room to grab her free hand. "He's not a bad man. I don't want you to put him in jail."

Though her anger was lethal, Tory gave Tod's hand a reassuring squeeze. "I'm just going to talk to him, Tod."

"He'll be crazy mad if you do, Tory. I don't want him to hurt you either."

"He won't, don't worry." She smiled, seeing by the expression in Tod's eyes that she'd already been forgiven. "Go get the broom now. I'll be back soon."

"Tory, please..."

"Go on," she said firmly.

Phil waited until the boy had disappeared into the back room. "You're not going."

Tory sent him a long look, then pulled open the door. Phil spun her around as she stepped outside. "I said you're not going."

"You're interfering with the law, Kincaid."

"The hell with that!" Infuriated, Phil pushed her back against the wall. "You're crazy if you think I'm going to let you go out there."

"You don't *let* me do anything," she reminded him. "I'm sworn to protect the people under my jurisdiction. Tod Swanson is one of my people."

"A man who punches a kid isn't going to hesitate to take a swing at you just because you've got that little piece of tin on your shirt."

Because her anger was racing, Tory forced herself to speak calmly. "What do you suggest I do? Ignore what I just saw?"

Frustrated by the image of Tod's thin face, Phil swore. "I'll go."

"You have no right." She met his eyes squarely. "You're not the law, and what's more, you're an outsider."

"Send Merle."

"Don't you hold with no woman sheriff, Kincaid?"

"Damn it, Tory." He shook her, half in fear, half in frustration. "This isn't a joke."

"No, it's not," she said seriously. "It's my job. Now, let go of me, Phil."

Furious, Phil complied, then watched her stride to her car. "Tory," he called after her, "if he puts a hand on you, I'll kill him."

She slipped into the car, driving off without looking back.

Tory took the short drive slowly, wanting to get her emotions under control before she confronted Swanson. She had to be objective, she thought, as her knuckles whitened on the steering wheel. But first she had to be calm. It wasn't possible to do what she needed to do in anger, or to let Phil's feelings upset her. To live up to the badge on her shirt, she had to set all that aside.

She wasn't physically afraid, not because she was foolishly brave, but because when she saw a blatant injustice, Tory forgot everything but the necessity of making it right. As she took the left fork toward the Swanson ranch, however, she had her first stirring of self-doubt.

What if she mishandled the situation? she thought in sudden panic. What if her meeting with Swanson only made more trouble for the boy? The memory of Tod's terrified face brought on a quick queasiness that she fought down. No, she wasn't going to mishandle it, she told herself firmly as the house came into view. She was going to confront Swanson and at the very least set the wheels in motion for making things right. Tory's belief that all things could be set right with patience, through the law, had been indoctrinated in childhood. She knew and accepted no other way.

She pulled up behind Swanson's battered pickup, then climbed out of the sheriff's car. Instantly a dog who had been sleeping on the porch sent out angry, warning barks. Tory eyed him a moment, wary, then saw that he came no farther than the edge of the sagging porch. He looked as old and unkempt as the house itself.

Taking a quick look around, Tory felt a stir of pity for Tod. This was borderline poverty. She, too, had grown up where a tightened belt was often a rule, but between her mother's penchant for neatness and the hard work of both her parents, their small ranch had always had a homey charm. This place, on the other hand, looked desolate and hopeless. The grass grew wild, long over-due for trimming. There were no brightening spots of color from flowers or potted plants. The house itself was frame, the paint faded down to the wood in places. There was no chair on the porch, no sign that anyone had the time or inclination to sit and appreciate the view.

No one came to the door in response to the dog's barking. Tory debated calling out from where she stood or taking a chance with the mangy mutt. A shout came from the rear of the house with a curse and an order to shut up. The dog obeyed, satisfying himself with low growls as Tory headed in the direction of the voice.

She spotted Swanson working on the fence of an empty corral. The back of his shirt was wet with sweat, while his hat was pulled low to shade his face. He was a short, stocky man with the strong shoulders of a laborer. Thinking of Tod's build, Tory decided he had inher-ited it, and perhaps his temperament, from his mother.

"Mr. Swanson?"

His head jerked up. He had been replacing a board on the fence; the hand that swung the hammer paused on the downswing. Seeing his face, Tory decided he had the rough, lined face of a man constantly fighting the odds of the elements. He narrowed his eyes; they passed briefly over her badge.

"Sheriff," he said briefly, then gave the nail a final whack. He cared little for women who interfered in a man's work.

"I'd like to talk to you, Mr. Swanson."

"Yeah?" He pulled another nail out of an old coffee can. "What about?"

"Tod." Tory waited until he had hammered the nail into the warped board.

"That boy in trouble?"

"Apparently," she said mildly. She told herself to overlook his rudeness as he turned his back to take out another nail.

"I handle my own," he said briefly. "What's he done?"

"He hasn't done anything, Mr. Swanson."

"Either he's in trouble or he's not." Swanson placed another nail in position and beat it into the wood. The sound echoed in the still air. From somewhere to the right, Tory heard the lazy moo of a cow. "I ain't got time for conversation, Sheriff."

"He's in trouble, Mr. Swanson," she returned levelly. "And you'll talk to me here or in my office."

The tone had him taking another look and measuring her again. "What do you want?"

"I want to talk to you about the bruise on your son's face." She glanced down at the meaty hands, noting that the knuckles around the hammer whitened.

"You've got no business with my boy."

"Tod's a minor," she countered. "He's very much my business."

"I'm his father."

"And as such, you are not entitled to physically or emotionally abuse your child."

"I don't know what the hell you're talking about." The color in his sun-reddened face deepened angrily. Tory's eyes remained calm and direct.

"I'm well aware that you've beaten the boy before," she said coolly. "There are very strict laws to protect a child against this kind of treatment. If they're unknown to you, you might want to consult an attorney."

"I don't need no damn lawyer," he began, gesturing at Tory with the hammer as his voice rose.

"You will if you point that thing at me again," she told him quietly. "Attempted assault on a peace officer is a very serious crime."

Swanson looked down at the hammer, then dropped it disgustedly to the ground. "I don't assault women," he muttered.

"Just children?"

He sent her a furious glance from eyes that watered against the sun. "I got a right to discipline my own. I got a ranch to run here." A gesture with his muscular arm took in his pitiful plot of land. "Every time I turn around, that boy's off somewheres."

"Your reasons don't concern me. The results do."

With rage burning on his face, he took a step toward her. Tory held her ground. "You just get back in your car and get out. I don't need nobody coming out here telling me how to raise my boy."

Tory kept her eyes on his, although she was well

aware his hands had clenched into fists. "I can start proceedings to make Tod a ward of the court."

"You can't take my boy from me."

Tory lifted a brow. "Can't I?"

"I got rights," he blustered.

"So does Tod."

He swallowed, then turned back to pick up his hammer and nails. "You ain't taking my boy."

Something in his eyes before he had turned made Tory pause. Justice, she reminded herself, was individual. "He wouldn't want me to," she said in a quieter tone. "He told me you were a good man and asked me not to put you in jail. You bruise his face, but he doesn't stop loving you."

She watched Swanson's back muscles tighten. Abruptly he flung the hammer and the can away. Nails scattered in the wild grass. "I didn't mean to hit him like that," he said with a wrench in his voice that kept Tory silent. "Damn boy should've fixed this fence like I told him." He ran his hands over his face. "I didn't mean to hit him like that. Look at this place," he muttered, gripping the top rail of the fence. "Takes every minute just to keep it up and scrape by, never amount to anything. But it's all I got. All I hear from Tod is how he wants to go off to school, how he wants this and that, just like—"

"His brother?" Tory ventured.

Swanson turned his head slowly, and his face was set. "I ain't going to talk about that."

"Mr. Swanson, I know something about what it takes to keep up a place like this. But your frustrations and your anger are no excuse for misusing your boy."

He turned away again, the muscles in his jaw tightening. "He's gotta learn."

"And your way of teaching him is to use your fists?"

"I tell you I didn't mean to hit him." Furious, he whirled back to her. "I don't mean to take a fist to him the way my father done to me. I know it ain't right, but when he pushes me——" He broke off again, angry with himself for telling his business to an outsider. "I ain't going to hit him anymore," he muttered.

"But you've told yourself that before, haven't you?" Tory countered. "And meant it, I'm sure." She took a deep breath, as he only stared at her. "Mr. Swanson, you're not the only parent who has a problem with control. There are groups and organizations designed to help you and your family."

"I'm not talking to any psychiatrists and do-gooders."

"There are ordinary people, exactly like yourself, who talk and help each other."

"I ain't telling strangers my business. I can handle my own."

"No, Mr. Swanson, you can't." For a moment Tory wished helplessly that there was an easy answer. "You don't have too many choices. You can drive Tod away, like you did your first boy." Tory stood firm as he whirled like a bull. "Or," she continued calmly, "you can seek help, the kind of help that will justify your son's love for you. Perhaps your first decision is what comes first, your pride or your boy."

Swanson stared out over the empty corral. "It would kill his mother if he took off too."

"I have a number you can call, Mr. Swanson. Someone who'll talk to you, who'll listen. I'll give it to Tod."

His only acknowledgment was a shrug. She waited a

moment, praying her judgment was right. "I don't like ultimatums," she continued. "But I'll expect to see Tod daily. If he doesn't come to town, I'll come here. Mr. Swanson, if there's a mark on that boy, I'll slap a warrant on you and take Tod into custody."

He twisted his head to look at her again. Slowly, measuringly, he nodded. "You've got a lot of your father in you, Sheriff."

Automatically Tory's hand rose to her badge. She smiled for the first time. "Thanks." Turning, she walked away. Not until she was out of sight did she allow herself the luxury of wiping her sweaty palms on the thighs of her jeans.

Chapter 9

Tory was stopped at the edge of town by a barricade. Killing the engine, she stepped out of the car as one of Phil's security men approached her.

"Sorry, Sheriff, you can't use the main street. They're filming."

With a shrug Tory leaned back on the hood of her car. "It's all right. I'll wait."

The anger that had driven her out to the Swanson ranch was gone. Now Tory appreciated the time to rest and think. From her vantage point she could see the film crew and the townspeople who were making their debut as extras. She watched Hollister walk across the street in back of two actors exchanging lines in the scene. It made Tory smile, thinking how Hollister would brag about this moment of glory for years to come. There were a dozen people she knew, milling on the streets or waiting for their opportunity to mill. Phil cut the filming, running through take after take. Even with the distance Tory could sense he was frustrated. She frowned, wondering if their next encounter would turn into a battle. She couldn't back down, knowing that she had done the right thing—essentially the only thing.

Their time together was to be very brief, she mused. She didn't want it plagued by arguments and tension. But until he accepted the demands and responsibilities of her job, tension was inevitable. It had already become very important to Tory that the weeks ahead be unmarred. Perhaps, she admitted thoughtfully, too important. It was becoming more difficult for her to be perfectly logical when she thought of Phil. And since the night before, the future had become blurred and distant. There seemed to be only the overwhelming present.

She couldn't afford that, Tory reminded herself. That wasn't what either one of them had bargained for. She shifted her shoulders as her shirt grew hot and damp against her back. There was the summer, and just the summer, before they both went their separate ways. It was, of course, what each of them wanted.

"Sheriff…ah, Sheriff Ashton?"

Disoriented, Tory shook her head and stared at the man beside her. "What—? Yes?"

The security guard held out a chilled can of soda. "Thought you could use this."

"Oh, yeah, thanks." She pulled the tab, letting the air out in a hiss. "Do you think they'll be much longer?"

"Nah." He lifted his own can to drink half of it down without a breath. "They've been working on this one scene over an hour now."

Gratefully, Tory let the icy drink slide down her dry throat. "Tell me, Mr.—"

"Benson, Chuck Benson, ma'am."

"Mr. Benson," Tory continued, giving him an easy smile. "Have you had any trouble with any of the townspeople?"

"Nothing to speak of," he said as he settled beside her against the hood. "Couple of kids—those twins."

"Oh, yes," Tory murmured knowingly.

"Only tried to con me into letting them on the crane." He gave an indulgent laugh, rubbing the cold can over his forehead to cool it. "I've got a couple teenagers of my own," he explained.

"I'm sure you handled them, Mr. Benson." Tory flashed him a dashing smile that lifted his blood pressure a few degrees. "Still, I'd appreciate hearing about it if anyone in town gets out of line—particularly the Kramer twins."

Benson chuckled. "I guess those two keep you busy."

"Sometimes they're a full-time job all by themselves." Tory rested a foot on the bumper and settled herself more comfortably. "So tell me, how old are your kids?"

By the time Phil had finished shooting the scene, he'd had his fill of amateurs for the day. He'd managed, with a good deal of self-control, to hold on to his patience and speak to each one of his extras before he dismissed them. He wanted to shoot one more scene before they wrapped up for the day, so he issued instructions immediately. It would take an hour to set up, and with luck they'd have the film in the can before they lost the light.

The beeper at his hip sounded, distracting him. Impatiently, Phil drew out the walkie-talkie. "Yeah, Kincaid."

"Benson. I've got the sheriff here. All right to let her through now?"

Automatically, Phil looked toward the edge of town. He spotted Tory leaning lazily against the hood, drinking from a can. He felt twin surges of relief and annoyance. "Let her in," he ordered briefly, then shoved the radio back in place. Now that he knew she was perfectly safe, Phil had a perverse desire to strangle her. He waited until she had parked in front of the sheriff's office and walked up the street to meet her. Before he was halfway there, Tod burst out of the door.

"Sheriff!" He teetered at the edge of the sidewalk, as if unsure of whether to advance any farther.

Tory stepped up and ran a fingertip down the bruise on his cheek. "Everything's fine, Tod."

"You didn't…" He moistened his lips. "You didn't arrest him?"

She rested her arms on his shoulders. "No." Tory felt his shuddering sigh.

"He didn't get mad at you or…" He trailed off again and looked at her helplessly.

"No, we just talked. He knows he's wrong to hurt you, Tod. He wants to stop."

"I was scared when you went, but Mr. Kincaid said you knew what you were doing and that everything would be all right."

"Did he?" Tory turned her head as Phil stepped beside her. The look held a long and not quite comfortable moment. "Well, he was right." Turning back to Tod, she gave his shoulders a quick squeeze. "Come inside a minute. There's a number I want you to give to your father. Want a cup of coffee, Kincaid?"

"All right."

Together, they walked into Tory's office. She went directly to her desk, pulling out a smart leather-bound address book that looked absurdly out of place. After flipping through it, she wrote a name and phone number on a pad, then ripped off the sheet. "This number is for your whole family," she said as she handed Tod the paper. "Go home and talk to your father, Tod. He needs to understand that you love him."

He folded the sheet before slipping it into his back pocket. Shifting from foot to foot, he stared down at the cluttered surface of her desk. "Thanks. Ah…I'm sorry about the things I said before." Coloring a bit, he glanced at Phil. "You know," he murmured, lowering his gaze to the desk again.

"Don't be sorry, Tod." She laid a hand over his until he met her eyes. "Okay?" she said, and smiled.

"Yeah, okay." He blushed again, but drew up his courage. Giving Tory a swift kiss on the cheek, he darted for the door.

With a low laugh she touched the spot where his lips had brushed. "I swear," she murmured, "if he were fifteen years older…" Phil grabbed both her arms.

"Are you really all right?"

"Don't I look all right?" she countered.

"Damn it, Tory!"

"Phil." Taking his face in her hands, she gave him a hard, brief kiss. "You had no reason to worry. Didn't you tell Tod that I knew what I was doing?"

"The kid was terrified." And so was I, he thought

as he pulled her into his arms. "What happened out there?" he demanded.

"We talked," Tory said simply. "He's a very troubled man. I wanted to hate him and couldn't. I'm counting on him calling that number."

"What would you have done if he'd gotten violent?"

"I would have handled it," she told him, drawing away a bit. "It's my job."

"You can't—"

"Phil—" Tory cut him off quickly and firmly "—I don't tell you how to set a scene. Don't tell me how to run my town."

"It's not the same thing and you know it." He gave her an angry shake. "Nobody takes a swing at me when I do a retake."

"How about a frustrated actor?"

His eyes darkened. "Tory, you can't make a joke out of this."

"Better a joke than an argument," she countered. "I don't want to fight with you. Phil, don't focus on something like this. It isn't good for us."

He bit off a furious retort, then strode away to stare out the window. Nothing seemed as simple as it had been since the first time he'd walked into that cramped little room. "It's hard," he murmured. "I care."

Tory stared at his back while a range of emotions swept through her. Her heart wasn't listening to the strict common sense she had imposed on it. No longer sure what she wanted, she suppressed the urge to go to him and be held again. "I know," she said at length. "I care too."

He turned slowly. They looked at each other as they had once before, when there were bars between them—

a bit warily. For a long moment there was only the sound of the whining fan and the mumble of conversation outside. "I have to get back," he told her, carefully slipping his hands in his pockets. The need to touch her was too strong. "Dinner?"

"Sure." She smiled, but found it wasn't as easy to tilt her lips up as it should have been. "It'll have to be a little later—around eight?"

"That's fine. I'll see you then."

"Okay." She waited until the door had closed behind him before she sat at her desk. Her legs were weak. Leaning her head on her hand, she let out a long breath.

Oh, boy, she thought. Oh, boy. The ground was a lot shakier than she had anticipated. But she couldn't be falling in love with him, she reassured herself. Not that. Everything was intensified because of the emotional whirlwind of the past couple of days. She wasn't ready for the commitments and obligations of being in love, and that was all there was to it. Rising, she plugged in the coffeepot. She'd feel more like herself if she had a cup of coffee and got down to work.

Phil spent more time than he should have in the shower. It had been a very long, very rough twelve-hour day. He was accustomed to impossible hours and impossible demands in his job. Characteristically he took them in stride. Not this time.

The hot water and steam weren't drawing out the tension in his body. It had been there from the moment when Tory had driven off to the Swanson ranch, then had inexplicably increased during their brief conversation in her office. Because he was a man who always dealt well with tension, he was annoyed that he wasn't doing so this time.

He shut his eyes, letting the water flood over his head. She'd been perfectly right, he mused, about his having no say in her work. For that matter he had no say in any aspect of her life. There were no strings on their relationship. And he didn't want them any more than Tory did. He'd never had this problem in a relationship before. Problem? he mused, pushing wet hair out of his eyes. A perspective problem, he decided. What was necessary was to put his relationship with Tory back in perspective.

And who better to do that than a director? he thought wryly, then switched off the shower with a jerk of the wrist. He was simply letting too much emotion leak into the scene. Take two, he decided, grabbing a towel. Somehow he'd forgotten a very few basic, very vital rules. Keep it simple, keep it light, he reminded himself. Certainly someone with his background and experience was too smart to look for complications. What was between him and Tory was completely elemental and without strain, because they both wanted to keep it that way.

That was one of the things that had attracted him to her in the first place, Phil remembered. Hooking a towel loosely around his waist, he grabbed another to rub his hair dry. She wasn't a woman who expected a commitment, who looked for a permanent bond like love or marriage. Those were two things they were both definitely too smart to get mixed up with. In the steam-hazed mirror Phil caught the flicker of doubt in his own eyes.

Oh, no, he told himself, absolutely not. He wasn't in love with her. It was out of the question. He cared, naturally: She was a very special woman—strong, beautiful, intelligent, independent. And she had a great deal of simple sweetness that surfaced unexpectedly. It was that one quality that kept a man constantly off-balance. So he cared about her, Phil mused, letting the second towel fall to the floor. He could even admit that he felt closer to her than to many people he'd known for years. There was nothing unusual about that. They had something in common that clicked—an odd sort of friendship, he decided. That was safe enough. It was only because he'd been worried about her that he'd allowed things to get out of proportion for a time.

But he was frowning abstractedly at his reflection when he heard the knock on the door.

"Who is it?"

"Room service."

The frown turned into a grin instantly as he recognized Tory's voice.

"Well, hi." Tory gave him a look that was both encompassing and lazy when he opened the door. "You're a little late for your reservation, Kincaid."

He stepped aside to allow her to enter with a large tray. "I lost track of time in the shower. Is that our dinner?"

"Bud phoned me." Tory set the tray on the card table they'd used before. "He said you'd ordered dinner for eight but didn't answer your phone. Since I was starving, I decided to expedite matters." Slipping her arms around his waist, she ran her hands up his warm, damp back. "Ummm, you're tense," she murmured, enjoying the way his hair curled chaotically around his face. "Rough day?"

"And then some," he agreed before he kissed her.

He smelled clean—of soap and shampoo—yet, Tory found the scent as arousing as the darker musky fragrance she associated with him. Her hunger for food faded as quickly as her hunger for him rose. Pressing closer, she demanded more. His arms tightened; his muscles grew taut. He was losing himself in her again, and found no power to control it.

"You really are tense," Tory said against his mouth. "Lie down."

He gave a half chuckle, nibbling on her bottom lip. "You work fast."

"I'll rub your back," she informed him as she drew away. "You can tell me all the frustrating things those nasty actors did today while you were striving to be brilliant."

"Let me show you how we deal with smart alecks on the coast," Phil suggested.

"On the bed, Kincaid."

"Well..." He grinned. "If you insist."

"On your stomach," she stated when he started to pull her with him.

Deciding that being pampered might have its advantages, he complied. "I've got a bottle of wine in the cooler." He sighed as he stretched out full length. "It's a hell of a place to keep a fifty-year-old Burgundy."

"Don't be a snob," Tory warned, sitting beside him. "You must have worked ten or twelve hours today," she began. "Did you get much accomplished?"

"Not as much as we should have." He gave a quiet

groan of pleasure as she began to knead the muscles in his shoulders. "That's wonderful."

"The guys in the massage parlor always asked for Tory."

His head came up. "What?"

"Just wanted to see if you were paying attention. Down, Kincaid." She chuckled softly, working down his arms. "Were there technical problems or temperament ones?"

"Both," he answered, settling again. He found closing his eyes was a sensuous luxury. "Had some damaged dichroics. With luck the new ones'll get here tomorrow. Most of the foul-ups came during the crowd scene. Your people like to grin into the camera," he said dryly. "I expected one of them to wave any minute."

"That's show biz," Tory concluded as she shifted to her knees. She hiked her dress up a bit for more freedom. Opening his eyes, Phil was treated to a view of thigh. "I wouldn't be surprised if the town council elected to build a theater in Friendly just to show your movie. Think of the boon to the industry."

"Merle walked across the street like he's sat on a horse for three weeks." Because her fingers were working miracles over his back muscles, Phil shut his eyes again.

"Merle's still seeing Marlie Summers."

"Tory."

"Just making conversation," she said lightly, but dug a bit harder than necessary into his shoulder blades.

"Ouch!"

"Toughen up, Kincaid." With a laugh she placed a loud, smacking kiss in the center of his back. "You're not behind schedule, are you?"

"No. With all the hazards of shooting on location, we're doing very well. Another four weeks should wrap it up."

They were both silent for a moment, unexpectedly depressed. "Well, then," Tory said briskly, "you shouldn't have to worry about the guarantor."

"He'll be hanging over my shoulder until the film's in the can," Phil muttered. "There's a spot just to the right…oh, yeah," he murmured as her fingers zeroed in on it.

"Too bad you don't have any of those nifty oils and lotions," she commented. In a fluid movement Tory straddled him, the better to apply pressure. "You're a disappointment, Kincaid. I'd have thought all you Hollywood types would carry a supply of that kind of thing."

"Mmmm." He would have retorted in kind, but his mind was beginning to float. Her fingers were cool and sure as they pressed on the small of his back just above the line of the towel. Her legs, clad in thin stockings, brushed his sides, arousing him with each time she flexed. The scent of her shampoo tickled his nostrils as she leaned up to knead his shoulders again. Though the sheet was warm—almost too warm—beneath him, he couldn't summon the energy to move. As the sun was setting, the light shifted, dimming. The room was filled with a golden haze that suited his mood. He could hear the rumble of a car on the street below, then only the sound of Tory's light, even breathing above him. His muscles were relaxed and limber, but he didn't consider telling her to stop. He'd forgotten completely about the dinner growing cold on the table behind them.

Tory continued to run her hands along his back,

thinking him asleep. He had a beautiful body, she mused, hard and tanned and disciplined. The muscles in his back were supple and strong. For a moment she simply enjoyed exploring him. When she shifted lower, the skirt of her dress rode up high on her thighs. With a little sound of annoyance she unzipped the dress and pulled it over her head. She could move with more freedom in her sheer teddy.

His waist was trim. She allowed her hands to slide over it, approving its firmness. Before their lovemaking had been so urgent, and she had been completely under his command. Now she enjoyed learning the lines and planes of his body. Down the narrow hips, over the brief swatch of towel, to his thighs. There were muscles there, too, she discovered, hardened by hours of standing, tennis, swimming. The light mat of hair over his skin made her feel intensely feminine. She massaged his calves, then couldn't resist the urge to place a light kiss on the back of his knee. Phil's blood began to heat in a body too drugged with pleasure to move. It gave her a curiously warm feeling to rub his feet.

He worked much harder than she'd initially given him credit for, she mused as she roamed slowly back up his legs. He spent hours in the sun, on his feet, going over and over the same shot until he'd reached the perfection he strove for. And she had come to know that the film was never far from his thoughts, even during his free hours. Phillip Kincaid, she thought with a gentle smile, was a very impressive man—with much more depth than the glossy playboy the press loved to tattle on. He'd earned her respect during the time he'd been in Friendly, and she was growing uncomfortably certain he'd earned something more complex. She wouldn't think of it now. Perhaps she would have no choice but to think of it after he'd gone. But for now, he was here. That was enough.

With a sigh she bent low over his back to lay her cheek on his shoulder. The need for him had crept into her while she was unaware. Her pulse was pounding, and a thick warmth, like heated honey, seemed to flow through her veins.

"Phil." She moved her mouth to his ear. Her tongue traced it, slipping inside to arouse him to wakefulness. She heard his quiet groan as her heart began to beat jerkily. With her teeth she pulled and tugged on the lobe, then moved to experiment with the sensitive area just below. "I want you," she murmured. Quickly she began to take her lips over him with the same thorough care as her fingers.

He seemed so pliant as she roamed over him that when a strong arm reached out to pull her down, it took her breath away. Before she could recover it, his mouth was on hers. His lips were soft and warm, but the kiss was bruisingly potent. His tongue went deep to make an avid search of moist recesses as his weight pressed her into the mattress. He took a quick, hungry journey across her face before he looked down at her. There was nothing sleepy in his expression. The look alone had her breath trembling.

"My turn," he whispered.

With nimble fingers he loosened the range of tiny buttons down the front of her teddy. His lips followed, to send a trail of fire along the newly exposed skin. The plunge of the V stopped just below her navel. He lingered there, savoring the soft, honey-hued flesh. Tory felt herself swept through a hurricane of sensation to the heavy, waiting air of the storm's eye. Phil's hands cupped her upper thighs, his thumbs pressing insistently where the thin silk rose high. Expertly he unhooked her stockings, drawing them off slowly, his mouth hurrying to taste. Tory moaned, bending her leg to help him as torment and pleasure tangled.

For one heady moment his tongue lingered at the top of her thigh. With his tongue he gently slipped beneath the silk, making her arch in anticipation. His breath shot through the material into the core of her. But he left her moist and aching to come greedily back to her mouth. Tory met the kiss ardently, dragging him closer. She felt his body pound and pulse against hers with a need no greater than her own. He found her full bottom lip irresistible and nibbled and sucked gently. Tory knew a passion so concentrated and volatile, she struggled under him to find the ultimate release.

"Here," he whispered, moving down to the spot on her neck that always drew him. "You taste like no one else," he murmured. Her flavor seemed to tremble on the tip of his tongue. With a groan he let his voracious appetite take over.

Her breasts were hard, waiting for him. Slowly he moistened the tips with his tongue, listening to her shuddering breathing as he journeyed from one to the other—teasing, circling, nibbling, until her movements beneath him were abandoned and desperate. Passion built to a delicious peak until he drew her, hot and moist, into his mouth to suckle ravenously. She wasn't aware when he slipped the teddy down her shoulders, down her body, until she was naked to the waist. The last lights of the sun poured into the room like a dark red mist. It gave her skin an exotic cast that aroused him further. He drew the silk lower and still lower, until it was lost in the tangle of sheets.

Desperate, Tory reached for him. She heard Phil's sharp intake of breath as she touched him, felt the sudden, convulsive shudder. She wanted him now with an intensity too strong to deny.

"More," he breathed, but was unable to resist as she drew him closer.

"Now," she murmured, arching her hips to receive him.

Exhausted, they lay in silence as the first fingers of moonlight flickered into the room. He knew he should move—his full weight pushed Tory deep into the mattress. But they felt so right, flesh to flesh, his mouth nestled comfortably against her breast. Her fingers were in his hair, tangling and stroking with a sleepy gentleness. Time crept by easily—seconds to minutes without words or the need for them. He could hear her heartbeat gradually slow and level. Lazily he flicked his tongue over a still-erect nipple and felt it harden even more.

"Phil," she moaned in weak protest.

He laughed quietly, enormously pleased that he could move her so effortlessly. "Tired?" he asked, nibbling a moment longer.

"Yes." She gave a low groan as he began to toy with her other breast. "Phil, I can't."

Ignoring her, he brought his mouth to hers for long, slow kisses while his hands continued to stroke. He had intended only to kiss her before taking his weight from her. Her lips were unbearably soft and giving. Her breath shuddered into him, rebuilding his passion with dizzying speed. Tory told herself it wasn't possible as sleepy desire became a torrent of fresh need.

Phil found new delight in the lines of her body, in the heady, just-loved flavor of her skin. A softly glowing spark rekindled a flame. "I want a retake," he murmured.

He took her swiftly, leaving them both staggered and damp and clinging in a room speckled with moonlight.

"How do you feel?" Phil murmured later. She was close to his side, one arm flung over his chest.

"Astonished."

He laughed, kissing her temple. "So do I. I guess our dinner got cold."

"Mmm. What was it?"

"I don't remember."

Tory yawned and snuggled against him. "That's always better cold anyway." She knew with very little effort she could sleep for a week.

"Not hungry?"

She considered a moment. "Is it something you have to chew?"

He grinned into the darkness. "Probably."

"Uh-uh." She arched like a contented cat when he ran a hand down her back. "Do you have to get up early?"

"Six."

Groaning, she shut her eyes firmly. "You're ruining your mystique," she told him. "Hollywood Casanovas don't get up at six."

He gave a snort of laughter. "They do if they've got a film to direct."

"I suppose when you leave, you'll still have a lot of work to do before the film's finished."

His frown mirrored hers, although neither was aware of it. "There's still a lot to be shot in the studio, then the editing… I wish there was more time."

She knew what he meant, and schooled her voice carefully. "We both knew. I'll only be in town a few weeks longer than you," she added. "I've got a lot of work to catch up on in Albuquerque."

"It's lucky we're both comfortable with the way things are." Phil stared up at the ceiling while his fingers continued to tangle in her hair. "If we'd fallen in love, it would be an impossible situation."

"Yes," Tory murmured, opening her eyes to the darkness. "Neither of us has the time for impossible situations."

Chapter 10

Tory pulled up in front of the ranch house. Her mother's geraniums were doing beautifully. White-and-pink plants had been systematically placed between the more common red. The result was an organized, well-tended blanket of color. Tory noted that the tear in the window screen had been mended. As always, a few articles of clothing hung on the line at the side of the house. She dreaded going in.

It was an obligation she never shirked but never did easily. At least once a week she drove out to spend a strained half hour with her mother. Only twice since the film crew had come to Friendly had her mother made the trip into town. Both times she had dropped into Tory's office, but the visits had been brief and uncomfortable for both women. Time was not bridging the gap, only widening it.

Normally, Tory confined her trips to the ranch to
Sunday afternoons. This time, however, she had driven
out a day early in order to placate Phil. The thought
caused her to smile. He'd finally pressured her into
agreeing to his "home movies." When he had wound up
the morning's shoot in town, he would bring out one of
the backup video cameras. Though she could hardly see
why it was so vital to him to put her on film, Tory decided it wouldn't do any harm. And, she thought wryly,
he wasn't going to stop bringing it up until she agreed.
So let him have his fun, she concluded as she slipped
from the car. She'd enjoy the ride.

From the corral the palomino whinnied fussily. He
pawed the ground and pranced as Tory watched him.
He knew, seeing Tory, that there was a carrot or apple
in it for him, as well as a bracing ride. They were both
aware that he could jump the fence easily if he grew
impatient enough. As he reared, showing off for her,
Tory laughed.

"Simmer down, Justice. You're going to be in the
movies." She hesitated a moment. It would be so easy
to go to the horse, pamper him a bit in return for his
unflagging affection. There were no complications or
undercurrents there. Her eyes drifted back to the house.
With a sigh she started up the walk.

Upon entering, Tory caught the faint whiff of bee's
wax and lemon and knew her mother had recently polished the floors. She remembered the electric buffer her
father had brought home one day. Helen had been as
thrilled as if he'd brought her diamonds. The windows
glittered in the sun without a streak or speck.

How does she do it? Tory wondered, gazing around
the spick-and-span room. How does she stand spending

each and every day chasing dust? Could it really be all she wants out of life?

As far back as she could remember, she could recall her mother wanting nothing more than to change slip-covers or curtains. It was difficult for a woman who always looked for angles and alternatives to understand such placid acceptance. Perhaps it would have been easier if the daughter had understood the mother, or the mother the daughter. With a frustrated shake of her head she wandered to the kitchen, expecting to find Helen fussing at the stove.

The room was empty. The appliances winked, white and gleaming, in the strong sunlight. The scent of fresh-baked bread hovered enticingly in the air. Whom did she bake it for? Tory demanded of herself, angry without knowing why. There was no one there to appreciate it now—no one to break off a hunk and grin as he was scolded. Damn it, didn't she know that everything was different now? Whirling away, Tory strode out of the room.

The house was too quiet, she realized. Helen was certainly there. The tired little compact was in its habitual place at the side of the house. It occurred to Tory that her mother might be in one of the outbuildings. But then, why hadn't she come out when she heard the car drive up? Vaguely disturbed, Tory glanced up the stairs. She opened her mouth to call, then stopped. Something impelled her to move quietly up the steps.

At the landing she paused, catching some faint sound coming from the end of the hall. Still moving softly, Tory walked down to the doorway of her parents' bed-room. The door was only half closed. Pushing it open, Tory stepped inside.

Helen sat on the bed in a crisp yellow housedress. Her blond hair was caught back in a matching kerchief. Held tight in her hands was one of Tory's father's work shirts. It was a faded blue, frayed at the cuffs. Tory remembered it as his favorite, one that Helen had claimed was fit only for a dust rag. Now she clutched it to her breast, rocking gently and weeping with such quiet despair that Tory could only stare.

She'd never seen her mother cry. It had been her father whose eyes had misted during her high school and college graduations. It had been he who had wept with her when the dog she had raised from a puppy had died. Her mother had faced joy and sadness with equal restraint. But there was no restraint in the woman Tory saw now. This was a woman in the depths of grief, blind and deaf to all but her own mourning.

All anger, all resentment, all sense of distance, vanished in one illuminating moment. Tory felt her heart fill with sympathy, her throat burn from her own grief.

"Mother."

Helen's head jerked up. Her eyes were glazed and confused as they focused on Tory. She shook her head as if in denial, then struggled to choke back the sobs.

"No, don't." Tory rushed to her, gathering her close. "Don't shut me out."

Helen went rigid in an attempt at composure, but Tory only held her tighter. Abruptly, Helen collapsed, dropping her head on her daughter's shoulder and weeping without restraint. "Oh, Tory, Tory, why couldn't it have been me?" With the shirt caught between them, Helen accepted the comfort of her daughter's strong arms. "Not Will, never Will. It should have been me."

"No, don't say that." Hot tears coursed down her

face. "You mustn't think that way. Dad wouldn't want you to."

"All those weeks, those horrible weeks, in the hospital I prayed and prayed for a miracle." She gripped Tory tighter, as if she needed something solid to hang on to. "They said no hope. No hope. Oh, God, I wanted to scream. He couldn't die without me…not without me. That last night in the hospital before…I went into his room. I begged him to show them they were wrong, to come back. He was gone." She moaned and would have slid down if Tory hadn't held her close. "He'd already left me. I couldn't leave him lying there with that machine. I couldn't do that, not to Will. Not to my Will."

"Oh, Mother." They rocked together, heads on each other's shoulders. "I'm so sorry. I didn't know—I didn't think…I'm so sorry."

Helen breathed a long, shuddering sigh as her sobs quieted. "I didn't know how to tell you or how to explain. I'm not good at letting my feelings out. I knew how much you loved your father," she continued. "But I was too angry to reach out. I suppose I wanted you to lash out at me. It made it easier to be strong, even though I knew I hurt you more."

"That doesn't matter now."

"Tory—"

"No, it doesn't." Tory drew her mother back, looking into her tear-ravaged eyes. "Neither of us tried to understand the other that night. We were both wrong. I think we've both paid for it enough now."

"I loved him so much." Helen swallowed the tremor in her voice and stared down at the crumpled shirt still in her hand. "It doesn't seem possible that he won't walk through the door again."

"I know. Every time I come in the house, I still look for him."

"You're so like him." Hesitantly, Helen reached up to touch her cheek. "There's been times it's been hard for me even to look at you. You were always his more than mine when you were growing up. My fault," she added before Tory could speak. "I was always a little awed by you."

"Awed?" Tory managed to smile.

"You were so smart, so quick, so demanding. I always wondered how much I had to do with the forming of you. Tory—" she took her hands, staring down at them a moment "—I never tried very hard to get close to you. It's not my way."

"I know."

"It didn't mean that I didn't love you."

She squeezed Helen's hands. "I know that too. But it was always him we looked at first."

"Yes." Helen ran a palm over the crumpled shirt. "I thought I was coping very well," she said softly. "I was going to clean out the closet. I found this, and... He loved it so. You can still see the little holes where he'd pin his badge."

"Mother, it's time you got out of the house a bit, starting seeing people again." When Helen started to shake her head, Tory gripped her hands tighter. "Living again."

Helen glanced around the tidy room with a baffled smile. "This is all I know how to do. All these years..."

"When I go back to Albuquerque, why don't you come stay with me awhile? You've never been over."

"Oh, Tory, I don't know."

"Think about it," she suggested, not wanting to push.

"You might enjoy watching your daughter rip a witness apart in cross-examination."

Helen laughed, brushing the lingering tears briskly away. "I might at that. Would you be offended if I said sometimes I worry about you being alone—not having someone like your father to come home to?"

"No." The sudden flash of loneliness disturbed her far more than the words. "Everyone needs something different."

"Everyone needs someone, Tory," Helen corrected gently. "Even you."

Tory's eyes locked on her mother's a moment, then dropped away. "Yes, I know. But sometimes the someone—" She broke off, distressed by the way her thoughts had centered on Phil. "There's time for that," she said briskly. "I still have a lot of obligations, a lot of things I want to do, before I commit myself…to anyone."

There was enough anxiety in Tory's voice to tell Helen that "anyone" had a name. Feeling it was too soon to offer advice, she merely patted Tory's hand. "Don't wait too long," she said simply. "Life has a habit of moving quickly." Rising, she went to the closet again. The need to be busy was too ingrained to allow her to sit for long. "I didn't expect you today. Are you going to ride?"

"Yes." Tory pressed a hand down on her father's shirt before she stood. "Actually I'm humoring the director of the film being shot in town." Wandering to the window, she looked down to see Justice pacing the corral restlessly. "He has this obsession with getting me on film. I flatly refused to be an extra in his production, but I finally agreed to let him shoot some while I rode Justice."

"He must be very persuasive," Helen commented.

Tory gave a quick laugh. "Oh, he's that all right."

"That's Marshall Kincaid's son," Helen stated, remembering. "Does he favor his father?"

With a smile Tory thought that her mother would be more interested in the actor than the director. "Yes, actually he does. The same rather aristocratic bone structure and cool blue eyes." Tory saw the car kicking up dust on the road leading to the ranch. "He's coming now, if you'd like to meet him."

"Oh, I…" Helen pressed her fingers under her eyes. "I don't think I'm really presentable right now, Tory."

"All right," she said as she started toward the door. In the doorway she hesitated a moment. "Will you be all right now?"

"Yes, yes, I'm fine. Tory…" She crossed the room to give her daughter's cheek a brief kiss. Tory's eyes widened in surprise at the uncharacteristic gesture. "I'm glad we talked. Really very glad."

Phil again stopped his car beside the corral. The horse pranced over to hang his head over the fence, waiting for attention. Leaving the camera in the backseat, Phil walked over to pat the strong golden neck. He found the palomino avidly nuzzling at his pockets.

"Hey!" With a half laugh he stepped out of range.

"He's looking for this." Holding a carrot in her hand, Tory came down the steps.

"Your friend should be arrested for pickpocketing," Phil commented as Tory drew closer. His smile of greeting faded instantly. "Tory…" He took her shoulders, studying her face. "You've been crying," he said in an odd voice.

"I'm fine." Turning, she held out the carrot, letting the horse pluck in from her hand.

"What's wrong?" he insisted, pulling her back to him again. "What happened?"

"It was my mother."

"Is she ill?" he demanded quickly.

"No." Touched by the concern in his voice, Tory smiled. "We talked," she told him, then let out a long sigh. "We really talked, probably for the first time in twenty-seven years."

There was something fragile in the look as she lifted her eyes to his. He felt much as he had the day in the cemetery—protective and strong. Wordlessly he drew her into the circle of his arms. "Are you okay?"

"Yes, I'm fine." She closed her eyes as her head rested against his shoulder. "Really fine. It's going to be so much easier now."

"I'm glad." Tilting her face to his, he kissed her softly. "If you don't feel like doing this today—"

"No you don't, Kincaid," she said with a quick grin. "You claimed you were going to immortalize me, so get on with it."

"Go fix your face first, then." He pinched her chin. "I'll set things up."

She turned away to comply, but called back over her shoulder. "There's not going to be any of that 'Take two' business. You'll have to get it right the first time."

He enjoyed her hoot of laughter before he reached into the car for the camera and recorder.

Later, Tory scowled at the apparatus. "You said film," she reminded him. "You didn't say anything about sound."

"It's tape," he corrected, expertly framing her. "Just saddle the horse."

"You're arrogant as hell when you play movies, Kincaid." Without fuss Tory slipped the bit into the palomino's mouth. Her movements were competent as she hefted the saddle onto the horse's back. She was a natural, he decided. No nerves, no exaggerated gestures for the benefit of the camera. He wanted her to talk again. Slowly he circled around for a new angle. "Going to have dinner with me tonight?"

"I don't know," Tory considered as she tightened the cinches. "That cold steak you fed me last night wasn't very appetizing."

"Tonight I'll order cold cuts and beer," he suggested. "That way it won't matter when we get to it."

Tory sent him a grin over her shoulder. "It's a deal."

"You're a cheap date, Sheriff."

"Uh-uh," she disagreed, turning to him while she wrapped a companionable arm around the horse's neck. "I'm expecting another bottle of that French champagne very soon. Why don't you let me play with the camera now and you can stand next to the horse?"

"Mount up."

Tory lifted a brow. "You're one tough cookie, Kincaid." Grasping the saddle horn, Tory swung into the saddle in one lazy movement. "And now?"

"Head out, the direction you took the first time I saw you ride. Not too far," he added. "When you come back, keep it at a gallop. Don't pay any attention to the camera. Just ride."

"You're the boss," she said agreeably. "For the moment." With a kick of her heels Tory sent the palomino west at a run.

She felt the exhilaration instantly. The horse wanted speed, so Tory let him have his head as the hot air whipped at her face and hair. As before, she headed toward the mountains. There was no need to escape this time, but only a pleasure in moving fast. The power and strength below her tested her skill.

Zooming in on her, Phil thought she rode with understated flair. No flash, just confidence. Her body hardly seemed to move as the horse pounded up dust. It almost seemed as though the horse led her, but something in the way she sat, in the way her face was lifted, showed her complete control.

When she turned, the horse danced in place a moment, still anxious to run. He tossed his head, lifting his front feet off the ground in challenge. Over the still, silent air, Phil heard Tory laugh. The sound of it sent shivers down his spine.

Magnificent, he thought, zooming in on her as close as the lens would allow. She was absolutely magnificent. She wasn't looking toward him. Obviously she had no thoughts about the camera focused on her. Her face was lifted to the sun and the sky as she controlled the feisty horse with apparent ease. When she headed back, she started at a loping gallop that built in speed.

The palomino's legs gathered and stretched, sending up a plume of dirt in their wake. Behind them was a barren land of little more than rock and earth with the mountains harsh in the distance. She was Eve, Phil thought. The only woman. And if this Eve's paradise was hard and desolate, she ruled it in her own style.

Once, as if remembering he was there, Tory looked over, full into the camera. With her face nearly filling the lens, she smiled. Phil felt his palms go damp. If a man had a woman like that, he realized abruptly, he'd need nothing and no one else. The only woman, he thought again, then shook his head as if to clear it.

With a quick command and a tug on the reins, Tory brought the horse to a stop. Automatically she leaned forward to pat his neck. "Well, Hollywood?" she said lazily.

Knowing he wasn't yet in complete control, Phil kept the camera trained on her. "Is that the best you can do?"

She tossed her hair behind her head. "What did you have in mind?"

"No fancy tricks?" he asked, moving around the horse to vary the angle.

Tory looked down on him with tolerant amusement. "If you want to see someone stand on one foot in the saddle, go to the circus."

"We could set up a couple of small jumps—if you can handle it."

As she ruffled the palomino's blond mane, she gave a snort of laughter. "I thought you wanted me to ride, not win a blue ribbon." Grinning, she turned the horse around. "But okay," she said obligingly. At an easy lope she went for the corral fence. The horse took the four feet in a long, powerful glide. "Will that do?" she asked as she doubled back and rode past.

"Again," Phil demanded, going down on one knee. With a shrug Tory took the horse over the fence again. Lowering his camera for the first time, Phil shaded his eyes and looked up at her. "If he can do that, how do you keep him in?"

"He knows a good thing when he's got it," Tory stated, letting the palomino prance a bit while she rubbed his neck. "He's just showing off for the camera. Is that a wrap, Kincaid?"

Lifting the camera again, he aimed it at her. "Is that all you can do?"

"Well..." Tory considered a moment, then sent him a slow smile. "How about this?" Keeping one hand loosely on the reins, she started to unbutton her blouse.

"I like it."

After three buttons she paused, catching her tongue between her teeth. "I don't want you to lose your G rating," she decided. Swinging a leg over the saddle, she slid to the ground.

"This is a private film," he reminded her. "The censors'll never see it."

She laughed, but shook her head. "Fade out," she suggested, loosening the horse's girth. "Put your toy away, Kincaid," she told him as he circled around the horse, still taping.

"Look at me a minute." With a half smile Tory complied. "God, that face," he muttered. "One way or the other, I'm going to get it on the screen."

"Forget it." Tory lifted the saddle to balance it on the fence. "Unless you start videotaping court cases."

"I can be persistent."

"I can be stubborn," she countered. At her command the palomino trotted back into the corral.

After loading the equipment back in the car, Phil turned to gather Tory in his arms. Without a word their mouths met in long, mutual pleasure. "If there was a way," he murmured as he buried his face in her hair, "to have a few days away from here, alone..."

Tory shut her eyes, feeling the stir...and the ache. "Obligations, Phil," she said quietly. "We both have a job to do."

He wanted to say the hell with it, but knew he

couldn't. Along with the obligations was the agreement they had made at the outset. "If I called you in Albuquerque, would you see me?"

She hesitated. It was something she wanted and feared. "Yes." She realized abruptly that she was suffering. For a moment she stood still, absorbing the unexpected sensation. "Phil, kiss me again."

She found his mouth quickly to let the heat and pleasure of the kiss dull the pain. There were still a few precious weeks left, she told herself as she wrapped her arms tighter around him. There was still time before... with a moan she pressed urgently against him, willing her mind to go blank. There was a sigh, then a tremble, before she rested her head against his shoulder. "I have to put the tack away," she murmured. It was tempting to stay just as she was, held close, with her blood just beginning to swim. Taking a long breath, she drew away from him and smiled. "Why don't you be macho and carry the saddle?"

"Directors don't haul equipment," he told her as he tried to pull her back to him.

"Heave it up, Kincaid." Tory swung the reins over her shoulder. "You've got some great muscles."

"Yeah?" Grinning, he lifted the saddle and followed her toward the barn. Bicks was right, Phil mused, watching her walk. She had a way of moving that drove men mad.

The barn door creaked in protest when Tory pulled it open. "Over here." She moved across the concrete floor to hang the reins on a peg.

Phil set down the saddle, then turned. The place was large, high-ceilinged and refreshingly cool. "No animals?" he asked, wandering to an empty stall.

"My mother keeps a few head of cattle," Tory explained as she joined him. "They're grazing. We had more horses, but she doesn't ride much." Tory lifted a shoulder. "Justice has the place mostly to himself."

"I've never been in a barn."

"A deprived child."

He sent her a mild glance over his shoulder as he roamed. "I don't think I expected it to be so clean."

Tory's laugh echoed. "My mother has a vendetta against dirt," she told him. Oddly, she felt amusement now rather than resentment. It was a clean feeling. "I think she'd have put curtains on the windows in the loft if my father had let her."

Phil found the ladder and tested its sturdiness. "What's up there?"

"Hay," Tory said dryly. "Ever seen hay?"

"Don't be smug," he warned before he started to climb. Finding his fascination rather sweet, Tory exerted the energy to go up with him. "The view's incredible." Standing beside the side opening, he could see for miles. The town of Friendly looked almost neat and tidy with the distance.

"I used to come up here a lot." Tucking her hands in her back pockets, Tory looked over his shoulder.

"What did you do?"

"Watch the world go by," she said, nodding toward Friendly. "Or sleep."

He laughed, turning back to her. "You're the only person I know who can turn sleeping into an art."

"I've dedicated quite a bit of my life to it." She took his hand to draw him away.

Instead he pulled her into a dim corner. "There's something I've always wanted to do in a hayloft."

With a laugh Tory stepped away. "Phil, my mother's in the house."

"She's not here," he pointed out. He hooked a hand in the low V where she had loosened her blouse. A hard tug had her stumbling against him.

"Phil—"

"It must have been carrying that saddle," he mused, giving her a gentle push that had her falling backward into a pile of hay.

"Now, wait a minute…" she began, and struggled up on her elbows.

"And the primitive surroundings," he added as he pressed her body back with his own. "If I were directing this scene, it would start like this." He took her mouth in a hot, urgent kiss that turned her protest into a moan. "The lighting would be set so that it seemed one shaft of sunlight was slanting down across here." With a fingertip he traced from her right ear, across her throat, to the hollow between her breasts. "Everything else would be a dull gold, like your skin."

She had her hands pressed against his shoulders, holding him off, although her heart was beating thickly. "Phil, this isn't the time."

He placed two light kisses at either corner of her mouth. He found it curiously exciting to have to persuade her. Light as a breeze, his hand slipped under her blouse until his fingers found her breast. The peak was already taut. At his touch her eyes lost focus and darkened. The hands at his shoulders lost their resistance and clutched at him. "You're so sensitive," he murmured, watching the change in her face. "It drives me crazy to know when I touch you like this your bones turn to water and you're completely mine."

Letting his fingers fondle and stroke, he lowered his mouth to nibble gently at her yielding lips. *Strong, self-sufficient, decisive.* Those were words he would have used to describe her. Yet, he knew, when they were together like this, he had the power to mold her. Even now, as she lifted them to his face to urge him closer, he felt the weakness come over him in thick waves. It was both frightening and irresistible.

She could have asked anything of him, and he would have been unable to deny her. Even his thoughts could no longer be considered his own when she was so intimately entwined in them. The fingers that loosened the rest of her buttons weren't steady. He should have been used to her by now, he told himself as he sought the tender skin of her neck almost savagely. It shouldn't be so intense every time he began to make love to her. Each time he told himself the desperation would fade; yet, it only returned—doubled, tripled, until he was completely lost in her.

There was only her now, over the clean, country smell of hay. Her subtly alluring fragrance was a contrast too exciting to bear. She was murmuring to him as she drew his shirt over his head. The sound of her voice seemed to pulse through his system. The sun shot through the window to beat on his bare back, but he only felt the cool stroking of her fingers as she urged him down until they were flesh to flesh.

His mouth devoured hers as he tugged the jeans over her hips. Greedily he moved to her throat, her shoulders, her breasts, ravenous for each separate taste. His mouth ranged over her, his tongue moistening, savoring, as her skin heated. She was naked but for the brief swatch riding low on her hips. He hooked his fingers beneath it, tormenting them both by lowering it fraction by fraction while his lips followed the progress.

The pleasure grew unmanageable. He began the wild journey back up her body, his fingers fumbling with the snap of his jeans until Tory's brushed them impatiently away.

She undressed him swiftly, while her own mouth streaked over his skin. The sudden change from pliancy to command left him stunned. Then she was on top of him, straddling him while her lips and teeth performed dark magic at the pulse in his throat. Beyond reason, he grasped her hips, lifting her. Tory gave a quick cry as they joined. In delight her head flung back as she let this new exhilaration rule her. Her skin was shiny with dampness when she crested. Delirious, she started to slide toward him, but he rolled her over, crushing her beneath him as he took her to a second peak, higher than the first.

As they lay, damp flesh to damp flesh, their breaths shuddering, she knew a contentment so fulfilling, it brought the sting of tears to her eyes. Hurriedly blinking them away, Tory kissed the curve of his shoulder.

"I guess there's more to do in a hayloft than sleep."

Phil chuckled. Rolling onto his back, he drew her against his side to steal a few more moments alone with her.

Chapter 11

One of the final scenes to be filmed was a tense night sequence outside Hernandez's Bar. Phil had opted to shoot at night with a low light level rather than film during the day with filters. It would give the actors more of a sense of the ambience and keep the gritty realism in the finished product. It was a scene fraught with emotion that would lose everything if overplayed. From the beginning nothing seemed to go right.

Twice the sound equipment broke down, causing lengthy delays. A seasoned supporting actress blew her lines repeatedly and strode off the set, cursing herself. A defective bulb exploded, scattering shards of glass that had to be painstakingly picked up. For the first time since the shooting began, Phil had to deal with a keyed-up, uncooperative Marlie.

"Okay," he said, taking her by the arm to draw her away. "What the hell's wrong with you?"

"I can't get it right," she said furiously. With her hands on her hips she strode a few paces away and kicked at the dirt. "Damn it, Phil, it just doesn't *feel* right."

"Look, we've been at this over two hours. Everybody's a little fed up." His own patience was hanging on by a thread. In two days at the most, he'd have no choice but to head back to California. He should have been pleased that the bulk of the filming was done—that the rushes were excellent. Instead he was tense, irritable and looking for someone to vent his temper on. "Just pull yourself together," he told Marlie curtly. "And get it done."

"Now, just a damn minute!" Firing up instantly, Marlie let her own frustration pour out in temper. "I've put up with your countless retakes, with that stinking, sweaty bar and this godforsaken town because this script is gold. I've let you work me like a horse because I need you. This part is my ticket into the big leagues and I know it right down to the gut."

"You want the ticket," Phil tossed back, "you pay the price."

"I've paid my dues," she told him furiously. A couple of heads turned idly in their direction, but no one ventured over. "I don't have to take your lousy temper on the set because you've got personal problems."

He measured her with narrowed eyes. "You have to take exactly what I give you."

"I'll tell you something, Kincaid—" she poked a small finger into his chest "—I don't have to take anything, because I'm every bit as important to this movie as you are, and we both know it. It doesn't mean a damn who's getting top billing. Kate Lohman's the key to this picture, and I'm Kate Lohman. Don't you forget it, and don't throw your weight around with me."

When she turned to stride off, Phil grabbed her arm, jerking her back. His eyes had iced. The fingers on her arm were hard. Looking down at her set face, he felt temper fade into admiration. "Damn you, Marlie," he said quietly, "you know how to stay in character, don't you?"

"I know this one inside out," she returned. The stiffness went out of her stance.

"Okay, what doesn't feel right?"

The corners of her mouth curved up. "I wanted to work with you," she began, "because you're the best out there these days. I didn't expect to like you. All right," she continued, abruptly professional, "when Sam follows me out of the bar, grabs me, finally losing control, he's furious. Everything he's held in comes pouring out. His dialogue's hard."

"You haven't been off his back since he came into town," Phil reminded her, running over the scene in his mind. "Now he's had enough. After the scene he's going to take you back to your room and make love. You win."

"Do I?" Marlie countered. "My character is a tough lady. She's got reason to be. She's got enough vulnerabilities to keep the audience from despising her, but she's no pushover."

"So?"

"So he comes after me, he calls me a tramp—a cold, money-grabbing whore, among other things—and my response is to take it—damp-eyed and shocked."

Phil considered, a small smile growing. "What would you do?"

"I'd punch the jerk in the mouth."

His laugh echoed down the street. "Yeah, I guess you would at that."

"Tears, maybe," Marlie went on, tasting victory, "but anger too. She's becoming very close to what he's accusing her of. And she hates it—and him, for making it matter."

Phil nodded, his mind already plotting the changes and the angles. Frowning, he called Sam over and outlined the change.

"Can you pull this off without busting my caps?" Sam demanded of Marlie.

She grinned. "Maybe."

"After she hits you," Phil interrupted, "I want dead silence for a good ten seconds. You wipe your mouth with the back of your hand, slow, but don't break the eye contact. Let's set it up from where Marlie walks out of the bar. Bicks!" He left the actors to give his cinematographer a rundown.

"Quiet.... Places.... Roll...." Standing by the cameraman's shoulder, Phil watched the scene unfold. The adrenaline was pumping now. He could see it in Marlie's eyes, in the set of her body, as she burst out the door of the bar onto the sidewalk. When Sam grabbed her, instead of merely being whirled around, she turned on him. The mood seemed to fire into him as well, as his lines became harsher, more emotional. Before there had been nothing in the scene but the man's anger; now there was the woman's too. Now the underlying sexuality was there. When she hit him, it seemed everyone on the set held their breath. The gesture was completely unexpected and, Phil mused as the silence trembled, completely in character. He could almost feel Sam's desire to strike her back, and his inability to do so. She

challenged him to, while her throat moved gently with a nervous swallow. He wiped his mouth, never taking his eyes from hers.

"Cut!" Phil swore jubilantly as he walked over and grabbed Marlie by the shoulders. He kissed her, hard. "Fantastic," he said, then kissed her again. "Fantastic." Looking up, he grinned at Sam.

"Don't try that on me," Sam warned, nursing his lower lip. "She packs a hell of a punch." He gave her a rueful glance. "Ever heard about pulling right before you make contact?" he asked. "Show biz, you know."

"I got carried away."

"I nearly slugged you."

"I know." Laughing, she pushed her hair back with both hands.

"Okay, let's take it from there." Phil moved back to the cameraman. "Places."

"Can't we take it from right before the punch?" Marlie asked with a grin for Sam. "It would sort of give me a roll into the rest of the scene."

"Stand-in!" Sam called.

In her office Tory read over with care a long, detailed letter from an opposing attorney. The tone was very clear through the legal terms and flowery style. The case was going through litigation, she thought with a frown. It might take two months or more, she mused, but this suit wasn't going to be settled out of court. Though normally she would have wanted to come to terms without a trial, she began to feel a tiny flutter of excitement. She'd been away from her own work for too long. She would be back in Albuquerque in a month.

Tory discovered she wanted—needed—something complicated and time-consuming on her return.

Adjustments, she decided as she tried to concentrate on the words in the letter. There were going to be adjustments to be made when she left Friendly this time. When she left Phil. No, she corrected, catching the bridge of her nose between her thumb and forefinger. He was leaving first—tomorrow, the day after. It was uncomfortably easy to see the hole that was already taking shape in her life. Tory reminded herself that she wasn't allowed to think of it. The rules had been made plain at the outset—by both of them. If things had begun to change for her, she simply had to backpedal a bit and reaffirm her priorities. *Her* work, *her* career, *her* life. At that moment the singular possessive pronoun never sounded more empty. Shaking her head, Tory began to read the letter from the beginning a second time.

Merle paced the office, casting quick glances at Tory from time to time. He'd made arrangements for Marlie to meet him there after her work was finished. What he hadn't expected was for Tory to be glued to her desk all evening. No expert with subtleties, Merle had no idea how to move his boss along and have the office to himself. He peeked out the window, noting that the floodlights up the street were being shut off. Shuffling his feet and clearing his throat, he turned back to Tory.

"Guess you must be getting tired," he ventured.

"Hmmm."

"Things are pretty quiet tonight," he tried again, fussing with the buttons on his shirt.

"Um-hmm." Tory began to make notations on her yellow pad.

Merle lifted his eyes to the ceiling. Maybe the direct approach would do it, he decided. "Why don't you knock off and go home."

Tory continued to write. "Trying to get rid of me, Merle T.?"

"Well, no, ah…" He looked down at the dusty tips of his shoes. Women never got any easier to handle.

"Got a date?" she asked mildly as she continued to draft out her answer to the letter.

"Sort of…well, yeah," he said with more confidence.

"Go ahead, then."

"But—" He broke off, stuffing his hands in his pockets.

Tory looked up and studied him. The mustache, she noted, had grown in respectability. It wasn't exactly a prizewinner, but it added maturity to a face she'd always thought resembled a teddy bear's. He still slouched, and even as she studied him, color seeped into his cheeks. But he didn't look away as he once would have done. His eyes stayed on hers so that she could easily read both frustration and embarrassment. The old affection stirred in her.

"Marlie?" she asked gently.

"Yeah." He straightened his shoulders a bit.

"How are you going to feel when she leaves?"

With a shrug Merle glanced toward the window again. "I guess I'll miss her. She's a terrific lady."

The tone caused Tory to give his profile a puzzled look. There was no misery in it, just casual acceptance. With a light laugh she stared back at her notes. Odd, she thought, it seemed their reactions had gotten reversed somewhere along the line. "You don't have to stay, Merle," she said lightly. "If you'd planned to have a late supper or—"

"We did," he interrupted. "Here."

Tory looked up again. "Oh, I see." She couldn't quite control the smile. "Looks like I'm in the way."

Uncomfortable, he shuffled again. "Aw, Tory."

"It's okay." Rising, she exaggerated her accommodating tone. "I know when I'm not wanted. I'll just go back to my room and work on this all by myself."

Merle struggled with loyalty and selfishness while Tory gathered her papers. "You could have supper with us," he suggested gallantly.

Letting the papers drop, Tory skirted the desk. With her hands on his shoulders, she kissed both of his cheeks. "Merle T.," she said softly, "you're a jewel."

Pleased, he grinned as the door opened behind them. "Just like I told you, Phil," Marlie stated as they entered. "Beautiful woman can't keep away from him. You'll have to stand in line, Sheriff," she continued, walking over to hook her arm through Merle's. "I've got first dibs tonight."

"Why don't I get her out of your way?" Phil suggested. "It's the least I can do after that last scene."

"The man is totally unselfish," Marlie confided to Tory. "No sacrifice is too great for his people."

With a snort Tory turned back to her desk. "I might let him buy me a drink," she considered while slipping her papers into a small leather case. When he sat on the corner of her desk, she cast him a look. "And dinner," she added.

"I might be able to come up with some cold cuts," he murmured.

Tory's low, appreciative laugh was interrupted by the phone. "Sheriff's office." Her sigh was automatic as she listened to the excited voice on the other end.

"Yes, Mr. Potts." Merle groaned, but she ignored him. "I see. What kind of noise?" Tory waited while the old man jabbered in her ear. "Are your doors and windows locked? No, Mr. Potts, I don't want you going outside with your shotgun. Yes, I realize a man has to protect his property." A sarcastic sound from Merle earned him a mild glare. "Let me handle it. I'll be there in ten minutes. No, I'll be quiet, just sit tight."

"Sheep thieves," Merle muttered as Tory hung up.

"Burglars," she corrected, opening the top drawer of her desk.

"Just what do you think you're going to do with that?" Phil demanded as he saw Tory pull out the gun.

"Absolutely nothing, I hope." Coolly she began to load it.

"Then why are you—? Wait a minute," he interrupted himself, rising. "Do you mean that damn thing wasn't loaded?"

"Of course not." Tory slipped in the last bullet. "Nobody with sense keeps a loaded gun in an unlocked drawer."

"You got me into that cell with an empty gun?"

She sent him a lazy smile as she strapped on a holster. "You were so cute, Kincaid."

Ignoring amusement, he took a step toward her. "What would you have done if I hadn't backed down?"

"The odds were in my favor," she reminded him. "But I'd have thought of something. Merle, keep an eye on things until I get back."

"Wasting your time."

"Just part of the job."

"If you're wasting your time," Phil began as he stopped her at the door, "why are you taking that gun?"

"It looks so impressive," Tory told him as she walked outside.

"Tory, you're not going out to some sheep ranch with a gun at your hip like some modern-day Belle Starr."

"She was on the wrong side," she reminded him.

"Tory, I mean it!" Infuriated, Phil stepped in front of the car to block her way.

"Look, I said I'd be there in ten minutes. I'm going to have to drive like a maniac as it is."

He didn't budge. "What if there is someone out there?"

"That's exactly why I'm going."

When she reached for the door handle, he put his hand firmly over hers. "I'm going with you."

"Phil, I don't have time."

"I'm going."

Narrowing her eyes, she studied his face. There was no arguing with that expression, she concluded. "Okay, you're temporarily deputized. Get in and do what you're told."

Phil lifted a brow at her tone. The thought of her going out to some secluded ranch with only a gun for company had him swallowing his pride. He slid across to the passenger seat. "Don't I get a badge?" he asked as Tory started the engine.

"Use your imagination," she advised.

Tory's speed was sedate until they reached the town limits. Once the buildings were left behind, Phil watched the climbing speedometer with growing trepidation. Her hands were relaxed and competent on the wheel. The open window caused her hair to fly wildly, but her expression was calm.

She doesn't think there's anything to this, he decided

as he watched the scenery whiz by. But if she did, his thoughts continued, she'd be doing exactly the same thing. The knowledge gave him a small thrill of fear. The neat black holster at her side hid an ugly, very real weapon. She had no business chasing burglars or carrying guns. She had no business taking the remotest chance with her own well-being. He cursed the phone call that had made it all too clear just how potentially dangerous her position in Friendly was. It had been simpler to think of her as a kind of figurehead, a referee for small-town squabbles. The late-night call and the gun changed everything.

"What will you do if you have to use that thing?" he demanded suddenly.

Without turning, Tory knew where his thoughts centered. "I'll deal with that when the time comes."

"When's your term up here?"

Tory took her eyes from the road for a brief two seconds. Phil was looking straight ahead. "Three weeks."

"You're better off in Albuquerque," he muttered. *Safer* was the word heard but not said. Tory recalled the time a client had nearly strangled her in his cell before the guards had pulled him off. She decided it was best unmentioned. Hardly slackening the car's speed, she took a right turn onto a narrow, rut-filled dirt road. Phil swore as the jolting threw him against the door.

"You should have strapped in," she told him carelessly.

His response was rude and brief.

The tiny ranch house had every light blazing. Tory pulled up in front of it with a quick squeal of brakes.

"Think you missed any?" Phil asked her mildly as he rubbed the shoulder that had collided with the door.

"I'll catch them on the way back." Before he could retort, Tory was out of the car and striding up the porch steps. She knocked briskly, calling out to identify herself. When Phil joined her on the porch, the door opened a crack. "Mr. Potts," she began.

"Who's he?" the old man demanded through the crack in the door.

"New deputy," Tory said glibly. "We'll check the grounds and the outside of the house now."

Potts opened the door a bit more, revealing an ancient, craggy face and a shiny black shotgun. "I heard them in the bushes."

"We'll take care of it, Mr. Potts." She put her hands on the butt of his gun. "Why don't you let me have this for now?"

Unwilling, Potts held firm. "I gotta have protection."

"Yes, but they're not in the house," she reminded him gently. "I could really use this out here."

He hesitated, then slackened his grip. "Both barrels," he told her, then slammed the door. Tory heard the triple locks click into place.

"That is not your average jolly old man," Phil commented.

Tory took the two shells out of the shotgun. "Alone too long," she said simply. "Let's take a look around."

"Go get 'em, big guy."

Tory barely controlled a laugh. "Just keep out of the way, Kincaid."

Whether she considered it a false alarm or not, Phil noted that Tory was very thorough. With the empty shotgun in one hand and a flashlight in the other, she checked every door and window on the dilapidated ranch house. Watching her, he walked into a pile of empty paint cans, sending them clattering. When he swore, Tory turned her head to look at him.

"You move like a cat, Kincaid," she said admiringly.

"The man's got junk piled everywhere," he retorted. "A burglar doesn't have a chance."

Tory smothered a chuckle and moved on. They circled the house, making their way through Potts's obstacle course of old car parts, warped lumber and rusted tools. Satisfied that no one had attempted to break into the house for at least twenty-five years, Tory widened her circle to check the ground.

"Waste of time," Phil muttered, echoing Merle.

"Then let's waste it properly." Tory shone her light on the uneven grass as they continued to walk. Resigned, Phil kept to her side. There were better ways, he was thinking, to spend a warm summer night. And the moon was full. Pure white, he observed as he gazed up at it. Cool and full and promising. He wanted to make love to her under it, in the still, hot air with nothing and no one around for miles. The desire came suddenly, intensely, washing over him with a wave of possession that left him baffled.

"Tory," he murmured, placing a hand on her shoulder.

"Ssh!"

The order was sharp. He felt her stiffen under his hand. Her eyes were trained on a dry, dying bush directly in front of them. Even as he opened his mouth to say something impatient, Phil saw the movement. His fingers tightened on Tory's shoulder as he automatically stepped forward. The protective gesture was instinctive, and so natural neither of them noticed it. He never thought: This is my woman, and I'll do anything to keep her from harm; he simply reacted. With his body as a shield for hers, they watched the bush in silence.

There was a slight sound, hardly a whisper on the air, but Tory felt the back of her neck prickle. The dry leaves of the bush cracked quietly with some movement. She reached in her pocket for the two shells, then reloaded the shotgun. The moonlight bounced off the oiled metal. Her hands were rock steady. Phil was poised, ready to lunge as Tory aimed the gun at the moon and fired both barrels. The sound split the silence like an axe.

With a terrified bleat, the sheep that had been grazing lazily behind the bush scrambled for safety. Without a word Phil and Tory watched the dirty white blob run wildly into the night.

"Another desperate criminal on the run from the law," Tory said dryly.

Phil burst into relieved laughter. He felt each separate muscle in his body relax. "I'd say 'on the lamb.'"

"I was hoping you wouldn't." Because the hand holding the gun was shaking, Tory lowered it to her side. She swallowed; her throat was dry. "Well, let's go tell Potts his home and hearth are safe. Then we can go have that drink."

Phil laid his hands on her shoulders, looking down on her face in the moonlight. "Are you all right?"

"Sure."

"You're trembling."

"That's you," she countered, smiling at him.

Phil slid his hand down to her wrist to feel the race of her pulse. "Scared the hell out of you," he said softly.

Tory's eyes didn't waver. "Yeah." She was able to smile again, this time with more feeling. "How about you?"

"Me too." Laughing, he gave her a light kiss. "I'm not going to need that badge after all." And I'm not going to feel safe, he added silently, until you take yours off for the last time.

"Oh, I don't know, Kincaid." Tory led the way back with the beam of her flashlight. "First night on the job and you flushed out a sheep."

"Just give the crazy old man his gun and let's get out of here."

It took ten minutes of Tory's diplomacy to convince Potts that everything was under control. Mollified more by the fact that Tory had used his gun than the information that his intruder was one of his own flock, he locked himself in again. After contacting Merle on the radio, she headed back to town at an easy speed.

"I guess I could consider this a fitting climax to my sojourn to Friendly," Phil commented. "Danger and excitement on the last night in town."

Tory's fingers tightened on the wheel, but she managed to keep the speed steady. "You're leaving tomorrow."

He listened for regret in the statement but heard none. Striving to match her tone, he continued to stare out the window. "We finished up tonight, a day ahead of schedule. I'll head out with the film crew tomorrow. I want to be there when Huffman sees the film."

"Of course." The pain rammed into her, dazzlingly physical. It took concentrated control to keep from moaning with it. "You've still quite a lot of work to do before it's finished, I suppose."

"The studio scenes," he agreed, struggling to ignore twin feelings of panic and desolation. "The editing, the mixing... I guess your schedule's going to be pretty tight when you get back to Albuquerque."

"It looks that way." Tory stared at the beams of the headlights. A long straight road, no curves, no hills. No end. She bit the inside of her lip hard before she trusted herself to continue. "I'm thinking about hiring a new law clerk."

"That's probably a good idea." He told himself that the crawling emptiness in his stomach was due to a lack of food. "I don't imagine your caseload's going to get any smaller."

"No, it should take me six months of concentrated work to get it under control again. You'll probably start on a new film the minute this one's finished."

"It's being cast now," he murmured. "I'm going to produce it too."

Tory smiled. "No guarantors?"

Phil answered the smile. "We'll see."

They drove for another half mile in silence. Slowing down, Tory pulled off onto a small dirt road and stopped. Phil took a quick glance around at nothing in particular, then turned to her. "What are we doing?"

"Parking." She scooted from under the steering wheel, winding her arms around his neck.

"Isn't there some legality about using an official car for illicit purposes?" His mouth was already seeking hers, craving.

"I'll pay the fine in the morning." She silenced his chuckle with a deep, desperate kiss.

As if by mutual consent, they went slowly. All pleasure, all desire, was concentrated in tastes. Lips, teeth and tongues brought shuddering arousal, urging them to hurry. But they would satisfy needs with mouths only first. Her lips were silkily yielding even as they met and increased his demand. Wild, crazy desires whipped through him, but her mouth held him prisoner. He touched her nowhere else. This taste—spiced honey, this texture—heated satin—would live with him always.

Tory let her lips roam his face. She knew each crease, each angle, each slope, more intimately than she knew her own features. With her eyes closed she could see him perfectly, and knew she had only to close her eyes again, in a year, in ten years, to have the same vivid picture. The skin on his neck was damp, making the flavor intensify as her tongue glided over it. Without thinking, she ran her fingers down his shirt, nimbly loosening buttons. When his chest was vulnerable, she spread both palms over it to feel his quick shudder. Then she brought her mouth, lazily, invitingly, back to his.

Her fingertips sent a path of ice, a path of fire, over his naked skin. Her mouth was drawing him in until his head swam. His labored breathing whispered on the night air. Wanting her closer, he shifted, cursed the cramped confines of the car, then dragged her across his lap. Lifting her to him, he buried his face against the side of her neck. He fed there, starving for her until she moaned and brought his hand to rest on her breast. With torturous slowness he undid the series of buttons, allowing his fingertips to trail along her skin as it was painstakingly exposed. He let the tips of his fingers bring her to desperation.

The insistent brush of his thumb over the point of her breast released a shaft of exquisite pain so sharp, she cried out with it, dragging him closer. Open and hungry, her mouth fixed on his while she fretted to touch more of him. Their position made it impossible, but her body was his. He ran his hands over it, feeling her skin jump as he roamed to the waistband of her jeans. Loosening them, he slid his hand down to warm, moist secrets. His mouth crushed hers as he drank in her moan.

Tory struggled, maddened by the restrictions, wild with desire, as his fingers aroused her beyond belief. He kept her trapped against him, knowing once she touched him that his control would shatter. This night, he thought, this final night, would last until there was no tomorrow.

When she crested, he rose with her, half delirious. No woman was so soft, no woman was so responsive. His heart pounded, one separate pain after another, as he drove her up again.

Her struggles ceased. Compliance replaced them. Tory lay shuddering in a cocoon of unrivaled sensations. She was his. Though her mind was unaware of the total gift of self, her body knew. She'd been his, perhaps from the first, perhaps only for that moment, but there would never be any turning back. Love swamped her; desire sated her. There was nothing left but the need to possess, to be possessed, by one man. In that instant she conceded her privacy.

The change in her had something racing through him. Phil couldn't question, couldn't analyze. He knew only that they must come together now—now, while there was something magic shimmering. It had nothing to do with the moonlight beaming into the car or the eerie silence surrounding them. It concerned only them and the secret that had grown despite protests. He didn't think, he didn't deny. With a sudden madness he tugged on her clothes and his own. Speed was foremost in his mind. He had to hurry before whatever trembled in the tiny confines was lost. Then her body was beneath his, fused to his, eager, asking.

He took her on the seat of the car like a passionate teenager. He felt like a man who had been given something precious, and as yet unrecognizable.

Chapter 12

A long sleepy time. Moonlight on the back of closed lids...night air over naked skin. The deep, deep silence of solitude by the whispering breathing of intimacy.

Tory floated in that luxurious plane between sleep and wakefulness—on her side, on the narrow front seat, with her body fitted closely against Phil's. Their legs were tangled, their arms around each other, as much for support as need. With his mouth near her ear, his warm breath skipped along her skin.

There were two marginally comfortable beds back at the hotel. They could have chosen either of them for their last night together, but they had stayed where they were, on a rough vinyl seat, on a dark road, as the night grew older. There they were alone completely. Morning still seemed very far away.

A hawk cried out as it drove toward earth. Some

small animal screamed in the brush. Tory's lids fluttered up to find Phil's eyes open and on hers. In the moonlight his irises were very pale. Needing no words, perhaps wanting none, Tory lifted her mouth to his. They made love again, quietly, slowly, with more tenderness than either was accustomed to.

So they dozed again, unwilling to admit that the night was slipping away from them. When Tory awoke, there was a faint lessening in the darkness—not light, but the texture that meant morning was close.

A few more hours, she thought, gazing at the sky through the far window as she lay beside him. When the sun came up, it would be over. Now his body was warm against hers. He slept lightly, she knew. She had only to shift or murmur his name and he would awaken. She remained still. For a few more precious moments she wanted the simple unity that came from having him sleep at her side. There would be no stopping the sun from rising in the east—or stopping her lover from going west. It was up to her to accept the second as easily as she accepted the first. Closing her eyes, she willed herself to be strong. Phil stirred, dreaming.

He walked through his house in the hills, purposely, from room to room, looking, searching, for what was vague to him; but time after time he turned away, frustrated. Room after room after room. Everything was familiar: the colors, the furniture, even small personal objects that identified his home, his belongings. Something was missing. Stolen, lost? The house echoed emptily around him as he continued to search for something vital and unknown. The emotions of the man in the dream communicated themselves to the man dreaming. He felt the helplessness, the anger and the panic.

Hearing him murmur her name, Tory shifted yet closer. Phil shot awake, disoriented. The dream slipped into some corner of his mind that he couldn't reach.

"It's nearly morning," she said quietly.

A bit dazed, struggling to remember what he had dreamed that had left him feeling so empty, Phil looked at the sky. It was lightening. The first pale pinks bloomed at the horizon. For a moment they watched in silence as the day crept closer, stealing their night.

"Make love to me again," Tory whispered. "Once more, before morning."

He could see the quiet need in her eyes, the dark smudges beneath that told of patchy sleep, the soft glow that spoke clearly of a night of loving. He held the picture in his mind a moment, wanting to be certain he wouldn't lose it when time had dimmed other memories. He lowered his mouth to hers in bittersweet goodbye.

The sky paled to blue. The horizon erupted with color. The gold grew molten and scarlet bled into it as dawn came up. They loved intensely one final time. As morning came they lost themselves in each other, pretending it was still night. Where he touched, she trembled. Where she kissed, his skin hummed until they could no longer deny the need. The sun had full claim when they came together, so that the light streamed without mercy. Saying little, they dressed, then drove back to town.

When Tory stopped in front of the hotel, she felt she was in complete control again. No regrets, she reminded herself, as she turned off the ignition. We've just come to the fork in the road. We knew it was there when we started. Turning, she smiled at Phil.

"We're liable to be a bit stiff today."

Grinning, he leaned over and kissed her chin. "It was worth it."

"Remember that when you're moaning for a hot bath on your way back to L.A." Tory slid from the car. When she stepped up on the sidewalk, Phil took her hand. The contact threatened her control before she snapped it back into place.

"I'm going to be thinking of you," he murmured as they stepped into the tiny lobby.

"You'll be busy." She let her hand slide on the banister as they mounted the stairs.

"Not that busy." Phil turned her to him when they reached the top landing. "Not that busy, Tory," he said again.

Her courtroom experience came to her aid. Trembling inside, Tory managed an easy smile. "I'm glad. I'll think of you too." *Too often, too much. Too painful.*

"If I call you—"

"I'm in the book," she interrupted. Play it light, she ordered herself. The way it was supposed to be, before… "Keep out of trouble, Kincaid," she told him as she slipped her room key into its lock.

"Tory."

He stepped closer, but she barred the way into the room. "I'll say goodbye now." With another smile she rested a hand on his cheek. "It'll be simpler, and I think I'd better catch a couple hours' sleep before I go into the office."

Phil took a long, thorough study of her face. Her eyes were direct, her smile easy. Apparently there was nothing left to say. "If that's what you want."

Tory nodded, not fully trusting herself. "Be happy,

Phil," she managed before she disappeared into her room. Very carefully Tory turned the lock before she walked to the bed. Lying down, she curled into a ball and wept, and wept, and wept.

It was past noon when Tory awoke. Her head was pounding. Dragging herself to the bathroom, she studied herself objectively in the mirror over the sink. Terrible, she decided without emotion. The headache had taken the color from her cheeks, and her eyes were swollen and red from tears. Dispassionately, Tory ran the water until it was icy cold, then splashed her face with it. When her skin was numb, she stripped and stepped under the shower.

She decided against aspirin. The pills would dull the pain, and the pain made it difficult to think. Thinking was the last thing she felt she needed to do at the moment. Phil was gone, back to his own life. She would go on with hers. The fact that she had fallen in love with him over her own better judgment was simply her hard luck. In a few days she would be able to cope with it easily enough. Like hell you will, she berated herself as she dried her skin with a rough towel. You fell hard, and some bruises take years to heal…if ever.

Wasn't it ironic, she mused as she went back into the bedroom to dress. Victoria L. Ashton, Attorney at Law, dedicated to straightening out other people's lives, had just made a beautiful mess of her own. And yet, there hadn't been any options. A deal was a deal.

Phil, she said silently, I've decided to change our contract. Circumstances have altered, and I'm in love with you. I propose we include certain things like commitment and reciprocal affection into our arrangement, with options for additions such as marriage and children, should both parties find it agreeable.

She gave a short laugh and pulled on a fresh shirt. Of course, she could merely have clung to him, tearfully begging him not to leave her. What man wouldn't love to find himself confronted with a hysterical woman who won't let go?

Better this way, she reminded herself, tugging on jeans. Much better to have a clean, civilized break. Aloud, she said something potent about being civilized as she pinned on her badge. The one thing she had firmly decided during her crying jag was that it was time for her to leave Friendly. Merle could handle the responsibilities of the office for the next few weeks without too much trouble. She had come to terms with her father's death, with her mother. She felt confident that she'd helped in Tod's family situation. Merle had grown up a bit. All in all, Tory felt she wasn't needed any longer. In Albuquerque she could put her own life in motion again. She needed that if she wasn't going to spend three weeks wallowing in self-pity and despair. At least, she decided, it was something she could start on. Naturally she would have to talk to the mayor and officially resign. There would be a visit to her mother. If she spent a day briefing Merle, she should be able to leave before the end of the week.

Her own rooms, Tory thought, trying to work up some excitement. The work she was trained for—a meaty court case that would take weeks of preparation and a furnace of energy. She felt suddenly that she had a surplus of it and nowhere to go. Back in the bath, she applied a careful layer of makeup to disguise the effects of tears, then brushed her hair dry. The first step was the mayor. There was no point putting it off.

It took thirty minutes for Tory to convince the mayor she was serious and another fifteen to assure him that Merle was capable of handling the job of acting sheriff until the election.

"You know, Tory," Bud said when he saw her mind was made up, "we're going to be sorry to lose you. I guess we all kept hoping you'd change your mind and run. You've been a good sheriff, I guess you come by it naturally."

"I appreciate that—really." Touched, Tory took the hand he offered her. "Pat Rowe and Nick Merriweather are both fair men. Whoever wins, the town's in good hands. In a few years Merle will make you a fine sheriff."

"If you ever change your mind…" Bud trailed off wanting to leave the door open.

"Thanks, but my niche in the law isn't in enforcement. I have to get back to my practice."

"I know, I know." He sighed, capitulating. "You've done more than we had a right to expect."

"I did what I wanted to do," she corrected.

"I guess things will be quiet for a while, especially with the movie people gone." He gave a regretful glance toward the window. Excitement, he mused, wasn't meant for Friendly. "Come by and see me before you leave town."

Outside, the first thing Tory noticed was the absence of the movie crew. There were no vans, no sets, no lights or packets of people. Friendly had settled back into its yawning pace as though there had never been a ripple. Someone had written some graffiti in the dust on the window of the post office. A car puttered into town and stopped in front of the hardware store. Tory started to cross the street, but stopped in the center when she was hailed. Shielding her eyes, she watched Tod race toward her.

"Sheriff, I've been looking for you."

"Is something wrong?"

"No." He grinned the quick-spreading grin that transformed his thin face. "It's real good, I wanted you to know. My dad…well, we've been talking, you know, and we even drove out to see those people you told us about."

"How'd it go?"

"We're going to go back—my mom too."

"I'm happy for you." Tory brushed her knuckles over his cheek. "It's going to take time, Tod. You'll all have to work together."

"I know, but…" He looked up at her, his eyes wide and thrilled. "He really loves me. I never thought he did. And my mom, she wondered if you could come out to the house sometime. She wants to thank you."

"There isn't any need for that."

"She wants to."

"I'll try." Tory hesitated, finding that this goodbye would be more difficult than most. "I'm going away in a couple of days."

His elated expression faded. "For good?"

"My mother lives here," she reminded him. "My father's buried here. I'll come back from time to time."

"But not to stay."

"No," Tory said softly. "Not to stay."

Tod lowered his gaze to the ground. "I knew you'd leave. I guess I was pretty stupid that day in your office when I…" He trailed off with a shrug and continued to stare at the ground.

"I didn't think you were stupid. It meant a lot to me." Tory put out a hand to lift his face. "*Means* a lot to me."

Tod moistened his lips. "I guess I still love you—if you don't mind."

"Oh." Tory felt the tears spring to her eyes and pulled him into her arms. "I'm going to miss you like crazy. Would you think I was stupid if I said I wish I were a fourteen-year-old girl?"

Grinning, he drew away. Nothing she could have said could have pleased him more. "I guess if you were I could kiss you goodbye."

With a laugh Tory brushed a light kiss on his lips. "Go on, get out of here," she ordered unsteadily. "Nothing undermines the confidence of a town more than having its sheriff crying in the middle of the street."

Feeling incredibly mature, Tod dashed away. Turning, he ran backward for a moment. "Will you write sometime?"

"Yes, yes, I'll write." Tory watched him streak off at top speed. Her smile lost some of its sparkle. She was losing, she discovered, quite a bit in one day. Briskly shaking off the mood, she turned in the direction of her office. She was still a yard away when Merle strolled out.

"Hey," he said foolishly, glancing from her, then back at the door he'd just closed.

"Hey yourself," she returned. "You just got yourself a promotion, Merle T."

"Tory, there's— Huh?"

"Incredibly articulate," she replied with a fresh smile. "I'm resigning. You'll be acting sheriff until the election."

"Resigning?" He gave her a completely baffled look. "But you—" He broke off, shaking his head at the door again. "How come?"

"I need to get back to my practice. Anyway—" she stepped up on the sidewalk "—it shouldn't take long for me to fill you in on the procedure. You already know just about everything. Come on inside and we'll get started."

"Tory." In an uncharacteristic gesture he took her arm and stopped her. Shrewdly direct, his eyes locked on hers. "Are you upset about something?"

Merle was definitely growing up, Tory concluded. "I just saw Tod." It was part of the truth, and all she would discuss. "That kid gets to me."

His answer was a slow nod, but he didn't release her arm. "I guess you know the movie people left late this morning."

"Yes, I know." Hearing her own clipped response, Tory took a mental step back. "I don't suppose it was easy for you to say goodbye to Marlie," she said more gently.

"I'll miss her some," he admitted, still watching Tory critically. "We had fun together."

His words were so calm that Tory tilted her head as she studied him. "I was afraid you'd fallen in love with her."

"In love with her?" He let out a hoot of laughter. "Shoot, I ain't ready for that. No way."

"Sometimes being ready doesn't make any difference," Tory muttered. "Well," she said more briskly, "since you're not crying in your beer, why don't we go over some things? I'd like to be in Albuquerque before the end of the week."

"Ah...yeah, sure." Merle glanced around the empty street. "I gotta talk to somebody first over at, um...the hotel," he announced. "Be right back."

Tory shot him an exasperated glance as he loped across the street. "Well," she murmured, "some things never change." Deciding she could spend the time packing her books and papers, Tory walked into the office.

Seated at her desk, casually examining the .45, was Phil Kincaid. She stopped dead, gaping at him. "Sheriff," he said mildly, giving the barrel an idle spin.

"Phil." She found her voice, barely. "What are you doing here?"

He didn't rise, but propped his feet up on the desk instead. "I forgot something. Did you know you didn't unload this thing last night?"

She didn't even glance at the gun, but stood rooted to the spot. "I thought you'd left hours ago."

"Did you?" He gave her a long, steady look. The cold water and makeup had helped, but he knew her face intimately. "I did," he agreed after a moment. "I came back."

"Oh." So now she would have to deal with the goodbye a second time. Tory ignored the ache in her stomach and smiled. "What did you forget?"

"I owe you something," he said softly. The gesture with the gun was very subtle, but clear enough.

Only partially amused, Tory lifted a brow. "Let's call it even," she suggested. Wanting to busy her hands, she went to the shelf near the desk to draw out her books.

"No," he said mildly. "I don't think so. Turn around, Sheriff."

Annoyance was the least painful of her emotions, so Tory let it out. "Look, Phil—"

"In the cell," he interrupted. "I can recommend the first one."

"You're out of your mind." With a thud she dropped the books. "If that thing's loaded, you could hurt someone."

"I have some things to say to you," he continued calmly. "In there." Again he gestured toward the cell.

Her hands went to her hips. "All right, Kincaid, I'm still sheriff here. The penalty for armed assault on a peace officer—"

"Shut up and get in," Phil ordered.

"You can take that gun," Tory began dangerously, "and—"

Her suggestion was cut off when Phil grabbed her arm and hauled her into a cell. Stepping in with her, he pulled the door shut with a shattering clang.

"You *idiot!*" Impotently, Tory gave the locked door a furious jerk. "Now just how the hell are we supposed to get out?"

Phil settled comfortably on the bunk, propped on one elbow, with the gun lowered toward the floor. It was just as empty as it had been when Tory had bluffed him. "I haven't anyplace better to go."

Fists on hips, Tory whirled. "Just what is this all about, Kincaid?" she demanded. "You're supposed to be halfway to L.A. Instead you're propped up at my desk. Instead of a reasonable explanation, you throw that gun around like some two-bit hood—"

"I thought I did it with such finesse," he complained, frowning at the object under discussion. "Of course, I'd rather have a piece with a bit more style." He grinned up at her. "Pearl handle, maybe."

"Do you have to behave like such a fool?"

"I suppose."

"When this is over, you're going to find yourself locked up for months. Years, if I can manage it," she added, turning to tug uselessly on the bars again.

"That won't work," he told her amiably. "I shook them like crazy a few months ago."

Ignoring him, Tory stalked to the window. Not a soul on the street. She debated swallowing her pride and calling out. It would look terrific, she thought grimly, to have the sheriff shouting to be let out of one of her own cells. If she waited for Merle, at least she could make him swear to secrecy.

"All right, Kincaid," she said between her teeth. "Let's have it. Why are you here and why the devil are we locked in the cell?"

He glanced down at the gun again, then set it on the edge of the bunk. Automatically, Tory judged the distance. "Because—" and his voice had altered enough to lure her eyes to his "—I found myself in an impossible situation."

At those words Tory felt her heart come to a stop, then begin again at a furious rate. Cautiously she warned herself not to read anything into the statement. True, she remembered his use of the phrase when talking about love, but it didn't follow that he meant the same thing now.

"Oh?" she managed, and praised herself for a brilliant response.

"'Oh?'" Phil pushed himself off the bunk in a quick move. "Is that all you can say? I got twenty miles out of town," he went on in sudden fury. "I told myself that was it. You wanted—I wanted—a simple transient relationship. No complications. We'd enjoyed each other—it was over."

Tory swallowed. "Yes, we'd agreed—"

"The hell with what we agreed." Phil grabbed her shoulders, shaking her until her mouth dropped open in shock. "It got complicated. It got very, very complicated." Releasing her abruptly, he began to pace the cell he had locked them both into.

"Twenty miles out of town," he repeated, "and I couldn't make it. Even last night I told myself it was all for the best. You'd go your way, I'd go mine. We'd both have some great memories." He turned to her then; although his voice lowered, it was no calmer. "Damn it, Tory, I want more than memories of you. I need more. You didn't want this to happen, I know that." Agitated, he ran a hand through his hair, while she said nothing. "I didn't want it, either, or thought I didn't. I'm not sure anymore. It might have been the first minute I walked in here, or that day at the cemetery. It might have been that night at the lake or a hundred other times. I don't know when it happened, why it happened." He shook his head as though it was a problem he'd struggled with and ultimately given up on. "I only know I love you. And God knows I can't leave you. I tried—I can't."

With a shuddering sigh Tory walked back to the bars and rested her head against them. The headache she had awoken with was now a whirling dizziness. A minute, she told herself. I just need a minute to take it in.

"I know you've got a life in Albuquerque," Phil continued, fighting against the fluttering panic in his stomach. "I know you've got a career that's important to you. It isn't something I'm asking you to choose between. There are ways to balance things if people want to badly enough. I broke the rules. I'm willing to make the adjustments."

"Adjustments..." Tory managed before she turned back to him.

"I can live in Albuquerque," he told her as he crossed the cell. "That won't stop me from making movies."

"The studio—"

"I'll buy a plane and commute," he said quickly. "It's been done before."

"A plane." With a little laugh she walked away, dragging a hand through her hair. "A plane."

"Yes, damn it, a plane." Her reaction was nothing that he had expected. The panic grew. "You didn't want me to go," he began in defense, in fury. "You've been crying. I can tell."

A bit steadier, Tory faced him again. "Yes, I cried. No, I didn't want you to go. Still, I thought it was best for both of us."

"Why?"

"It wouldn't be easy, juggling two careers and one relationship."

"Marriage," he corrected firmly. "Marriage, Tory. The whole ball of wax. Kids too. I want you to have my children." He saw the change in her eyes—shock, fear? Unable to identify it, Phil went to her again. "I said I love you." Again he took her by the shoulders. This time he didn't shake her but held her almost tentatively. "I have to know what you feel for me."

She spent a moment simply looking into his eyes. Loved her? Yes, she realized with something like a jolt. She could see it. It was real. And more, he was hurting because he wasn't sure. Doubts melted away. "I've been in an impossible situation, I think, from the first moment Merle hauled you in here."

She felt his fingers tense, then relax again. "Are you sure?" he asked, fighting the need to drag her against him.

"That I'm in love with you?" For the first time a ghost of a smile hovered around her mouth. "Sure enough that I nearly died when I thought you were leaving me. Sure enough that I was going to let you go because I'm just as stupid as you are."

His hands dove into her hair. "Stupid?" he repeated, drawing her closer.

"'He needs his own life. We agreed not to complicate things. He'd hate it if I begged him to stay.'" She smiled more fully. "Sound familiar?"

"With a slight change in the personal pronoun." Phil pulled her close just to hold her. *Mine,* they thought simultaneously, then clung. "Ah, Tory, last night was so wonderful—and so terrible."

"I know, thinking it was the last time." She drew back only enough so their mouths could meet. "I've been giving some thought to it for a while," she murmured, then lost the trend of thought as they kissed again.

"To what?"

"To…oh, to moving to the coast."

Framing her face with his hands, Phil tilted it to his. "You don't have to do that. I told you, I can—"

"Buy a plane," she finished on a laugh. "And I'm sure you can. But I have given some thought lately to moving on. Why not California?"

"We'll work that out."

"Eventually," she agreed, drawing his mouth back to hers.

"Tory." He held her off a moment, his eyes serious again. "Are you going to marry me?"

She considered a moment, letting her fingers twine in his hair. "It might be wise," she decided, "since we're going to have those kids."

"When?"

"It takes nine months," she reminded him.

"Marriage," he corrected, nipping her bottom lip.

"Well, after you've served your sentence...about three months."

"Sentence?"

"Illegal use of a handgun, accosting a peace officer, improper use of a correctional facility..." She shrugged, giving him her dashing grin. "Time off for good behavior, you should be out in no time. Remember, I'm still sheriff here, Kincaid."

"The hell you are." Pulling the badge from her blouse, he tossed it through the bars of the window. "Besides, you'll never make it stick."

* * * * *

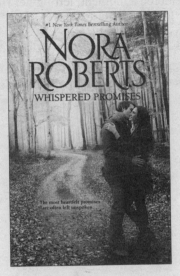

There's nowhere better to spend the holidays than
with *New York Times* bestselling author

SUSAN MALLERY

in the town of Fool's Gold, where love is always
waiting to be unwrapped...

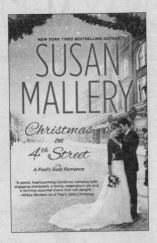

Available now wherever books are sold!

"Susan Mallery is one of my favorites."
— #1 *New York Times* bestselling author Debbie Macomber

www.SusanMallery.com

REQUEST YOUR FREE BOOKS!

2 FREE NOVELS
FROM THE ROMANCE COLLECTION
PLUS 2 FREE GIFTS!

YES! Please send me 2 FREE novels from the Romance Collection and my 2 FREE gifts (gifts are worth about $10). After receiving them, if I don't wish to receive any more books, I can return the shipping statement marked "cancel." If I don't cancel, I will receive 4 brand-new novels every month and be billed just $6.24 per book in the U.S. or $6.74 per book in Canada. That's a savings of at least 22% off the cover price. It's quite a bargain! Shipping and handling is just 50¢ per book in the U.S. and 75¢ per book in Canada.* I understand that accepting the 2 free books and gifts places me under no obligation to buy anything. I can always return a shipment and cancel at any time. Even if I never buy another book, the two free books and gifts are mine to keep forever.

194/394 MDN F4XY

Name	(PLEASE PRINT)	
Address		Apt. #
City	State/Prov.	Zip/Postal Code

Signature (if under 18, a parent or guardian must sign)

Mail to the **Harlequin®** Reader Service:
IN U.S.A.: P.O. Box 1867, Buffalo, NY 14240-1867
IN CANADA: P.O. Box 609, Fort Erie, Ontario L2A 5X3

Want to try two free books from another line?
Call 1-800-873-8635 or visit www.ReaderService.com.

* Terms and prices subject to change without notice. Prices do not include applicable taxes. Sales tax applicable in N.Y. Canadian residents will be charged applicable taxes. Offer not valid in Quebec. This offer is limited to one order per household. Not valid for current subscribers to the Romance Collection or the Romance/Suspense Collection. All orders subject to credit approval. Credit or debit balances in a customer's account(s) may be offset by any other outstanding balance owed by or to the customer. Please allow 4 to 6 weeks for delivery. Offer available while quantities last.

Your Privacy—The Harlequin® Reader Service is committed to protecting your privacy. Our Privacy Policy is available online at www.ReaderService.com or upon request from the Harlequin Reader Service.

We make a portion of our mailing list available to reputable third parties that offer products we believe may interest you. If you prefer that we not exchange your name with third parties, or if you wish to clarify or modify your communication preferences, please visit us at www.ReaderService.com/consumerschoice or write to us at Harlequin Reader Service Preference Service, P.O. Box 9062, Buffalo, NY 14269. Include your complete name and address.

NORA ROBERTS

28594	O'HURLEY'S RETURN	___ $7.99 U.S.	___ $9.99 CAN.
28592	O'HURLEY BORN	___ $7.99 U.S.	___ $9.99 CAN.
28590	SWEET RAINS	___ $7.99 U.S.	___ $9.99 CAN.
28588	NIGHT TALES:		
	NIGHT SHIELD & NIGHT MOVES	___ $7.99 U.S.	___ $9.99 CAN.
28587	NIGHT TALES:		
	NIGHTSHADE & NIGHT SMOKE	___ $7.99 U.S.	___ $9.99 CAN.
28586	NIGHT TALES: NIGHT SHIFT &		
	NIGHT SHADOW	___ $7.99 U.S.	___ $9.99 CAN.
28583	WORTH THE RISK	___ $7.99 U.S.	___ $9.99 CAN.
28171	FOREVER	___ $7.99 U.S.	___ $9.99 CAN.
28169	HAPPY ENDINGS	___ $7.99 U.S.	___ $9.99 CAN.
28168	CHANGE OF HEART	___ $7.99 U.S.	___ $9.99 CAN.
28167	CHARMED & ENCHANTED	___ $7.99 U.S.	___ $9.99 CAN.
28165	CAPTIVATED & ENCHANTED	___ $7.99 U.S.	___ $9.99 CAN.
28164	FIRST IMPRESSIONS	___ $7.99 U.S.	___ $9.99 CAN.
28162	A DAY AWAY	___ $7.99 U.S.	___ $9.99 CAN.
28161	MYSTERIOUS	___ $7.99 U.S.	___ $9.99 CAN.
28160	THE MacGREGOR GROOMS	___ $7.99 U.S.	___ $9.99 CAN.
28158	ROBERT & CYBIL	___ $7.99 U.S.	___ $9.99 CAN.
28156	DANIEL & IAN	___ $7.99 U.S.	___ $9.99 CAN.
28154	GABRIELLA & ALEXANDER	___ $7.99 U.S.	___ $9.99 CAN.
28150	IRISH HEARTS	___ $7.99 U.S.	___ $9.99 CAN.
28133	THE MacGREGORS: SERENA & CAINE	___ $7.99 U.S.	___ $9.99 CAN.

(limited quantities available)

TOTAL AMOUNT	$	_____
POSTAGE & HANDLING	$	_____
($1.00 FOR 1 BOOK, 50¢ for each additional)		
APPLICABLE TAXES*	$	_____
TOTAL PAYABLE	$	_____

(check or money order—please do not send cash)

To order, complete this form and send it, along with a check or money order for the total above, payable to Harlequin Books, to: **In the U.S.:** 3010 Walden Avenue, P.O. Box 9077, Buffalo, NY 14269-9077; **In Canada:** P.O. Box 636, Fort Erie, Ontario, L2A 5X3.

Name: _____
Address: _____ City: _____
State/Prov.: _____ Zip/Postal Code: _____
Account Number (if applicable): _____

075 CSAS

*New York residents remit applicable sales taxes.
*Canadian residents remit applicable GST and provincial taxes.

Silhouette®
Where love comes alive™

SNR1013BL